"This book is about the timeless effects of war on a soldier," writes Ray Moore, retired psychologist, who served a portion of his career at the very hospital used as the setting for much of this story. Dr. Moore went on to say, *"Symptoms of Post-Traumatic Stress Disorder were recorded in 490 BCE by Herodotus in his descriptions of the battle of Marathon."*

The Works of Roland Cheek

nonfiction

Montana's Bob Marshall Wilderness

Learning To Talk Bear
- so bears can listen

The Phantom Ghost of Harriet Lou
- and other elk stories

Dance On the Wild Side

My Best Work Is Done at the Office

Chocolate Legs
- sweet mother, savage killer?

fiction

Echoes of Vengeance

Bloody Merchants War

Lincoln County Crucible

Gunnar's Mine

Crisis On the Stinkingwater

The Silver Yoke

THE DOGGED AND THE DAMNED

One Soldier's War at Home

by Roland Cheek

a Skyline Publishing Book

Copyright © 2009 by Roland Cheek

Printed in the United States of America

First Printing - October, 2009

Publisher's Cataloging in Publication

Cheek, Roland, 1935--
    The Dogged and the Damned / Roland Cheek.
       p. cm.
    ISBN 978-0-918981-14-1
    1. USA--World War II, New Guinea--Fiction. 2. Mikhail Baranovitch (fictitious character)--Fiction. 3. War Hero. 4. Battle Fatigue (P.T.S.D.). 5. Fugitive. 6. Outdoor Survival.
    I. Title

      2009
  ISBN 978-0-918981-14-1
Library of Congress Control Number   (pending)

Skyline Publishing, P.O. Box 1118, Columbia Falls, MT 59912
http://www/rolandcheek.com
email: roland@rolandcheek.com

FOR SELENE, WITH LOVE

Post Traumatic Stress Disorder was known as *"Soldier's Heart"* during the Civil War, *"Combat Fatigue"* or *"Shell Shock"* in World War I, and *"Battle Fatigue"* in the aftermath of World War II.

Whatever PTSD may have been formerly called, the illness means the traumatic event persists as a dominating psychological experience, typically causing a person to experience flashbacks of the event from other stimuli.

- Psychiatric Disorders.com

ACKNOWLEDGMENTS

Any book is the inevitable product of many often faceless individuals; all the more so when a great deal of time elapses between conception and fruition. Mark Worsley, a long-time outdoors companion of mine, was the first of these contributors-- over 40 years ago--when, learning of my interest, he researched newspaper files on the Steve Solavitch saga that inspired, and eventually led to, *The Dogged and the Damned*.

Another of my long-ago Oregon friends, Willis Weaver, was, a decade ago, kind enough to guide me through the labyrinth of canyons and mountains making up the south portion of Oregon's Douglas County, where my fictional character Mikhail Baranovitch was first run to ground after becoming a fugitive.

Too, there was one of my first heroes, Perry Wright, the rugged North Umpqua woodsman/guide, who, along with Jessie, his bride of over five decades, spent untold hours lecturing a young wannabee on survival in the wilds.

Later, serendipity took a hand as my efforts to find a mainstream publisher for *The Dogged and the Damned* dimmed in the face of general apathy from Manhattan's Mount Olympus editors and agents. At that moribund period, while working out at an athletic club in Whitefish, Montana, I chanced to strike up a casual conversation with--*get this!*--a retired psychologist who had actually served both internship and his residency at-- *still holding on to your seat?*--the United States Veteran's Hospital at Roseburg, Oregon--so central to this story. The stranger showed an interest when I mentioned my novel about a soldier who'd undergone treatment at his former hospital.

Dr. Ray T. Moore agreed to read the work. The encouragement he provided at that critical moment was the element needed to kick me into a decision to self-publish this book.

Chapter 1

"Today, we'll talk about Buna, Michael. Please take a seat."

The patient did as instructed, glancing out the office window where a steady drizzle fell; a drizzle he'd watched for hours from his own room's window.

The psychiatrist continued to shuffle through a stack of papers, pausing from time to time to read a passage or study a diagram. Michael stared at the man, through him, to another place and time....

This drizzle, steady though it might be, is only the drip of a leaky faucet compared to what beat down on us in New Guinea.

Private Mikhail Baranovitch flew into the jungle airstrip at Wanigela on October 16, one soldier among a compliment of replacements for the 128th Regiment of the 32nd Infantry Division; a division depleted by malaria and dengue fever and yellow jaundice. The flight over the mountains from Port Moresby was quick, during a break in the weather, no more than an hour. Private Baranovitch wished he could've had a window to view all the mountains towering from lift-off to touch-down. Fortunately, he was crammed into a space alongside the B-17's port waist turret and the gunner let him take a quick glance out. In the hazy distance was a lofty peak tipped in white. He asked the gunner if the white was snow or limestone, but the man merely shook his head before shoving Michael back to his seat so the airman could reassume his post at the twin 50-calibers.

"All right Michael," the doctor said as he laid the papers to his desk, "tell me about Buna. Were you transported by troop ship?"

The patient's laugh was a sharp bark. "That came later. Actually, the next day."

"The day after *what*, Michael?"

"The day after we flew in."

"I see. So you arrived in New Guinea by air."

"No."

"Michael, I'm trying to help you. You say you flew in to New Guinea, but you never arrived by air. How could that be?"

"We went to Port Moresby by ship, then flew across to Wanigela in a B-17."

"I see. Now we're getting somewhere."

"Then they put us on small ships they called trawlers to go to Pongani."

The doctor rifled through the papers on his desk, found the one he searched for, then began to read. As he did, Michael's mind spun backward....

We marched from Wanigela to the sea carrying duffel bags and weapons. From the beach, we loaded into outrigger canoes paddled by Papuan natives who took us out to two trawlers anchored offshore. Me and fifty-five other men boarded the King John. Forty-six additional replacements were shoe-horned into a smaller sister ship, the Timoshenko.

The trawlers coasted along what he overheard an officer say was uncharted waters off Cape Nelson. All afternoon and most of the night, they coasted. It was during the night, while he watched the phosphorescent water curling from the King John's bow that the newspaper guy said, "Where're you from soldier?"

He turned to see this gruff old guy somebody said was a reporter from the *New York Times* standing at his side. The reporter was as tall as Michael and quite a bit beefier. The younger man said, "Butte, sir. Montana."

"You don't need to 'sir' me, soldier. My war was the last one and I never rose far enough in rank for anyone to do it then, either."

Michael said nothing to that, so the reporter asked, "Why you here, son?"

The soldier saw the man had out a notebook and a stub of pencil. He didn't know what the guy wanted to hear, so he said, "Same reason the rest of 'em are, I suppose."

The *Times* guy smiled. "How old are you?"

"Comin' twenty."

He smiled again. "Nineteen. How long you been nineteen, private?"

"A month. A month and a week, more or less."

"So you weren't drafted, were you?"

"No."

"When did you join?"

"Last January."

He jotted something else down. "Well, private," he said, "despite what you say, you're not like most of these soldiers. Most of them were drafted. So you joined because of 'Pearl'?"

"No, I joined because of my coach. And my papa."

The *Times* guy didn't seem to hear. Or maybe didn't care. Instead he stared down at the purling bow wave and asked, "Are you scared?"

Michael chuckled. "Scared? Of what? So far, I got to spend most of the winter outdoors in boot camp at Fort Lewis. Then I got a train ride to Frisco, took a pleasure cruise to Australia, a ferry ride to Port Moresby, then caught a plane to Wanigela. After Wanigela, natives paddled me around in an outrigger canoe; now I'm on a slow boat coasting over green coral reefs and into deep bluewater bays in the South Pacific. Over yonder is Tahiti and overhead every star in the whole universe sprinkles down. And to top it off, all the guys on this boat—every one of which seem nice—will do to go on a camp-out with. Frankly, Mister ..."

"Durham. Barnaby Durham."

"... I ain't never had it so good, and never would've, or even could've if I'da stayed in Butte, Montana. Hell, this is an adventure. A south seas adventure."

Barnaby Durham scribbled for quite a while. He still stood by Michael's side, but the journalist wasn't paying any attention to the bow wave or reef colors in the moonlight. The young soldier wasn't even sure if the guy knew when the trawler crew cut the engines and dropped anchor. But ...

"Michael, I asked you a question."

Michael's eyes cleared and there was Dr. Henderson with eyebrows arched and chewing on a lip. "I'm sorry, what was the question?"

"I asked why they took you to Pongani?"

"They didn't."

"I thought you said that was where your outfit was going."

"Was. But I didn't get there."

The doctor shook his head, puzzled. "So your outfit never got to Pongani. So where ..."

"The outfit—most of 'em anyway—got there. I didn't."

"Why didn't you get to Pongani, Michael?"

"Got blowed off the boat. Had to swim for shore. Barney didn't make it to Pongani, either. Nor did he make it home,. Shell fragment in the head, I guess."

"Shell fragment? Tell me about it, Michael."

"Course I haven't made it back home yet, either. I still got a chance, though. Barney don't."

"Where's home, Michael?"

"Montana."

"Butte?"

"Nope. Nothing left for me at Butte. Mama and Papa are both gone. But there's lots of places in Montana besides Butte. I always liked Kalispell, every time we played up there."

The doctor propped elbows to desktop and tapped fingertips together. "Tell me what happened on the boat."

"It was the airplane."

"Did the airplane bomb you?"

"Yes."

"So you were still in the boat, on the water, when the Jap plane came over."

"Wasn't Jap. It was one of ours."

"One of ours! You mean the plane was American?"

"Yes. He made one pass to drop a couple that missed, then came back around.

That time, I got a few bursts off before I was blowed into the water."

"At an American plane? A few bursts? What were you firing?"

"My B.A.R."

"So you handled the Browning Auto Rifle. I planned to get to that later. But right now I want to know about the results of the 'friendly fire' from the American plane."

"He strafed us as well as bombed us. Wasn't friendly at all."

"So he came in low?"

"Yes."

"And you were blown into the water. Is that right?"'

"Barney was my friend."

"Of course he was, son. How far from shore were you?"

"Two miles, more or less. It's hard to tell on the water. At least it's hard for me to tell how far it is to any place when I'm looking over water."

"No doubt. But the boat was sunk?"

"Nope. Lots of guys injured and a few killed. But the boat made it to the Pongani beach. So did the other boat."

"And is that when you got your first Purple Heart?"

"The six other boats coming up a week later didn't make it, though. At least most of 'em didn't. That time it was Japs. Japs are better at dropping bombs than Americans."

Dr. Henderson scanned a file lying near to hand, then looked up. "Michael, this says you were wounded at Mendaropu on November 18. Is that the action between"—the doctor paused to glance at his notes—"your trawler and the American plane?"

"Mendaropu is where I caught up with my regiment. I reached 'em a couple of days later. They were still setting up camp when I hobbled in. By then, the shrapnel in my back hurt like hell."

"Hit by 'friendly fire,' yet you got a Purple Heart for it," the doctor mused. "I didn't know they gave medals for being shot by your own side."

"I told 'em I didn't want it. Told 'em all I wanted was for them to pull out the bomb piece. But the sergeant said they all were so pissed off at the Air Corp that the officers wanted to decorate the only guy on board who fired back."

"Were you the only one blown from the boat, Michael?"

"It wouldn't have happened if I had been holding to the rail, instead of my B.A.R."

"Were you the only one blown from the boat, Michael?"

"Barney was a good old guy. Went through the First War without too many scratches. Then got hit in the head by fragments from the same bomb that got me,

I guess. Life's a bitch, ain't it, Doc."

"She certainly is, Michael, a red-titted bitch! Were any others blown from the boat?"

"Couple others, I guess. Neither of 'em made it to Mendaropu. One of 'em was Callaway, from some place in Oklahoma I think. He seemed like an okay guy, too. If you ever see him, let him know I asked about him."

"So you swam two miles to shore. Why didn't you swim for the boat?"

The patient's laughter was explosive. When he ran down, the doctor asked, "What was so funny, Michael?"

"You. Asking why I didn't swim for the boat—and it hi-jinking all over that bay trying to dodge more bombs."

"Were any more dropped?"

"Not that I know of. Four was probably all that plane carried. But I'll tell you, the King John headed up the bay lickety-split for shore in case any more 'friends' showed up."

Doctor Henderson studied the patient, then said, "So you dragged yourself out on the beach. You had no idea where you were. You didn't know if Jap patrols would come screaming out of the jungle. You didn't know which way to go, nor what it'd look like when you got there. You were wounded, and had no idea how severely. Were you scared?"

"No. I was hungry, though. We only had some C-rations on board the trawler. And I worked up an appetite during the swim."

"And you'd lost everything."

"No, I still had my belt knife. And I had my pants. Everything else I jettisoned in the water. Boots, socks, shirt."

"Knife. Do you mean your bayonet?"

Again the patient snorted. "No place for a bayonet on a B.A.R, doc. They give special weapons people jungle knives."

"I'm curious, Michael, why didn't you jettison the knife, too. Wouldn't it have been easier to swim without the knife?"

"Maybe. But sharks—there're sharks in the Solomon Sea. Everybody knows that. We never saw any from the King John, though. But I was bleeding and I didn't know how bad. If a shark come along, I might need something to make it more even."

"And a jungle knife would've made things even against a shark?"

"Better'n nothing. Better than my fists, way I figured."

Dr. Henderson smiled. He thought a moment, then said, "So you reached the beach. What did you do then?"

"Got the hell off the sand. Scrambled into the jungle. Then I found some moss and laid in it to try and stop the bleeding."

"Did it?"

"I guess. Leastways it was pretty well quit when I woke up."

"So you went to sleep?"

Mikhael Baranovitch pushed suddenly to his feet. "I don't want to talk any more. I want to go back to my room."

Dr. Henderson glanced out his office window and said, "It's pretty much quit raining, Michael. Would you like to take a walk around the hospital with me? The air would be especially sweet right now."

"Yes."

Dr. Henderson took a wide-brimmed, flat-crowned canvas hat filled with a multitude of hand-tied dry flies of assorted colors, sizes, and bizarre tastes from his closet, turning the hat around and around, admiring its adornments, pausing to fluff a fly here, stroke another there. Michael stared down at the freckled man's few strands of grayish red hair raked across a sunburned dome; the squirrely fuzz over the ears appeared as a light blend of cayenne pepper speckled with salt. The face was speckled, too: freckled and puffed and florid. The patient suspected the doctor's ruddy complexion wasn't entirely from sun or an Anglo-Saxon heritage. Then the portly little psychiatrist settled the hat in place, glanced up and said, "Ready?"

An old soldier, perhaps a World War I veteran, leaned on a cane at the building's double entrance doors, then hobbled out behind them. The sidewalks were pretty much empty so soon after the rain. The pair stood out: the tall, broad-shouldered, lean-hipped younger man wearing the blue cotton shirt and trousers issued to patients and the basketball-shaped older man with sunburned arms looking for all the world like small diameter pipes poking from a red-flowered Hawaiian shirt. To complete the outlandish ensemble, the doctor wore khaki British officer's tropical shorts, and sandals over off-white, calf-length stockings. Henderson's knees were sunburned, too. Overall, Michael thought the doctor emitted a faint pink, like light coming from a dim shuttered window in a seedy cathouse. He liked the doctor, perhaps even understood and appreciated the man's unconventional nature. It'd been weeks earlier when the orderly first led him into the psychiatrist's office....

"Oh my," a portly, ruddy, ridiculous little man sitting behind a clean army-issue steel desk noted the way Michael ducked at the doorway and said, "you're a big bastard, hmm?"

That first interview began on the wrong foot in other ways, too, like when the doctor opened the file accompanying his new patient: "Says here your name is Mikhail" (he pronounced it Mick-hale). "Is that right?"

The prisoner—and that's how he thought of himself since Morotai—felt no urge to reply until the doctor pointed out that the rules of war obligated prisoners to give certain information to their captors. "Michael Baranovitch," he muttered. "Busted back to "buck." And I don't remember my serial number."

That's when the doctor's chair rollers screeched and he came around the desk, holding out a hand, smiling, and saying, "Michael, it's good to have you here. Our objective is to help you recover. We can do that, too, with your help."

He doubted it. When he'd been led into this prison or asylum or whatever it is—his third since Morotai—they'd climbed two flights of stairs, passed through a security door, and started down a hallway when he and his orderly escort met two other orderlies pushing a gurney. A man covered to the neck with a white sheet was strapped to the gurney. The man's face was long and cross-hatched with careworn wrinkles. Amid the wrinkles was a scattering of white beard stubble. The gurney rider's pop-eyes seemed filled with fear. Those eyes followed Michael until the gurney rolled from sight.

Upon placing him in his room, the orderly had bolted the door from the outside. The prisoner strode to his cell's window and dialed into the asylum's distant sounds—a series of piercing screams and a hyena cackle coming from another direction. He'd noted the fourth floor's barred windows on his way into the building; from that, plus the crazed sounds wafting into his room, he knew they'd stuck him near the lunatics' floor.

The screaming stopped abruptly, but the hyena was joined by another, probably from the same pack.

The street through the hospital grounds was wet, with water standing in puddles on the pavement. A passing vehicle splashed the pair. The doctor shook his fist, but Michael who took the brunt of the spray, seemed not to notice. "This ... this is the first time I've been allowed to walk outside in ..." He paused to glance down at his portly companion, "... I don't remember how long."

Birds were beginning to chirp and robins began work on nightcrawlers emerging onto the watersoaked lawn. "I'm interested in your early life, Michael," the doctor said when they were halfway around the main hospital building.

"I don't want to talk no more," the patient muttered.

Dr. Henderson chuckled. "Oh? I thought you might wish to know that I've sent to Butte, asking for your school records."

The patient faltered, then took up the pace, walking faster and faster, until the doctor was panting, yet still falling farther behind. As they neared completion of their first circle, approaching the steps to the main entrance, Dr. Henderson shouted, "All right, Michael, that's enough! We'll go in now."

Wrought-iron metal benches perched each side of the entry walkway. Michael collapsed onto one. Tears ran freely down his face. He did not glance up as the doctor approached. "Please let me sit here for a little while, Doctor. I won't do anything bad. I promise."

Henderson pulled off his hat, eyeing him closely. "All right, Michael. Sit here for, say, half an hour. I'll tell Daniel to keep an eye on you. He'll tell you when your time is up. After that, you'll have to return to your room. Okay?"

"Yes."

The doctor disappeared into the building as a soft rain again began falling.

It was during Michael's second session with the psychiatrist that the lightning storm struck. Dr. Henderson had just asked if he'd finished high school. When told no, the doctor said, "Shame on you. The army could've wallowed along without your help for a few more months. He was chuckling at his own joke when there was a flash and a deafening crack and the room lights blinked, then went out. Light still leaked in from around the window blinds, but it wasn't much. The doctor opened the blinds. Michael was at his side in a heartbeat. Both men seemed excited by the lowering dark clouds and the black wisps trailing beneath.

"Looks like tornado weather to me, Michael. Or it would be if we were somewhere besides the 'One Hundred Valleys of the Umpqua'."

There was another flash and another not-quite-so-deafening blast somewhere to the north and east. "You know, if lightning strikes one of those maples, a limb could come through this window," the doctor said, shivering. "Exciting, isn't it?" He was even more excited when he helped the big man raise the windows so the wind-blown rain could pelt their faces.

A quarter-hour passed and the shower dribbled to a stop. Again, Michael and Dr. Henderson strolled outside. Again, Michael was permitted to sit unattended on the same wrought-iron bench. A wrinkled, gray-haired man in blue thrust his head out the main doors, peered up at the leaden sky, then crept outside, peering fitfully over his shoulder, as if being pursued. The man nodded at Michael just as a city transit bus pulled to the curb with a hiss of airbrakes, debarking passengers. At the air's "hissss," the gray-haired old soldier screamed, "INCOMING!" and threw himself to the grass, covering his head with hands and forearms.

Michael helped the old man to his feet, then became alarmed at the crazy lights dancing in the other's eyes. They met Daniel as Michael helped the old man up the building's steps. The orderly took note of the older soldier's wet, grass-stained shirt and trousers and said, "Heard 'em comin' again, huh Chester?"

As the orderly took the old man by the arm, he said to the younger one, "You should change clothes, too, Michael."

Chapter 2

"Michael, it's good to see you again. I've thought of you most of the week and frankly, I'm concerned."

"Why?" the man who thought as a prisoner asked as he sank into his chair.

"I'm concerned because I seem to be the only person in the hospital you talk with."

"Daniel."

"I'll grant you that. Daniel says you'll respond to him if he asks you a direct question. But Daniel only works eight hours per day. The other orderlies and the cafeteria ladies tell me you'll only respond to questions, and then in monosyllables. All of them say you eat alone, nor do you take notice of other patients, even if they sit down by you. As far as I know, you've never spoken willingly to others, nor initiated a conversation with another person. All in all, Michael, I'd say my concern is well-founded."

The patient twisted in the chair to stare at the window.

"Is there some reason why you don't talk to others, son?"

"No," Michael said. "I just can't think of anything to say."

The doctor frowned, eyes magnified by the round, steel-framed spectacles. "Look at me, son." When Michael did so, the doctor said, "Did you have any hobbies, Michael? Any interests? Did you build model airplanes? Read adventure novels? Do crossword puzzles? Ride touring bikes? Play football? Hang out at the drug store? Fish? Hunt?"

"Yes."

"'Yes'? Yes to what?"

"Yes to all of 'em. Except the touring bike. Mine was a used Hawthorne without a chain guard or fenders. It wasn't much fun to ride in the rain or if the street was wet." He paused, then added, "Sometimes I'd tape a playing card to a wheel brace so the card rat-a-tat-tatted against the bicycle spokes. Sounded a lot like the reel-type mowers we're hearing outside right now."

"You see? You have interesting stories. I'll bet others would love to hear some of them. And other people have interesting stories, too, and would love for you to listen. Why don't you give them a chance. Start with Daniel. Or Jack. Or Charles, William, or Frank. Start with the orderlies. They're trained to listen. No one will laugh at you. In fact, I'll bet they'll be fascinated to hear about you getting blown from the, uh, King John, was it?"

"Yes."

The doctor glanced back to his desk, pulled a yellow notepad before him and paged through it. "All right, we left last week with you blown from the King John, wounded, swimming to the beach, and hiding in the jungle. You had no idea where you were, or how to join your companions. You feared Japanese patrols and you were hungry, thirsty, and afraid. Right?"

"No. I wasn't afraid. I had my knife. And down in Queensland, they taught us how to use it."

"All right, you weren't afraid. But you were wounded and with no way to dress your wound."

"The shrapnel was still there. I could feel it. But I didn't want to pull on it, because I couldn't see it and could barely reach it." The patient paused, thinking, then blurted, "I guess I was afraid, wasn't I."

"So what did you do?"

"Went to sleep. Then started walking."

"Which direction?"

"Northwest. That's the way the boat went. So that must be where I'd be sure to find Japs. And that was what they were paying me for—to fight Japs."

"Did you stay in the jungle?"

"Pretty much. On the edge of it, anyway."

"What did you do for food and water?"

"Ate coconuts."

"Coconuts! How did you get them?"

"When I came to the plantation ..."

"A plantation? There should've been someone there.

"I didn't see anybody. But I did find a rice sack laying under a coconut palm. It had Japanese lettering on it, so I decided I didn't want to see nobody around there. After dark, though, I climbed a tree and knocked down some coconuts."

"Climbed a tree? A coconut palm? That must have been quite a trick! Even for an unwounded man."

"Not really. I'd been told how natives tied a string between their big toes and used it and their arms to ratchet up a tree. I didn't have a string, but I did have a knife and the rice sack. So I cut a band off its top, twisted it and tied it around my ankles. Worked fine."

"I'd call that fascinating, son. Simply fascinating."

"Then I drank some coconut milk and threw a half-dozen in the rice sack, slung 'em over my shoulder, and took to hiking up the beach in the dark. After I got a fair distance away from the plantation, I cracked a couple of nuts and cut out the meat with my knife. Actually, I did fine."

"And you found your outfit at Mendaropu?"

"Yeah. I could hear activity ahead and I didn't know whether it was us or them. So I pussy-footed through the jungle until I saw a bunch of guys—Americans—head out to the beach to swim in the ocean. I wandered out and joined 'em."

"Were they happy to see you?"

"They made out like I was a hero, which I wasn't. The field doc took out the bomb splinter and he gave me a couple of days off. Then they moved me up into the line."

"The line. At Mendaropu?"

"Yeah. They gave me an M-1 and fit me into a bunch of guys just off-loaded from a half-dozen other trawlers. Those poor bastards had tried to walk to Pongani from Wanigela and nearly drowned in a bunch of swamps before they turned back. I got put into "F" Company, on what we were told was the forward line. I don't know why, though, 'cause one thing there wasn't was Japs."

"I keep hearing 'Pongani', Michael, but nobody gets there. Why is that?"

The patient shrugged. "I guess it was by-passed, maybe because no Japs was there. All's I know is they wanted it for an airfield, and I guess they put one there eventually because before we finished at Buna, our planes were buzzing over our lines morning, noon, and night."

"From Pongani."

"Yeah. Or from Dobodura or Wanigela."

While the doctor busied writing, Michael's mind wandered: Command had ordered patrols out from Mendaropu, but all they found was mosquitos, swamps, and dysentery. Nobody had anything but bayonets to hack through the jungle with. Mud was plentiful and the rainy season hadn't even started. Mostly, though, he remembered Mendaropu for its tedium. He liked the guys he served with—mostly National Guardsmen from Wisconsin. Those Wisconsin boys talked of Pabst and Leinenkugle and the Green Bay Packers. Michael wasn't on a first-name basis with any particular brand of beer (although he'd once got away with a six-pack of Great Falls Select after a ball game with the Bisons), but one thing he could damn sure do—and do well—was talk football with partisans from Curly Lambeau's country.

"The Principal of your Butte school sent me an old 'Bulldogs' Yearbook, Michael." The patient's eyes slowly focused from a spot over the doctor's head to the book the man held in his hand. "It's from 1940, instead of 1941, so it covers the fall and winter of 1939, through the spring of '40. That's when you were—let's see—a sophomore."

Michael seemed riveted by the book.

"It said you were a standout football player, Michael—second-string all-state, as a matter of fact. As a sophomore, that's phenomenal. Especially as a lineman." The patient frowned. "The accompanying letter says you fulfilled every bit of promise during the following year: first-string all-state, led the team in tackles, was the Bulldogs' top blocker. It also said your team went undefeated and that your grades averaged a B-plus."

Michael's eyes dropped to his folded hands, where he began kneading the knuckles.

"Then it said the following year college recruiters watched every game you played—until you quit the team halfway through its schedule. That was your senior year, man! The writer said Notre Dame and Southern California were after you! Said your grades fell and you left school in January to enlist in the army."

A tear squeezed from the big man's eyes.

"Michael, please tell me what happened."

"Can I go now?"

"Why won't you talk about it, Michael?"

"I want to go now."

The psychiatrist closed the Butte Yearbook and said, "Very well. So you liked to fish."

The voice was surprisingly tiny—almost a squeak: "Yes."

"Did you flyfish?"

"No."

"Where did you fish?"

"In the water."

Dr. Henderson smiled. "And what did you think while you were fishing, Michael?"

The patient's brow furrowed and he cupped his chin in a hand. The furrows vanished and the man's black eyes glistened. "I can't remember thinking anything."

"Good answer, son. And you hunted, too?"

"Yes."

"For deer?"

"And elk."

"Any birds?"

"No. Except for chunking fool hens from trees with rocks."

Dr. Henderson shuffled through folders on his desk, then asked, "Can we go back to Buna, Michael?"

"No."

"Why not?"

"Because I'm through now. I want to go back to my room." He stood.

"All right, Michael. But first I want to give you these." The doctor picked up a stack of comic books from the floor and handed them to the patient. "Read those, Michael, then bring them back and I'll give you more."

Mickey Mouse topped the pile, with Donald Duck directly beneath, and Bugs Bunny below that. Michael smiled as he leafed through them, then suddenly held out his hand. Surprised and tremendously pleased, Dr. Henderson took it. After Mikhail Baranovitch had taken his leave, the psychiatrist scribbled **PROGRESS!!** in bold letters across his notepad. Then wrote: **May 23, 1950.**

Daniel reported in on his way off shift that Baranovitch was sitting quietly on his cot reading comic books. William Hefferman, working swing shift, reported the same thing on his log. So did John Wilder, from the graveyard shift.

The following morning, Mikhail Baranovitch knocked on Dr. Henderson's open office door, carrying a stack of comic books. The doctor waved Michael in.

"I...I just thought I'd return these," Michael said, stacking the comic books on a corner of Dr. Henderson's desk. There was a prolonged silence, then Michael said, "Well, I'll go now."

The doctor said, "These belong to my son. But I'll bet he has more. If so, I'll bring them in tomorrow. Okay?"

"Yes, sir. Thank you."

"And in the meantime, son, why don't you stop by the lounge. I'll bet they have copies of the local paper, and probably of the two Portland papers, too. There should be some comic strips in them."

"Yes, sir. I'll do that." The following day, Dr. Henderson had another stack of comic books delivered to Mikhail Baranovitch's room. In it were Spiderman and Batman and Superman comics. There were also more Donald Ducks and Mickey Mouses and Bugs Bunnys, as well as Yosemite Sam, the Coyote and the Road Runner, Tom & Jerry mice, Tweety Bird canary, and Sylvester the cat. There was also a comic book depicting Japanese savagery in the Philippines, and the heroism of captive Filipino and American soldiers on the Bataan March. Daniel plucked the war story from the restroom wastebasket only minutes after dropping the comics off to the patient.

"Well, Michael, we missed our regular weekly meeting didn't we? You knew Memorial Day fell on Tuesday last week, didn't you? And I'll be damned if I could find another suitable time slot for us to visit. But we'll make up for it this week, won't we?"

"Yes."

"Very well. Ah-hum."

Michael stared out the window, as he'd been doing all morning, first from his window, then the main lobby windows, and finally from the common lounge. The lounge was large, its ceiling high. Card tables lined one wall. There were sofas, easy chairs, straight-back chairs, even a couple of recliners. Some patients were in wheelchairs, and it was obvious to Michael that several of the loungers had neither mental or physical capacity to travel the building without help. Not a few glanced at the newcomer, dismissed him, and returned to stare at each other with puzzled faces. One crew-cut man, standing in a corner, wore a heavy coat though the day was warm. He held a coat collar over his mouth as he snickered into it. His eyes were filmy, as if nothing lay behind....

"It's a beautiful day, isn't it?" Dr. Henderson said.

It took a moment before the patient focused on the doctor. But he soon gazed away.

"Look at me, please."

Michael turned again to the doctor.

"I must say, I'm very happy with reports I'm getting on you. I'm told you're spending time in the lounge; you're actually reading there every morning—is that correct?"

"Yes."

"The papers, right?"

"Yes."

"All of them, right?"

"Yes."

"And I'm told you devour them. Daniel said you read the sports section as well as the comics."

"Yes."

"And even society pages and advertising?"

"But not politics. I don't like politics."

"No, not politics. I share your low regard for both donkeys and elephants, my boy."

The doctor paused, hoping for his patient to initiate a topic. Finally he said, "Well, let's get back to business, Michael. Let's talk again about Buna."

The patient began kneading his knuckles.

"When did you move out on Buna?" When he received no reply, the doctor gently said, "It was a month after you arrived at Mendaropu, wasn't it?"

"We didn't have enough to eat," Michael mumbled. "Some of the guys blamed it on officers getting it all, but the problem was in supply—they had too many of us at Mendaropu to supply, either by air or by trawler."

"So you weren't getting enough to eat?"

"And I'd lost my B.A.R when I got blowed out of the King John, so I was mostly naked."

"Naked? Do you mean no clothes?"

"No. No firepower."

"So they didn't have a replacement B.A.R?"

Michael shook his head, opening up memories: They not only didn't have replacement firepower, they never had any oil or hardly any rags to keep what we had clean. Even replacement shirts were hard to find, and I never did find another pair of size-14 boots. Had to cut the toes from a pair of 12s and let 'em hang out. It was clear up to Embogo and beyond before I even found a replacement helmet— picked up one from a guy who didn't need it no more. Got his cigarettes and some M-1 ammo, too. And on the nineteenth, when we went after Cape Endaiadere, I got another B.A.R when the guy packing it was cut in half by two chattering Nambus coming from bunkers hidden in the jungle and tall grass.

My problem was how to get the B.A.R without getting chopped up myself. Hell, the thing was laying there in easy sight, not more than twenty steps away. Problem was, I could see the bunker slits and imagined the Nambu snouts wandering back and forth, looking for another American to eat. Way I figured, I had one advantage in them not knowing I didn't want their bunker; all I wanted was that B.A.R. But how to exploit that little difference in interest? So I laid out two grenades side by side. Then I pulled the pins on both, snatched up one and flung it with my best pitch to the left of the left bunker, then grabbed up the second and flung it as far as I could to the right of the right bunker. I was moving before either grenade exploded. One Nambu started up my direction, then when the grenade to its right front went off, swung in that way. The other Nambu was already spraying its left front when I reached the Browning and started back.

"Michael."

Does no good to do a broken-field when you're dealing with machine guns. Only thing'll help then is how fast you can accelerate from ought-to-forty, and I was doing a hundred and ten when I pitched the Browning behind my mango tree and dove for cover.

"Michael! Are you there?"

So many Nambu bullets gouged and chopped and slashed at the mango that I thought for a minute the Nips were trying to cut it down. But after awhile they quit and I got a chance to reach my new B.A.R and look it over.

"Yoo-hoo! Michael!"

The patient jerked, eyes clearing.

"What were you thinking about, Michael?"

"About my new B.A.R."

"So they gave you a new one?"

Not exactly. The guy using it didn't want it no more."

"I see. That was when you ran into resistance?"

Ran into resistance, did he say? Well, that's one way to put it. Mildly. But there wasn't anything mild about it—they stopped us cold.

"You ran into quite a bit of enemy resistance, I gather from reading about the battle for Buna. You were with the 1st Battalion, moving up the coast. Heading for Cape Endaiadere?"

"Yes."

"And this happened on the nineteenth?"

"Yes."

"So what happened then?"

"We had nothing to eat. Had nothing all day—not even K-rations. Besides that, we were out of ammunition."

"All right. You ran up against tough resistance when you thought you'd have a cakewalk. There was little food and you were running out of ammunition. What did you do then?"

"I didn't fire my B.A.R."

"Oh? Why not?"

"I only had a few rounds—however many in it when the guy who had it got killed. But that's not the reason I didn't fire it."

"So why *didn't* you fire your B.A.R, Michael?"

"I was afraid to. It had rust all over it. Even the barrel was filthy. When I tried to cock it, it jammed. That night when we pulled back I cleaned it. Stayed up half the night working on it. Borrowed some cooking oil to get me by, then wiped it all off with my shirt. I took the firing mechanism all apart, too, and cleaned it. The next morning it was ready."

"So then did you go back to face those bunkers?"

"No."

"I see. You were put into another sector, right?"

"No. We were still supposed to advance up the coast. But there was no use trying to hammer through those interlaced bunkers with nothing more than machine guns and M-1s. Mortars couldn't blow 'em out by dropping rounds on top of 'em, and we had no artillery. Flame throwers didn't get to us until later on, up the coast. Tanks could've done it. But we had none."

"Well, Michael, what did you do?"

The patient shrugged. "The problem wasn't mine. It belonged to the coach. We did the best we could, but when the game plan is wrong, all you can do is keep your head down and wait."

Dr. Henderson glanced thoughtfully at the ceiling. Then he said, "So your casualties were high?"

"You might say that. Is twenty percent high?"

"My God!"

"That's how many we lost to dengue fever and malaria before the nineteenth. By the twenty-third, we'd lost another thirty percent. One of every two of those were dead, the others wounded."

"Michael, those are extremely high casualties." The doctor paused, then said, "You told me the Japanese had constructed formidable defense lines with interlaced bunkers. Did they have snipers in the trees?"

Did they have snipers in the trees? Michael thought. Hell, they had 'em in the ground, too. Trapdoor snipers, we called 'em. Once on patrol, we got into a firefight with a Jap patrol and when it was over and we walked past the dead Japs, two of 'em jumped up and killed Bruno and Jackson and ran off. They would've got away if I hadn't ran 'em down with the B.A.R and blowed their guts all over the jungle.

Michael laughed when he remembered that he almost paid the big price for that one; if he hadn't wheeled back to his squad when he did, the sniper's bullet would've taken him in the top of his head. The patient laughed again. That Jap's mistake was shooting straight down. Wasn't but one place the sniper could be, so I sprayed that treetop with a full clip. Wasn't sure I got him 'til the blood started dripping through the leaves.

"Michael, let's try this one more time: were there Jap snipers in the trees?"

"Yes."

"Is that how you got your second Purple Heart?"

"Yes. But I didn't want that one either. He mostly missed and I didn't."

"Where did you take that one, son?"

"Aw, it's just a long, white streak from my left shoulder down my back, through the cheek of my left butt. Wasn't nothing. They sent me back onto the line on Thanksgiving Day."

Dr. Henderson glanced at his watch, then came to his feet. "Goddamn it, Michael, I don't want this to end, but I've got three other patients to see today."

The big man shook his head and grinned up at the doctor. "All my bullets caught me in the rear, Doc. What does that tell you?"

Chapter 3

The day was blistering. Despite a bright red bandanna, rolled and tied around his balding head, sweat coursed down the pudgy doctor's face. An electric fan perched on a desk corner, blowing out across the room toward the open window. Rising, smiling, and bouncing around his desk, Dr. Henderson said, "Ah, Michael, a bloody hot day, eh?"

The patient nodded and edged to the window.

"'Bloody' is a vile word to the Aussies," the doctor continued, "did you know that?" Then he chuckled. "But of course you knew that. You were stationed in Australia, and fought with the Kiwis in New Guinea."

"Kiwis are New Zealanders."

"That's right. Of course. And Aussies were what?"

"'Diggers'. But I just called them Ozzies."

Dr. Henderson smiled, propped elbows on the windowsill, and cleared his throat. "So let's ..."

Not noticing, Michael said, "Just like we called mosquitoes 'mozzies' and dysentery 'the shits'."

The doctor smiled up at the solemn patient and said, "Ah-hum. That's very interesting, Michael." Turning for his desk, he added, "Why don't you take a seat and we'll go on from where we left off last week at Cape Endaiadere."

"We didn't talk about Endaiadere last week."

The doctor nodded. "Yes, you're right. We talked about the battle for Buna. But you see, I've been reading about that, both in your records and from library research, and the initial objective for your outfit, the 128th, was to secure Cape Endaiadere. Isn't that right?"

"We were covered with dirt and slime, down with fever, starved like dogs, living in a tidal swamp, plagued by mosquitoes and flies, and under fire most of the time from an enemy we couldn't see." He paused, then added, "And damned near demoralized from seeing our buddies cut down in front of us, sometimes by our own planes."

"Go on, Michael," Dr. Henderson said.

"Their bunkers were built of coconut logs and reinforced with plate metal tops and barrels filled with sand. We had no way to knock 'em out, and we couldn't get around them because another one of the bastards was dug in off to the side and covering the first one's approach. There were more, too, enfilading other directions."

"Please continue."

"No artillery. No tanks. Mortars were ineffective against 'em. And the last thing we wanted was to ask the goddamn air jockeys to hit us again."

"Hit, Michael? Do you mean bombs. Are you saying that American planes dropped bombs on you, or are you talking about the incident when you were blown from the King John?" Terrible memories! The patient's eyes slitted and his mouth corners reached for his jawline. "Twice!" he snarled. "They bombed us twice! Got Charley and Brill in the line next to me."

Dr. Henderson, scribbling furiously in his notepad, was startled to hear additional voluntary revelations from his patient: "And the rain! God, did it rain. We waited 'til the rainy season *started* before we launched our attack. Why couldn't we have waited until the dry season. By then, we could've had the equipment we needed. The bastards!"

Dr. Henderson paused, leaned back in his swivel chair. A fly buzzed his nose. Another lit on his sweat-stained bandanna. "You mean the generals?"

"God, did it rain. You never seen the like, Doc. Drummed down twenty-four hours a day, day after day. Once in awhile, though, the heavens really opened and it dumped like a whole herd of Holsteins pissing on a milking room floor. A man couldn't see three feet in that downpour. That was when I got the idea that a guy might crawl ahead through the slime and mud and sheets of blinding Holstein piss and toss a grenade into a bunker slit."

"And you did that, Michael?"

"Good thing I was smart enough to get behind the bunker before attacking it, and not try to dash back to our line. Every bunker in that jungle opened up when the one I tossed the grenade into blew. It was that train ride to Divide that taught me that. Remember?"

"The train ride?"

"Yeah, the one where I hopped the freight out of Butte, then got afraid to jump off. Didn't we talk about that? Where I learned to be smart and alive, rather than dumb and dead?"

The doctor had wriggled forward in his chair. But he leaned back again, swung the chair in a full circle, then studied the patient through his wire-rim glasses. "I don't recall, Michael. Give it to me again."

"Then the Holsteins quit pissing and the cats-and-dogs-rain took over and I laid snuggled up tight against that blowed-out bunker wall without moving, face pressed into the mud mindful that the next thing I might feel was a bayonet in the back. Well, I laid there for maybe a half-hour, until another deluge came along. Then I crawled to the next bunker and did it again."

"Great God! Is that when you made corporal?"

"Then with two enfilading bunkers out on one side, our guys could snake around and outflank the position. That's where my B.A.R. came in handy, holding Jap reinforcements off until my outfit got there."

The doctor pitched his notepad back to his desk and said, "Michael, have you any idea what you've been saying? You've just used quite precise military terms: 'enfilade', 'outflank', 'demoralize'. Where did you pick up those terms?"

The patient's face went blank and his voice toneless: "Same place you did, Major. Either somebody told me about 'em, or I read 'em somewhere. There's no other way to learn. No other place for a person to know most things, is there?"

Dr. Henderson rocked while studying the man across from him. "Tell you what, Michael, why don't we walk down to the river. It's bloody hot outside and most of our way will be under a blistering sun. But I'll bet we can find some shade beneath a riverside oak and perhaps there'll be a breeze there. What do you say?"

The smile was quick, the "Yes" barely audible.

The doctor pulled a pith helmet from his closet shelf. Then he held out his floppy canvas fishing hat full of dry flies to Michael. They made a ludicrous pair as they hiked the sidewalk to the South Umpqua River bridge: the big broad-shouldered man in patient's blues—shirt, trousers, stockings; the short, pudgy man wearing scotch-plaid Bermuda shorts that hung below his knees and a baby blue Hawaiian shirt with prints of bright red anthuriums flowering it. In addition, the short man wore an African pith helmet perched over a bright red bandanna rolled as a sweat band. The taller patient had on a floppy gray canvas hat that was at least two sizes too small for him. Passing autos slowed so passengers could point to the pair and laugh and wave. Even a city transit bus trundled by at a crawl so the driver and his half-dozen riders could get a clearer view.

Michael and Dr. Henderson ignored the bus and its passengers. They saw no passing vehicles, strolling patients, or visiting ladies sitting with patient-husbands beneath maple trees. Instead, they were content to stroll silently together, though the younger man opened ears to the chirp of gray squirrels and the beat of bird wings.

After they left the bridge and sidewalk to drop down to the stream, after they found perches on riverside rocks in the shade of overhanging oaks, the doctor said, "I'm very pleased with your progress, Michael. You know that, don't you?"

Michael picked up a fallen twig and broke it into tiny bits, feeding them one by one into the stream.

"When you first came to see me," the doctor continued, "you wouldn't speak at all. Then it was only in toneless monosyllables, and finally as brief sentences

The Dogged and the Damned

replying to questions. Today, however, you began volunteering information. And you, sir, demonstrated considerable thoughtfulness and depth in that information. I believe, Michael, that you are making enormous strides toward recovery."

The patient pulled off the doctor's fishing hat and laid it at his side. The pith helmet was placed beside it.

"What you need to do now, son, is to join the outside world, seek out others, talk to them, laugh, sing. I'll bet you're more widely read than I supposed. Is that right?"

The larger man sighed. "I don't know what you supposed."

The doctor pointed across the stream. "Look at the mallards! A drake and a hen weaving along shore—see them?"

The patient nodded, then turned back to the doctor. "Are you trying to say something with the clothes you wear?"

Dr. Henderson roared, then wriggled his sandals. "So I'm unorthodox?"

"For an officer, you're the queerest I ever saw."

"And the shirt is gaudy and clashes with the Bermuda shorts?"

Michael said, "I just asked. I don't want to make you mad."

"Well, at the very least I'm comfortable. Army spit and polish was never my style, Michael. When I had to wear it, I did—and I had to wear it all the way through North Africa and India and France. But they relaxed officer dress codes after the war ended and I relaxed with them. Do you think my current style at odds with my profession as a major in a military hospital?"

"I don't know."

"So tell me, were you promoted because of your rainstorm grenade initiative against the bunkers?"

"Yes. Captain Baldwin put in for me, and Sergeant Stans endorsed it, too."

"Tell me about Captain Baldwin."

"He got wounded at Aitape. He was a good guy. I think he still is. But I don't know where he is. I was wounded, too, and never found out what happened to him 'til later."

"So you liked him?"

"Yes. As an officer and as a person." The patient paused, then added, "He stopped my court-martial."

"Oh? How did he do that if he was wounded?"

"I don't know. Wrote a lot of letters, I guess. Sergeant Stans told me his wife is—was anyway—a senator's daughter."

"Michael, are you ready for Morotai? How it happened that Captain Sarbones leveled those charges against you?"

"No."

21

"All right. Let's go back to Cape Endaiadere. You took out those two bunkers in the rainstorm and your squad? platoon? company? flanked the Japanese strong point; then what happened?"

"We ran into another one. That's when Walker and Thomas got it."

"How far apart were the two strong points?"

"I don't know. Maybe a couple of hours of crawling time. Me and Lucky Cosmos had to stay at the two knocked out bunkers until more of our guys came up. The sarge said my B.A.R might better serve there. Anyway, when the rest of the guys came up, me and Lucky took off after our outfit."

"What happened to the other bunkers you bypassed, Michael?"

"After we bypassed them, the rest of the Japs cleared out; it was during the next rain squall. At least they weren't there when the next squad poked into 'em."

"So you ran into another strong point—was it hidden, with enfilading bunkers, too?"

"Yeah. Between the two airfields—the old strip and the new strip. At least that new strong point was up out of the swamp and we could dig rifle pits. But it was clear across a big patch of kunai grass to get to 'em and the Japs had burned the grass down to stubble for a couple of hundred yards in front. So there went my pissing Holsteins idea. Besides, the rain tapered off and anybody would've been dumb and dead to try it then."

"What did you do?"

"Soon as I got my foxhole dug, I went to sleep."

"Weren't you worried about a counter attack?"

"No. The burned-out kunai worked both ways."

"So, tell me how your squad took the next set of bunkers."

"Didn't." Then Michael stirred the water at his foot with the toe of his oxford. "Is it all right if I soak my feet in the river, Doctor?"

"Of course! In fact, I'll join you."

Michael rolled up his trouser legs and waded out to his knees. The doctor followed, then playfully splashed his patient. The patient splashed back and soon there was a full-fledged water fight that left both men soaked and giggling like children.

At last, still chuckling, Dr. Henderson returned to his rock to slip on stockings and sandals. "I'm afraid all good things must end, Michael. It's past time for us to return."

Chapter 4

There were eight chairs at the cafeteria table; six were empty. At one end sat Lawrence Jacobs, a small, gray-haired, gray-faced, World War I vet who'd been gassed in the Argonne Forest. The chair on the opposite side, opposite end was occupied by Mikhail Baranovitch. "Good afternoon, Michael." Dr. Henderson said, ambling up. "Hello Lawrence. Mind if we join you?" The doctor carried a cup of coffee; the lanky, gaunt, white-haired man with him carried a tray filled with food.

Lawrence Jacobs' smile was gap-toothed. "You're always welcome, Doc." Michael waved a casual hand at the empty chairs.

The newcomers pulled out chairs in Jacobs' row, across from Michael, but before they took seats, Dr. Henderson introduced the stranger as Weyland Jones. Jones, Michael noted, was not dressed in hospital blues. "Michael is the gentleman I was telling you about, Weyland. He has some fascinating stories."

Though Michael shook hands, his glance was brief. It was long enough, however, to tell him that Jones' face was swarthy with prominent cheek bones and a five-o'clock-shadow. In addition, the hand Jones offered was gnarled and calloused, with dirt beneath the fingernails. The man's smile was broad, though, with two rows of even, glistening teeth.

"So where did you serve, Michael?" Weyland asked as he took his chair.

"New Guinea."

"Oh really. I was there, too."

Michael stared at his plate, picking at his food.

Dr. Henderson said, "Michael was at Buna."

"Now isn't that a coincidence," the newcomer said. "I was at Buna, too."

Michael looked up in interest as Jones asked, "What outfit?"

Michael swallowed, then said, "128th."

"I was with the 126th." The man grinned infectiously and added, "Actually I was with the Mendendorp Force."

Michael dropped his spoon. Holy shit! he thought. This is one of the "Ghost Mountaineers," the guys who climbed over the Owen Stanley Range from Port Moresby via the Kapa Kapa trail. This is one of the ones who edged along cliff walls and hung onto vines so they wouldn't fall over thousand-foot cliffs. It took three weeks for these poor bastards just to cross the mountains, then when they came out weak, filthy, mud-caked, and half-starved on the other side, they had to march forty more miles through swamp and jungle to get to the battle. Michael murmured, "The Ghost Mountain outfit?"

Again the broad smile. "That was us. It was an experience. But given my druthers, I'd druther do that one twice more than go into Buna once, even if I did have to crawl for seven hours just to make the last 2,000 feet to the top."

"Your battalion was physically destroyed," Michael muttered.

"Well, yeah. But most of my buddies came out at the end of the Kapa Kapa Trail. All too few came back from Buna."

Lawrence Jacobs moved around the table to take a place at Michael's side. As he did, Dr. Henderson said, "Weyland was one of our patients. And he still checks in from time to time. He has a farm out of Sutherlin."

Michael seemed fascinated by the gaunt farmer. He asked, "Where did you go in?"

"At Buna village."

"Which time?"

"Well, I was there on December 2, then again on the 5th."

Michael sighed. "They bombed you, too, didn't they?"

Jones nodded. "We not only got hit by our own planes, but by our own artillery. Most of us just plain quit after that, some collapsed from nervous exhaustion, crying like babies and shaking all over from head to foot."

Dr. Henderson said, "Weyland wound up at 'Huggins Roadblock'."

"No!" Michael cried.

"Yeah," Jones said. "Started out to be just a supply party. We got into a scuffle just to get through. Then when we did, the door closed behind us. The whole idea for the attack on December five was to relieve us."

Quiet descended on the table. Then Michael shook his head and said, "You got balls the size of grapefruits, soldier."

Jones laughed. Dr. Henderson said, "Well, gentlemen, I have to get back to the office." He eyed Michael thoughtfully, then said to the World War I veteran, "Lawrence, how about walking me to my office? I've got something to talk to you about."

Jacobs leaped to his feet, beaming.

After the doctor and Jacobs had gone, Weyland Jones said, "What about you? Dr. Henderson told me you got a battlefield promotion and a medal at Buna."

"You got a medal, too, if you were with Huggins."

Jones smiled. "Okay. It's something I'm proud of. Now, how about you? If you were with the 128th, that means you probably came up the coast, headed for Endaiadere."

24

Michael nodded. "What we thought we were after was airfields. But after we got 'em we got re-routed to Giropa Point."

"Via the coast? Or from 'The Triangle'?"

"God no! Up the coast. Them guys in The Triangle had it worst of all."

"Oh I don't know," Jones mused. "They had it bad, all right. And I'm glad I wasn't there. But my guys had it bad at Buna Village and your guys had it bad at Endaiadere and Giropa, and we both had it bad at Buna station."

Michael nodded, muttering, "The ones who got through The Triangle went to Buna Station, too." The blue-clad patient pushed his empty plate aside while Weyland Jones continued eating.

Jones asked, "Where you from?"

Michael said, "Now, or then?"

"Then."

"Montana. Butte."

"I'm told it's a pretty place."

"Not Butte. But it was home."

"You want to go back there?"

"No, not now. Both my folks are dead. Butte people are fine, but I want to live where there's trees on the mountains."

Weyland Jones took a pack of cigarettes from his pocket, shook a few loose and offered one to Michael. Michael wagged his head. "Kicking the habit was the one good thing to come out of my hospital time."

Jones struck a match. "There are mountains around here."

Michael smiled. "Not like in Montana."

"Maybe you haven't seen the Cascades."

"I seen Rainier from Fort Lewis. They're still not like my Montana mountains."

Jones drew deeply, then said, "So where were you wounded?"

Michael said, "In the butt and in the back."

"I mean what action?"

"Which time?

"How many Purple Hearts you got?"

"Three. They didn't give me one for Morotai until later." He hesitated, then added, "And that was way too late."

"Tell me about Morotai."

"No."

"Okay," Jones said. "What do you want to know about me?"

"You from around here?"

"Long time. The first Jones came in with the Applegates, back in '44. That's *eighteen forty-four.* Settled up at Yoncalla. My daddy had a farm out at Umpqua. Lost it in '37. I signed up in '39. Made noncom in '41. That's how come I wound up with the 126th. Then I got busted over a bar fight in Brisbane and still wound up with the 126th."

The two men fell silent. Jones drew thoughtfully on his Lucky Strike while Michael studied him as if the ex-patient had a secret to unlock. Then Jones said, "The medal—what is it?"

"Was," Michael said. "I don't have it any more. None of 'em."

"Why?"

"I threw 'em in the ocean as soon as I could hobble to the beach on Espiritu Santo. Purple Hearts, too."

Weyland Jones gazed thoughtfully around the dining room. Shrewdly, he never asked Michael why he'd thrown his citations away, but said instead, "Tell me about how you earned them."

One of the serving ladies bustled up to pick up their trays and plates and cups. "You boys are supposed to deposit these at the counter on your way out."

"Are we through?" Weyland Jones said, feigning surprise.

She laughed and slapped his shoulder with a napkin. "Weyland, what ever will I do with you?"

Michael envied their easy repartee.

After she'd gone, Jones said, "Back to your medals...."

Mikhail Baranovitch pushed back from the table and said, "I don't want to talk about it now."

Jones came to his feet, too, holding out a hand. Michael took it and said with feeling, "Thank you."

The Sutherlin farmer pulled out a notepad and jotted his name and telephone number, ripped out the page and handed it to Michael. "We'll probably bump into each other from time to time. I come here for medicine and physical checkups. When I'm here I'll look you up. Meanwhile, feel free to call me anytime you want. We have a lot in common, you see. Where you are now is where I once was." Tears came into the drawn face of the gaunt man. "That's why I know what you're going through."

At the doorway, Jones gripped Michael's shoulder, "God speed," he said and strode away.

"Isn't Weyland Jones an interesting fellow?" Dr. Henderson said when he and Mikhail Baranovitch settled onto a wrought iron sidewalk bench for their next weekly interview.

"Uh-huh."

"Would you like to know how long he was a patient in our hospital before being restored to health?"

"Yes."

"Twenty-two months. Broke down in Luzon in 1945. Came to us before the war ended because his family was here. His recovery set no speed record, but it was a damned good average. We want you to do the same, Michael."

His patient stared across the lawns at a distant ridgeline. "I want that, too."

The doctor followed his gaze. "That's Mount Nebo, Michael. At least the far left point is. They say there are wild goats up there who predict the weather for the people in Roseburg. Can you believe that?"

"Thank you for introducing us, sir."

"You're welcome. I'd recommend you seize every opportunity to talk to Weyland. He has as many interesting stories to tell as you do. And the most important thing is he knows enough to be sympathetic to you, no matter what mood strikes." The patient said nothing, continuing to gaze at the distant ridge. "Will you? Will you talk to Weyland when you can?"

"Yes," Michael said, "I'll try."

Dr. Henderson clapped the patient on the knee and said, "Okay, time to get back to work. When we last left off, your patrol was blocked by another nest of bunkers and snipers between the two airfields on Endaiadere. Is that right?"

"Yes."

"So how did you get by them?"

"They finally brought up a field gun and knocked out three pillboxes before they used up all their ammunition. But it was enough for us to circle past the bunkers and take them out from the rear with gasoline and a match."

Without thought, Dr. Henderson cried, "How horrible!"

The patient's response was explosive, leaping to his feet, he thundered, "Is there a good way to die!" He faced the reddening doctor squarely and shouted, "IS THERE? IS THERE?"

"No, no. Of course not. I'm sorry Michael."

The patient subsided to stare down at his toes.

"Michael, would you like to stroll down to the river?"

"No."

The pudgy man wearing suntans pushed to his feet and said, "Well, I would. Come along now."

Obediently, the patient followed. Before they were halfway to the bridge, they trudged side by side. After they reached the structure they walked to the other side of the river, where rows of thirty-foot cedar trees, limbs nearly touching, brushed close-cut grass. Michael parted the limbs and disappeared among the trees while the doctor smiled indulgently.

When they continued on, Dr. Henderson pointed through the trees at another red brick building, much smaller than their hospital complex. "That's the old hospital, Michael. They now call it the 'Old Soldiers Home.' It was built, I believe shortly after the turn of the century to house recovering Spanish-American War veterans. Isn't that interesting?"

"Yes."

They strolled on until their sidewalk bumped into a busy east-west thoroughfare. "That's it, Michael. We've walked to the south edge of the hospital grounds. Perhaps later we can explore the north grounds, too. Would you like that?"

"Yes."

A car turned from the busy street onto the one slicing through the hospital complex. A paperboy pedaled by on his bicycle—a "Hawthorne" Michael saw—with a slack newspaper bag hanging from its handlebars. The boy waved. Both Michael and the doctor waved in return.

As the two men re-crossed the river, Dr. Henderson said, "So you'd seized the two airfields. Was your mission then complete?"

"No."

"You still had Cape Endaiadere ahead, didn't you?"

"No. The Japs abandoned it after they lost the airfields; they pulled back to Giropa Point."

"So that became your objective?"

"Yes."

Each man walked with his head down, hands behind his back. Michael, anticipated the doctor. "They had bunkers in depth blocking us from Giropa Point, too. That's one thing about the Japs, they hedged all the time. I'll bet they prepared those defenses just in case, while they marched over the mountains, on Port Moresby."

Dr. Henderson smiled. "Go on, son."

"We wanted tanks to take care of the bunkers. Instead, they sent five open Bren-gun carriers to break through."

They came to the hospital entrance and Dr. Henderson sat down on the same bench he'd left forty minutes earlier. Michael took a seat beside him. "And?" the doctor said.

"It was a slaughter. Those poor bastards never had a chance. The ground was uneven, with stumps all around and their carriers got hung up. They were assaulted with hand grenades, machine guns, and bombs that stuck on the sides of the machines."

"It must have been bad."

"Hell, they knocked all five of 'em out in fifteen minutes. Killed thirteen of the twenty crew members and wounded the rest." Michael lapsed into momentary silence, then added, "And they got a bunch of us who followed in support."

The doctor pushed to his feet and said, "Unfortunately, I have no more time, Michael. You may stay out here for an hour. I'll tell Daniel. But before I go, I must know what happened after the Bren-gun carriers were knocked out?"

Michael shrugged. "The Japs pulled out. I guess they killed so many of us that they wound up without anything left to kill us with. So they pulled back to Buna Station."

Chapter 5

For a guy as reticent as Mikhail Baranovitch, he turned positively garrulous during the days following his stroll with Dr. Henderson to the Old Soldiers Home. He no longer waited for the cafeteria line to thin, but entered it with others. He even responded to their comments like, "Nice day," or questions such as, "How goes it?" There were days when Michael put together an entire sentence—or even two—with a half dozen fellow patients. Sometimes he smiled and "Tsk-tisked" when a fellow patient moaned about his teeth hurting or his toes curling.

Baranovitch could often be found in the common lounge, quietly reading, devouring each of the three newspapers delivered daily to the reading room, or a magazine or book. It wasn't that the man initiated contact with other patients, but that he no longer shunned them. If another patient sat down beside Michael while the big man read the newspaper, he'd offer a section to the newcomer. If the newcomer made comment on events transpiring in the outside world, Michael laid his paper across his knees and listened politely. Occasionally, if the other's comment concerned sports or outdoors activities such as hunting or fishing, Michael might softly offer his point of view.

Weyland Jones stopped by on Saturday and the two men sat on one of the benches flanking the hospital's entry steps, quietly exchanging Buna experiences. Weyland accompanied Michael back to the main lobby and again pressed his phone number on his blue-clad friend, saying, "Remember to call me anytime you want, buddy."

On Sunday morning, Michael entered the common lounge at five minutes after six. There were two other patients already there. Michael found the Portland *Oregonian* and nodding to the other men, selected an overstuffed chair by the window. His eye settled on bold, three-inch type blazoned across the top of the paper's front page:

NORTH KOREA LAUNCHES ATTACK ACROSS 38TH PARALLEL - SEOUL THREATENED!

Michael leaped to his feet, ripped off the front page, wadded it into a ball and threw it at the open doorway. "Hey!" the patient to his right shouted; the other shrank into his chair. Baranovitch rushed into the hallway, kicking at the wadded newspaper as he passed. He took the stairs three at a time, ran down the long hall, darted into his room, and flung himself on his bunk. Later, when Lloyd, the weekend orderly working the day shift passed by and glanced in his room, Michael stood quietly by the window, nose pressed to the glass.

Mikhail Baranovitch did not report for breakfast that Sunday morning. Neither did he attend the noon meal. He didn't come to supper, either. Ralph, the evening orderly, reported that Baranovitch gazed out his window all during his shift. And when the night orderly, David, passed by on his first round, he saw Mikhail Baranovitch peering into the inky night. Twice more during the night, David passed the room and found Mikhail Baranovitch at his window. David passed along his findings to his regular weekday superior.

"Michael."

The patient glanced from the window, then returned to stare out onto the hospital grounds.

"Michael, what's happening?" Daniel laid a hand on the big man's shoulder and said, "Come along and let's go to breakfast."

The patient meekly followed, listlessly offering nothing as Daniel filled his plate with hotcakes and sausage and eggs and hashbrowns, then snared two cups of coffee. They found an isolated table and Daniel sat quietly while the blue-clad man scraped the plate clean. Then he asked, "What's wrong, Michael?"

The patient shook his head.

"Is it Korea, Michael?"

The patient stared down at his empty plate.

"Do you wish to go back to your room, Michael?"

"Yes."

Daniel returned at noon to assist Michael to the cafeteria. And Sam, the evening orderly, came for Michael at six p.m. Michael handled his own tray the following morning, responding with a simple "Yes" or "No" to the serving ladies questions. Again, he and Daniel sat apart from the others.

"It's the war in Korea, isn't it, Michael? It's upset you, hasn't it?"

"Barney was a nice guy."

Daniel didn't have the foggiest idea who Barney was, but he said, "He sure was, Michael. A very nice guy. You know, the war in Korea has upset lots of people. Nobody wants it. But when it's forced on us, what can we do?"

"Kill Japs. That's what they paid me to do. And that's what I did."

"Only these are North Koreans." The orderly thought about it a moment, shrugged, and said, "Same difference, maybe."

Daniel collected Michael at noon and after they'd finished their lunch, the orderly took the patient to Dr. Henderson's office.

The room was in considerable disarray. File drawers were open, half-filled cardboard boxes were pushed beneath the window and against the wall. Dr. Henderson's pith helmet lay upon one of the boxes of file folders. The canvas fishing hat was turned on its crown atop a black leather medical bag. A pair of field glasses perched on a desk corner.

Dr. Henderson wore a freshly pressed suntan uniform, with the gold oak leaves of a major pinned to his blouse collar. He was on hands and knees, rummaging in the lowest drawer of a file cabinet. Another man, tall, stooped, acerbic-appearing, with wild gray hair and a large between-the-eyes mole leaned in a corner, watching. The new man stared at the orderly and his charge, saying nothing.

Daniel cleared his throat. Dr. Henderson looked around, pushed to his feet and, while dusting his hands, said, "Ah, Michael. Good to see you again. Come on in." He gestured to the new man and said, "This is Dr. Smith."

Dr. Henderson then waved at the orderly and his patient, "And this is Daniel and the patient I spoke with you about, Michael Baranovitch." Dr. Smith made no move; Daniel acknowledged him with a soft, "Hello." Michael's attention was entirely on the Major.

Dr. Henderson dismissed Daniel, then placed a hand on Michael's shoulder and chuckled. "I'm being called up, Michael. Can you imagine an old duffer like me being called to active duty."

Shutters on Michael's eyes descended, turning them vacant.

Dr. Henderson led him to the chair, but he continued to stand woodenly between it and the desk.

"I guess there's an urgent need for doctors, Michael, no matter their age. And no matter whether he practices surgery. I'm trained as a doctor. They need doctors, so I have to go.

"Besides," the doctor added, "maybe I'll find adventure, too."

The man in blue began to sway on his feet, imperceptibly at first, but rocking back and forth, farther and farther.

Dr. Henderson said, "The bastards took Seoul last night. We're sending in troops, but it's questionable if we can even hold on to the peninsula. There are apparently a lot of casualties."

Tears squeezed from Michael's clinched eyes to drop on the floor between his feet.

Dr. Henderson glanced at the other doctor, then said, "I won't be gone long, Michael. Certainly no longer than a year. The only regrettable thing is, I won't, during the interim, participate in your recovery. Instead, that delightful duty will belong to Dr. Smith. He's a local doctor who will assume responsibility for some of my patients. You are one of them."

Michael continued to rock, eyes closed. More tears squeezed out to streak through stubble on his unshaven face.

"My wife and son fail to applaud my leaving, also, Michael. Did I tell you of them? My son is—or will be—entering high school this year. And my wife is a radiant lady I met while still in college, back during the depths of the Great Depression."

The patient's rocking began to ebb.

"So you see, everyone will suffer in this. But when the other bastard jabs you in the eye, what can you do but jab him back."

"I killed Japs," Michael said. "That's what I did."

"That's right. And you were very good at it, son." Dr. Henderson glanced out the window and said, "What do you say you and I go out and sit on a bench?"

The day was cloudy, but warm. Dr. Henderson leaned back against the wrought iron and said, "I've been hearing disturbing reports about you, Michael, ever since Korea broke. You have to be led to the cafeteria. Are you hiding in your room?"

"No." Then before Dr. Henderson could say more, Michael added, "Maybe."

"Shit happens, Michael. There's nothing you can do about global events. The only thing you can do is learn to cope with them."

"Yes."

"I know you well enough to know you're not afraid for yourself. Therefore, you must be afraid for others. Is that not the problem, Michael?"

"I don't know."

Dr. Henderson stared out across the street, to the east. He asked, "Do loud noises frighten you, Michael?"

"I don't think so."

"Does stupidity frighten you?"

"No."

"Does stupidity anger you?"

"Sometimes."

"Does stupidity that gets somebody else killed anger you?"

"Yes."

"Does it infuriate you?"

"Yes."

"Really infuriate you?"

"YES! YES! YES! YES!"

"Enough for you to want to make the stupid one stop doing stupid things to your friends?"

The patient jerked back against the iron bench's back, crossed his arms and legs, and said nothing. His lips, however, pinched into a thin line and his eyes

33

flashed sparks.

Dr. Henderson smoothed the wrinkles in one trouser leg and said, "The world's not a perfect place, Michael. There are stupid people. Some of them, unfortunately, rise to command. Just as there are smart people who rise to command that aren't competent to command in their sphere. All humanity does not improve linearly. You must understand that. The world does not just grow better day by day, person by person. Instead, humanity moves steadily forward in jerks. Some people are smart and good, some dumb but good. Other people are smart and bad, while yet others are dumb and bad. On the average, however, the world gets better from one generation to the next. We must believe that.

"Hitler was a bad man. So was Mussolini. So was Japanese militarism bad. But that didn't make all Germans or Italians or Japanese bad people, just as one rotten officer doesn't make the entire command structure bad. It is true that today there are good people dying because there are bad decisions being made. But that doesn't make every decision that's being made bad. Some are good. Our men are going into battle in Korea because a good decision was made about a bad situation caused by bad people. In actual combat, by and large, our people will be handled deftly in order to achieve good results." Dr. Henderson glanced up at Michael, then continued: "Good will win out, Michael, you'll see. But I fear there are many hard rows to hoe before our good wins over their bad. What we must do—all we can do—is live through their bad. And we must, in our own way, try to strike such blows as we can against the bad, just as you did in your own way against Japanese aggression in the last war.

The doctor paused, then continued: "Now, what about you? How does all the foregoing apply to you? I don't know and neither do you."

Michael blurted, "Does that mean we should *always* follow a bad order? *Always?*"

The doctor straightened the other trouser leg. "That's a much more complex question, Michael. The guard who followed an order to bayonet a fallen prisoner on the Bataan Death March was morally wrong. And Nazi guards who gassed innocent people by the trainloads can in no way be defended for following Hitler's orders. But, 'Soldier, take that beach' against a hail of gunfire, or 'Soldier, take that mountain against emplaced guns'—I don't know."

Michael muttered, "Once? Twice? How about ten? Twenty? Fifty times?"

The doctor shook his head. "I don't know, Michael. I know what military regulations say. But I don't know what's right. Perhaps someday you and I will be able to come up with a few answers. Right now, however, I must go back to my office and complete packing." He stood. "Why don't you come with me so you and Dr. Smith can get acquainted."

Back in his office, Dr. Henderson turned over his two chairs to Dr. Smith and Michael. Smith, sitting across the desk from his patient, opened Michael's files and said, "All right, Mikhail, tell me about yourself."

Michael studied the binoculars lying on the desk's near corner. "Let's see, you were in the Pacific. Were you employed against the Japanese?" When he received no response, Dr. Smith said, "Mikhail? Mikhail!" And he reached across the desk to snap his fingers.

Dr. Henderson, carrying a cardboard box, paused at the door. "It's probable he won't answer unless he's called Michael?"

Startled, Smith looked down at the file. "But it says 'Mikhail' as plain as day." Dr. Henderson was gone.

When Henderson returned, the other doctor paced angrily at the side of the desk. "You're right about him not talking. He has yet to speak, even when I called him Michael."

Dr. Henderson sighed. Then he said, "Michael, would you help me carry a box out to my car?"

The blue-clad patient jumped up. On their way to Henderson's gray Buick coupe, the Doctor said, "Michael, you must be patient with Dr. Smith, just as you were with me. Remember that he's here to help you, just as I was—and will soon be again. Professionally, Smith may not be as competent as we'd like, but his intentions are honorable and he does have training that might be of benefit to you."

"Like Captain Sarbones?"

"Who?"

"Captain Sarbones. The officer I wanted to kill."

Chapter 6

Mikhail Baranovitch opened the door, then snapped to attention and saluted. "At ease, soldier," the major said, striding past him and into the room.

"They said you were gone," Michael said. "They said you left for Korea."

Dr. Henderson chuckled. "Actually, I'm to leave tomorrow for San Francisco. I just stopped by to tie up a few loose ends. Then I found the pitcher of roses you'd left on my old desk. Dr. Smith seemed upset that you might have prowled outside at night in order to pick them. He also said the stems were cut and he concluded from that fact that you had some sort of a knife."

Michael, still at the door, hung his head.

"Dr. Smith also told me you simply won't talk to him, so I thought I'd pop up and perhaps we could discuss it. Can we?"

"I don't know."

"Of course you do, Michael. You're upset because of the war in Korea. Then you became more upset when you discovered I'm leaving. So now you've regressed in your recovery when you should be working for continued improvement."

Dr. Henderson glanced around, then sat on Michael's tightly made cot and said, "Why don't you sit down beside me and let's talk about it, son."

After Michael took a seat the doctor said, "I'm not indispensable to your mental well-being, Michael. And no one should be. You assist in guiding your ability to recognize what's salient in your life and what isn't. It's true that I'll be gone for a period. And it's also true that you will go to sleep every night, wake up every morning, eat breakfast, lunch, and dinner every day whether I'm present in your life or not."

The blue-clad man focused on the floor between his oxfords, but the doctor knew he listened.

"Michael, I think we were making huge strides in treating you simply by helping you confront your beasts from the past. I just wish we'd had a little more time because I believe you could've progressed steadily on until complete restoration. Another month, perhaps two, and I would've felt confident enough to give you the freedom of the hospital grounds for a couple of hours each day." He saw the patient nodding and became more encouraged. "What you must do, Michael, is continue your progress, to hell with Dr. Smith. He's there to help you and you'll be in error if you don't at least try to pick the good things he has to offer, even though you may choose to reject the rest. Do you see?"'

Michael continued to nod.

"Good boy!" The doctor pulled himself up by gripping Michael by the shoulder and said, "Daniel told me you have an excellent view from your window, is that right, Michael?"

"Yes." The patient followed the doctor.

Halfway to the window, however, the doctor faltered. At the window, he didn't bother to glance outside, but picked up a pair of binoculars from the sill. He turned them over in his hands, then murmured, "These are my Zeiss glasses aren't they, Michael?"

The big man pressed his nose to the glass and said, "It wasn't right, Barney getting killed when all that happened to me was getting blown off the boat."

The doctor shook his head. "I missed them, son, but I thought I'd already packed them in one box or another." Then he harshly said, "Look at me, Michael."

The big man turned and stared down at the portly officer. "You do know that it's wrong to take another person's property don't you?"

"Barney was a nice guy."

"But Barney wouldn't have liked you to take another man's property."

"The captain would have let me."

"No, Michael. The captain wouldn't have let you. I'm a major and I outrank him. And I just said so."

When the man in blue said nothing, Dr. Henderson sighed. "Michael, I don't know why some things are the way they are. But I do know that we are all at risk some way or the other every day. Shit happens. When shit happens, most people live through it and go on with their life in the best way they can. Other people, however, are overwhelmed by the shit and cannot go on. Most of the unavoidable shit is manageable, though, even when it's unavoidable. How? Because, more often than not, it's natural. When you recognize that, then you're on the road to managing it. Dammit, man, that's what I wanted to lead you to. I wanted you to be able to recognize that what you experienced, while perhaps unavoidable, was to some degree natural—and manageable. Then came this sonofabitchin' Korea."

Dr. Henderson sighed and shrugged his shoulders. "Michael, did you hear what I said?"

"Yes."

"Do you understand that it's very important that you try to work with Dr. Smith?"

"Maybe."

"Goodby, son." The doctor held out his hand. "Hasta la vista."

Michael seized the hand and surprised Dr. Henderson by saying "Adios"—until the doctor remembered that the big man had spent many months in recovery at the former Spanish Island of Espiritu Santo.

Dr. Smith did not choose to see Michael the following Tuesday. Instead, Daniel, while accompanying the patient to the noon meal, told him the psychiatrist had fallen so far behind that he had to reschedule Michael for the following week. While Daniel and Michael loitered over ham and macaroni, two other orderlies, on Dr. Smith's instruction, searched Michael's room until they found the scissors he'd used to cut long-stem roses for Dr. Henderson.

The scissors led to Michael being confined to his room for the remainder of that week, his food brought to him. His door was not locked however, because it was necessary for him to use the hall bathroom. Thus the night orderlies ignored Michael if he roamed upper-floor halls, but held fingers over their lips and cautioned him against descending to the main floor. In addition, Daniel brought the pseudo-prisoner whichever of the Portland newspapers he could spirit from the common lounge.

For his part, Michael was surprised by the numbers of fellow patients frequenting the restroom during the wee hours of the morning. He wondered if the new doctor had introduced some virulent strain of insomnia into the hospital.

Dr. Smith scowled up at Michael when Daniel delivered him for consultation on July 18. "Sit down, soldier," he said after first spending several seconds staring at him. "I trust you've learned the penalty for hiding weapons in your room."

When the big man made no move to sit, nor even acknowledged the psychiatrist's presence, Dr. Smith ordered Daniel to make the patient sit. When Daniel leaned forward and whispered, "Please," the big man dropped abruptly into his chair.

The doctor continued to study Michael, then opened a file folder and said, "All right, Mikhail, I want a report from you on what happened at Morotai."

Michael met the doctor's sharp eyes head on. But he was looking through him, thinking about what a dumb bastard this dumb bastard is. He wondered what the dumb bastard would do if he knew about the paring knife he'd just picked up in the cafeteria?

Daniel laid a hand on Michael's shoulder as the doctor said, "I can't very well help you, young man, if you won't cooperate."

The patient figured that worked two ways. He decided Smith was a screwed up refugee from a failed circumcision, where his parents should've sued the doctor for throwing the wrong piece away.

"Cowardice is pretty serious stuff, you know, even if it was swept under the rug. I assume you have an explanation?"

Michael's eyes met Smith's head on. The last shrink didn't have to have an explanation and neither did the investigating team at Espiritu Santo. Or the ones in San Francisco. But you figure you'll get it out of me? Hell, you bastard, you might be able to outthink me, but you can't outwait me.

"All right, Mikhail, you're not leaving here until you talk to me."

Michael's broad grin broke his face in two. "Ah now, this is something I know how to do," he said while thrusting to his feet, wheeling, smile still firmly in place, starting for the door. Daniel made as if to block him, but the smile vanished and Michael shook his head. His friend stepped aside.

Back in his room, Michael slipped the paring knife in his shoe and stared out the window.

The following week he refused to follow Daniel for his weekly psychiatric visit and, as a result, his minimum security privileges were revoked. In addition, he was placed behind lock and key in his old third-floor room overlooking the boiler room chimney.

It was Weyland Jones who was instrumental in getting Michael released from the high-security wing, and when Daniel came for him, the orderly was chortling. "You should've seen him, Michael. Man, did sparks fly. Maybe you heard Weyland shouting clear up here. He called that excuse for a shrink every name in the book, including a bunch I hadn't heard before. Then when Smith threatened to recommit him, Weyland went right over the desk. Took three orderlies to break it up."

Upon entering his former room, Michael strode directly for his window looking out over the greensward.

"Then when Smith went to press charges, half the hospital staff ganged up on him, including the other psychiatrist. Weyland's two brothers came down from Sutherlin and by the time the sheriff got here, Smith was out of the building lock, stock, and barrel. Dr. Harrow signed your transfer form. He's also agreed to take your case and will see you next Tuesday." Daniel paused at the door. "You will see Dr. Harrow, won't you?"

"Yes."

The orderly smiled. "I'll come for you at noon. We'll eat together in the cafeteria. All right?"

"Yes."

Dr. Harrow was a prune of a man, weathered from age, hard work, and genetics. His desk was overflowing and untidy. Michael thought the new doctor untidy, too, despite his suntanned uniform, which also carried the oak leaves of a major. "Come in Michael—it is Michael, is it not?"

The patient nodded, shuffling into the room.

"Please take a chair, son." The chair was covered in leather. The room was the same size as Dr. Henderson's office, but it occupied the northeast corner of the building. Across the street, further northeast, was the carpentry shop where patients who'd reached trusty status could hone woodworking skills. Michael sat gingerly, perched on the edge of the chair.

"I had occasion to discuss your case with Dr. Henderson, before he left. He felt you are special and he was quite hopeful for you." Michael said nothing, though Dr. Harrow allowed him time to comment if he wished. "I'm aware of the problems you had with Dr. Smith and want you to know the rest of the staff apologizes for whatever might've happened."

"Why aren't you in Korea, too?"

The question took Dr. Harrow by surprise, but he chuckled. "I'm a little old, Michael. Too old. In fact, I'm overdue for retirement. Korea postponed that. But it'll end someday and then I can retire and spend more time in my orchards."

Michael nodded. "I would like that, too."

"Would you now? Have you had any experience as an orchardist?"

Michael laughed. "In Butte, Montana?"

Dr. Harrow studied the patient. The doctor's eyes were disconcerting, set in his brown, crinkled face. Though faded, they had distinctive dark rings around the pupils. Michael found them interesting, so much so that he leaned forward and cocked his head. The doctor retreated further into his chair, but said, "It's all right, Daniel."

Michael heard the orderly's footfalls as he retreated down the hall. Meanwhile he continued his fascination with Dr. Harrow's eyes. Then they blinked and Michael dropped his head to stare at the floor.

"All right, Michael—let's see, that's Baranovitch, isn't it?"

"Yes."

"Tell me, Michael, have you given any thought to what we have to do to bring you back to the point you were when Dr. Henderson left."

"No."

"Why don't we do that now?"

Michael shrugged.

"What were you two talking about at the end? You see, there's no reason for us to have to go over ground you and Dr. Henderson plowed before. In other words, there's no need for us to re-invent the wheel."

When Michael shrugged again, Dr. Harrow said, "I really haven't had time to do more than glance at your file. You were in New Guinea?"

"Yes."

"You saw action there?"

"Yes."

"Had you and Dr. Henderson talked about your battle, or battles, there?"

"Yes."

The doctor spread his palms. "Which ones?"

"Buna."

"Ah yes, Buna. I've treated other patients who fought at Buna. In fact, I seem to remember that Weyland Jones was in that one, too."

"He was Ghost Mountain."

Dr. Harrow and Mikhail Baranovitch talked about the patient's Montana hometown, where Michael had gone to boot camp, the route he took to reach New Guinea, and something about the outfit he served with. But when the doctor inquired about other theaters he might have been in, the younger man turned mute. He remained mute, too, when Dr. Harrow asked about other New Guinea campaigns, after Buna.

So Dr. Harrow went elsewhere. He told Michael of his service in France during World War I, about the trenches, massive artillery duels, poorly equipped hospitals and the fantastically beautiful French women. Finally the doctor glanced at his watch, stood, held out his hand and said how pleased he was to meet Michael and how well he thought the interview went.

As he left, Michael laid a paring knife on a corner of the doctor's overflowing desk.

Chapter 7

Dr. Harrow glanced up as the orderly paused at the open door. "Come in Daniel, I presume Michael is with you?"

"Sure 'nough, sir," Daniel said as he strode into the room followed by the patient. "And he's as antsy as a kid primed to play his first pinball machine."

Dr. Harrow's smile was toothy, and split his wrinkled and tanned face as if it were cleaved. "Do come." He waved idly to the padded armchair and said, "Please take a seat, Michael. I'll be finished here in a moment." To the orderly, he said, "Daniel, thank you for bringing Mr. Baranovitch. It would be all right if you went on about your duties. I'll ring the desk when I need you to return."

"Right, sir." Daniel retreated.

The paring knife was in the exact same spot Michael had left it--on the corner of the doctor's desk. When he glanced around, the doctor had his head down, apparently working on a report. Michael wondered if he'd even spotted the knife among the mass of papers, pencils, books, magazines, and file folders littering the desktop. The patient pocketed the knife, then returned to stare at the top of Dr. Harrow's tangled gray-haired head.

The doctor penned his signature with a flourish, threw the report in an "out" box and turned his wrinkled face to Michael. Again, the faded eyes with the dark rings around the pupils were disconcerting. However, another toothy cleavage allowed the patient to relax, sinking back into his leather armchair.

"I trust you've had a good week, son?"

"Yes."

The doctor suddenly asked, "Michael, are you getting enough exercise?"

"No."

"Would you like more?"

"I would like to go for a walk," Michael replied. "Can we?"

Dr. Harrow smiled. "We have an exercise room, Michael. Perhaps you don't know about it. Do you?"

The big man shook his head.

"It's at the west end of the main floor. I can have Daniel give you an introduction to our physical therapist, Mr. Terwilliger. After Terwilliger shows you around the facility and how to properly use the equipment, I'll write an order giving you access to the room during hours. Would you like that?"

"I ... I think so. Maybe."

Dr. Harrow's smile vanished and he straightened abruptly. His eyelids fell, and he gripped the desktop with both hands, knuckles whitening. Then he released the desk, opened his eyes and smiled. "Well, young man, what shall we talk about today."

Michael shrugged, then asked, "Do you have an apple orchard?"

Dr. Harrow stood and leaned forward against his desk. "Oh yes. I have twelve trees of Johnathans and two delicious. But I have other types of fruit, also: peaches, pears, prunes, cherries. Then there are hazel nuts, and walnuts. About twelve acres, actually."

Michael's eyes drifted to the window. "Is it a lot of work?"

Dr. Harrow chuckled. "Well, let's just say it keeps me out of the taverns late of night."

"Can you tell me about raising an orchard?"

Again Dr. Harrow chuckled. "That's a unique way of putting it, Michael-- 'raising an orchard'. But it might be a better explanation than 'orchardist'. The answer, of course, is yes, I'd be pleased to tell you about raising an orchard."

And so Dr. Harrow stood behind his desk, waxing eloquently on his role as an orchardist. He explained that in his orchard, cherries are the first fruit to bear, followed quickly by peaches and pears, then by apples and prunes. "The nuts come last, especially walnuts."

"I like cherries," Michael said.

"Alas, my boy, cherries are all gone by now. So are most of the peaches. But pears are in the middle of their harvest. And apples and prunes are beginning to ripen."

"Why aren't you out in your orchard now, gathering, or whatever you do with an orchard?"

Dr. Harrow nodded. "'Pick' is what it's called. Picking fruit. The reason I'm not out there right now," the doctor continued, "is because of the war in Korea. I'd planned to take three months leave--and I would be into the picking now. But when Dr. Henderson was called up, that leave was, of necessity, canceled. Then when Dr. Smith proved so incompetent, that left the hospital dreadfully short of psychiatric counselors. Fortunately, the government has agreed to retain a knowledgeable overseer at my orchard, and hopefully he's performing adequately at hiring pickers and managing them."

"Can I go help you pick?"

Dr. Harrow smiled. "I'm sorry, Michael. Not now. Perhaps someday, after you've recovered. Right now, however, we must help you to re-enter life. Isn't that right?"

"Yes. But if the fruit isn't picked at the right time, don't it spoil?"

"That's right, son."

"And I could help."

Again, Dr. Harrow smiled. He rifled through the papers on his desk until he found a "Baranovitch" folder. He opened it and began paging. As he did, Michael asked, "Just picking fruit--that's not all there is to raising an orchard, is it."

Dr. Harrow laid the folder atop other papers on the overflowing desk and said, "Oh no, Michael. There's pruning and spraying. Then to really care for an orchard, one must properly cultivate between the rows—you know, get rid of the weeds. Old trees must periodically be ripped out and ..."

The doctor's eyes closed, his mouth pinched tightly, and he again gripped his desktop with both hands.

"Doctor Harrow?" Michael said, coming to his feet.

The doctor's eyes opened and he released the desktop. "...and new seedlings planted."

"Can I get something for you, doctor?"

Dr. Harrow's smile was faint. "Perhaps a glass of water."

Michael bumped into Daniel as he hurried to the cafeteria. "It's Dr. Harrow," he said. "He needs water. Maybe you'd better see him." When Michael returned with a glass of water, Dr. Harrow was shuffling about his office. Daniel stood just inside the doorway, hands at his side. Dr. Harrow downed the water, then handed the glass back.

"More?" Michael asked.

When Dr. Harrow nodded, Daniel said, "I'll get a pitcher."

Dr. Harrow returned to his desk and sat gingerly in his swivel chair. Michael took the armchair he'd used earlier, saying, "We could talk about Salamaua, if you wanted."

The plethora of deep wrinkles on the doctor's worn face, twisted into a momentary grin. "I'm afraid, son, that we've talked so much about my orchards that little time is left for us to plow New Guinea ground you cultivated a decade ago."

Daniel hurried in with the pitcher of water, and the doctor drank two more glassfuls before sighing and leaning back in his chair with eyes closed. Michael glanced at Daniel and both men shrugged simultaneously.

When next Dr. Harrow opened his eyes and leaned forward to slide out a desk drawer, he muttered, "Where are those forms?" Finally locating a pad, he scribbled on it, tore off the top one and held it out to Daniel. "Please convey Mr. Baranovitch to the exercise room and tell Will Terwilliger I'd like him to show this patient the facility and how to use its equipment. Tell him, too, that I'm authorizing Michael to utilize the facility any time during its open hours."

Michael took it that the session was over. He came to his feet, then stood awkwardly for a moment before saying, "I'd like to bring you more water, sir."

Dr. Harrow glanced at the half-full pitcher, then smiled and shook his head. "Next time, perhaps. Meanwhile you'll do us both a lot of good if you'll return the knife to wherever you found it."

The therapist, Will Terwilliger, was small and wiry, but well set-up. He wore canvas tennis shoes, white cotton trousers, a white t-shirt, and horn-rimmed glasses. When Daniel and Michael entered the exercise room—more a gymnasium, Michael thought—the therapist was leaning at a stand-up writing desk and had a rolled up hand towel draped around his neck. He strode quickly to the newcomers. The man's curly dark hair was wet with perspiration.

"Afternoon, Will," Daniel said. "I'd like to introduce you to Michael Baranovitch. Doctor Harrow asked me to bring him by." The therapist's smile was a younger version of Dr. Harrow's toothy grin—only Terwilliger's never quite reached his eyes. The hand the therapist extended was without callouses, but its grip was firm as he pumped the patient's hand. "Welcome, Michael. Do they call you Mike?"

Michael said, "Yes. I also answer to 'Bar'."

Terwilliger turned to Daniel. "And did Doctor Harrow say what he wished for me to do with this guy?" Michael thought his voice had a nasal twang to it—like that of the New Englanders in his old 128th Regiment.

Daniel handed Dr. Harrow's authorizing form to the therapist. "I take it that he thinks Michael should have access here for some sort of fitness regimen. Said I should ask you to show the patient around, maybe explain the use of the equipment."

"I can do that," Terwilliger said, studying Dr. Harrow's authorization. "Looks like he's to have ready access during hours."

"I'd guess that's what the doctor had in mind," Daniel said.

"What happens when we're finished. Is he to find his own way to his room?"

Daniel and the therapist both looked at the patient. "I can find my room," Michael said.

After Daniel returned to other duties, Will Terwilliger led Michael around the exercise facility. He showed him the exercycle and how to set the machine's timer, as well as its dial to control pedal resistance. Then the two men moved to the treadmill. Terwilliger demonstrated how to control speed and slant. From there, they went to the weight machine and how to add weights for more muscle demand. There were dumbbells and ankle weights and spring-loaded handgrips.

There was a basketball backboard and net at one end of the thirty-by-fifty room, and a basketball lying on the floor. As they moved past the ball, the therapist lightly flipped it with the toe of his tennis shoe so that it rolled up his leg to his knee; there he grasped it with both hands, set himself for a brief second, then swished the ball through the net from twelve feet. "Ever play, Michael? You're big enough to go power forward."

"No. Just in make-up games is all. Maybe a little intramural. Football is what I played in school."

"Oh? And where was that?"

"Montana. Butte."

"What position? Tackle, I suppose, huh?"

"Yeah."

"Were you any good?"

"As good as I could be."

"And how good was that?"

"Can I go back and get on the treadmill?"

Fifteen minutes on the treadmill dismayed Michael. In high school, he'd been the swiftest lineman on the team, as well as the most tireless. If coach wanted four laps, Michael always ran five. If running wind-sprints was the day's exercise, and a half-dozen was acceptable, Michael regularly ran eight while others did six.

At boot camp, it was always Mikhail Baranovitch who finished a route march first, Mikhail Baranovitch who performed calisthenics faultlessly and tirelessly. And in New Guinea, it was Mikhail Baranovitch who carried special weapons, extra ammo, and helped others slog through mud during the march.

Now, however, after fifteen minutes on the treadmill, his legs felt shaky. It was the first time he fully realized how much six years of confinement had sapped his vitality. He set the timer for another fifteen minutes, and upped the incline another ten degrees.

When at last he stepped off, Will Terwilliger was there with a towel for Michael to wipe sweat. The patient gasped, "Little off ... my game.... Must've ... let myself ... get soft."

Terwilliger's mouth widened into the toothy grin. This time the smile also twinkled the therapist's eyes. "Not too many patients can go that far, that long."

"Can I try the weight machines now?"

The therapist shrugged. "Harrow's authorization gives you carte blanche. But I suspect I'd better monitor you to make sure you don't take on too much the first time out."

Michael stooped to read the weights already loaded on the machine, then added another two hundred pounds.

"That's too much," the therapist said. "Three hundred pounds is beyond reach for even a guy as big as you."

The Dogged and the Damned

"I used to do it. Used to do more."

Terwilliger took off four of the twenty-five pound weights. "Okay, go ahead and try two hundred first. Then we'll see."

Michael lay down on the platform, positioned his head in the cradle, set his heels in the slots, seized the grips, and with dark eyes boring into the therapist, lifted two hundred pounds without obvious strain.

"Not bad," Terwilliger said. "Now do it ten more times and we'll see."

Up down. Up down. After five, Michael repositioned himself, then did five more. "Still want more weight?" the therapist asked. Michael shook his head, then did five more.

"We had a weight set-up just like that in Butte," Michael said when he emerged from the platform. "But I'm a lot weaker now than I was at seventeen."

"How long were you in the hospital?" the therapist asked, again handing him a towel.

"I don't know. Since Morotai, I guess."

"Where's Morotai?"

"Near New Guinea."

"World War II New Guinea?"

"Yes."

The therapist whistled. "That's five or six years! You're lucky you got any muscles at all." Just then, the doors to the exercise room opened and an orderly led another blue-clad patient in. The second patient hobbled with a cane and looked as wild-eyed as a jackrabbit plopped down in the middle of an empty stadium parking lot. Terwilliger said, "Well, here's Briney for his exercise. I'll have to leave you now."

Michael said, "Can I go back to the treadmill?"

"Good Lord, man, haven't you had enough?"

"My legs stopped trembling. I think I can do more."

The therapist shrugged. "Go ahead. I'll try to keep an eye on you, but I can't guarantee it. Don't do too much your first time out. That's an order I can't give, but one I want you to take. Are you listening?"

"Yes."

The therapist finally shooed Mikhail Baranovitch from the gym when he locked the doors at five o'clock.

The patient returned to his room exhausted, falling asleep immediately, missing supper. He showered when he awoke at three in the morning, napped until breakfast, ate, then was waiting at the exercise room doors when Will Terwilliger arrived at eight-thirty. "Mike, what am I going to do with you?" he said as he unlocked the doors. "It looks to me like you're a glutton for punishment and will overdo it if I let it happen."

"No I won't, honest."

"How do you feel?"

"Okay. It was the first good night's sleep I've had in a long time."

The therapist stared thoughtfully up at the patient, then said, "I'd like you to come back to the examination room and let me check you over, see where you are physically."

"All right."

Stripped of his clothes, and with only a detested hospital gown to cover him, Michael sprawled face down on the examination table. Terwilliger pulled the gown up, preparing to knead the patient's muscles. "Jesus Christ!" he exclaimed. "Are these all bullet holes?"

"No. One of 'em was shrapnel."

"I can't believe what I'm seeing!"

"It's not as bad as you think--only two of 'em came out the front."

"Only two of them came out the front, he says! Mike, you are either the luckiest man alive, or the unluckiest. My God!"

"I guess you see they all went in the back."

Terwilliger laughed. "Were you running away?"

"One happened while I was going to war." Michael fell silent for a period as the therapist began staccato-pounding his back with the edges of his hands. Then he added, "One came from a tree climber...."

"A sniper?"

"... One happened while I was trying to get me and my captain back to our own lines..."

"Je-e-sus!"

"... And the rest came when I decided it was time to go home."

Chapter 8

"Can I get you a glass of water, sir?"

Dr. Harrow glanced up from the report he was reading and smiled. "No thank, you son. But it was decent of you to ask."

After Michael had taken his seat, Dr. Harrow said, "It certainly seems, by the reports, that you're seizing the opportunity for exercise."

"Yes, sir."

"Isn't six to eight hours per day excessive?"

"No. I'd let myself go, you see, and ..."

"You didn't, as you say, 'let yourself go', son, you were incapacitated. Severely incapacitated. Perhaps even lucky to be alive."

Michael said, "I could do better if I could walk outside."

Dr. Harrow chuckled. "And that might be in the offing, Michael; especially if you continue to improve, and don't take things belonging to others."

Michael hung his head and said nothing, so the doctor pulled some papers close to hand and said, "The last time we met you mentioned Salamaua. From what I've read, Salamaua—and Lae, too—were Australian operations."

Michael nodded. "That's pretty much true, until the 162nd landed at Nassau Bay. But I was detached from the 128th because we took a few artillery pieces in before our guys got there, and the Ozzies needed B.A.R men to cover 'em."

"I see ..."

"I volunteered, because after three months at Camp Cable, I wanted something to do."

"Tell me about ..."

"Besides, I liked the Ozzies. I'll tell you one thing, Doc, they're all *men* with a mile of guts and a sense of glory. Besides, they tend to think we're okay, too. And maybe most of us are. How's the picking going?"

"Uh huh, that's--what did you say?"

"I asked how the picking was going."

"Fine, fine."

"I suppose you're all through with the peaches and are getting right into the swing of pears?"

"Yes." Dr. Harrow glanced up, frowning. "Now tell me, Michael, how was your artillery deployed?"

"When will the prunes start falling?"

"They don't just fall, son. We shake them down."

"When will that begin?"

"Next week." The doctor shook his head and said, "Let's talk about Salamaua. When did you go in there?"

"Late in April, as I recall. We had destroyer escort. The B.A.R teams deployed first, followed by the 75s. The Ozzies had already secured the beach, so it was pretty much a cakewalk. How do you shake prunes?"

"How did the—ah—Ozzies utilize the guns? Wait a minute, how many guns were there?"

"Six. I suppose walnuts and ..."

"And how were they used."

"Well, as I recall, they took a couple up to the 'Pimple'."

"The Pimple?"

"Yes, sir. It was a hill that poked up above the jungle floor. Not much more than, well, a pimple. But the Ozzies had already been pushed back from it twice. I don't know why they wanted it so bad, but I'm not an officer. And maybe not knowing why the Ozzies needed it so bad is why I'm not officer material. Is that it, Doc?"

Dr. Harrow shook his head, so Michael asked again about the walnuts. "We're not talking about walnuts, Michael. Nor about peaches or prunes or pears."

"What about hazel nuts, then?"

"Nor hazel nuts."

"Cherries? Apples?"

"Nor cherries, nor apples. Michael, we're here to help *you*. We can't do that if we talk about what I'm doing all the time."

"Where'd you go to school, Dr. Harrow?"

The doctor rolled his eyes, then smiled. "University of Pennsylvania. I did pre-med there, too. Undergrad work was at Ohio Wesleyan. Now can we go back to Salamaua?"

There was something of triumph in Michael's smile as he nodded. "Our two 75s blasted every tree off the foreside of the Pimple, then moved around to the back. When they got through, there was no way an ant could hide there."

"Did the Japanese try to counter-attack your artillery? To silence it?"

"No. I think they had pulled out before we got there."

"And after the Pimple, what?"

"Well, there was Green Hill and Bobdubi Ridge. No doubt about it, the guns tilted the fight our way. But it was still the guys on the ground who had to clear out enough Japs that our guys could get the guns up and bearing."

Dr. Harrow leaned back in his chair, tapping the tips of his fingers together

50

and staring at the patient with those unsettling, dark-ringed, pale-pupiled eyes. "Michael, during the entire Salamaua operation, did you ever experience a moment when you felt personally threatened?"

"Not while I was with the guns, Doctor. Those guns were so precious to the Ozzies that they made sure they were safe. If we'd had guns like that at Buna, we would've made short work of that campaign. And even when they finally got a gun or two up to us, they never had enough rounds for them to be effective." Then he added, "At Buna, I mean."

"But you weren't with the guns through the entire Salamaua campaign?"

"No. After the 162nd Regiment landed back at Nassau Bay, I was supposed to be transferred to them."

"Nassau Bay ... *back* at Nassau Bay. Where was that?"

"East, along the coast. Fifty, sixty miles from Salamaua. The idea, so I was told, was to secure an advance base on the coast, within distance for landing craft to travel in one night. That way there was less danger in moving troops and supplies."

"But you never got to Nassau Bay?"

"No. Their operation went so smooth I never got to 'em until they reached Tambu Bay, which was their real objective, I guess."

"So you went into the line at Tambu Bay. Isn't Tambu Bay close to Salamaua?"

"Well, sort of, I guess. But I wasn't up front at Tambu, either. They went in with full companies, and I was the odd man out. Then, too, our guns—the ones I was with, plus eight others coming in with the 162nd—blasted everything growing off the first ridge, and then directed everything they had at Mount Tambu. The Tambu assault started around mid-August and lasted only four days. By the time they needed a slot filled for a B.A.R man, there wasn't any Japs left in that part of the country. Poor bastards."

"Poor bastards—you mean our guys? The Ozzies? The natives?"

"The Japs. They never had a thing left. Clothes hanging in shreds, shoes made of tree bark. One guy gave himself up just after I got to the platoon. He weighed 75 lbs. They were starved, had the shit pounded out of 'em with heavy guns, no supplies of their own trickling through. It was bad for them, Doc."

Dr. Harrow scribbled a passage into his notepad, then asked, "What happened next?"

"Well, the Ozzies did the rest. They took Salamaua within a couple, three weeks, and Lae five days after that. Then they moved on to Finschafen and I went back to the 128th."

"And they were still back in Australia ..." The doctor sorted through his notes.

"... at Camp Cable?"

No. By the time I got to 'em—sometime in November—they were beginning to stage on Goodenough Island."

"Goodenough Island. Where's that?"

Michael laughed. "I guess they didn't want us at Milne Bay any more; wanted to keep the comforts of Milne exclusive for Ozzies. So they stuck us on Goodenough."

"And it's ..."

"It's off the tail of New Guinea. We called it 'Barely Goodenough' Island." The doctor chuckled. Michael added, "That was a bum rap, though, because it was a decent place. It's just that the other guys were coming from Australia—which they liked—and going back to New Guinea—which they hated. And I was coming the other way. So Goodenough looked good enough to me."

"Were you glad to see your buddies."

"Yes." Then the patient smiled so radiantly it lit his entire face. "It was like old home week, Doc. Even Captain Baldwin welcomed me back—he was the company commander, you know." The patient's eyes seemed to soften. "He didn't cuss, did you know that? He sometimes got vexed and he'd use substitute words--like 'Sonofabeast!' or 'Fug!' But he wouldn't cuss. I always respected him for that."

Dr. Harrow penciled notes to his pad, then looked up with those unsettling eyes. "So you staged on Goodenough Island, then embarked for--where?"

"Saidor. We celebrated Christmas on Goodenough, but New Year's Day we were in a bunch of transports heading up the Solomon Sea. We were surrounded by destroyers. I was stuffed into one of the LCIs, but there was one LST running on one side and another LST on the other side."

"How long was the voyage, Michael?"

"I don't know. It rained all the time. And we were out in the open. It wasn't fun."

"Was the ocean rough?"

"Anyway, we hit the beach the day after New Year's. That's what they said."

"Was the landing opposed?"

"Only by our own fire."

"What precisely do you mean by that, soldier?"

"Dr. Henderson said I'm not a soldier any more. He said I don't have to salute you even if you wear the cluster."

Dr. Harrow chuckled. "And he was absolutely correct. I shouldn't have called you a soldier, Michael. But do tell me what you meant by your landing being opposed by 'our own fire'."

"Well, the LCIs went right in almost to shore to drop their ramps, but the LSTs stayed out to circle while we secured. We hit the beach running, see, then deployed; we didn't know what to expect. Our sector was Blue Beach. It was still raining cats and dogs and I guess the commanders expected the Japs to try to hit the force from the seaward side. So as soon as we got into the jungle without resistance, they deployed some of our automatic weapons and heavier stuff pointed out to sea. Then when the LSTs tried to come in with our tanks and heavy artillery, our guys thought they were Japs and started shooting at 'em."

"What happened then?"

"Well, they backed off and probably raised a little hell with headquarters. Then they came in."

"Meanwhile, you met no resistance?"

"One guy got killed on one of 'em, I heard later, and a couple injured on the other LST."

"But you actually met no enemy resistance?"

Michael settled back into his chair, thinking of the hell-hole that was Saidor. Saidor was surrounded on three sides by high mountains and cut by swamps along all the streams. The ground was soggy and too soft to support much heavy equipment. But it did have a couple of important features to recommend it: an airfield on dry ground, and it didn't have many Japs.

"Michael, I asked if you met any resistance."

"They made a pass at us with their aircraft, but that was mostly out in the bay. Then, too, our guys owned the air, so about all they could do was send in a Zero or two to strafe. Far as I can recall, a few of our guys got hit, but not many."

"Saidor, as I see on the map, was a leap up the coast. What was the objective? Was it to cut off enemy to the east?"

"We went after the airfield, first thing. Had it the first day, so the hairy ears could start working on it."

"'Hairy ears'? I don't understand."

"Engineers. They're the guys with hairy ears. They had to get the field open to take our planes and we hadn't done it a lot of good with our bombardment before we came ashore."

"I see ..."

"I guess they set up docks and build roads, too. It's a hell of an outfit, Doc, them hairy ears guys."

"So, in essence, Saidor was easy."

"To begin with. Then it toughened up some. The hairy ears had the airfield going in a week, so supply was easy. But there was a hell of a bunch of Japs between us and the Ozzies to the East, and they wanted to go home as bad as I did. Only thing was, their way home was past Saidor."

The doctor softly asked, "Can you be more explicit?"

"Can I be more what?"

"Explicit. What about your supply? You had an airfield. But what about the Japanese? How did they supply?"

Michael slowly shook his head. "Didn't, I guess. We had the air and controlled the sea. Like I said, there were no roads. Only trails. And to get any cargo along those, a man had to pack it on his back, or hire—or maybe force—natives to do it. Then when the native chiefs started comin' over to us...." Michael's voice fell to a whisper as his mind leaped ahead:

"We'd been at Saidor for a week when the natives started coming in. I happened to be right there in an outpost when the first one showed. One minute I stood up to piss and light a smoke, the next minute the bush right in front of me was gone and this ugly little black bastard was standing there, leaning on a spear, ankles crossed. He actually did have a bone through his nose, but it wasn't no hambone or nothing—just a little one. I later found out it was a child's little finger bone, but right then I felt naked, and it was him didn't have no clothes!"

His mind outran the voice: The guy laid his spear on the ground and all of a sudden more of 'em appeared in front of near every bush around our post. Casey seen me looking strange, so he popped his head up to look around, screamed and went for his greaser. "Hold it!" I said. And when he collapsed against the sidewall of that foxhole, staring up at me with eyes that wouldn't fit on a dinner plate, I turned back to the first headhunter and held up my hand with the palm out. "How," I said, just like in the movies, where Hopalong Cassidy meets the Comanche nation.

"Tell me more about the natives coming over to our side, Michael. Did you know anything about them?"

"They were Tultuls, and somebody else told me Luluais. I guess I might have been one of the first white guys they approached, although farther east the Kanga Force that raided behind Jap lines for two years had been active and must have had contact with the natives. So maybe these guys knew their invaders was fighting among themselves."

"They approached you. Why you?"

"I was on the perimeter, I guess. Why they picked me, I don't know. They wouldn't have had to. Those guys could go anywhere they wanted in that jungle and we never woulda been the wiser. But I guess I was their guy."

"What did you do?"

"Took them back to the command post. Captain Baldwin was tickled pink to see 'em."

"Tell me, Michael, did that mean the natives were previously working for the Japanese, but now began working for the Americans?" The patient's mind spun backward: The whole bunch of 'em—and there must have been twenty—never would win any beauty contests; even in Butte. They had scars all over their chests and backs and legs, even faces. They'd most likely done it to themselves, then rubbed in ashes or dirt or maybe some kind of juice to color 'em blue. Beauty kind of snuck away from their women, too, though Charlie Lockerbie swore on a stack of bibles that it didn't make no difference after the moon went down.

"I asked, Michael, if the natives began working for our side?"

"Maybe. But I didn't see it if they did. Actually, we didn't really need 'em much. With our boats running up and down the coast and making deliveries to any forward posts, there really wasn't that much need for porters. I think what it meant the most when they came to see us was they were no longer working for the Japs.

"I see."

"I'd guess we paid 'em for doing nothing, because once I was helping back at the landing zone, and a crate broke open. It was loaded with beads, knives, razors, and mirrors, along with some bright-colored yard goods."

"So the natives were pacified?"

"Not altogether. There was a raid on our outpost at Bilau, and it was confirmed that natives led the Japs to our position. We were lucky, I guess, 'cause a Jap tripped a hand grenade I'd booby-trapped fifty yards in front of our position. We beat the bastards off, but it was nip-and-tuck for awhile. Then Captain Baldwin said we'd better get across the Mot River—did I tell you it was in flood? God, Doc, you never seen such rain! They said twelve inches fell during a single night. I wished I'da had some bunkers to attack that night."

"Bunkers to attack?" said Dr. Harrow. I don't understand."

Michael smiled. "That's the trouble with talking to a whole bunch of doctors, instead of just one."

It was Dr. Harrow's turn to smile. "I want to know how you got back across the Mot if it was in flood."

"Captain Baldwin. He's uncanny—or at least he was. Got a nose for everything. And he hedged every bet. When we crossed the first time, we ferried it in a handful of native dugouts. Then when we established our outposts another couple of miles farther along, he sent patrols back to search up and down the Mot, scrounging everything floatable: dugouts, logs, driftwood, and stacked them at a narrow crossing. Then he set a guard. So when we retreated, it was easy to pick up our flotilla and get away."

"Did you retreat under fire?"

"No. Again, like I told you, the captain had a nose for it. When that Jap squad ran into our outpost, and my booby grenade got tripped, and the big firefight took place, and we held the post, the captain came up to take a look. There was a bunch of dead Japs there. All of the dead ones had bayonets fixed on their rifles and they also carried knee mortars and grenades. On top of that, their weapons were all new and in top condition. Besides, they didn't carry no packs or canteens. So he figured they hadn't come far. When the captain stood up after picking through the pockets of one or two of the Japs for any useful information, he said, 'They've got to have a camp nearby. Corporal, what do you say we live to fight another day'."

"And?"

"And so, we lived to fight another day."

"Were there any repercussions from Captain Baldwin's decision?"

"Not that I know of. Especially not after the east side of the Mot became a killing ground, filled with our dead bodies."

"Such as?"

"Colonel Clarkson bought the farm over there, along with twenty-two others of his 1st Battalion. All told, we lost more'n a hundred guys over there. And all the time, Captain Baldwin kept telling 'em to draw a line at the Mot and hold the bastards there. But no, the powers that be didn't already have enough real estate of their own. Far as I know, the Japs still held the east side of the Mot clear up until an Ozzie non-com waved at me from across the river. That was a couple of weeks into February."

"So tell me more about Saidor."

Michael laughed, seemingly at ease. "We had a counter-strike up the coast, maybe a couple of weeks after we got there. Report was the Japs were running barges near Cape Iris. Said there were up to eight barges steaming around the cape and were being strafed by our planes in the moonlight. Everybody in reach was scrambled.Then when daylight came, they discovered the 'enemy' barges were dummies our guys had put up on the beach to distract Jap planes. Our planes strafed 'em, our boats shelled 'em, and our troops let 'em have it with every automatic weapon we could reach." Michael continued to chuckle for several seconds, then sobered and added, "The Japs ignored the dummies."

The doctor studied his notes, then raised his head and said, "I take it, not many Japanese made it past your Saidor roadblock."

"I don't know. I know that, at the end, the few prisoners we got was walking dead. The only food they had was native plants and animals. Most of 'em didn't have any equipment, and nothing but rags for clothes. I brought three prisoners to command in one day. They was just wandering around in the brush. Two of 'em carried backpacks with no food and little water. None had weapons, except for bayonets they carried on their belts. They had cut-up truck tires for sandals. Wasn't one of 'em weighed a hundred pounds."

Michael fell silent. Dr. Harrow said, "That's it?"

"That's it."

"So now we go to Aitape?"

Michael again stared at his feet. "It wasn't right, Barney I mean. How could that happen to such a nice old guy?"

Dr. Harrow looked up from his notepad to see Michael wringing his hands. "I'm sorry, son. I don't know Barney. Who's he?"

"Standing right there beside me, shaking his fist while I shook my B.A.R. By rights, he might've taken the one meant for me." Then the big man buried his face in his hands sobbing audibly.

Dr. Harrow came around the desk and laid a hand on Michael's shoulder until the patient quit sobbing. Then the doctor told Michael to sit quietly while he went after a pitcher of water for both of them.

After Michael and the doctor had both drunk glassfuls of water, Dr. Harrow said, "I believe we've covered sufficient ground today, son. I've asked Daniel to join us because I want him to know I'm relaxing conditions of your restraint a little more. Will Terwilliger has nothing but praise for the exercise regimen you are developing with him. He feels you are reliable."

Daniel strolled in and Dr. Harrow said, "Daniel thinks you are reliable, and I think you are reliable. Therefore I'm going to give you unrestricted access to the halls of this building. That means, Michael, that you are responsible for keeping your own schedule. No one will come for you for breakfast, lunch, or dinner. You can continue to come and go at the exercise room. And most of all, it means you are responsible for keeping your appointments at your treatment sessions in my office. Can we count on you?"

"I don't have a watch, sir."

"That shouldn't be a problem, Michael. There are enough clocks scattered throughout this building that you can follow the time. Next Tuesday at 1:30. Can you be here on your own?"

"Yes."

After Michael and Daniel had gone, Dr. Harrow studied his hands for several minutes, then pulled his yellow pad from the desk corner and began scribbling:

Patient Mikhail Baranovich's problem not with Salamaua, nor Saidor, nor with Australians. Suspect one trauma may lay with his next campaign Aitape. At least he became distraught at its mention.

After he'd finished, the doctor went to the library and took out an official volume on the New Guinea campaign. Back in his office, he checked the Index for Aitape, turned to the correct page, and began to read.

Michael lay upon his room's cot, hands clasped behind his head, dark eyes boring holes in the ceiling. Had Dr. Harrow but known, he might have been pleased to learn Michael was engaged in his own study of Aitape. But unlike the doctor, the patient needed no library volume to recollect the hell and horror that transpired in that godforsaken place.

Chapter 9

"Mike! You're late. Two days late, actually." Will Terwilliger was shooting free throws when Mikhail Baranovitch entered the exercise room. The therapist's shooting percentage, the patient knew from past observation, was astonishingly high. The patient also knew such an exceptional average came as a result of constant practice. Michael, an athlete himself, knew one when he saw one.

"So where you been, big guy?"

Michael said, "I didn't feel like working out."

The truth was that his memories of Aitape had made him physically ill—with stomach cramps, diarrhea, and a debilitating headache. Daniel became alarmed when Michael never attended breakfast, or the noon meal the day after his visit with Doctor Harrow. He checked the records and found the patient had not eaten supper the evening before. "What's wrong, Michael?" Daniel had asked, knocking softly, then entering Mikhail Baranovitch's darkened room.

The reply was a low moan. "It's Barney."

"What about Barney, Michael?"

"He's hurt."

"But he's better now. Michael, I want to look at you. I'm going to raise this shade. Okay?"

The patient swung his feet to the floor and sat up just as Daniel lost control of the window shade so it flap-flap-flapped around its spool. The orderly turned to see Michael clapping his palms over his ears. "Headache, Michael?"

"Yes."

"Hold on, I'll bring some aspirins."

Later, the orderly led the patient down to the cafeteria. The following morning, Mikhail Baranovitch returned to the workout gym where Will Terwilliger said he'd missed him.

Michael headed directly for the treadmill, where he set the timer for fifteen minutes, draped his towel over a parallel safety bar, stepped on the machine and flipped the switch. The therapist drifted over. "I've been talking to the doc about you. He said according to your record that you were an all-state football player in Montana."

Michael's eyes switched to the therapist, then returned to the blank wall directly before his treadmill.

"Did I tell you I was a quarterback in high school and college?" Michael's gaze returned to Terwilliger; somewhere deep inside the dark pupils was a glint of interest. The therapist added, "Worcester's Loyola High, then Holy Cross." He added, "In Boston."

Michael bent over to flip the incline switch to medium. He asked, "Single wing or 'T'?"

"Both. My high school coach was pretty traditional, so it was mostly single wing. I didn't mind that, though, because it gave me a chance to run more."

"Was you any good?"

Terwilliger still carried the basketball, rolling it around in his hands. "Good enough to win district two years running. Made it to the quarterfinals in state my senior year."

Michael smiled. "Well, that says your team was good. And it says you weren't altogether *bad*. But it doesn't say *you* was necessarily outstanding."

The therapist smiled, bounced the ball twice, and said, "I was all right." Then his grin widened to show his teeth. "I would've ran rings around you."

Michael chuckled. He reached down to twist the treadmill button to maximum incline, then said, "I'da had you before you got up to speed." Terwilliger's eyes glistened. Michael, beginning to pant, added, "And if you went to the other side, I'da overhauled you from behind."

Grinning himself, the therapist asked, "What was your speed in the forty?"

"Four—gasp--four was my—gasp--best ever." Then the machine clicked off, coasting down. With sweat coursing down Michael's face, he said, "Four-six was my average."

The smile vanished from the therapist's face. "That's fast. It's a wonder some college didn't take you."

Michael re-set the treadmill for more speed, left it on maximum incline, clicked the timer for another fifteen minutes, and punched the "on" button. Staring at the wall, the patient thought, they would have--if they'd had the chance. Half the colleges in the West, and some in the East had alumni or coaches scouting the team during my junior and senior years. Enough to make a guy proud. Coach was proud, too. And in his own way, even Papa was proud. Sweat beaded Michael's brow and trickled in rivulets down his face. The only places his blue shirt wasn't wet with sweat was the outside of his pocket and the outside fold of his collar. He shook his head. Trouble was, all three of us was too proud. And none with any give. Coach O'Malley had this fixation that his star tackle was going to Notre Dame, and that was that.

"Shaughnessey's here again, Baranovitch," O'Malley growled when the ruddy-faced coach came through the locker room before the Kalispell game. "He says to tell you, if you stay consistent you'll get a free ride onto Leahy's team."

Michael stared down at his bare toes. He hadn't pulled on his jersey or the padded knee pants, so he resembled a gladiator, clad only in the shoulder harness, hip discs, and a jockstrap. O'Malley turned at his office door. "You hear what I said, Baranovitch? I want you to tear Bannion and Markson and King limb from limb." Michael glanced at coach and slipped his jersey over his head. When his eyes, nose, and mouth popped through the neck hole, O'Malley had his hands on his hips, staring down the line at him. "Well?"

"Well what?" the youth asked.

"Are you going to play like God had ye by the throat?"

Michael grinned and shook his head. "No, but I'll do my best—that much I know." He could tell his reply angered O'Malley. Coach was accustomed to getting his own way—one of the privileges of being a winning coach in football-crazed Butte. On the other hand, even a martinet with near-limitless power over his players had sideboards when it came to controlling a star player of Mikhail Baranovitch's caliber—especially when the player was the son of that crazy Slav, Stefan Baranovitch.

Suddenly the machine clicked off! Michael blinked and stared down at the switch. Will Terwilliger's hand was on the "off" button. The therapist murmured, "You're going at it too hard, Mike. You need to build yourself back, but you don't have to do it all at once."

Deliberately, Michael reached out a sausage-sized forefinger and pushed the "on" button. Terwilliger bounced the basketball twice while staring up at him, then turned and walked away. The machine still had six and one-half minutes left to cycle.

You don' need to go to no college to work underground," Stefan Baranovitch told his son. "You go to college an' you get all snooty. Too good for you momma and you papa." The elder Baranovitch poked his own chest with a thumb and said, "I make a good living in the mines and that's what you will do, too."

Michael held his father's flashing black eyes while swallowing and saying nothing. In those days his eyes were on a level with the eyebrows of his father. In those days he was among the biggest and toughest football players in the state, with arms corded with muscles much like his father's, thighs as big around as most of his teammates' waists, and shoulders even more broad than those of Stefan Baranovitch.

But there, the comparisons stopped. Except for a scar over an eyebrow where, as a freshman, he'd been beaten with a two-by-four by a maddened teammate, and one on the chin where a Billings linebacker had kicked him with a cleated shoe when he was a sophomore, Michael's face was unblemished. On the other hand, Stefan Baranovitch's was a mass of scar tissue—a matter of considerable pride to the brawler from the bowels of Butte.

In those days, when a call came in to the stationhouse that Stefan Baranovitch was on a tear, the desk sergeant routinely dispatched two paddywagons. Not because two wagons would be needed to bring in so many drunks and disorderlies, but because two wagons were needed to haul sufficient numbers of constables to subdue the "crazy Slav." Yes, Stefan Baranovitch was a man of considerable pride who wore his battle scars as badges. The "crazy Slav," feared no man and, though there were many workmen plying Butte's underground adits and shafts and drifts and winzes who also dwelled beyond fear of mortal man, few went out of their way to cross a Slavic devil who routinely seemed to go crazy mad during a brawl.

Michael couldn't help it, he shivered. But still, he held eye contact. Then Stefan Baranovitch's scarred and rutted face broke into a gap-toothed grin and he gripped his son by a shoulder and squeezed, picked up his lard-pail lunch bucket and left for work.

Michael looked down where his mother sat, knitting needles clicking. A slip of a woman, she never even looked up. But she said, "You don' pay him no mind, Michael. You wanna go to college and get smart, you go."

Something intruded on Michael's thoughts and, with a jerk, he saw he plodded on a treadmill that wasn't running. Will Terwilliger leaned against the weight machine, toothy grin shining. The therapist glanced at his watch and said, "It cycled off a minute and twenty seconds ago." Michael took his towel from the parallel hand bar and wiped his face, then shuffled to a bench, suddenly very tired.

Terwilliger sauntered over. "Man, you were lost in your own world. Was it football or women?"

Michael stared vacantly up at the grinning therapist. "I miss Barney," he said.

"I've got bad news for you, Michael," Daniel said. "Doctor Harrow had to close up shop today. Got something wrong inside, I guess. Told me to tell you he'll have to skip a week with you."

Michael hung his head, clearly disappointed.

"However," Daniel continued, "he said to tell you he called Weyland Jones to see if he could get away this afternoon. The Doc left a note at the front desk giving Weyland permission to take you anywhere he wishes on the grounds."

The blue-clad patient's head slowly ratcheted up, and he seemed almost to sniff the air. "I can go outside?"

"With Weyland. Weyland said to tell you he'll have his noon meal with you."

"Now? Can we go now?"

Daniel laughed. "Not now. It's only ten-thirty. Be another hour or two before Weyland gets here. Said he was laying down his raspberry canes; said he'll be in as soon as he can."

It was a long two hours that Mikhail Baranovitch waited for the white-thatched Sutherlin farmer. But when Weyland at last came striding into the lobby, Michael flashed him a huge smile. "Great to see you, Michael," the farmer said, shaking hands and slapping the larger man's back. Then Weyland clapped his hands and said, "What's for dinner? What say we go down to the cafeteria and heckle the girls?"

As always, the rail-thin farmer was a hit with the ladies. "Corrine," he said, as she served the mashed potatoes, "you just get prettier every day."

"Go on," the plump blonde replied. "You've kissed the blarney stone too many times. Besides, these days I got my cap set for your partner." Michael blushed as Corrine plopped two servings of potatoes and two generous slices of roast beef on his plate.

Michael and Weyland took a table in a far corner. Only Kelsey Park and Ogden Christopher were there, both sitting in their wheelchairs and being spoon-fed by orderlies. Kelsey's head lolled and he slobbered with each spoonful, but his eyes lit with the company and he tried to wave. All the quadriplegic Ogden could do was wag his head like a puppet—along with a broadband smile that lit his face in welcome. After they'd all finished, and Kelsey and Ogden had been wheeled away to the lounge, the Sutherlin farmer pushed his chair back, pulled a kitchen match and a small clasp knife from his pocket, shaved the match end to toothpick-size and said, "So, what do you think of Doctor Harrow?"

Michael said, "I like him a lot. Not as much as Doctor Henderson, but a lot."

"Ol' Henderson was quite a guy wasn't he?"

"He's not as old as Doctor Harrow."

"No, that's true. Kinda ribald, though, where Harrow is serious."

"Doctor Harrow is sick."

"Sick?" Weyland Jones quit picking his teeth and leaned forward. "Harrow's sick? How is he sick?"

"I don't know. But he is."

The farmer again tilted his chair against the wall and stared at a florescent light fixture on the ceiling above the cafeteria counter. "You're probably right," he mused. "The guy's doing double duty and trying to keep his farm alive." Jones snapped the toothpick in half, pitched the remnants on his empty food tray and added, "He's no spring chicken any more either, but he's one tough old bird."

When Michael nodded, Jones said, "He'll probably outlive both of us." Then the farmer pushed to his feet, picked up his tray and utensils and said, "Speaking of Doctor Harrow, he was supposed to leave us authorization at the front desk for you and me to walk around the grounds. What do you say to us checking?"

It'd been nearly three months since Mikhail Baranovitch had been outside and his head began swiveling the moment he and Weyland Jones descended the hospital steps. It was a warm, partly cloudy September day. The huge maples had begun to turn and an occasional leaf drifted down. Michael snatched twice at the first one, missing it both times. Then he chased another and caught it, giggling aloud, then chased another as it drifted down, falling to his knees as he caught it.

Weyland sauntered after, smiling at Michael's exuberance. When the patient paused to peer closely at his latest catch, the farmer said, "It's a fine time of year, isn't it, Michael?"

"Uh huh."

"My favorite."

"Uh huh." Then Michael looked up at his friend and said, "I like spring, too."

"Spring's nice, yes."

"And so is summer. And winter's okay."

"Yeah." Weyland stared over Michael's shoulder, across the greensward of the hospital grounds. "What you're really saying is that it's great to be alive, aren't you?"

Michael dropped his leaves, clambered to his feet, thrust both hands in his pockets and said, "Yeah."

They ambled on, passing a blue-clad patient sitting on an iron bench, feeding peanuts to a hesitant gray squirrel. One of the patient's trouser legs was empty and pinned above the knee. The man's crutches leaned on the bench at his side. Tears squeezed from Michael's eyes and trickled down to drip from his nose.

Weyland murmured, "We gotta get you out of here, Michael."

"I could help you lay down your raspberries."

"That's not what I mean ..."

"We could go now."

Weyland laughed. "No, Michael. Your pass only allows you out on the grounds in company with me. What I mean is that we've got to get you well enough to leave the hospital. Then you can go where you want, when you want."

"But I want to go now."

"Well, friend, you can't go now. Not until the doctors say you are cured. What you can do, though, is help them get to that point. Like telling them about your experiences that brought you to the hospital."

Their stroll had taken them almost to the river bridge. Michael began walking faster, but the farmer easily matched him stride for stride. They crossed the bridge to the south. When they reached Harvard Avenue the patient faltered; Weyland took his elbow and said, "Let's go this way, Michael. I haven't walked over here in years."

So they strolled across the fresh-mown grass, past the Old Soldier's Home, to the plot beyond that was filled with white crosses. Michael glanced at Weyland in alarm as the farmer led him into the cemetery. But Jones continued down one row, then back up another. After they'd strolled in somber silence for several minutes, Weyland murmured, "You see, Michael, we're not the only ones to give something for our country." He paused. "Look here, Spanish American War. Back behind us was a whole row of World War I guys." Weyland strolled on. Michael followed. "It's tough, ain't it?" the farmer muttered. "But these guys gave a little more than you and me. We've still got a chance to get back into the world. These guys have none."

"Like Barney," the larger man murmured.

Weyland paused at the Grave of the Unknown Soldier. "Tell me about Barney," he said.

Chapter 10

Patient: MIKHAIL BARANOVITCH

Physically, patient recovering remarkably well, working out aggressively in exercise room. Some improvement psychologically, but we have much ground to plow to get him beyond his dark side. I believe one intial blockage occurred during his experience at Aitape. Then, of course, there was his court-martial from Morotai.

First things first: Aitape. Patient experiencing considerable difficulty addressing that operation. Each time Aitape is mentioned, he exhibits signs of stress.

It's possible we've identified a first signal that a particular conversation is becoming stressful to the patient by his mentioning his friend "Barney". He may be using "Barney" as a defense mechanism to deflect conversational direction from points he wishes to defer, or more probably, ignore.

"Barney," research discloses, was in reality New York Times war correspondent, Barnaby Durham, who was killed by "friendly fire" while standing at Mikhail's side during his first action. It's probable, "Barney" was the first person the patient saw killed and it may have affected him deeply.

On the other hand, it's possible "Barney" is nothing more than a readily accessible defense line Mikhail employs when approaching periods of deep distress. Whatever the reason for its use, it's a tool for marking progress during this patient's treatment.

During recovery, Mikhail has made friendship beachheads with orderly Daniel Fields and recovered former patient, nearby farmer Weyland Jones. The patient also has a fine workout arrangement with therapist William Terwilliger. All three men express confidence in the patient's reliability. Jones and Fields both recommend giving Baranovitch limited unattended access to the grounds.

Our next stage must be exploring Aitape in sufficient depth to uncover the trauma that occurred there. Perhaps an offer to permit the patient outside access will provide sufficient motivation for Mikhail to tentatively enter presently locked recesses of his own mind.

Signed,
Dr. Archibald Harrow
V.A. Hospital
Roseburg, Oregon
Sept. 19, 1950

Dr. Harrow re-read his typed notes, then slid them into the expansion folder that was stamped "Mikhail Baranovitch". The folder also included Dr. Henderson's voluminous files on the patient. Harrow rubbed his temples and wished he had time to read all of Henderson's work on Baranovitch. The doctor took a pill bottle from his desk drawer, shook two shiny red tablets into his hand and popped them in his mouth, took a swallow of water from the glass on his desk, glanced at the clock, saw it was almost 1:30, and leaned back to await Mikhail Baranovitch. Promptly upon the clock's half-hour ding, the patient knocked.

"Oh, do come in, Michael. The door's open. The only time you must knock is if the door is closed." The doctor pushed to his feet, motioning the patient to a chair.

"I'm sorry we missed last week, Michael. But I understand you and Weyland Jones had a splendid visit. Walked the grounds, did you?"

"Yes."

"Weyland tells me you enjoy being outside a great deal. And Daniel tells me you and Doctor Henderson sometimes took walks during your consultation with him. Is that right?"

"Yes."

"Perhaps we might see if we can arrange a little more outside time for you." Michael's eyes lit. "Could I? I mean, would you do that?"

Dr. Harrow smiled his toothy grin. "I might. Better said, I could. And I would if you continue to show improvement. And today that means we need to begin talking about Aitape."

The excitement in Michael's eyes slowly dimmed, and he studied his hands. But when he opened his mouth to tell Dr. Harrow about Barney, the doctor beat him to it. "Barney wasn't at Aitape, son. You were. You and lots of other soldiers."

"Lots of Japs, too," the big man muttered.

"When did you go in?"

Michael took a deep breath and murmured, "Our Regiment disembarked in mid-May."

"When did the Aitape operation begin?"

67

"I don't know. Three weeks before, more or less."

The doctor made a notation on his tablet. "So you missed the worst of it?"

"Missed the worst of it?" Michael murmured. "Missed the worst of it? Doctor, you must be out of your mind!"

"I'm sorry, son. I should be more circumspect. You said there were a lot of the enemy at Aitape. I just assumed the initial landing would've been difficult and the later operations easier. Apparently that assumption is incorrect?"

"They had fifty thousand men stationed at Wewak. The Japs' whole Eighteenth Army was at Wewak. We bypassed 'em to hit Aitape. We bypassed Wewak because they didn't have much in place at Aitape to stop us."

"Why Aitape, Michael?"

"Airfield. Every time we hit someplace, it was for an airfield." Michael's mind sprinted ahead: If we had to hit an airfield, it was a hell of a lot better to go after one that didn't have many Japs around it. Aitape fit that score starting out, I guess, except for one thing. There was a bunch of the slant-eyed little bastards within walking distance.

"Michael, I asked if the Aitape airfield was lightly defended?"

The patient's eyes fell on Dr. Harrow's fascinating black-ringed pupils and was trapped by them.

"I wasn't there, but the guys I talked to said it was a cakewalk. They said what Japs were there ran off into the jungle, and that they secured the airstrip on the first day."

"So the airfield was near the beach."

"It was eight miles inland—at a place called Tadji Plantation."

"And they made the entire eight miles in one day! They certainly did encounter little resistance."

Michael nodded. "They had this road, see?"

The younger man gnawed at his lower lip. "Then they started getting pressure from the east—from Wewak, so they put a line up on the Driniumor to keep the Japs from the airfield."

"Driniumor?"

"A river. Wasn't much of a river—not even as big as the Mot, over in Saidor. But it'd be all right with me if I never see or hear of it again."

Dr. Harrow's eyes were steady. "I'm afraid it's important that we do talk about it, Michael."

"Barney ..."

"Barney's not here, son. You are. And me. And it's very important to both of us that we talk about what went on at the Driniumor. If it helps you come to grips with your problems, you can get more and more freedom."

Michael studied the man across from him for perhaps a minute, then softly continued: "They put out a defense line on the Driniumor, then threw up an outpost about ten miles across the Driniumor, at a place called Nyaparake. Then they moved a couple of companies a few miles even further east by patrol boats. From the minute they got there, those companies came under attacks that got heavier and heavier every day. Are you through shaking prunes, now?"

Dr. Harrow smiled and nodded.

"So I guess it's hazel nuts and walnuts, huh?"

"What happened to those companies, Michael?"

"Do you dry walnuts?"

"Michael, what happened to those two companies that were the furthest outpost toward Wewak?"

The patient swallowed. "Barney ..."

"Remember, Barney isn't here. I'm here and you were there. What happened to those companies?"

"They got cut up. One of 'em was Bottcher's outfit."

"Bottcher? I'm not familiar with that."

"Bottcher's roadblock. At Buna."

"I see."

"Captain Baldwin really liked him."

"Yes?"

"And that was good enough for me. If Captain Baldwin liked him, so did I. He was a German who fought against the Fascists in Spain. A blocky guy. Tough as nails and meaner'n hell. I'm glad he never played football for Kal...."

"Michael," Dr. Harrow cut in, "what happened to the advanced companies. You said they got cut up. Were they wiped out?"

"We saw 'em—what was left of 'em—coming back as we moved up to Nyaparake. It made you wonder."

"So you were moved up to Nyaparake. When was that?"

"On the twentieth. We got there just in time to get hit by a banzai attack. Turned out Bottcher's guys were still withdrawing and he asked Captain Baldwin to provide a fighting rear guard." The patient smiled wryly then and said, "Hell, I didn't hardly get to see Nyaparake except looking over my shoulder."

"So you were retreating?"

"I hope to shout. But Captain Baldwin, he was everywhere, picking out the best defensive ground, then moving us back each time, just before the cheese got binding."

"You liked Captain Baldwin very much, didn't you?"

Michael's eyes widened. "What do you mean *liked*? What do you mean *didn't*

I? Has anything happened to him? Why wouldn't I still like him?"

It was the doctor's turn to be flustered. "Oh! I'm sorry. Somewhere I got the idea that Captain Baldwin was ... was ... but he wasn't, is that right?"

"I'm through now. I don't want to talk no more."

"I think we need to talk about what happened at Nyaparake, Michael."

"I don't want to."

The doctor pulled a slip of paper from the file on his desk and held it up for the patient to see. "This is an authorization slip, Michael, for you to walk unattended about the grounds for an hour each Monday. I want you to have the opportunity to do this thing, but I also want to know what happened during your withdrawal from Nyaparake."

Michael's lips pinched tight, but he took a deep breath. "They kept trying to surround us, but we stayed close to the beach where we had covering fire from our patrol boats. Lots of time, over the next few days, we had to fight our way through a line of Japs in order to keep our retreat going. But the little bastards didn't have time to throw up pillboxes before we got there to dig 'em out, so we were hitting them before they got ready for us. Besides, we weren't green any more. And we were heading back to safety, instead of into their nest. Wasn't nobody nowhere that could stop us from getting back to our lines."

When Michael fell silent, the doctor asked, "So you pulled back across the Driniumor?"

"No. We pulled back to Yakamul."

"What happened then?"

Michael sighed. "I don't want to talk any more today."

Dr. Harrow made a big show of picking up the authorization slips on his desk. Then he looked up and said, "Michael, I think it's important for us to continue this today."

Michael's eyes narrowed to slits and he replied through clinched teeth, "Dr. Harrow, I admire you a bunch. And I know you're sick. And I wouldn't hurt your feelings for nothing. But ..." he pushed to his feet "... you can take those fucking pieces of paper and shove 'em up your ass!"

Chapter 11

Patient: MIKHAIL BARANOVITCH

Went too far, pushed too hard during today's session. Mikhail obviously has his own inner sword lines and I tried unsuccessfully to push him beyond them. The circumstance was an action that took place in the battle for Aitape, at a place called Nyaparake. Apparently Mikhail's outfit was in retreat and I insisted we continue when he obviously thought we'd covered enough ground for today. The irony of it is the patient probably was right, especially in this case.

The peculiar thing is that I feel the particular operation Mikhail Baranovitch and I are presently exploring isn't the traumatic one we're seeking. I suspect there's much more to the battle for Aitape than the fighting retreat from Nyaparake that we've thus far discussed.

Unfortunately, I probably won't live long enough to see this patient cured.

Signed,
Dr. Archibald Harrow
V.A. Hospital
Roseburg, Oregon
September 26, 1950

It was the following morning when the orderly found Michael on the exercise room treadmill. Will Terwilliger stood nearby, dribbling his ever-present basketball and talking with the patient. Noting the paper Daniel carried, the therapist said, "Whatcha got for me this time?"

"Not a thing, Will. This is for Michael."

Michael hit the off-button and stepped off as the machine coasted down. The orderly handed him the paper, saying, "Doctor Harrow asked me to show this to you before I handed it in to the desk. I got to tell you I'm pleased."

Michael took the paper, scanned it quickly, then, visibly overcome, moved to a bench and, face twisted and shoulders bobbing, sobbed and collapsed against the wall.

"What is it?" Terwilliger whispered to Daniel.

Daniel grinned at the therapist and shouted so loudly he might've been heard in the cafeteria, "It's authorization for the big guy to walk the grounds without escort three hours a week!"

"All right!" the therapist cried, slapping the orderly's back.

Daniel took the paper from Michael's trembling fingers and laid a hand on his shoulder. "This is Wednesday, Michael," he said. "And this authorization is for an hour after lunch, Monday, Wednesday, and Friday. So that means after lunch today, you're free to go outside for an hour. Would you like that?"

The patient looked up with tear-filled eyes and nodded.

That first day, Michael surprisingly spent his outside hour sprawled in the shade of the big maples, staring dreamily up at a cloudless sky, watching an occasional leaf fall, thrilled by the iridescent colors and beams of sunlight through the trees. The gray squirrels fascinated him, as did the pigeons and robins. Once he heard the wild goose cry and scrambled out into the street to look overhead and see a flight of honkers heading for rice paddies in the San Joaquin Valley.

Michael saw Daniel three times during that hour; on the entry steps, once leading another patient back inside, and once staring down from an upstairs window. And when his hour was up, Michael met the orderly as he pushed through the main doors into the lobby.

"Hey, Michael!" Daniel said. "Great timing. I was just coming to get you."

On Friday, Michael walked over the river bridge to Harvard Avenue, then found himself in the cemetery and, though he knew none of them, read every name. Again, he entered the main hospital building at 2:30 pm on the dot.

Monday, he strolled the other way, north to the busy Garden Valley Road, where he turned around and strode past the administration building on his way to the river. Again, he was prompt to return at the end of his hour. In all hours between, he exercised in the gym or, when not sleeping or eating, could be found quietly reading in the lounge.

On Tuesday, promptly as the wall clock "dinged" half past one, Michael entered Dr. Harrow's office and took a seat. So silent was he that the doctor continued working at his desk for several minutes before he looked up at the clock and saw his patient. "Michael! My God man, you gave me a fright! How long have you been sitting there?"

"I don't know."

"Well, you're here now and it's ten minutes past the half hour. Were you on time?"

"I think so."

Doctor Harrow peered at him for several moments before saying, "Michael, about last week ..."

"We pulled back to Yakamul, where we were reinforced with elements from Company A, under the command of Captain Herrick."

The Dogged and the Damned

The doctor picked up a pencil, pulled his yellow pad in front of him, and began making notes.

"Herrick Force was joined by a mostly headquarters company, so a lot of 'em were fresh, but with no battlefield experience. Herrick's outfit threw up a defense perimeter at Yakamul to block the Japs. Then the Battalion Command sent "Baldwin's Bunch"—that's us—to patrol south, into the interior, along the Harech River. The idea was for us to make sure no Japs moved through the jungle to bypass the Yakamul defense."

"I see," the doctor prompted.

"Well, all hell broke loose."

"You ran into the enemy in strength?"

"Not for us. For the 'Herrick Force'. They had Japs on 'em like fleas on a dog. I wasn't there, but some of the survivors said it was hell. The Japs hit 'em in company-sized waves—one, two, three. Herrick had A Company's perimeter dug in just ahead of a small stream, with the headquarters outfit behind, as reserve. Well, artillery began ranging on 'em—and that damn sure got the attention of the generals back at the ranch!"

"I don't understand," Dr. Harrow said. "What's the significance of the artillery?"

The patient took a deep breath and said, "They wasn't s'posed to have any. They wasn't s'posed to be able to move anything heavy through the jungle from Wewak. But they did. And Herrick's outfit come under mortar fire, too."

Dr. Harrow held up a hand, and said, "Michael, how far was Yakamul from"—he paused to page back to previous notes—"the Driniumor Line?"

"'Bout two miles, as I recall...." Michael shifted in his chair to stare vacantly out the office's window, remembering how if anyone was qualified to recall, he was damn sure the one; crossed those miles twice, I did—part of 'em more. Most of the time, what bushes left were bent and busted, and if they had any tattered leaves, they were died red with blood—ours and theirs. The last time, me and the captain left ours. Mostly the captain's.

"Ahem, Michael, would you like a glass of water?"

The dark eyes returned from the window to focus on the riveting ones of the doctor. "I'll go get a pitcher."

"Be kind enough to bring two glasses, would you please?"

When Michael returned, he poured for both, drank his, and took his seat.

"All right, Michael, you were saying about Herrick's force coming under heavy mortar and artillery fire...."

"And banzai waves. Under cover of the banzai attacks, artillery salvos, and mortar fire, another company of Japs crossed the stream and got around 'em and hit the headquarter's outfit from the rear. They got a wedge between A Company and the headquarters outfit, then turned on A Company from the rear."

When the patient paused, the doctor deliberately picked up his water glass and took a sip.

"There was another attack along the beach, too, and then the headquarters outfit was overrun and A Company started taking fire from the hill where the headquarters outfit had been."

Again, Dr. Harrow took a sip of water.

"All the Herrick outfit could do was to run for it, across the little stream, heading for the beach."

Dr. Harrow coughed gently, and Michael pulled out a handkerchief and wiped sweat from his own face, though it was a mild fall day outside and the room was cool.

"Where were you and your outfit while this was going ... no wait, how long was Herrick's command under attack?"

"A day and two nights."

"All right, and where was 'Baldwin's Bunch' while Herrick was under attack?"

"Where we was supposed to be—up the Harech River, clear into the foothills of a big mountain range. At least that's where we was when the call came in for us to get the hell back to Yakamul to help out there."

Dr. Harrow tapped the yellow tablet with his pencil. "And if I might be permitted to ask, how long did it take you to get back to Yakamul?"

Michael thought for a minute or two, counting on his fingers. At last he said, "A full day and half the night. It started to rain a couple hours after night fell. See, Doc, in New Guinea there wasn't nothin' like a gentle rain. Nor a day-long shower. When it started to rain, it came in buckets. Then all of a sudden it'd quit. Maybe for an hour or two. Then it'd come again in buckets."

"So you attacked under cover of the rain?"

"Sorta. That and it was night, too. Anyway, it was pouring down when we went into position. But it quit before we hit 'em. That's the way it was when the captain squatted there with a stick, drawing us a map of Yakamul in the mud. He did it in the light of a flashlight, showing us where A Company had been and the little stream and the hill where the headquarters company had been wiped out.

"Well, Yakamul had been overrun, too, and the remnants of Herrick's outfit was fighting for their lives at the beach—we could hear it going on. Small arms fire, and the like. Mortars, too. Knee mortars they was—so they were theirs, not ours. It sounded desperate up there, and it turned out to be even worse than it sounded."

The doctor quit scribbling, too absorbed with Michael's tale to continue.

"We was wore out, too, but the captain looked around at the lieutenants and non-coms and said, 'I do believe the Japs lost us, boys. They haven't got a notion that we're here, so we're going in like the mill-tails of hades, you hear?' Then he looked at me and said, 'Bar, when it starts, I want you to lead and I don't want you to take your finger off that trigger of yours until the weapon runs dry. I'll be timing you, boy, and if it don't start up again in five seconds, I'll bust you back to Buck, you hear?'

"Well, I heard. I also heard all the ruckus up ahead of us, toward the beach and it wasn't too hard to guess that we was heading into trouble.

"The captain said, 'When we start to advance, we'll do so quietly—as quiet as we can. But when the first shot is fired, I want all of you to start howling like the wrath of God and I'll be double-dimwitted if we won't kick the stuffing out of them sonsaboobies'."

"So it was a night attack?" Dr. Harrow murmured.

"Yeah. That's why we pulled it off. The Japs are masters of night attacks, but they don't think we got the guts. I was the first one to bump into a Jap. Stepped on the booger while pushing through some tangled vines and creepers. He said 'Uh'—I think he might've been asleep—and he jerked and twisted around."

Dr. Harrow took another deep pull on his water glass as he studied his patient. He decided Mikhail Baranovitch was drifting into the recesses of his mind and he took another pull on his water. "Can you continue, son?"

"I could barely make out his rifle off to one side, and he was reaching for it, screaming, when I shot him. Twice. He bumped up and down each time, and his fingers still kept on reaching for that rifle, even as the life ran out of him. That's all I remember about that—at least it's all I want to remember!"

Dr. Harrow said, "That's fine, son."

"Well, the captain fired a 'Very' shell and then Herrick's outfit fired some and pretty quick there was lights all over that blasted-out jungle, and Japs was scattering all over the place, trying to get the hell out of Dodge."

"So you broke through?"

"Yeah, no problem. We caught a little fire around the fringes, but whatever reserves the Japs had was already sent on up to the Driniumor, and they didn't have anything to stop us except the scared little bastards we'd already set on fire. And them ones wasn't eager to stay around."

Dr. Harrow said, "I'd imagine the Herrick Force was glad to see you."

Michael stared at his lap. Wasn't much left to be glad to see us, but the ones still able was glad. The first foxhole had a guy laying in the bottom, half-in, half-out of muddy water. He was trying to get a drink by dipping the mud with his helmet with one hand, while holding his guts in with ...

"Michael?"

"The first one I bumped into was a corporal who was trying to hold his guts in with his fingers. He looked up at me and said, 'It's about time the cavalry got here, soldier.' I think that guy was beyond caring whether I came from Tokyo or Toledo."

Dr. Harrow took another sip of water. When Michael finally looked up, the doctor raised an eyebrow, smiled, and said, "Barney would've been proud."

Tears welled in the big man's eyes.

"I've been getting good reports about your visits to the grounds, son. Daniel says you are punctual in returning. He says you seem well-refreshed by the exercise and the experience. Is that right?"

"Uh huh."

"I'm very gratified. Perhaps we can give you even more freedom soon."

Tears spilled over to run down the big man's face as the import of the Doctor's words registered. Then there was the broad, dimpled smile.

"There is just one other thing I wish to add, son."

The dimpled smile faded.

"We will only progress at your speed. If you reach back in your memory and confront something you don't wish to talk about at the particular time, it's not something having to be done today, tomorrow, or even next week."

Michael studied his clasped hands. Dr. Harrow cleared his throat and continued: "But you do realize that someday, you must confront those very things that you are hesitant to let surface. It is those things you must confront if you are eventually to get well. And by confronting those things, you'll win our confidence to allow you more and more freedom."

When the patient continued to sit with his head bowed, Dr. Harrow asked, "Michael, do you hear?"

The voice was little more than a squeak, "Yes."

"Then, young man, I believe our session today is over. Thank you for the water and for being so forthcoming."

The patient pushed to his feet and turned to leave. But at the door, he turned back. "Doctor Harrow, sir ..."

"Yes?"

"Might it be possible to allow me my hour outside right after breakfast?"

The doctor smiled. "I will see to it, Michael."

Chapter 12

"Those white pants won't stay white very long in this kind of weather." The boy looked up in surprise. He held a chain guard for his bicycle in place with one hand while trying to start a nut on a holding bolt with the other. Mikhail Baranovitch bent down. "Here, let me hold the guard for you."

The boy nodded and soon threaded a nut to the bolt, screwing it finger-tight. Then he threaded a nut to the rear bolt. "They're corduroys," he said of his trousers, as if that had anything to do with their off-white color, especially since he knelt on one knee to the wet pavement.

Michael smiled and pointed to the paperbag hanging from the handlebars. "I used to deliver the *Montana Standard* when I was your age. That's in Butte."

The boy said, "Where's that?"

"Montana," the big man said. "You heard of Montana?"

"Yeah. But I never figure to go there."

"Why not. You don't know what you're missing."

The boy finished tightening the last nut, stood, straddled his bicycle, thumped the kickstand back and said, "Thanks for your help, mister. But I got school to go to, and I'm late.

Michael shoved his hands in his pockets and said, "That's a good bike, isn't it, a Hawthorne?"

The boy pushed off and started pedaling. Over his shoulder he said, "Aww, it's a Monkey Ward and I'd rather have a Schwinn."

Earlier, Michael had grabbed a cup of coffee and a quick platter of pancakes for breakfast, scarfed it down like a starving man and hurried to the front desk, where Gladys smiled at him and waved him on for his first early morning walk. He strode down the hospital steps, paused and breathed deeply of the brisk air, then strolled away to the river bridge, and across it to Harvard Avenue. A soft rain fell, more mist than moisture. The boy had his bicycle pulled under a maple tree, kneeling beside it as Michael ambled up. Now he stared after the boy as the youngster pedaled away, envying the youth his freedom.

Then the boy swung around, crossed the busy street and pedaled back to him. "I've got one copy of yesterday's paper left in this bag," the boy said. "I'll sell it to you for a nickel."

Michael turned his pockets inside out and spread his palms. "If I had a nickel I'd give it to you whether you'd trade me a paper or not."

The boy grinned, reached into his papersack and handed Michael a damp copy of *The Daily News* for September 26, 1950. "You can owe me the nickel, mister. How's that?"

Michael took the paper, crossed his heart, and held out his hand. The boy solemnly shook it, then pedaled away. Michael rolled the paper and thrust it in his hip pocket. Then he strolled through the cemetery, ambled back to the bridge, and found his way down to the river. There, he took a seat on the same boulder where he'd perched during one of his last visits with Dr. Henderson.

It was later that afternoon when Jasper Meacham, exiting his shower, spotted Michael with his hand in Jasper's trousers pocket. The World War I veteran stood dripping on the concrete floor, shouting, "Hey you! What the hell're you doin'?"

Michael jerked his hand back. "Barney told me to hang the pants back up."

Jasper was slight, wrinkled, and badly worn from a gas attack on the Somme. But like many small men, especially as they age, he was also crotchety and quick to anger. He shoved past Michael, looking—In his birthday suit—for all the world like a plucked chicken. "You sonofabitch," the little man shouted, shaking a fist and jerking his trousers from their wall peg at the same time, "if you stoled anything, I'll shove this fist up your ass and pull your pecker out your bung hole."

Other heads thrust from shower numbers four and seven.

Michael mumbled, "It was Barney," as Jasper slipped his wallet and his handkerchief and comb from the rear pockets, then reached into a front pocket for a handful of change. "By God, it's lucky for you, you lightfingered bastard; it's all there, else me and the boys would cut you up into pieces so small you'd hafta be strained through a dish towel."

Michael's head remained hanging, while Jasper Meacham, grumbling beneath his breath, dried and dressed. Two other patients entered and two left while Michael stood abjectly by. On his way out Jasper said loudly enough for anyone to hear, "That big bastard is a sneak thief. Watch him like a hawk."

Michael followed Jasper out and down the hall, then turned into his own room. In its safety, he shook his head at the little man's anger. After all, Michael was putting change back into Jasper's pocket; not, as the little man supposed, stealing from him. Then Michael opened his fist and stared at the shiny coin. "All I wanted, he muttered, "was five cents." He plucked the nickel from his palm and held it between thumb and forefinger. "That little guy had a bunch of coins bigger than this one. What was he carrying on about?"

On Friday, Michael waited for the kid from ten after seven until almost eight o'clock. Finally, in order to stay inside his allotted hour, he gave up and jogged all the way back to the hospital. Daniel waited for him, opening the door as the blue-clad patient arrived. "What time is it, Michael?" he asked.

The big man stopped half way through the door, eyes widening. "I'm not late. I know I'm not late."

"How do you know you're not late, Michael? Do you have a watch?"

"Yes."

"Can I see it?"

Clearly hesitant, the patient pulled a watch from his shirtpocket.

"That's a lady's watch, Michael. Isn't that a little unusual for you to have a lady's watch?"

"No."

"No? Why would you have a lady's watch, Michael?"

"To tell time." When Daniel said nothing, Michael added, "I only have an hour. I have to be back on time or the doctor won't let me out."

"Come on in and close the door, Michael."

When Michael did so, Daniel took him by the arm, guiding him to the near-empty cafeteria, then to an isolated corner.

After they were seated, Daniel said, "Gladys told me she lost her watch a week ago. She said she broke her band and had it laying on her desk."

"Barney ..."

"Jasper told me that you were going through his pockets in the showers."

The big man's head sank until his chin rested on his chest. Daniel sighed. "Michael, you do know it's wrong to steal."

After a long period of silence, Daniel whispered, "Michael, you know it's wrong to steal, don't you?"

"Yes."

"Why did you do it?"

"I needed a watch and Gladys wasn't using hers."

"But Michael, it is still hers. Just because you need something doesn't mean you have the right to take anything that belongs to another person."

Michael bit the inside of his cheek. "But if I need something ..."

Daniel held up a hand. "It's still not right to take it from someone else. I can keep the thing with Gladys's watch quiet. I'll tell her I found it someplace. But Jasper is blabbing all over the hospital that you were going through his pockets. Since he says nothing was missing, maybe what he's telling will be forgotten."

The patient stared at the floor until Daniel said, "I might keep this from Doctor Harrow, so far. But if it continues, Michael, I won't have any choice but to tell him."

"NO-O-O!" Those few others lounging in the cafeteria swiveled their heads at the big man's anguished cry.

* * *

Monday morning was heavy with frost, but Michael nevertheless stood at the junction of the hospital drive and Harvard, shoulders hunched against the cold, breath fogging against the morning air. The kid pedaled past at seven-fifteen and Michael waved him over to give him his nickel.

"I could bring you another in the morning," the kid said. But Michael shook his head. "No money. I can't."

"I'll trust you. You're a good credit risk."

Michael shook his head again, then turned and with shoulders hunched and hands in his pockets, walked toward the river bridge and the hospital.

As he'd told the boy, Michael had once had a paper route. A delivery boy had to be fourteen-years-old to deliver papers in Butte, but Michael applied for a route upon completing the sixth grade. No one at the *Mining Gazette* thought to ask the oversized youngster his age.

Michael kept at it, too, until the autumn of his eighth-grade-year when *Gazette* pressmen went on strike and as the struggle raged the newspaper closed. He wandered past the cinder field where the high-schoolers practiced football.

Coach O'Malley snarled at him when he chased after an errant punt and returned it panting to the flustered sophomore who'd shanked it from the side of his foot.

"Hey! You cowturd," O'Malley yelled, "you wanta run around this field, get enough guts to sign up for football."

But when the sophomore punter told O'Malley that Michael was only an eighth-grader, the coach's tone changed. "Come here, kid," he called, waving.

When Michael hesitated, pointing a forefinger at his own chest, the coach snarled, "Yeah, you. Now, get over here!"

The youngster shuffled forward, still unsure. The three punters and the linemen snapping them balls watched, grinning.

"Not too swift, are you?" O'Malley said in a flat voice. "How old are you?"

"M-me?" Michael stammered. "Almost fourteen, sir."

O'Malley eyed the youngster as if he was appraising a side of beef. "What grade?"

"Eighth, sir."

"What school?"

"School? Junior High. Right here."

"How big are you?"

"I don't know."

"Well, how tall are you?"

80

Michael shuffled his feet. "I don't know." He held out a hand at eye-level. "Maybe about this tall."

The punters laughed.

"Shit," the coach said. "I don't suppose you know how much you weigh, either?"

"No."

O'Malley grinned at the punters. "You wanta play football?"

"Yes." Then Michael added, I played at Daly School in the sixth grade."

"Why aren't you playing Junior High ball?"

"I'm delivering papers."

Michael knew he'd said the wrong thing when O'Malley turned to the punters and snarled, "Get busy." Then the coach's eyes swept back to the eighth-grader. "You can deliver papers or you can play football. You can't do both."

Michael could, though. He quit the afternoon *Gazette* and got a job at the bigger morning paper, rising at 5:00 a.m. every day, rain or shine, to deliver the *Montana Standard* before school. The youngster tried to go out for Junior High football, too. But "cuts" had already been made and Michael was told to come back next year. So he spent his afternoons hanging around the high school practice field. And O'Malley seemed to take no note—even when Michael began hitting the tackling dummies and shoving around the blocking frames.

And when ninth grade rolled around and Michael had grown another two inches and put on twelve more pounds, O'Malley had him practicing with the high schoolers, even though ninth graders weren't eligible for varsity competition.

"You stick with me, Baranovitch," the coach said, "and I'll teach you this game."

And when Michael said that maybe he could get in some game time by playing junior high football, mentioning that coach Smythe had asked him to come out for his team, O'Malley snapped, "To hell with that fruitcake. He coulda had you last year, but no. 'Rules aren't made to be broken!' That's what the sonofabitch told me he said to you when you tried to get on his team last year."

Coach O'Malley even suited up Michael for home games, and had the freshman sitting on the bench, though Mikhail Baranovitch was listed on no programs, and saw no game time.

O'Malley did throw the youngster into intrasquad scrimmages, however, always on defense and usually against Butte High School's first team. And the coach pulled no punches—might even be considered brutal—In his criticism of the fifteen-year-old's play against the veteran team's offense: "Goddamn it, Baranovitch! You let Snell trap you again! Are you too damn dumb ever to learn this game?" Then, with the young player near tears, he began striking back, using his hands and forearms and shoulders to fend off the older player. After all, Snell hardly outweighed him, even though the eighteen-year-old (some said nineteen) wore a scraggly beard and moustache.

Then Snell muttered something about Stefan Baranovitch and bridged Michael's nose with the heel of his hand. So, on the very next play, Michael was off before the snap of the ball, elbowing the unprepared Snell flat on his back, and walking the length of the older player with his cleats. The freshman's mistake was that he also took down a surprised tailback, smashing him to the ground with a diving tackle. Michael was benched for the rest of that practice, even though Coach O'Malley seemed more amused than angered by the freshman's aggression.

It was the following morning when retribution visited; that was when a still angry Richard Snell waited for Michael outside *Montana Standard*'s distribution office and beat the younger boy with a two-by-four until he was unconscious. But when practice began, Michael was there with two black eyes and a broken nose. And when the first scrimmage began, Michael was there, too, tapping the second-string right tackle on the shoulder and lining up across from a surprised—and perhaps fearful—Richard Snell.

Michael heard O'Malley shouting from across the field as Demarest, the second-string tackle trotted to the sidelines, but it made no difference—he still slammed into Snell with everything he had, carrying the older player to the ground, punching and punching and punching, until four other players and O'Malley pulled him off.

Richard Snell's attack outside *Montana Standard*'s distribution office ended Mikhail Baranovitch's newspaper delivery days, but it ushered in Stefan Baranovitch's demand for his son to enter the mines. "I tell you one thing," the father said, "in the mines, you learn soon how to fight."

Michael shook a head filled with black eyes and swollen nose. "No, papa, I want to finish high school, play football."

Stefan Baranovitch's laughter sounded as though it came from the bottom of a deep well. "Play?" the older man said when he stopped laughing. "Them eyes and that nose, they don't look like you was playing."

"Stefan Baranovitch," Michael's mother piped up, "I've seen you worse, more times than not."

"He goes to the mines," the older man growled.

"He's only fifteen."

"He'll pass for twenty. You want to feed him forever?"

Alexia Baranovitch folded her arms and said, "He'll go to no mine. Not now. Maybe not forever."

Her husband folded his arms, too, and thrust out his jaw. "You would test me on this, woman?"

She shook her head so hard the bun pinned to its back fell loose. "This is no test, husband. If you think so, you make big mistake." Michael lifted his head and stared through swollen slits at his mother.

Stefan shouted, "Mistake, woman? You say I make mistake. What is this—a war in my own home."

"Papa, don't," Michael muttered, causing his father to return attention to his son.

"And what will you do if I don't?" the older man said. When Michael failed to reply, Stefan Baranovitch laughed and said, "Will you fight me over it? Ha, ha! No, you won't fight me. Right now you can't fight me. But you will never fight me. You know why? Because I kick the shit out of you, that's why."

Then Stefan Baranovitch wheeled, snatched his lunch pail from the kitchen table and stomped from their home.

Chapter 13

Dr. Harrow studied Mikhail Baranovitch as the patient ducked his head to enter the doctor's office. He noted how Baranovitch shuffled to the visitor's chair, head hanging; how the big man dropped heavily into his place without being bidden. Harrow leaned back in his swivel chair, clasping gnarled hands over his sunken midsection and murmured, "Michael, I'm the recipient of some disquieting things that's being said about you." A tear trickled down the patient's face and he began kneading his knuckles. "Jasper Meacham stopped me in the hallway the other day."

A heavy silence descended, broken when Dr. Harrow pushed back his chair, went to the open door, and softly closed it. When he returned, he remained standing behind his desk, staring with piercing eyes at a patient who avoided looking anywhere but at his shoes. "I asked Daniel if there was any truth in what Jasper said. Do you wish to know what Daniel told me?" Another tear trickled out, coursing down Michael's rough-stubbled cheek. He shook his head.

"Daniel said you'd found Gladys's watch and returned it to him, so he *felt* there was nothing to what Jasper said."

Mikhail Baranovitch looked up in surprise. Even the hands on the wall clock seemed to pause. Finally the older man reached into a desk drawer and pulled out a pocketwatch, dangling it from its chain. "I ... ahh ... found this old watch languishing in a cupboard at home. I quit using it when my daughter gave me this gold-plated beauty." Harrow pushed back his left sleeve and twisted his arm so the shiny wristwatch glistened from the light of the 100-watt overhead.

Michael glanced at Harrow's wristwatch, but shifted back to the swinging pocketwatch as if hypnotized. Harrow extended the watch across the desk and said, "Would you like to have it?" Like his arm was ratcheted by a gear with missing teeth, Michael slowly reached for the dangling pocketwatch. There were more tears. "Thank you," he squeaked.

Harrow settled into his chair. "Indeed, it's my pleasure. The last time I wound it, which was some time ago, it lost a couple of minutes each day, so you might wish to measure it against the lobby clock to keep it straight." The faded eyes with their disquieting black rings continued to study Michael as the younger man's attention was wholly riveted on this most prized gift. The patient wound it, then lifted it to an ear. A great smile spread across his broad Slavic face.

"Now Michael," the doctor said, "is there anything else you need that we're not providing?"

Michael's lips pursed. "Money. I need money."

Dr. Harrow said, "How much money do you need?"

"A nickel."

The doctor laughed. "A nickel! Come on, Michael, do you need money? How much? And what would you do with it?"

The patient's face turned red, and Dr. Harrow saw he'd thoughtlessly ridiculed the younger man. "You're not joking are you? Five cents is all you want?"

Still flushed, Michael stubbornly said, "I need a nickel is all, but I won't tell you what for."

"Well, son," Harrow reached into his pocket, pulling out a handful of change, "take this and use it wisely."

Michael looked at the assorted change Harrow held in the palm of his hand, then plucked out a nickel, ignoring the rest. When the coin was safely in his own pocket, the patient said, "If I had any way to make some money is when I can pay you back."

Dr. Harrow eyed Baranovitch, then said, "Michael, do you know that patients who assist our gardeners are paid a nominal fee for their work?"

"No-o-o," the big man said, clearly interested.

"Most of the work season is over, though there are still leaves to be raked and bulbs to be dug. Would you like me to talk to the head groundskeeper about helping him? I believe gardener helpers are paid at the rate of twenty-five cents an hour."

"Would you do that?"

Harrow scribbled a note on his scratch pad, then turned his black-rimmed pupils on his patient. "Yakamul," he said.

Almost before the word was out of the doctors mouth, Michael blurted, "They took what was left of the Herrick Force away, evacuated them from the beach. Our wounded, too. There wasn't many Herricks left—took only one lighter."

"What about the Baldwin Bunch, Michael? They left your outfit surrounded on three sides by Japanese?"

Mikhail Baranovitch stared through the doctor, seeing a littered beach from an ethereal world, sand pitted and thrown up from hundreds of artillery and mortar rounds. He remembered the blasted jungle, devoid of leaves, with only broken-off stumps and logs lying crisscrossed in a tangled welter. Over it all was his recollection of the various shades of red: bright red of fresh blood, dull red of dried blood, washed-out red of rained-on blood. Still staring through the doctor, Michael muttered: "We'd put the fear of God in the yellow bastards...."

"But they were still out there, weren't they, Michael?" the doctor prompted at his patient's pause.

"Yeah, they were out there. Thousands of 'em. And they were like a beehive a horse had kicked over." He hiccupped. "Like I said last week, Tokyo had already bypassed the Herrick Force with most of a couple of divisions, anxious, I suppose to get on to the Driniumor, maybe cross it and attack our holding force at the Aitape airfield."

The doctor paused with his notepad and pen, not wishing to move Baranovitch faster than the reminiscing soldier wished to go. "Course we threw sand in that cog when we perched across their supply route. So it didn't take 'em long to send a force back to route us out." Michael's thoughts outpaced his tongue: Yeah they did. And they had even more of the bees buzzing up from their big base at Wewak, wanting to get to the Driniumor. And their best way was over the top of us.

Doctor Harrow cleared his throat. "But you were blocking their supply?"

Michael nodded, hiccupping again.

"So you were almost certain to get hit--and soon. What did you do to prepare for your ordeal?"

Michael eyes swept to the ceiling and he smiled. "That Captain Baldwin! Even while the lighter was evacking the Herrick Force, he put us to pulling blasted logs into a half circle, maybe a hundred yards long, with the beach behind us. Then we started throwing sand over all that, digging out a trench behind the logs. Doc, you wouldn't believe it! That captain was everywhere—him and the two lieutenants we had left: Wellman and Gray. And when Jap faces started popping out of the blasted-off land behind us we throwed 'em a homecoming party they couldn't forget."

"So you were pinned down, miles from any help...."

"We still had our gunboats in the bay. Least we did until the Japs ranged their artillery on 'em." Then Michael gave a half-laugh, half-cry. "On us, too—they wanted us out of there, bad."

"And things kept heating up for you...."

"I hope to shout. But we were dug in there all day and into the next night."

"How about your own supply? Food? Ammunition?"

"A couple of lighters came in that first night, in the middle of a rainstorm. The Japs could hear 'em, but they couldn't see 'em. They tried a couple of their own flares, but their propellants didn't carry far enough for the lights to reach our supply craft. Besides it helped us kill the Japs crawling up on us."

"I'll bet the supplies those lighters brought was welcome."

Michael nodded, then said, "All except for one piece of resupply. They brought in a light colonel to buck us up. I was at the captain's command post when that colonel came crab-running up. He was spotless, with fresh-ironed suntans. And he was scared shitless. Him and Baldwin saluted. Then the colonel—I never

86

The Dogged and the Damned

did learn his name—said, 'Headquarters feels it's imperative to our Driniumor defense line that you hold here, Captain'."

Dr. Harrow thoughtfully rubbed his chin, certain that the patient teetered on a memory precipice. He wanted a drink of water, sorely *needed* a drink of water. But it would be unconscionable to interrupt Michael now. Instead, the doctor let his queer unblinking eyes do the prompting. Mikhail Baranovitch's story:

"For how long?" Captain Baldwin asked the staff colonel.

"Forever, if there's need," replied the colonel.

"That's no answer, sir, Captain Baldwin growled. "We're only one shot-up company against the Good Lord only knows how many Japs they're bringing up out there. Look around! Better yet, walk around! You can see there's no line of any consequence left. We might hold with reinforcements, but without 'em...." Baldwin trailed off, then, "I'll ask again, sir, how long are we expected to hold?"

"Captain, your orders are that you're not to retreat. Ever."

"Retreat!" Baldwin cried. "Where would we retreat to? They're around us now like flies. Our backs are to the water with only a couple of patrol craft between us and survival. And when they range in those big guns a little better, it'll be suicide to bring any kind of craft in here to take us out."

Michael told how the half-dozen men in the command post fell silent as thousands of surrounding throats began the chants that would ultimately lead to a suicide charge. He told how the colonel had asked, "What's that?"

Every man in the post, from buck privates up, looked at him in contempt. Captain Baldwin said, "That, Colonel, stems from the liquid courage those Japs are taking in preparation for a banzai charge."

The whites of the colonel's eyes glistened. He reiterated the order he'd been sent to deliver, and picked up his map case to leave. Then Michael told how a Jap artillery salvo fell on their tiny pocket and the beach behind it. "Wasn't much damage done," the patient said, "except to the colonel's lighter. It and its coxswain went to greener pastures."

"So was the colonel there when ..."

Michael laughed. "Yeah, he was still on the radio trying to call in some more transport for his green and yellow ass when the banzai came. Then with every weapon we had, and every weapon they had, and every weapon our patrol craft had firing as fast as they could, that colonel quit tryin' to call out, and started tryin' to crawl under."

A silence fell in the northeast corner office of the ground floor of the Veteran's Hospital in Roseburg, Oregon. Finally Dr. Harrow asked, "Is this something you can continue with today, Michael? Can you tell me about the Japanese attack?"

Michael saw neither the doctor or the room, nor heard the muted sounds of

87

the hospital. But he began to speak....

They came. They came first with a whisper, like insects, like army ants on the move. Then it took on a rumble and you could feel 'em coming even through the sand....

"Li-i-ights!" the captain yelled, firing his own Very pistol into the air. Lieutenant Wellman did the same from the left and then the flares popped open and there was this blue light, like around a street lamp in San Francisco when the fog rolls in. And there they were. It looked like they was trying to jump over the jackstrawed logs and brush, coming as silent as they could, their faces pale and smooth, dark eyes glistening, coming in clusters and waves.

"F-I-I-I-RE!" screamed Captain Baldwin, and his command was drowned in the din. I first thought the Japs were hurling themselves down to take shelter, but then I saw that they were tumbling like wheatstraw from a threshing machine. My weapon went dry, and as I fumbled for another magazine, a second wave washed over the first and made it halfway to our trench before I could open up again.

Jorgenson grunted on my left and I see Marble hanging over the same log he'd been firing over on my right. A grenade bumped against the log I tucked behind, then bounced back toward the thrower. I dropped back of my log and the grenade went off and throwed sand and chunks of wood all over. The captain ran by, flinging grenades as fast as he could pull the pins and the ground in front of our position erupted and I jumped back up to fire again. So did a couple of other guys on my right that we called Rogers and Hammerstein 'cause their real names—Rogett and Hargesheimer sounded a bunch familiar to classical music lovers.

Then the Japs started coming over the top and there for a little bit I thought they would carry the day. I swung my B.A.R. to right and left, spraying the tops of our earthwork and suddenly both the flares and the Japs went out together.

The captain bent over his Very pistol, muttering, "Gollydobberung!"—did I tell you the captain just never cussed? Then he got another flare in and pointed the gun at the sky and soon another light exploded overhead. Nothing moved in front of us. "Wellman!" the captain screamed, staring out across the enemy line. But Lieutenant Wellman was beyond answering.

"Stacked up out there," I said. "Wonder how many of 'em are playing dead and will come if they get up another charge?"

"*When* they get up their next charge, soldier," Captain Baldwin said.

Rogers and Hammerstein shuffled through the sand to each slant-eye who'd made it into our trench, making sure with their bayonets that each of 'em had truly gone to lotus land.

When Captain Baldwin came back by, handing out extra grenades, I said,

"Barrel got a little hot back there, Cap'n—red hot."

Baldwin never paused, "Urinate on it, Bar." Then he spotted the colonel trying to raise Central Command on the radio. "Still trying to reach your relief, sir?" The colonel frowned. "Give me your coordinates, captain. If another wave comes at us, we'll be unable to stop them. That's when I'll call in our own artillery."

Harrow held up a hand while he scribbled. Then he quit and said, "Your losses, Michael? How fared the Baldwin Bunch?"

The big man's face was twisted as he struggled with the memory: The captain went along our line checking us for effectives. We were down another half of the half we had left after relieving the Herrick Force.

"You know how to use that jungle knife, Bar?" the captain asked as he passed back. When I nodded, he said,

"Good! You might need it."

"Where was the colonel, Michael?" Dr. Harrow asked.

"About then he was chasing after the captain. Seems he was determined to get our coordinates so's he could call in our own artillery on us."

"Did Captain Baldwin give them to him?"

"Wasn't much use after I sprayed our radio with my B.A.R."

Chapter 14

Dr. Harrow's mouth hung open upon Mikhail Baranovitch's disclosure that he'd destroyed, with a burst from his B.A.R., the Baldwin Bunch's only means of contact with Central Command. The doctor hitched up his lower jaw with visible effort and reached for his desk phone. After dialing, he said, "Gladys, this is Dr. Harrow. I wish you to tell Daniel to cancel my next appointment. Tell him I'm not to be disturbed until further notice ... Yes, thank you, Gladys ... no, nothing is wrong ... yes, I took my medicine ... yes, Gladys ... please, I must go now. Oh, one more thing—can you send over a pitcher of water and two glasses."

When the doctor replaced the phone in its cradle, he turned a bemused gaze on his patient. "Well, Michael, your method might have been a little unorthodox, but I presume it was effective."

"We didn't have to watch out for any of our own seventy-fives falling on us."

"What did the colonel say?"

"Wasn't much he could say. I told him I'd spotted a Jap moving over there. Told him I was sorry as hell about the radio, but I didn't see it when I went for the Jap."

"Were there any Japanese out there?" the doctor asked.

The younger man shrugged. "The colonel wasn't about to go poking around outside the command post. Leastways, not in the dark. Then when Rogers and Hammerstein told him they'd seen a Jap out there, too, all he did was sputter."

"Well, soldier, what did Captain Baldwin say about the radio?"

"Far as I know, doc, he's said nothing to this day. He did tell the colonel that he'd better pick up a loose rifle and lay out a supply of grenades."

Again a pall of silence descended. Harrow gave it plenty of time, then said, "Was there another banzai charge, Michael?"

"Was there another banzai charge?" the patient muttered. "I hope to shout...."

A full minute ticked by, then Dr. Harrow said, "Michael, I seem to be terribly dry. Do you mind if I go and hurry that pitcher of water?"

The patient appeared not to hear, raising his hands and staring at the palms. Then the hands began to tremble and Mikhail Baranovitch covered his eyes with them as Dr. Harrow tiptoed from the room. The doctor returned in only a few moments with a pitcher of water and two tumblers. He filled a glass, lifted one of the patient's hands from his face, and placed the glass in it. "There Michael," Dr. Harrow said, "drink this and we'll talk about what happens when an orchard sleeps."

The patient let the other hand fall, then drank off his water in one draught. Meanwhile, Dr. Harrow poured himself a glass of water and sipped while Michael regained his composure.

Minutes ticked by. Finally Michael whispered, "When an orchard sleeps, Dr. Harrow--that's beautiful."

Harrow nodded. "Orchards are beautiful, son; asleep or awake, they're single organisms."

"Is your orchard asleep now?"

"Not quite. This is early October. We've finished prunes, but the nuts are still ahead—filberts and walnuts."

"Filberts—is that like hazelnuts?"

Dr. Harrow nodded.

"I like hazelnuts."

"I'll bring in a bag of them for you," the doctor said, "when they're dry."

"We always had nuts at Christmas—walnuts and hazelnuts and almonds and niggertoes. I don't know where Mama got 'em, but we always had nuts then. Seemed like it couldn't be Christmas without 'em."

"Tell me about Christmas in Butte, Michael."

A huge smile. "There was snow, see? Butte's on this big hill, and most of the mines strung up lights on their galley frames. The store fronts all had their windows decorated, and the city maintenance crews strung lights across the streets and decorated the lightpoles with wreaths and other greenery." Then Michael's face turned puzzled and he said, "I don't know where they got all the tree boughs from; there wasn't no trees left close to Butte."

"So Christmas was a big thing in Butte?"

The patient laughed. "It might've been the *only* thing the Cornish and the Irish agreed on, Doc. Yeah, Christmas was big. All us kids roamed the streets, going from one shop to another. Some of those shops had candy out for us. One gumdrop for each kid. Some of the church groups or Odd Fellows or Knights of Columbus organized sleigh rides for kids. Carolers went from house to house, stomping their feet from the cold, and singing their hearts out just because they could. Or maybe because they were good."

"I see. It sounds wonderful the way you ..."

"And there was snowmen and snowforts and snowballs. One year, they had contests for the best snow sculpture."

"What was that like, Michael?"

"Montana Power won it with a manger and the baby Jesus and wise men and shepherds—the whole rack-a-frack. It was beautiful."

"It sounds like it, Michael."

"They had all the snow sculptures up on Copper Street, just off Montana Street. They were most of 'em life-size. Didn't take much of an imagination to see real donkeys and people and things into 'em." Dr. Harrow began writing on his notepad. Michael said, "They had to haul in snow, though."

Harrow glanced up. "Haul in snow?" The patient nodded. "Yeah. It was a big snow year, but Butte seldom gets much. And Montana Power's manger scene used up most of what the city street crews pushed up on the hill. Then the Parrot—that's a mine—started building a snow castle they figured would rival one built in Leadville—that's Colorado—back in the eighteen-hundreds. But when they took to hauling in snow from Pipestone and Elk Park, even the pockets of the richest mine in Butte ran out."

"Did they have sculpture contests every year, Michael?"

The big man shook his head. "Only in thirty-nine."

"And you were in high school then?"

Michael nodded.

"And you played football, right?"

Michael stared at the doctor, through the doctor. Then he said, "Tell me what happens when an orchard sleeps."

Dr. Harrow smiled, then spent the next half-hour talking about putting an orchard to bed; the disking and cultivating, the February pruning. He branched into theories on grafting, the use of fertilizers, and the application of chemicals for disease and pest control.

At the conclusion of his thirty-minute dissertation on orcharding, Dr. Harrow asked Mikhail Baranovitch if he'd like to continue with his account of the Yakamul battle.

Without batting an eye, Michael told how Captain Baldwin went to each of us and told us at the first sign of the coming attack, we was all to rush to our west perimeter. "All right, here's what we're going to do," the captain said, "We're going to attack them as they attack us. We're going to go at them in the jungle fringe at the edge of the beach. They'll be weaker there, because ..."

Michael told how the colonel broke in. "Captain!" he snarled, "that's contrary to your orders! You are to hold this position! I'm ordering you to do that."

Captain Baldwin glanced at his superior officer, then switched back to his men. "We're going to hit them near the beach because their charge will be weakest there—they're afraid of our gunboats."

"Captain!" the colonel broke in again. "There are thousands of Japs out there.

The Dogged and the Damned

You know that! What you're suggesting is suicide!"

"And if we wait here, Colonel, there'll be thousands of Japs here, too, and we'll all be dead. What I'm telling these men is our only chance for any of them to get out alive. Attacking will be so unexpected, it just might break through their own thin attack line."

"What then, Cap'n?" asked Johnny Drew in his South Carolina drawl.

Captain Baldwin smiled at the men around him. "Why, then, all we need do is run two miles to the Driniumor, hit the Jap holding force there in the back, convince our guys across the river that we're friendlies, then make a river crossing against hostile guns from both directions."

"Sounds like a turkey shoot to me," Drew drawled.

"I've heard enough!" the colonel said, drawing himself up. "Captain, I'm relieving you of command of this company. Lieutenant Gray, you are to take command."

The lieutenant knelt there, right by the side of the colonel. His eyes flicked from side to side, then he leaned toward Captain Baldwin and said, "How do we coordinate withdrawal from our perimeter Captain, and get to your launch point?"

"This is mutiny!" the colonel cried, his face reddening. "I'll see you are all court-martialed for this!"

"Only if you survive, Colonel," Private Drew said. "And I'd guess you or me, neither one, has much chance of seeing the sunrise."

"You are ordered to ..."

"What about our wounded?" Lieutenant Gray asked.

The captain shook his head. "They'll have to keep up. For those who can't, the only thing we can do is load their weapons and give them a couple of hand grenades each."

"Captain! Again I must warn you that this is insubordination! I'll ..."

Baldwin grinned. "Well, we're making a little headway, Colonel. A minute ago it was mutiny." He eyed the colonel from head to toe. "Maybe you'd like to stay here with the wounded, sir; take command of the post, so to speak, while we go after some help." After a few moments, Captain Baldwin said, "Sir?"

"It took a while for the Japs to brew up another potion of courage," Mikhail Baranovitch told Dr. Harrow. "The captain finally started fretting about 'em taking so long; guess he feared daylight would come before our own attack and cut into our odds of getting through.

"But they finally started their chants, and my heart started beating a little faster, just like before kickoff for the State Championship game." Harrow glanced

93

up in momentary interest, then returned to his writing pad. Michael said, "They came just like before. Only this time there wasn't much fire from our side—just a few of our wounded got off a few rounds. Meanwhile the rest of us—somewhere around thirty effectives—concentrated on our right side, right at the jungle line with the beach."

"But there wasn't much jungle left there. Is that correct?" Harrow prompted.

"That's right. But the Japs were afraid of taking fire there from our gunboats—on both beach perimeters."

"And you were planning to charge right into a sector that might've been blanketed by fire from your own boats?"

"Captain Baldwin said that's the sector that would have the fewest Japs in it because they didn't want to get ground up by the gunboats. He also thought they'd think it would be the one place we wouldn't hit because of running into our own stuff."

"And was Captain Baldwin right?"

Michael shrugged. "It's where we went."

"And obviously you got through?"

Again, the shrug.

"Can you tell me about the jump-off, Michael? How did Captain Baldwin's plan unfold?"

Michael slumped deeper into his chair and thrust trembling hands in his pockets. "I don't know; maybe our lack of return fire confused the Japs. First they were shooting and hollering their gibberish like mad. Then the shooting started falling off, and so did their shouting. I saw some of 'em coming over the earthwork behind us when the captain screamed, 'Up and at 'em, boys!' And we all leaped up and out, flinging our pineapples and charging right after ...""

"Wait a minute!" Dr. Harrow cried, holding up his hand. "You mean you threw hand grenades and ran right after them?"

Michael was nodding even before the doctor finished his question. "That was the plan. Captain Baldwin said some of us might get hit by stuff from our own grenades—as well as from the gunboats' fifty calibers. But he said there would be one supreme moment of confusion and we'd better be into it, firing every thing we had at that exact moment."

Dr. Harrow bent to his scratch pad. At last, he looked up and said, "What happened then, Michael?"

The patient raised his chin from his chest, almost as if he thought the doctor's question unnecessary. "We broke through. It was just like the captain said. Wasn't none of 'em expecting us to attack. When we come at 'em out of the sand and mud throwed up by our grenades, screaming like banshees and firing every piece of equipment on as auto-fire as we could get—well it surprised 'em. Like the captain said, their line was thin in that spot, and we was running like a herd of buffalo. We blowed a hole through their line and was into the untouched jungle behind 'em before they even knew what happened." Here Michael fell silent as he reconstructed their breakthrough from memory....

Yeah, sounds easy. But Laidlaw got cut down right alongside, Terry cartwheeled off to the left, and bullets and shrapnel was singing left and right, front and back, top to bottom. But it was quick and we was quick and then it was over—at least it seemed like it.

Dr. Harrow cleared his throat and Michael began again: "We killed quite a few of 'em on the way through and lost another half of our own. But we were out of the pocket!"

"The colonel, Michael?" Harrow murmured.

"Well, Doc, he was a little retarded in figuring out what he wanted to do. That made him slow to get started. The kind of action we was in didn't make it any safer for anybody lagging behind."

Dr. Harrow laid down his pen and paper. "Would you care for a drink?" The doctor leaned back in his chair and said, "I know I would. Could you pour for us?"

The big man poured their glasses full. Dr. Harrow beamed when Michael handed him a glass with a steady hand.

After the two men had finished their water, the doctor picked up his pad and pen and said, "So you'd broken through the Japanese line, into hostile territory, still two miles from your own lines on the Driniumor?"

"Yeah."

"And it was still dark?"

"Yeah, but before we got to the Driniumor, there were streaks of light in the east. It was our luck that it started to rain again, though."

"How long did it take you to get to the Driniumor, Michael?"

"I don't know. Maybe a half-hour. Maybe an hour. I know the captain kept us together, kept us moving. Did I tell you he found a trail first thing?"

"Even so, that's incredible time to cover two miles of jungle, isn't it?"

Michael said that was so. "But, tell the truth, Doc, maybe you never had all the mill-tails of hell after you like we figured we had."

"And did they catch you?"

Michael smiled. "I never found out if they even tried. Maybe all they wanted was for us to get off their supply route."

"But you were heading for another line of Japanese, weren't you? Along the Driniumor river? And wouldn't that have been a more formidable line?"

Michael poured another glass of water for each of them, emptying the pitcher, nodding to himself the entire time. Then he picked up the story: "That's true. But the captain stopped us before we got to their next line and told us that he doubted if the Japs even knew we were nearby. He said it was our luck that it looked like the first Japs hadn't followed us, hadn't got into any fire-fights with us. So it might be that the Japs we headed for hadn't heard that we were coming. Then he told us to catch our breaths because the next Japs we bumped into would surely be their Driniumor River line. 'As soon as we bump into the first one, I want every man-jack of you to charge at 'em again, just like you did back yonder, firing everything you got. And when you reach the Driniumor, you run across it screaming Yankee Doodle at the top of your lungs! Got it?'

"Well, we got it. Wasn't long after that when we come on a Jap supply station. Cooking rice, they was. We went through 'em like the wrath of God. I was trying to measure my clips to have enough when we got to the Driniumor, but God there was a bunch of Japs, and I didn't bring enough. So I flung my B.A.R. aside and went the last hundred yards waving my jungle knife and screaming like I did once against Kalispell in the playoffs."

"And your group got through?"

"Yeah, most of us. Credit it to sheer surprise. It began with every Jap face turned toward us in surprise, and ended with the backs of their heads and helmets as they fled the swath we cut."

"And at the river?"

"Yankee Doodle did the job for us. When I hit the water, they were laying down a covering fire that a fly couldn't a-buzzed through. I was splashing water fifteen feet on each side of me, and Lieutenant Gray was doing the same thing on my right and Rogers and Hammerstein on my left."

"How many made it, Michael?"

The patient shrugged. "I don't really know; some were wounded and I never saw them again, others were left behind at the Yakamul, and some died at the Driniumor crossing. Maybe ten, maybe a dozen. Reason I don't know is because they were all gone when I came back."

Dr, Harrow laid down his pad and pen. "Came back? I don't understand. Came back from where, Michael?"

"Back from across the Driniumor. I went back for Captain Baldwin. He never made it across."

Chapter 15

Progress Report

Patient: Mikhail Baranovitch

BREAKTHROUGH!!! Both in my own understanding of a possible treatment method, and the patient's willingness, when it's properly applied, to recall traumatic occurrences. May be on cusp of penetration into one action that contributed to the patient's psychological breakdown.

What an experience! Aitape itself is merely the campaign; but the battles! First at Yakamul, secondly on the Driniumor, and finally when Mikhail Baranovitch returned across enemy lines to rescue his captain. Presently we've covered his company's fighting withdrawal from the Yakamul pocket, and their surprise breakthrough of enemy lines at the Driniumor—the entire context for both of these affairs are sufficient for a fair-sized volume, but so much ground was covered in this most recent consultation that I'll confess my own frailties precluded continuing, even though the patient may have been cajoled into doing so.

The breakthrough in treatment for this patient came by discovering that Mikhail Baranovitch readily responds to carrots, but vehemently resists the stick. It was the gift of a second-hand watch and a nickel—A NICKEL, FOR GOD'S SAKE!—that brought Mikhail around to discussing the two final actions, at the Yakamul pocket and on the Driniumor River. With luck—provided my own internal devils hold off—we'll get to the first of Baranovitch's traumas during our next session.

Problem: It may be that the patient has some sort of compulsion to steal. However, rather than basic kleptomania, Mikhail feels a very real need and thinks his only solution is by stealing from others. Fortunately Mikhail Baranovitch's desires are modest. And perhaps, if we can reach and treat the man's underlying problems, he will feel no need to take items not belonging to him.

In short, such successful treatment I've been able to accomplish with this patient is to discover his utmost desire, then, if possible, grant it to him, while, at the same time leading him to open his mind to past events that led to his illness. This time it was through a worn-out pocketwatch and five cents. (I'd love to know more about that nickel!).

Signed,
Dr. Archibald Harrow
V.A. Hospital
Roseburg, Oregon
October 3, 1950

It was Jasper Meacham again—his angry screeching caterwauled down the second-floor hallway, carried around its corners and reverberated through its wings. Daniel and two other orderlies ran to investigate.

What they found was Jasper with his nose nearly against Mikhail Baranovitch's chest, forefinger tapping at the bigger man and shouting, "So you admit it you overstuffed shitass! You admit you stoled from me." Daniel was first on the scene. Michael slumped against the wall, head hanging in abject penitence as the little man stabbed at him with a rigid finger.

"What's the matter, Jasper?" Daniel said as Larsen Volkamen and Ring Sanders dashed up.

Jasper gave Michael a final push with the flat of his hand. "You know what this big shithead just did?" the little man said while holding out a five-cent piece between thumb and forefinger.

"He said he took this out of my pocket that day I caught him rifling my clothes."

The three orderlies milled uncomprehendingly, staring first at Jasper, then at the nickel. "He really is nuts, ain't he?" Jasper said in his loudest whine.

Daniel studied Michael. The big man leaned against the poorly lit hallway wall, eyes on the floor. Daniel said, "Larsen, why don't you and Ring take Jasper down to the lounge. Maybe he'll want to spend that nickel on a coke. If not, tell him the treat's on me." After the other three disappeared, Daniel said, "Okay, Michael, he's gone."

A here this-moment, gone-the-next smile flashed across Mikhail Baranovitch's face as he straightened from his slouch and eyed the orderly. "Don't worry. I won't hurt him."

Daniel smiled and said, "He can be grating, though, can't he?" Then he sobered and stared up at the bigger man, seemingly weighing what to say next. Michael beat him to it.

"I got the nickel from Dr. Harrow. He gave it to me an hour ago. He also gave me this." The patient pulled out Harrow's old pocketwatch and held it out to the orderly."

"I see," Daniel murmured. "At least I guess I do...."

Michael beat the orderly to the next question, too. "No, I won't tell you what

I needed the nickel for." The orderly's smile was as fleeting as was Michael's moments before. He patted the patient on the arm and walked away. As he did, Michael said, "Jasper don't mean nothing by getting on our nerves, Daniel. He just wants to feel bigger than he is."

True to his word, Dr. Harrow talked to the hospital's head groundskeeper about employing Mikhail Baranovitch on his crew. Gordon Smith waited on Friday for Michael to return from his morning walk. Smith introduced himself and said Dr. Harrow had suggested Mikhail Baranovitch (Smith was careful to pronounce the given name "Michael") for grounds duty. Would Michael care to join the crew?

Michael's heart leaped, but he said, "I'll do anything I can to help, but I'm only allowed out on Monday, Wednesday, and Friday for an hour each morning."

Smith smiled. "And how about more? I'm sure, if you're interested, that we can spring more yard time for you for our program. You see, Dr. Harrow ..."

"I can go now!" Michael blurted. "I've already had breakfast. And I don't need to eat before supper. I'll do anything you want and I'll do it good, sir. I swear I will. If you want me through the weekend, I'll work then, too."

Smith's smile broadened. "How about Monday, son? I'll talk to Dr. Harrow and get your papers fixed up by then. Say nine o'clock Monday—If its not raining."

"I'll work in the rain. It rained all the time in New Guinea. I'm not afraid of getting wet."

Smith chuckled. "Monday, then, it is. Meet me here in the lobby at nine, okay? We need help raking leaves. Did Dr. Harrow tell you we pay twenty-five cents per hour?"

"Yes sir. But I'll work for less if you don't think I do it good enough."

Mikhail Baranovitch returned from his hour walk on Monday morning by eight o'clock. For the next hour the man was like a caged lion, pacing the lobby, checking his pocketwatch every couple of minutes, dropping into a heavy oak lobby chair only to bounce up to pace again and check his watch.

Gordon Smith was several minutes late, and Gladys became sufficiently concerned at Michael's growing agitation that she called for Daniel on the loudspeaker. Smith arrived first.

"Sorry I'm running behind, Michael," Smith said. "But you'll probably find that's the way I generally run anyway."

When the patient only nodded, the groundskeeper said, "You ready to go to work?"

"Yes."

"Do good, Michael," Gladys called. Daniel waved encouragement, too.

Smith gave Michael a rake, pointing him to a front lawn inundated with maple leaves. "Rake 'em up in piles out by the street, Michael. Just keep 'em out of the way of cars and off the sidewalks. Some of the other boys will be along in a truck to haul 'em away."

Mikhail Baranovitch *attacked* the leaves like he was charging into hostile fire, wielding the rake with a vengeance, beginning next to the building and pulling together a long row of leaves that was soon up to his knees. By the time the blue-clad workman reached the sidewalk, the line was up to his thighs. Then he raced to one end and began dragging a tremendous pile back to the middle. In an hour and a half, when Gordon returned to check on his newest charge, Michael had leaves from the entire front yard of the main hospital building raked into one gigantic pile that stood nearly as high as his head and twenty feet in circumference. Smith laughed and said, "Now *that* is one hell of a pile of leaves, soldier."

When Michael grinned, the groundskeeper said, "But next time, how about raking them into, say, a half-dozen smaller piles? Probably be easier, wouldn't it? And it might be easier for the other guys to pick up."

So after Gordon Smith had instructed Michael to move down to the next building, then left to supervise elsewhere, Michael broke his huge pile into six smaller ones, all in a row along the sidewalk, about three feet apart. Then he went to the next building and did the same. And the next building.

Smith had to come for him at noon or Mikhail Baranovitch would've worked through the meal period. "What in the hell are we going to do with you, soldier?" the groundskeeper asked, laughing. "Don't you know you'll work yourself out of a job in a week?"

While Michael was at the noon meal, Smith picked up the man's rake and took it to the tool shed. But he failed to tell Michael that he was done for the day. So when the big man returned to his raking he discovered he had no tool. He began picking up late-falling leaves and carrying them individually to his piles. And when the truck came to haul the leaves away, Michael joined in their loading with glee, picking up armloads and throwing them up to the man in the truck bed who tramped the leaves into place.

It was Daniel who discovered Mikhail Baranovitch still at work picking up individual leaves as the orderly left at the end of his shift. "That's enough for today," he said, taking Michael's arm and leading the big man to the cafeteria for supper.

Smith failed to meet Michael the next morning, though the patient paced the lobby from six-thirty to eleven-forty. Finally Gladys again called for Daniel.

The Dogged and the Damned

"Did Gordon tell you he would meet you here this morning?" the orderly asked.

"No," Michael said. "I just thought...."

"Did he tell you he would use you every day?"

"No."

"Well, did he tell you he wouldn't use you every day?"

"No." The patient's replies grew weaker with each answer.

Daniel patted Michael on the shoulder, saying, "Obviously this is something we must get cleared up, friend. Meanwhile, it's getting close to lunch time. Then your session with Dr. Harrow comes after that. What say you go on to the cafeteria while I see if I can find Gordon and get it cleared up once and for all how much you're supposed to work."

The patient turned away, head hanging.

Daniel came for him at twenty minutes after one to lead him to Dr. Harrow's office. The head groundskeeper was there. "Good afternoon, Michael," Dr. Harrow said.

"I didn't mean to do wrong! I don't even know what it is that I done."

The three other men laughed. "There's nothing wrong, Michael," the doctor said. "Gordon says the only problem with you is that you do the work of three men and he doesn't know how he can keep you busy."

The groundskeeper nodded. "You don't know when to quit, son," he said. "I didn't know you worked all afternoon until Daniel told me a few minutes ago."

Mikhail Baranovitch visibly brightened. "I didn't do wrong by helping the other guys pick up leaves?"

Smith said, "No, no. In fact they tell me you helped a lot. Said they'd like to have you on their team all the time. But with all the leaves we've got down around the buildings, and the way you rake, I think I'd like to keep you on at that for awhile." The groundskeeper paused to blow his nose, then added, "That is, if you want to continue with us."

"I'd like that, sir."

Dr. Harrow said, "How much can you employ him, Gordon? I happen to know Michael enjoys being outside very much."

Smith said, "Well, I can try him every day if you'd like, Doc. But I'm not sure I can use him all day, every day."

"Then can you set up a regular schedule for Michael to meet you with your regular crew. I assume you give out instructions each morning."

"Sure, we can do that." The groundskeeper turned to Michael. "Can you meet me at my office at nine o'clock, son?"

"I guess. But I don't know where your office is, sir."

Daniel said, "I'll take you there in the morning, Michael. It's down by the motor pool. How about if I meet you in the lobby at five minutes to nine?"

Michael beamed, head bouncing.

There were a few minutes of small talk between the other three, then Daniel Fields and Gordon Smith took their leave. Dr. Harrow shuffled a few papers on his desk, looked up at Michael, and murmured, "Sit down, _Bar_."

The sudden use of his old nickname jolted Michael. He sank slowly into his chair. "You used ..."

Dr. Harrow's eyes crinkled. "I've known of it for some time, Michael. In fact, you even repeated it yourself when talking about how Captain Baldwin sometimes used it. I think it's a fine nickname, one deserving respect and professional admiration."

The patient sat a little straighter in his chair, though his face had turned expressionless. Dr. Harrow reached to one side of his desk and pulled a notebook to him. "By the way," he said, "Gordon really is impressed with your eagerness and willingness to work."

Michael nodded, but his eyebrows arched as he stared at the notebook.

Dr. Harrow sneezed, wiped his nose, and said, "It seems as though everyone is catching a cold." Then, "Let's see, Michael, last week we left off with you telling me you went back across the Driniumor for Captain Baldwin. Can we take up your story there?"

Chapter 16

The exhausted men of Baldwin's bunch, some wounded, all at their physical and psychological limit, gathered in a tiny clearing on the American-held side of Drinumor River. Mikhail Baranovitch slumped against the flattened front tire of a blasted half-track, adrenalin still pumping. Lieutenant Gray had fallen on his face nearby. Rogers and Hammerstein, along with a wounded Johnny Drew, sprawled on the other side of the glade.

"We made it, Bar," the lieutenant said, rolling over and sitting up. "We made it, man!"

Doorman and Kotynski shuffled into the clearing, each supporting the other. Blood trickled down Kotynski's right leg.

"I lost my B.A.R.," Michael muttered. "Threw it away when I ran out of mags." He grinned. "What will MacArthur do to me?"

"Tell MacArthur to go to hell!" Lieutenant Gray blurted. :Don't you understand, you jackass, we made it! WE MADE IT!" Michael struggled to his feet as a pair of medics ran into the clearing. He watched as one medic knelt by Drew, the other took Kotynski by the arm

"Sir," Michael said to Lieutenant Gray, "hadn't we better find Captain Baldwin? He'll probably want us to set up a perimeter or something."

The lieutenant shook his head. "I don't think Captain Baldwin made it. That's what ..." Lieutenant Gray's voice turned to a gurgle as he was dragged to his feet by the throat.

"What did you just say?" Michael snarled, releasing the lieutenant and adding, "Sir!"

Gray rubbed his throat. "Get a handle on yourself, soldier," he muttered. "I said I think Captain Baldwin bought the farm over there."

Baranovitch thrust his nose against the lieutenant's. "Did you see him go down?" he thundered. "Did you see him fall?"

Lieutenant Gray stepped back, face reddening. "I did not, corporal. No, I didn't see him fall. One minute he was running at my side; the next minute he wasn't. You know how it was—you can't be sure of anything."

Mikhail Baranovitch jerked out his jungle knife and wheeled. "Corporal!" the lieutenant cried, "Get your ass back over here!"

Michael snarled, "No way, Lieutenant. Ain't none of us followed orders much on this one. And I ain't about to 'til I find the captain."

Gray slumped against the blasted half-track and waved. "Go on, then," he said. "I hope to God you find him, but I'll put a dollar against a dime that you won't."

Hours spent searching for Captain Baldwin among the ranks of soldiers manning the Driniumor Line proved futile. Several of the men Michael talked to had watched their dash to freedom across the shallow river. None could remember a captain among their group.

It was an hour after darkness fell when Mikhail Baranovitch entered the tiny slough he thought led to an old crocodile nest. At least he *hoped* the little water trough led to an *old* nest.

"I don't know, corporal," the sentry said. "I ain't seen no crocs since I been pullin' duty here. Between us and the Japs, I reckon we killed 'em all off. But that don't mean there ain't one left in this river somewhere."

Michael slipped into the brown water, submerging and slowly crawling along the muddy bottom into the main watercourse. Clenched in his teeth was a length of quarter-inch carburetor hose cut from the half-track he'd leaned against earlier that morning. He was naked, covered with a black grease pulled from the half-track's gear case. His only weapon was a fisted jungle knife. Wrapped around his waist were three filled, thirty-caliber machine gun belts for weight. Twice during the crossing, Mikhail Baranovitch pushed to the surface, exposing his eyes and nose and taking controlled gasps of air. Then he'd sink again to crawl along the bottom of the shallow stream, breathing through his hose.

Mikhail Baranovitch's objective was a fallen mango tree whose blasted and leafless trunk lay half-submerged in the Japanese side of the river. It took forty-five minutes for him to reach the fallen trunk, then another thirty minutes to slip noiselessly from the water and into the jungle, marvelling all the while that his luck held.

Michael's luck was more the improbable nature of a single soldier crossing the river to slither among enemy lines than any particular lack of vigilance by Japanese sentries. The enemy was, after all, preparing for an attack of their own, interested only in defending against a massed spoiling attack. That one enemy soldier would crawl into their midst was unthinkable.

It took two additional hours for Michael to pause-and-crawl past the line of Japs entrenched on their side of the Driniumor. But at last, Michael felt he could rise to his hands and knees and creep farther into enemy territory.

He arrived in minutes at the Japanese supply site where Captain Baldwin had led them into their charge across the Driniumor. From there, Michael began the slow crawl back along their attack route to the river. As he recalled, they'd sprinted along a good footpath; a jungle track he easily found and followed. Twice he had to roll into the underbrush as Japanese patrols tramped by. The second time he did so, he rolled into the same hollow occupied by Captain Baldwin.

He struck the boots first, then bumped up against the cartridge belt of the tiny hollow's first occupant. There was a low groan. In an instant, Michael clamped a hand over the other man's mouth, pushing the knife point against the exposed neck. After sounds of the Japanese patrol faded, Michael released his clamp over the other's mouth and whispered, "Who are you?"

Again there was a groan. Still with the knife pressed against the unknown soldier's throat, Michael ran a hand over the other's clothing. There was a web belt and revolver holster. An officer! But Jap or Yank? The holster was empty. Michael reached up to feel the shoulder flaps. Two bars! "Captain?" he whispered. "Captain Baldwin?"

"Water," came the weak response.

Michael nearly laughed aloud. "Didn't bring no water," he whispered. "Figured instead to take you to it. First, though, I gotta find out where you're hit."

"Knee," Captain Baldwin muttered.

Michael felt down the captain's legs until he found the wounded knee. Broken bone thrust through the mud-splattered khakis. All the rescuer could do was cut a few short sticks, commandeer Baldwin's shirt, cut it into strips and lash an improvised splint into place. Each time the captain groaned, Michael covered his mouth and whispered to him.

"One time, Captain, up there in Elk Park out of Butte, I come on this little clump of purple wildflowers...."

Another Japanese patrol tramped by, then Michael pulled the captain to a sitting position.

"I studied some on them flowers--watched 'em all day," Michael whispered. He stripped off the captain's web belt, buckling it around his own middle. The belt carried a flare pistol. Michael checked it for load, then thrust it back into place. He also slipped his knife into the belt. Then he took the captain under the arms and lifted him, placing a shoulder between the officer's crotch, picking the wounded man up in a fireman's carry.

"Like I said, they was purple," he whispered, "but they had big yellow centers, maybe the size of a shirt button." Captain Baldwin's head lolled against the bulging biceps of Michael's arm. Michael parted the bushes and staggered onto the trail, creeping forward as nearly like a wraith as a two hundred and twenty pound man packing a hundred and seventy pound man could do.

"They closed up every night, but in the morning, after the sun came up, they opened up into the prettiest little bowl you ever saw...."

Again and again, sometimes alerted by Japanese chatter, sometimes sensing a nearby enemy, Michael drifted into the underbrush with his load. Occasionally he lowered the captain to the ground, then slipped silently into the jungle, knife at the ready. Eventually he worked to within a few yards of the river. It was here that his heart began to beat faster. Again he lowered the captain, then lay beside him gathering strength for a final dash. "Their leaves," he whispered into the captain's ear, "was thin and crinkled, and kinda fuzzy...."

At last he came stealthily to his feet, gathered up Captain Baldwin in his fireman's grip, took a deep breath, pulled out the Very pistol, and fired it upstream at a low arc. He was afraid for a moment that he'd allowed such a low trajectory that the flare wouldn't ignite before hitting the water, but at last it popped open, bathing its surroundings into one brief glare before plunging into the river.

With all eyes on both sides of the river jerked upstream, Michael hit the water running. "YANKEE DOODLE CAME TO TOWN," he bellowed, YANKEE DOODLE DANDY!"

Rifle muzzles began winking from the rear and bullets whizzed past. "MIND THE MUSIC ... AND ... THE GIRLS ..." He felt Captain Baldwin's body jerk. Then a machine gun opened up from the American side and rifle muzzles started winking over there, too. "AND WITH ... THE GIRLS ..."

Captain Baldwin jerked again and this time a sharp pain ripped into Michael's lower back! Someone was yelling from the American side, even over the roar of concentrated gunfire. "AND ... WITH ... THE GIRLS ..."

He was wobbling, but the American shoreline was only a few yards away. Again Baldwin jerked. Then Michael was at the jungle line; a man leaped into the water to help. Willing hands grasped him and dragged him and the captain into the jungle. "HE'S ... HAN ... dy!" he managed to gasp, then everything grew dim and blinked out.

Chapter 17

"Gladys," Dr. Harrow said into his desk phone, "another pitcher of water, please. Perhaps Daniel would be kind enough to bring it."

Mikhail Baranovitch seemed drained after his hour-long monologue about re-crossing the Driniumor with Captain Baldwin. But the man was strangely calm, slumping in his chair, eyes closed, breathing easily. After Daniel appeared with the water and he'd drank his fill, Michael straightened and smiled.

"Michael," Dr. Harrow said, "that's one of the most extraordinary accounts I've ever heard. Is that when you were awarded your Silver Star?"

"No," the patient said, shaking his head. "That was at Endaiadere. The one at the Driniumor was made out of bronze."

Dr. Harrow murmured, "The Silver Star *and* a Bronze Star, too—that's pretty heady stuff, soldier." The patient shrugged. "And you received another Purple Heart at Driniumor?"

"Yeah, but the captain took most of 'em intended for me. He got shot all to hell—three rounds, not counting the one he took in the knee before I got back to him."

"How about you, son? How badly were you hit?"

Michael shrugged again. "Lower left back with one that had already passed through the captain. Lost a little blood, I guess. But it wasn't much."

Harrow spun his chair around to stare out the window for a few moments, then spun back. "Did you see Captain Baldwin again?"

"They took him to the big hospital on Espiritu Santo, then to the States. I saw him when I got to Espiritu before he left. He came to my ward just after I got there and I guess I was pretty much out of it. Besides that, I was under guard."

Michael's eyes seemed to close as he struggled to remember. "Captain Baldwin, he eyed the guard, then said, 'How are you, Bar?' I remember mumbling, 'They was pasqueflowers ... them purple flowers with the yellow ... centers ... that closed up during the night and ... opened when the sun came out'."

The doctor pushed to his feet. "I'd like to continue this, Michael. But there is no way I can do it today." He smiled. I do want to congratulate you on making it past this giant hurdle, son. You've been most forthcoming, and I'm sure it will contribute a great deal to your future healing."

The patient said, "When I came to in the hospital at Aitape, they said I was still trying to sing Yankee Doodle."

Dr. Harrow chuckled, then said, "I presume you're enjoying your time working on the grounds."

"Yes, sir."

"And you will see Mr. Smith at his office in the morning."

"Yes, sir. Daniel is supposed to take me."

"Are you still working out in the gym?"

Michael's eyes flicked to the window. "Not as much as I should, sir. But if I get to spend more time outside, I'd rather do that."

The doctor nodded. "Of course. I can understand that."

Michael placed his hands on the arms of his chair. "You want me to go now, don't you?"

Dr. Harrow smiled and nodded.

The next several days passed swiftly for Mikhail Baranovitch. He turned into a one-man leaf-raking crew—a chore few others of the grounds crew welcomed. The big man was so dedicated to the task that he spent much of his Monday, Wednesday, and Friday free hour picking up leaves without a rake. Then one day he turned up with a rake, even though he wasn't to start work for two hours and Gordon Smith hadn't yet unlocked the tool shed.

"Michael," Daniel said, "where did you get the rake?"

"Found it," the patient mumbled.

"You found it?"

"Yes."

"Where did you find it, Michael?" The blue clad patient poked at the grass with the toe of his shoe. "Michael, where did you find the rake?"

"At a house."

Daniel blurted, "At a house! You mean, at a house outside the grounds?"

"I could see it across the road. It was just leaning there. Nobody was using it. I thought I could use it, then I'll take it back."

"Michael," Daniel said, "how long have you had this rake?"

"I don't know."

"Have you had it more than just today?"

"Yes."

"Where have you kept it?"

"Under my bed."

Daniel's mouth pinched and he swung his head to stare at Mount Nebo. Then he said, "Under your bed. You stole the rake from a house across the street from our grounds—which street, Harvard or Garden Valley?"

"Across the river--Harvard."

The Dogged and the Damned

"Shit!" The normally reticent orderly murmured, "All right, Michael. I'll have to go tell Gladys where we're going, then you and I are going to march across the river, across Harvard, and knock on the door of the house where you took this rake from. We're both going to tell whoever comes to the door that we're sorry we took something that doesn't belong to us, and we're going to throw ourselves on their mercy. Is that clear, Michael?"

"You mean you want to go for a walk across the river with me? That's great!"

Fifteen minutes later, the orderly and his patient mounted the steps and knocked on the door of a house sided with pale blue asbestos shingles. When an elderly gentleman opened the door, Daniel removed his cap and said, "Sir, we're returning this rake one of our patients took from you a few days ago...." Michael held out the rake so the owner could better see. "He's very sorry," Daniel continued. "He now recognizes the error of his act and swears on a stack of bibles that it won't happen again."

The elderly gentleman looked from one visitor to the other. "Tain't my rake," he said. "My rake is leaning against the side of my house. Used it just yesterday."

Daniel threw up his hands and stomped down the steps. They left the rake leaning where Michael found it.

Dr. Harrow was absent the following Tuesday, as well as the next. Though Michael missed his counseling visits, he kept so busy raking the grounds that he found little time to worry about his friend. Fortunately, Daniel had found him a rake that he could keep in his room for his very own. And with a permissible staff that allowed him to come and go almost as he wished, Michael spent most of the daylight hours either outside raking, or in the gym on workout machines.

"God, Daniel," Gordon Smith said, "he's even raking the gardens now that the leaves have all come down. He rakes the lawns, too; tells me he wants to get all the dead stuff out before new growth begins."

"Tell me when the teeth on his rake wears out so I can beg you for another," the orderly muttered.

"Hell, he's out there all hours," the chief groundskeeper said, "even Saturdays and Sundays."

Daniel shook his head.

"Well, I'm not paying him overtime. Even at twenty-five cents an hour, he'd break my bank."

The orderly laughed. "Have you seen his hands?" he asked. "They started as blisters; now they're turning into calluses."

* * *

When at last Mikhail Baranovitch was able to resume counseling, he was stunned at Dr. Harrow's appearance.

"Do come in, Michael," the doctor grated as the patient paused at the door. "I suspect you're alarmed at my appearance."

Warily, like a hesitant deer approaching an apple orchard patrolled by guard dogs, the patient shuffled into the room, eyeing the Doctor with each step: the gaunt face, sleeves hanging around arms that looked stick-like, hair that hung listless and was uncombed. After he seated himself, Michael said, "You don't look so good."

Harrow smiled. "I don't feel so good, either, son."

"What's wrong, sir?"

"Cancer. That's the diagnosis the doctors came up with up at Portland. Lung cancer, they say, though I haven't smoked in twenty years. Luck of the draw, Michael. They can't do anything about it and neither can I. They say I've got a few more months to go, so I figure I might as well spend that time working with my favorite people. Like you."

"You ought to be fishing."

Harrow chuckled. "Then I couldn't visit with you."

"We could go fishing together."

The doctor's smile turned into a grimace, then a gasp. At last the man was able to grate, "You do have a point."

The patient leaped to his feet. "I could ask Daniel for a fishing pole. He knows where all kinds of good stuff is."

Dr. Harrow stopped him with a wave. "Sit down, please. We need to talk about you."

After Michael settled back into his chair, the doctor said, "I'm not sure if I recall exactly where we were when we last visited. Let's see, I know you'd gone back over that river—New Guinea wasn't it? Brought out your friend, right?"

"Captain Baldwin."

"That's right, you'd gone back to rescue your captain. For that, they awarded you the Distinguished Service Cross, if I recall."

"The Bronze Star."

Dr. Harrow ran a hand over his face. "That's right," he said. "The Bronze Star. And you're properly proud of that, aren't you soldier?"

"No."

Dr. Harrow appeared not to have heard the response because he slid a notepad near to hand and said, "Your next action was where?"

Michael didn't answer, but the doctor seemed not to notice, clenching his eyes instead. After a few moments he opened them and said, "I see. And after that, where?"

The patient pushed from his chair. "I'm going now, Dr. Harrow. I'll see if I can get someone to look in on you."

"Oh! Is our time up? It seems as if we'd just begun."

Mikhail Baranovitch went directly to the front desk. "Dr. Harrow needs help," he said to Gladys. "He's a sick man."

She nodded. "We all know he's dying, Michael. But he insists on going ahead with his duties. And who can blame him? The poor man needs something to take his mind from his fate."

So Michael returned to Dr. Harrow's office. He strode in as the Doctor swallowed the last of a handful of pills. "Is your orchard asleep now?" he asked.

Dr. Harrow nodded. "I believe the last of the nuts came in while I was in Portland. Evan—that's my overseer—drove me through it just yesterday. I'd like to pull a few of the older pears and replant seedlings, but I'm not sure I have the energy at this point in my life."

"Was it a good year, crop-wise?" Michael asked.

The Doctor nodded. "I haven't sold all the nuts yet—still drying some. But the fruit went as well as could be expected without my being there as much as I wished. Actually the prunes were bumper, and with the war going on in Korea, prunes were priced high. Cherries and peaches were good, too. Pears did all right, though apples were down."

Daniel poked his head into the room to ask, "How you feeling, Doc?"

Dr. Harrow smiled, then winced. After recovering, he said, "I'm fine. Michael is doing quite splendidly in recounting his exploits on Luzon."

Daniel raised an eyebrow at Michael, but the patient shook his head. After the orderly retreated, Michael asked, "How many acres did you say you had in what, Doctor Harrow? Can you give me your acreage overall, then break it down by crop types?"

For the next half-hour, the patient drew the doctor-orchardist out, discussing yields, sales methods, and orchard care. Once, he went out for a pitcher of water. Twice he leaped up in alarm as Dr. Harrow's face turned white and the man began to choke. Finally Daniel appeared to tell them that another of Dr. Harrow's patients waited.

It was Wednesday, November first--payday! Michael accepted his check as if he received a religious icon, nodding and turning away without a word, shuffling back inside the hospital with his rake in one hand, his check in another, unaware that he passed Gladys, Daniel, the girls who called to him from the cafeteria.

Later, he asked Gladys if she knew where he could cash his check. She held out her hand saying, "Sure, I can do that here. How much is it?" He handed it to her. "Ooh," the woman cooed, "thirty-seven dollars and seventy-five cents. You've earned a bunch of money, Michael." He asked for his money in nickels. She laughed, handing him a twenty, ten, five, two ones, and fifteen nickels.

Michael waited during pelting rain at Hospital Road and Harvard Street from ten after seven until eight o'clock. The paperboy never pedaled past. At nine o'clock, Smith, the head groundskeeper turned him away from trying to rake.

The boy did ride past on Friday. Michael waved him over to ask if he had an extra paper?

"Nope," the boy said. "Sold 'em all yesterday. But I can save you one this afternoon if you'll meet me here about five. There's no school tomorrow, see? So I won't even go in until around three."

It all seemed confusing to Michael, so he hung his head and said he guessed he wasn't suppose to get his own newspaper.

"I can put you on my delivery route," the boy said. "I can drop off the last day's paper every morning on my way to school."

Michael nodded. Then he tried to pay the boy in advance for his coming Monday delivery.

"Naw. I can count on you. When you get the papers, pay me then."

The headline for Saturday's, November 4, 1950 issue of Roseburg's *The Daily News* (which Mikhail Baranovitch read on the following Monday) blazed:

**MACARTHUR SAYS NEXT OFFENSIVE WILL BE
A "HOME BY CHRISTMAS" ONE.**

Reading down the text, Michael saw that Uncle Sam's troops, aided by South Koreans, Australians, Canadians, Englishmen, and Turks were streaming northward through North Korea; toward some place called the Yalu River. As a result, when he strode into the noontime cafeteria, Michael confidently predicted to anyone who would listen that Dr. Henderson would be back in time for Christmas. So certain was the young man of Dr. Henderson's impending arrival that he asked Gladys to help him choose proper Christmas presents for Daniel, Dr. Harrow, and Dr. Henderson.

"Henderson! Why him?" she cried. "He's clear across the world, hon'."

"But he's coming home. I know he is."

Chapter 18

"**CHINESE HORDES CROSS THE YALU!**" blazed the Thanksgiving edition of *The Daily News*. Outside, raindrops made mushrooms on street puddles and the gutters ran full. Gladys and Michael leaned on the counter together, reading the alarming news she had already learned the evening before. Michael's face was impassive as he read that General MacArthur's airy-sounding "Home By Christmas" offensive was reeling back all across the Korean Peninsula in the face of Chinese armies in the hundreds of thousands.

Gladys looked up into Michael's expressionless face. "Well, big guy, it looks like Dr. Henderson might have to wait until Christmas of '51 to get that flowered shirt you bought."

Dr. Harrow also missed Christmas at the Veteran's Hospital, having been rushed once more to Portland as his cancer took a turn for the worse. He did return in late January for a visit, but this time the return was augmented by his son and daughter pushing his wheelchair through the lobby, and limited mostly to simple greetings to patients and staff. Michael shyly handed him the hatbox swathed in Christmas wrapping paper—elves and Santas and reindeer—and when the Doctor opened the box and saw the straw gardener's hat, tears coursed down his cheeks.

Only Daniel Fields, the surprise recipient of a Portland Beavers baseball cap, participated at the proper time in Mikhail Baranovitch's Christmas largesse. "How...?" the orderly began. But when he saw Gladys and the button-busting Michael giggling beneath the brightly colored ribbons and streamers, he nodded and smiled.

It was Gladys, however, who turned the tables on Michael by presenting the delighted patient with a pair of leather work gloves wrapped in bright red paper and tied with a candy-stripe ribbon into a big bow.

But Weyland Jones was the greatest yuletide hit when he lugged four gallon jugs of his best cider into the cafeteria to share with the staff and patients.

While Weyland's crowd were laughing and mixing and singing Christmas carols in the cafeteria, Michael improvised with a gift of a prized robin's nest to Gladys and a worn rake with a candy-stripe bow tied around the handle to Weyland.

The Sutherlin farmer seemed confused, then Daniel thumped his own chest with a thumb and mouthed "ours." Weyland's quick nod might have been missed, but the smile he flashed Michael would've played well on a Broadway billboard. Since the hospital's cafeteria party fell on Saturday afternoon, and the following day was Sunday, December 24, and Christmas Day fell on Monday, Michael was without a rake until Tuesday, when a Gerretsen Building Supply truck dropped a brand-spanking-new rake with a varnished handle and red-painted teeth off at the reception desk.

"Michael!" a breathless Gladys called as the forlorn patient wandered into the lobby a few minutes later. "Look what Santa Claus just dropped off for you. He said he was sorry to be late, but that he's running behind this season."

There was a big cream-colored tag wired to the handle. On it was printed: "MIKHAIL BARANOVITCH / MERRY CHRISTMAS."

Little progress had been made on Mikhail Baranovitch's treatment during his last several visits with Dr. Harrow. Instead the big blue-clad patient had mostly listened as Dr. Harrow filled in the blanks of his own life—his university training, his armed forces service, the marriage, the subsequent birth of their children, the tragic loss of his wife in an auto accident.

Though there was no progress on Michael's actual treatment, Dr. Harrow did use his few remaining weeks to complete reports on Michael's interviews and disclosures. Included within those reports were surprisingly accurate accounts of Baranovitch's service at Yakamul, and on the Driniumor Line. The Doctor's last service in Michael's behalf was to allow Daniel to thoroughly examine the patient's files.

"I know I'll not be with us much longer," Dr. Harrow told the orderly. "That's why I want you to know how far we've progressed on Michael's case." The doctor sighed and leaned back in his chair. "I'll want you to package these files after I'm gone, then store them. And if they fail to bring in a doctor that's suitable for Michael, you at least will know their content and can pass them on when a qualified doctor eventually appears."

"You feel Dr. Yerkes may not be suitable, then?" Daniel said. Dr. Yerkes, an unfortunate polio victim as a child, had recently arrived at the Roseburg facility. The young doctor came right out of the University of Oregon Medical School, and was to serve his internship at the hospital.

"No, certainly not. Charles is here as an intern. Michael's case is much too sensitive to entrust to a young and inexperienced doctor." Archibald Harrow then leaned back and closed his eyes. But before he opened them to lean forward and retch into his wastebasket, he said, "Let us hope Michael's next doctor will be Bryce Henderson."

* * *

Officially permitted outside the hospital building for an hour Monday, Wednesday, and Friday, as well as detailed to work on Smith's groundskeeping crew at the head groundskeeper's pleasure, Mikhail Baranovitch was in fact allowed a great deal of latitude. Gordon Smith, a disorganized man himself, loosely ran a groundskeeping crew of patients who had advanced sufficiently in their treatment to rate "trustee" status. Each workman of Smith's crew was allowed to come and go at their pleasure as long as they abided by certain rules: presence at breakfast, dinner, supper; in their proper rooms at curfew when hospital lights were dimmed; no belligerence. Baranovitch, while not yet fully authorized, so fulfilled all other criterions and was such a common sight working around the grounds that most of the staff considered him a bonafide trustee. Colonel Y. Herbert Corwin, the hospital director himself, was even seen occasionally chatting with the big patient during the director's arrivals and departures.

Dr. Archibald Joseph Harrow died peacefully at his Umpqua home on Wednesday, February 21, 1951. Michael learned of Harrow's passing when he saw Gladys weeping and Daniel packing the doctor's files. Dr. Harrow's obituary ran in Thursday's paper, which meant that Michael didn't read it until after his private paper delivery at Harvard and Hospital Drive on Friday morning. He learned that interment would be at the Umpqua Community Cemetery at 10 a.m. the following Monday. He also discovered from others that Umpqua was a community of one store, a church, and three houses eighteen miles out Garden Valley Road—the roadway that provided the northern border for the Roseburg Veteran's Home.

Mikhail Baranovitch arose from his bed at three o'clock on the morning Dr. Harrow was to be laid to rest. The man began hiking west amid a pelting rain. Michael walked rapidly—he assumed he could cover the eighteen miles in six hours. If he double-timed, he knew he could do it in less. He did it in less, arriving at the cemetery shortly after daylight. Fortunately the rain diminished to occasional showers. Clearing skies brought falling temperatures, however, and the lightly clad patient was cold as well as drenched. He solved his problem by running in place beside the freshly excavated grave. He was nearing exhaustion when the hearse and a long line of cars arrived. Daniel and Gladys and Will Terwilliger were in one of the first vehicles following the deceased's immediate family.

"I don't believe this!" Daniel cried as he leaped out. The orderly took Michael by an arm, whispering fiercely, "What in God's name do you think you're doing?"

Michael stared at him blankly. "Same thing you are."

"But you're not to leave the grounds!"

"I want to say goodby."

The orderly, dressed now in dark suit and tie, shook his head. "I know that, Michael, but you can't just walk away. It's not allowed."

Some of the newcomers were staring at Daniel and Michael as they exited their automobiles.

"My God, man, you're wet and freezing cold. You'll catch your death out here. When did you leave the hospital?"

"At three."

Daniel slapped himself on the forehead. "I don't believe this!" he said again. Weyland Jones hurried to them. "What did he do, walk all the way?" Daniel nodded. Weyland said, "Poor bastard. How could we have overlooked this?"

"His tit will be in the ringer over this," Daniel muttered.

"Why?" Anger flashed in the farmer's eyes. "Because he wants to attend the funeral of one of the few friends he's had? Don't be an ass, Daniel. What he's doing is one of the finest pieces of work I've ever seen anyone do—head screwed on straight, or not."

"All the same," Daniel tugged on Michael's arm, "I've got to get him in the car before anyone else sees him." He tugged again. "I'm sure Colonel Corwin will be here any minute. C'mon Michael." Steel fingers gripped Daniel's wrist, pulling the orderly's hand from the big man's arm. "Oh God," Daniel moaned, "there's the colonel."

The minister opened his book and waved to those hanging back. "Please gather closer, good people. I'm sure Dr. Harrow would take comfort in knowing his friends are all here."

Weyland put an arm around Michael's shoulders and said, "Let's take the preacher's advice. What do you say, big guy?"

Michael let himself be led closer. "Come on, Daniel," he whispered. "You can stand beside me, too."

Weyland drove Mikhail Baranovitch back to Roseburg. "You know, Michael, if you're a trustee, we're going to have to find you different clothes."

"I don't think I'm a trustee."

"If not, you should be."

"But I did something bad today."

Weyland glanced at his passenger. "Do you really think you did something bad?"

"No. But Daniel and Gladys and Colonel Corwin thinks so."

"Did Corwin even see you?"

"Yes. He nodded. That's when I had to hold Daniel up."

The Dogged and the Damned

"You know what, Michael," Weyland said, "I doubt if anybody's going to say anything about you attending your friend's funeral."

"I hope not. I wouldn't like that."

The farmer laughed. "Now *that* is a thought to consider. But I think the fact that Colonel Corwin also was at Espiritu Santo might have a bearing on the subject. I'll talk to him."

True to Weyland Jones' prediction, little was said of Mikhail Baranovitch's visit to Dr. Harrow's funeral. Therapist Will Terwilliger mentioned it during Michael's next visit to the workout room, but was quickly snuffed when the big man didn't even look at him as he sat the weight machine to three hundred pounds. Too, Gladys mentioned it when she whispered, "Good for you, Michael. That was a *sweet* thing to do."

And that was it.

Mikhail Baranovitch didn't even *see* Daniel for the next two weeks. He thought the lead orderly was in the building, and even heard the man's voice coming from the staff lounge, but it was mid-March before he actually encountered the orderly at their noon meal. Michael smiled and Daniel smiled and things were as they were before.

Colonel Corwin proved cordial enough, too, nodding and speaking as he always did when Michael was working near the director's private entrance.

The boy slowly pedaled his Hawthorne, keeping barely enough headway to stay upright. Michael planted tulip bulbs along Hospital Drive, digging holes with a hand trowel and lovingly setting each bulb as if it was a precious jewel. The boy paused to watch. After awhile he said, "I brought you your paper early. Got a nickel?"

Michael left the trowel sticking in the dirt and stood, brushing soil from his knees. "Why aren't you in school?"

"Spring break," the boy said. "We get a week off in the spring. Didn't you ever get a week off at Easter where you went to school—up in Montana?"

Michael nodded.

"Are you a patient here?"

"Yes."

"What's wrong with you? You look okay to me."

"I guess it's my head. They don't think my head is okay."

The boy reached across his handlebars, into the paperbag, then held out the day's paper. "Personally, I don't believe 'em."

The patient dropped a nickel in the boy's hand as he took his paper. "But you're not a doctor."

The boy flipped down his bike's kickstand and stepped off to sprawl in the grass. "They going to fix you up?"

Michael sprawled beside him. "That's why I'm here."

The boy mulled on that before saying, "Well, I hope they don't do it too quick. You're one of my best customers."

The older man sat up, waving a hand. "What's it like out there?" he asked.

The boy sat up and looked where he waved. "Out where?"

Michael quit waving and pointed. "That one."

The boy laughed. "That's Nebo. That's almost in our back yard. There's bigger mountains than that around here."

"But what's up there?"

"Oak trees and poison oak and goats. The view's good, though. You can see all up and down the valley, see into Roseburg. You get up there and you can see some really big mountains up the North Umpqua, like Mount Scott—If it's not foggy or hazy."

Michael stared as if entranced. "I'd like to see that."

The boy re-tied a loose shoestring, saying, "I go up there a lot. Maybe some day I could meet you up there and show you some goat trails. Or maybe we could take a look at where the high school kids paint their class numbers on cliff faces."

Michael picked up his trowel and thrust it into the lawn. "I can't. I'm not supposed to leave the grounds."

The boy pocketed Michael's nickel, then glanced up at the fourth floor of the main building where a hyena cackle came from behind the bars of an open window. "What's it like in there, mister?"

"What's it like?" Michael repeated. "Well, there's all kinds of people in there; most had hopes and dreams just like the ones rattling around in you." The big man pointed a finger at his temple while continuing, "But they took a few licks too many up here and now they're in the hospital to get fixed."

The hyena cackle came again and once more the boy glanced at the window. Michael said, "Some of 'em will never leave. For them, it's marking time. They're not here to get fixed, but to keep 'em from walking the streets and to keep 'em out of other people's hair. Me? I'm here to get fixed—at least that's what they tell me. But I'm not sure what I need that I can't find out here in the grass and under the trees." He glanced at the distant ridgeline. "Or up there."

The boy climbed on his bike, and said, "I think I'll just hike up there next Sunday. Prob'ly after lunch." He pedaled lazily away.

Chapter 19

The boy was sitting beneath the flagpole when Mikhail Baranovitch arrived. The man would've been earlier, but he spent the better part of an hour watching the half-wild band of long-haired domestic goats that called the mountain home.

"I wondered if you'd come," the boy said, hugging his knees. "I thought maybe you might figure this was all an April Fool's joke and stay away."

The blue-clad man breathed deep and turned a three-sixty, smiling. Above the man and boy, the Stars and Stripes snapped in a stout breeze. "That's Mount Scott over there," the boy said, pointing at a loaf-shaped, snow-capped mountain to the northeast.

The boy looked over his shoulder as a soft "ba-a-a" came from behind. "The goats followed you," he said. Michael took a seat by his friend. "You don't say much, do you?" the boy asked.

"That's the first time you've asked me a question."

"Well, do you?"

"Only when there's something worthwhile to say."

"How long will I have to wait?"

Michael grinned. "Not long—I think I've got something coming on now. Urp! Here it comes, listen close. It's beautiful. Thank you for inviting me."

The boy giggled and lay back on the barren hilltop, cupping his hands behind his head. "You know anything about girls?"

"No. Do you?"

"Well, I'm sure no expert," the boy said. Michael waited. "There's this girl, see? She lives next door and she spends most of her time at my mom's house. Mom says she's sweet on me, but I don't want her to be."

"Oh?" Michael said.

"I bought her a milkshake last summer and now I can't get rid of her."

The man looked down at the boy. "Sounds to me like you made a mistake."

Michael had wondered, too. Her name was Anna. The girl's father and mother always called her by both given names—Anna Karenina. It was, "Anna Karenina, love, will you come here a moment," or "How was school today, Anna Karenina?" Her full name was Anna Karenina Ormansky.

Anna's father had been an officer of the "White Army" in St. Petersburg during the communist revolution. That Captain Vladimir Ormansky escaped Mother

Russia one step ahead of the Red Army took skill and daring. That he managed also to extricate his wife and infant son from the burning city was considered miraculous.

Unfortunately, the son contracted typhoid fever during the family's dash to freedom through the turmoil of a Europe still teetering from the flames of World War I. But there were other children, all born in America; Anna Karenina was third of Vladimir and Sylvina Ormansky's six living children.

By the time of Anna Karenina's birth, Vladimir Ormansky had traded on his considerable military command experience to secure a position as head of the Anaconda Mining Company's security at Butte, Montana. By the end of the decade, Vladimir Ormansky, as the only candidate acceptable to both Irish and Cornish miners, had been offered command of Butte's City Police Force.

Later, Police Captain Vladimir Ormansky had occasion to wonder about the wisdom of accepting the city's offer. Had he, at the time, suspected the degree of torment heading his way by the drunken forays of a single miner, Captain Vladimir Ormansky repeatedly told listeners, he might have declined. Then to have his very daughter bring Stefan Baranovitch's son into Vladimir Ormansky's own home....

Mikhail Baranovitch thought Anna Karenina Ormansky the most beautiful girl in Butte High School. Butte Central, too, if one wanted to throw Catholic virgins into the watchable-girl mix. Michael became aware of Anna Karenina Ormansky in the second grade. She was tall then—taller than seven-year-old Michael—and oh! so blonde! She was also far beyond reach for the clumsy Slav kid with the square face and dark, wide-set eyes. As a second-grader, Michael hardly understood the significance of being a police chief's daughter, but the seven-year-old knew enough to know it was a police chief who commanded the men who regularly jailed the boy's father, and sometimes brought Stefan Baranovitch home drunk and still battling centuries-old wars between Serbs and Croats, Serbs and Turks, Serbs and Greeks, Serbs and Serbs.

Besides, Anna Karenina Ormansky was studious, easily the best speller and reader in class.

By grade four, the police chief's daughter was diagramming sentences and was teacher's pet. Michael didn't mind though because he was then madly in love with teacher.

He'd fallen for Miss Dorothy Brummel on the first day of school. Stefan Baranovitch's son's eyes remained fixed on the red-headed, green-eyed, full-lipped young woman as he worked his way to the head of the introduction line. And when Miss Brummel wrote Mikhail Baranovitch on her tablet, then looked up and said, "My, aren't you the handsome one," he fell hopelessly in love. And when she added, "I'll bet you're called Michael instead of Mikhail, aren't you?" there was no turning back.

Even when Miss Dorothy Brummel changed her name in mid-season to Mrs. Dorothy Rand, Michael, not fully understanding the significance of the name change, remained smitten.

One unusual outcome of that year was that the police chief's blond daughter began calling him Michael, too. And when fifth grade rolled around, bringing the ugly ancient Miss Hope as a teacher, the object of young Baranovitch's attention again focused on the class brain who was not only the police chief's daughter, but whose mother was a member of the school board, head of the Butte Library Commission, and the "go-to" person on Silver Bow County's March of Dimes Campaign.

Being in love with a girl with such illustrious parentage was no certain thing, however. Though Michael had sprouted a couple of inches and ten pounds, Anna Karenina still looked down on him in more ways than one. She had brains, so Michael studied harder. She didn't chase boys on the playground, so Michael stopped running and began ignoring the girls who did chase boys. She volunteered to wash blackboards after school; Michael volunteered the next afternoon. Still, the girl ignored him.

Then one day Anna Karenina Ormansky clapped when Michael spelled 'trigonometry' correctly in class and he beamed. But the following day, when they stood together in the cafeteria line, Anna Karenina said, "Michael, why don't you do something about your father? My father says your father causes him more grief than any ten other men in Butte."

Michael dropped his empty tray and utensils on the floor and stalked from the cafeteria.

Anna Karenina Ormansky's cheeks were flame-red when Mikhail Baranovitch shuffled into the classroom at the beginning of afternoon classes. But she avoided eye contact. And when the day ended the girl strode from the classroom, from Marcus Daly School, along the sidewalks of Butte, books tucked against budding breasts, nose in air, with all the indifference of a fifth-grade social and intellectual superior whose parents were among the most prominent citizens of Butte. Not that Anna Karenina would have been able to catch Michael's eye had she deigned to do so, for from the moment he dropped his aluminum lunch tray until the end of the school year—and through their sixth, seventh, eighth, and ninth grade years— the boy simply stared through her, as if she was a window or an open door.

Between fifth grade and their sophomore year in high school, Mikhail Baranovitch sprouted to six-foot-one and two hundred pounds, while Anna

Karenina Ormansky stood five-nine in her stocking feet, tipped the scales at one-twenty-five, and was inordinately proud of her twenty-two-inch waist.

During that same five-year period, Captain Vladimir Ormansky's Butte police force jailed Stefan Baranovitch twelve times for being drunk and disorderly, and four times for assault and battery. One of the assault and battery cases hospitalized three members of Butte's finest and resulted in a three-month jail term for the elder Baranovitch.

Anna Karenina Ormansky tried smiling at Mikhail Baranovitch once during their sixth grade year, and again during their first year of junior high school. And she even wrote a note she tucked into Michael's history class textbook during eighth grade. Still, the boy stared through her, or beyond. She wondered if there was another girl? But Anna Karenina was intelligent as well as attractive, and was in fact the leader of a clique of the most popular girls in her grade. As far as she could discern, Mikhail Baranovitch had yet to discover girls.

Though popular, Anna Karenina was too tall and too thin for cheerleading. She tried band, but was too exacting in her own practice and marching efforts to remain satisfied while engaging in a school activity filled with upwards of three dozen schoolmates, at least thirty of whom couldn't carry a tune in a wheelbarrow—and really didn't care that they couldn't. But when she quit band, Anna's instructor persuaded the girl to try for Drum Majorette, and it was there that the long-legged, high-stepping, baton-twirling Anna discovered her metier.

It was while she strutted routines as the band practice-marched on one end of the football field while the Bulldog football team did calisthenics on the other that she became aware Mikhail Baranovitch stared *at* her instead of *through* her—for the first time in five years.

"Look at that one," the boy said, pointing overhead. "Don't that one look like a ship? Look at it go!"

Michael laid back beside the boy to better see the scudding clouds. "There's one with a face that looks like Goofy's from the comics," he said.

The boy said, "Yeah. And look at the one over to the right. Don't it look like Mickey Mouse?"

They watched in silence for a while, then Michael said, "There's a roadster."

"I was just lookin' at it."

"And that one looks a little like Anna."

"Who?"

There came a day, two months into their sophomore year, when Anna Karenina, carrying an armload of books, caught Michael, crowding him back against his locker. Fire flashed from her blue eyes. "Isn't five years long enough for us to both hate the other over a misunderstanding?" she demanded. Tears blurred her fire, and finally put it out as they coursed down her face.

He didn't know what to do, so he put his arms around her while other kids passed them in the hallway and pretended not to notice. The bell rang and the hall emptied. And still he held her. She gazed up at him and said, "We'd better go."

"I haven't had any tardies this school year," he said, "so maybe we could stand here a little while longer." Then Mr. Fetterson, the Principle, came from a distant hallway and Michael released Anna Karenina and they went to separate classrooms with songs in their hearts and bubbles in their heads.

"I don't know your name, mister," the boy said.

"Michael," Mikhail Baranovitch dreamily replied. "You don't know my name either."

The man glanced at the boy. "Don't want to either."

"Why not?"

"Because you're my friend. That's good enough. Names just complicates things. Makes faces fuzzy way inside the head where memories are kept. If you tell me your name, I'll just forget it on purpose."

The boy sat upright. "I've already forgotten yours, and I don't want you to tell me again. Okay?"

"Okay." Michael sat up, too, then rolled to his feet, took out his pocketwatch and studied it. "Show me those whitewashed class numbers you told me about, then I've gotta go."

The following Sunday, Michael met the boy atop Mount Nebo again. On that day, they hiked the ridge west, until they overlooked the Lookingglass Valley.

When they parted at four o'clock, the boy said, "I don't know how to tell you this, but newspapers are going up to a dime the first of May. Don't worry about it, though, I'll still charge you a nickel."

The following morning, Michael converted his remaining nickels to dimes. But on Tuesday, when he tried to pay with a dime, the boy refused to take it. "No, no, no. The papers won't go up until the first of May. That's three weeks away. Besides, I told you I'd keep you on at the old rate."

Michael demurred, not wishing to have to ask Gladys to convert the dimes back to nickels. Finally a compromise was struck between the enterprising young merchant and his determined customer that Michael could pay the boy every two days. "But," the boy said drawing a line, "you'll have to keep track of it. I got enough to do." So Michael carefully folded a sheet of notebook paper, marked off a calendar and, with a stub pencil lifted from Gladys's counter, kept a meticulous daily record with which the boy could find no fault.

* * *

"I'm pretty sure Michael is leaving the grounds on Sundays," Daniel confided to Gladys. "Herb Stephens said he missed lunch the last two Sundays, and John Wilder searched for him and couldn't find him last Sunday afternoon."

"Oh, Daniel, I can't believe he's hurting anything if he is. Might he just be going down to the river somewhere?"

"He's not a trustee, Gladys, even though we all treat him like one. Besides, he's got the whole run of the grounds. Why does he need to leave it?"

"For Dr. Harrow's funeral," she said, ending it with a smile and her tongue actually pushing out her cheek.

"Aside from that, I mean. We should've taken him, that's a given. Apparently Colonel Corwin even thinks so. But I'm afraid if he gets accustomed to leaving the grounds that someday he won't come back."

Gladys shrugged. "Perhaps we've done all we can for him, especially if we can't even find a doctor to see him."

"He's got money now," Daniel said, still worrying his first bone. "He's worked quite a bit for Gordon over the last few months, and could have a lot. What's he doing with that?"

"Well," Gladys said, "aside from your baseball cap and Dr. Harrow's gardening hat for Christmas, and a Hawaiian shirt for Dr. Henderson—If and when that good doctor gets back—I've got the rest of it under lock and key in my cash drawer. If you really want to know how much, he now has one hundred and eight dollars and sixty cents in an envelope with his name on it. I counted it just yesterday. Made a note and dated it."

"But why does he want it?"

"He doesn't want it, Daniel. He just wants a few nickels or dimes to buy a paper from the only outside friend he has—other than Weyland. He doesn't know—nor care—how much money he's built up. He only wants to be outside. And given his choice, he'd like to be working."

"I still don't like it," the orderly said.

"Can you talk to him?"

"Yeah, I can do that. The only thing I'm not sure of is whether he listens to anything except his own inner music." Daniel studied Gladys, then added, "Besides, to tell you the truth, he scares me."

Gladys's laughter was still ringing in the red-faced orderly's ears as he left the lobby. That and her reply: "Well, honey, I can tell you he doesn't scare me! In fact, I'd like to hug him near to death; he's such a sweet dear. And probably, if they had the chance, so would half the girls in the cafeteria."

124

Chapter 20

"Michael, we think you've been leaving the grounds without permission." The two men sat on a bench in front of the main hospital building, the orderly clothed in white and leaning forward, the blue-clad man leaning back, legs crossed at the ankles, chin on chest, holding a rake, digging idly at the lawn grass with its tines.

Daniel continued, "I'm not going to ask if you've been off the grounds for fear you'd tell me you have and then I'd have put you on report. We should've made arrangements for you to go to Dr. Harrow's funeral and we didn't. That was our mistake. And we realize in order to pay your last respects you took what you felt was the only avenue available. But that does not give you carte blanche to come and go from the hospital any time you wish. Only a doctor can provide you with that opportunity by upgrading the terms of your commitment to that of a trustee. Okay?"

Michael stared at the toes of his worn oxfords. He said, "What does carte blanche mean?"

"It means kinda like coming and going whenever you want without asking anybody's by-your-leave."

"What if I ask and they say *no*."

"Then you can't go."

"So, if I don't ask, then they won't say *no*."

Daniel rolled his eyes. "Michael, you cannot leave the grounds. Period. You cannot leave the grounds. Do you hear me?"

"Okay." Daniel breathed a sigh of relief, until Michael added, "I wasn't planning to go for a hike this Sunday, anyway." The orderly threw up his hands

Even with the patient's assurance that he planned to stay on the grounds, Daniel still scheduled John Wilder to monitor Mikhail Baranovitch's movements on Sunday. Wilder said it was the most boring day he'd ever spent. As happened, a storm moved in from the Pacific and dropped buckets of rain. "Hell, Daniel," Wilder said, "all he did was sit in the lounge and read. Except when he went to the lavatory or the cafeteria."

So Daniel prepared carefully for the following Sunday, assigning *two* orderlies to keep tabs on the big patient. Those plans went awry, when Weyland Jones arrived early Sunday morning with a pass signed by Colonel Y. Herbert Corwin. The pass permitted Mikhail Baranovitch to leave the grounds in company with the Sutherlin farmer.

With the hospital's administrator—as well as much of the rest of the staff—apparently in the patient's corner, Daniel gave up monitoring the movements of Mikhail Baranovitch. That's why it was to everyone's consternation when Michael failed to return to his room on the evening of Sunday, May 20, 1951.

He didn't plan it. Like Topsy, the adventure grew until it took on a life of its own. First, he climbed Mount Nebo to say hello to his friends, the weather goats. The goats, as sometimes happened when a weather front was on its way in, proved skittish, trotting away from the man.

Michael scratched his head and followed. And when the goats dropped down the south side of Nebo Ridge, into the Fiedler Creek drainage, the man followed. Then the skies darkened and thunder murmured off to the west-southwest. Michael paused to turn his face into a rising breeze. Lightning flashed and thunder crackled much nearer. The wind whipped into a frenzy, followed by a deluge seemingly squeezed from a celestial sponge

He took shelter under a huge red oak tree. But the downpour increased until the oak leaves could hold it back no longer, huge drops leaking through the branches to splatter the huddled man.

Then the storm's leading edge of thunder and lightning moved eastward and the rain began to slacken. Through the trees, an old board-and-batten shack beckoned. The driveway, little more than two ruts, was weed-filled, unused. The building's single window and the door was boarded over. Shivering, the man pried on one of the rough boards with his fingers and, with it's nails rusted through, the wood fell off in his hands. Michael turned the door knob, the latch snapped free, and the door groaned open on rusty hinges. He jerked another of the one-by-twelve planks from the doorway and wormed through into the dusty, dingy, single-room cabin. Dusty it might've been, but it was dry and he was wet.

The room contained an iron bedstead which, in turn, embraced cobwebbed bedsprings. A dusty cookstove with cast metal scrollwork on the oven door purporting it to be a "Great Majestic" squatted in the middle of the room. A plank table was nailed to the wall along one edge and propped up with blocks of wood on the other. Two oak blocks served as chairs. Old newspapers and magazine pages had been tacked to the rough-board inside walls for insulation. Michael leaned close to read their dates in the gloom. Most of the papers and magazines seemed to have originated in the late-twenties, but there was one *Collier's* advertising page with a 1937 dateline on it.

Mice and rat turds, perhaps a half-inch deep in the corners, proved the cabin had not gone entirely unoccupied since the last human slept here. Two apple boxes were nailed to a wall for cupboards. Only one chipped porcelain bowl and a cracked pewter mug was still in the apple boxes; the rest of their contents lay broken on the floor. A 12-inch cast iron frying pan hung from a nail beside the apple boxes.

There was nothing else.

Michael took his pocketwatch from his soaked cotton trousers and stared at it. It's crystal face was fogged and unreadable. He moved near the open door, still staring. The rain began again. The big man laid the watch on the cabin's dusty table and wondered what to do next. Soon he stretched out on the bed springs and uncomfortable though it would be to most people, fell sound asleep as rain pounded the shake roof.

The skies were only just beginning to lighten in the east when Michael awakened. Outside, birds were flitting through the oak trees and singing their heads off amid clearing skies. Though his cotton shirt and trousers were dry, the face of the pocketwatch was still fogged. When he left the cabin, it was solid daylight and he carried the pewter mug, the chipped bowl, and the cast iron frying pan.

Michael drifted down the overgrown driveway until he hit a graveled road that showed recent traffic. He studied the graveled road, then deciding he was now a fugitive, skirted the road and climbed the hills even further south. Late that afternoon, he crossed a busy highway, then, safely ensconced on a low knob, watched as a sedan pulled away from a white bungalow. There were children in the sedan; a cocker spaniel dog leaped among them.

The thing that most caught Michael's attention, however, was a clothesline filled with drying clothes. A pair of men's overalls hung from that clothesline. Even from a distance, Michael could tell the overalls must have been worn by a big man. He wondered why the man would simply abandon the overalls like that. The overall's fit him perfectly.

Michael also wondered why the people would leave the house unattended, especially with a plate of cookies lying on a countertop. He ate several, then helped himself to a handful of stick matches as he left.

The following day, the moisture fogging Michael's pocketwatch began to clear. In celebration, he helped himself to a lunch from an unattended pickup parked on a forest road. Then he found an old log home tucked far up a remote little creek. A small meadow spread down the hill before the home, and a half-dozen fruit trees lined the winding driveway to the buildings.

The man shifted the heavy frying pan in his hand as he studied the house, then the graveled drive. There were no tire tracks since the rain. Off to one side, behind the house, was a car shed. It contained no vehicle. Both doors of the log home were locked, but none of the windows were latched. He chose a back window

Inside, he found an old Trapper Nelson pack frame hanging from a wall peg, and a Boy Scout packsack. There was a 12-inch butcher knife in a rack by the kitchen sink. He also helped himself to a small aluminum coffee pot and a pound of coffee, two tins of peaches, and a slab of bacon from a propane refrigerator. Mikhail Baranovitch was gone from the log home in ten minutes, striding swiftly uphill, toward the west.

Later that day, Michael killed a grouse with a rock. The bacon, the bird, the peaches! He patted his tummy, scattered the fire with a stick, then curled against the roots of a big Douglas fir tree and slept the sleep of the just.

"Any word on the big guy yet?" Gladys asked as the orderly leaned against the lobby counter.

Daniel shook his head. "I don't even know if we're going to look for him, other than with the standard issue notice to the Sheriff's Office." The orderly studied a broken fingernail, bit it smooth, then said, "I talked with Colonel Corwin yesterday. He said Michael's treatment seemed to be progressing well, from all reports reaching his desk. He said, "Perhaps the young man decided to go his own way in the world."

"He didn't take any of his money with him," the woman said. "I've still got over a hundred dollars belonging to him in my desk."

"No money. No clothes except what he had on his back...."

"And?"

Daniel shrugged. "He's been out a week now. If he tried to beg, somebody would see his inmate's uniform and call the law. It's unlikely he could get a job either. No money...."

"What are you saying, Daniel?"

"There's no way he can survive without stealing his way."

Douglas County is, by Oregon's standard, a relatively large county; it's the only one in the Beaver State encompassing an entire river valley—one hundred and fifty miles from the river's source in the snowcapped Cascade Mountains, to Pacific Ocean tidewater. The Umpqua drainage has two primary forks: the North Umpqua, draining much of the county's north and east, and the South Umpqua, draining Douglas County's south and southeastern portions.

Roseburg, its largest community and the seat of county government, lies near the geographic center of Douglas County and is the location of the Federal Veteran's Administrative Hospital from which Mikhail Baranovitch strayed. The townsite was originally platted eight miles up the South Umpqua River from its juncture with the North branch.

A Federal highway—U.S. 99—runs north and south through the county, from Portland and Puget Sound on the north, to California's inland valleys, and Los Angeles and San Diego on the south. The Southern Pacific Railroad maintained a line through the county, stretching north to the Columbia River and south over the rugged Siskiyou Mountains, along the California border.

Away from these travel arteries, Douglas County was sparsely settled, especially the eastern half, taken up mostly as the Umpqua National Forest. Also sparsely settled was its rural southwestern portion. It was to that southwestern sector that Mikhail Baranovitch gradually worked his way during the remainder of May, and the first two weeks of June, 1951.

By the time Baranovitch passed the hamlet of Riddle, he packed an enormous load composed of bedding, cooking and eating utensils, clothing, and food, all of which he'd pilfered from unattended homes and cabins en route. He also carried an axe in one hand and a Marlin 30-caliber carbine in the other. Even for a man his size, the load began to wear.

It was well after dark, on the outskirts of Riddle, when Mikhail Baranovitch watched an engine spot several boxcars at a sawmill. After positioning the boxcars, the engine huffed south, up the track. Besides the tender, and a caboose at the end, the engine trailed seven boxcars, and three empty flatcars equipped with stakes to hold logs destined for valley sawmills. As the engine puffed from the siding, the brakeman stepped up on the locomotive, leaving the rear of the little train unattended. As the cars picked up speed, Michael threw his pack, rifle, and axe on a flatcar, then leaped aboard.

The train rolled into a lonely canyon and remained there for many miles. Though the moon was in its last quarter, there was still sufficient light for him to make out occasional houses, all small, most isolated from its neighbors. He also made out a stream on one side of the track and a graveled road on the other. Finally the train slowed and Michael leaped from his perch. He watched the trainmen spot the flatcars on a siding, then the remainder of the train rattled into the distance.

The bench was small, tucked up the little canyon, and screened on its lower end by a growth of head-high firs. When he'd pushed through the saplings, Mikhail Baranovitch paused and contemplated the bench, finally deciding it'd been caused by a long-ago land slump. He leaned the rifle and axe against what he thought must be a live oak tree, then dropped his pack.

The man strolled around the bench, stroking his chin; it seemed maybe thirty feet wide and fifty long--big enough for his needs. He paused at one side of the little glade, where a tiny brook bubbled through sphagnum moss and salal leaves, then glanced up at the steep, fir-covered hillsides. Down below, he heard a logging truck laboring up the valley. He glanced above at the spreading limbs and leaves of the live oak and knew they'd help dissipate campfire smoke.

It took Mikhail Baranovitch the better part of two weeks to build his three-sided lean-to shelter. The reason it took so long was because the man, fearing cut stumps and scattered sapling tops might attract attention, chose to use material selected from a canyon to the south. There, he felled saplings, trimmed them, then packed them two by two to his embryo dwelling. He even chose different paths to his camp so as not to wear a defined trail to the refuge.

First came a ridgepole wedged into a fork in the live oak trunk, then lashed on the other end with bailing wire to the trunk of a 12-inch Douglas fir. A series of additional poles ran down from the ridgepole to the ground on one side. Bark was brought in from fallen giants of dead firs—long strips, sometimes four feet in length, a foot in width, and up to four inches thick. This bark was placed with its natural grooves running verticle and overlapping, like shingles, to those poles framing the back of Michael's shelter.

Then he brought an angled overhang three feet down the front and covered it with more bark. The big man constructed a pole bunk against the sloping back wall, and laid out his bedding. Lastly, he built a rock-lined firepit at the mouth of the shelter.

The result was a homey little lean-to of approximately fifteen feet square. True, the overlapping bark was hardly wind-proof, but even when a storm front moved through, breezes seldom reached into his deep and narrow little canyon. The thick fir bark proved heavy and solid and shed rain well.

Michael already knew snow was a seldom seen phenomenon in the inland valleys of western Oregon, but spring and early summer mosquitoes were something else. And until the dog days of August passed, his shaded, airless camp was a bloodsucker's delight. Therefore, Michael used his time to explore the puzzling mountain fastness farther west. And eventually Michael waded Cow Creek to penetrate the more densely forested country to the east, until he bumped into the valley carrying the north-south ribbon of U.S. Highway 99.

By the time he returned to cross Cow Creek, a heavy fall rainstorm brought a down-stream freshet that was difficult to wade. So, after doing so, Michael gathered up his tools and backpack, re-forded Cow Creek, and set about finding a suitable place to erect another isolated shelter—a home away from home that would allow him a comfortable retreat while exploring to the east, or when the stream was too high to safely ford.

Upon completion of his second shelter, Mikhail Baranovitch felt obliged to forage for the wherewithal to stock his new digs. He copped a blanket, a quilt, and a mess kit with U.S.A. stamped on it at the first unattended home he came to; a frying pan, coffee pot, and a shovel was lifted from the next. His foraging took him downstream almost to Riddle before he'd satisfactorily solved his more pressing needs.

Upon returning from equipping his second home, Michael explored the back of an empty pickup parked at the logging siding and found a pair of freshly oiled size-12 lace-up logging boots with new caulks in the soles. Back at his camp, he cut the toes out of the logger boots and made them his standard issue winter wear; as one could imagine, his hospital-issue oxfords were so tattered as to be nearly useless.

Perhaps the most overriding result of Mikhail Baranovitch's decision to build and equip a second home was a rash of petty thefts reported from the Cow Creek area in southern Douglas County. Nor could the fugitive miss the increase in vehicles belonging to the Douglas County Sheriff's Department traveling the rural Cow Creek Road.

Chapter 21

October rolled into November, and November into December. Christmas came and went, and the calendar turned into another year. Mikhail Baranovitch knew none of this, having lost all track of days, weeks, months, and even years—and caring not a whit. All the fugitive knew was that summer had been exceedingly dry, fall rains had come at last and, according to the watch given him by Dr. Harrow, the days had stopped shortening.

With year's-end approaching, Mikhail Baranovitch had been A.W.O.L from the Roseburg VA Hospital for over seven months. At the hospital's annual Christmas Party, Weyland Jones brought the subject up with Daniel and Will Terwilliger: "He's out there somewhere; I know he is."

The off-duty orderly swirled a glass of Weyland's cider, then asked, "So you think he's still alive?"

Jones snorted. "Of course he is. Anybody who's survived as much as he has: Us, Montana, New Guinea, hospitals all over the world—hell yes he's alive. Not only that, he's well. Boys, that guy's a survivor."

The therapist shook his head and stared up at the Sutherlin farmer through his thick glasses. "Not around here, he's not. Somebody would've spotted him by now. In order to get away as clean as he did, he had to have outside help."

As far as Mikhail Baranovitch knew, he'd never been spotted by another person during his months of freedom. Moving largely at night and avoiding roads and occupied buildings during daylight hours, Michael had watched other humans from a distance, but avoided contact.

He'd had to exercise considerable more caution during autumn's hunting season, and the onset of mountainsides crawling with red-clad hunters had, for the better part of a month, driven him to spending more daylight time in his two shelters. Hunting season did have it's "up" sides, though, such as the dressed deer carcass he found lying near the road where a hunter had, at dusk, carelessly left it while walking after his pickup truck, or the heavy red mackinaw coat another hunter apparently abandoned to hang in a tree while toiling up a mountainside.

After hunting season, the fugitive had more freedom to roam, yet found little reason to do so. He did visit a couple of boarded-up summer cottages to requisition a little salt and pepper, a can of vegetables and one of fruit, or perhaps a quilt as a cold front blew in from the northeast. But all in all, with two fully equipped shelters and no real need for extensive farm country foraging, even the specter of petty thefts that had plagued southern Douglas County in October and November waned until the year-around residents of the Cow Creek Valley lost their concern.

For his part, Michael alternated between both shelters, limiting himself mostly to wood gathering at some distance from the camps, then packing the pieces to add to his woodpiles.

He killed an occasional deer for meat. Once he discovered spawning salmon in a little side creek and managed to scoop one out on the bank. Grouse were numerous, but wild during the winter. Once, hungering for grouse, he made a midnight raid on the chicken coop of an isolated farm. There was no alarm from the house, despite the fluttering cacophony of frightened hens.

Spring arrived after what seemed like a winter filled with rain. All at once, so it seemed to the man, flowers popped from the ground, bees began buzzing, and ants stirring. He recognized many flowers and shrubs as similar to ones he'd found in Montana. But Michael had not seen others and sometimes would sit for hours studying wild azalea blooms, or smelling a rhododendron.

Though needing nothing, Michael took to cruising unattended cabins, perhaps just to feel he'd been near others of his kind. On the kitchen table of one cabin, he discovered an open book titled *Identifying Western Wildflowers*. He turned the book over in his hand, then sat down and began reading. When he left the cabin, *Identifying Western Wildflowers* was tucked beneath his overalls.

For the next several weeks, Mikhail Baranovitch studied the wildflower book, comparing the photographs and drawings against actual flowers found in the wild. He discovered that, though certain wildflowers began fading at lower elevations, he could follow them up mountainsides clear into early summer.

Eventually his flower book became tattered and worn. Pages loosened and began falling out. But while it was still legible, the man had learned from it—so much that he saw he had lots more to learn. He revisited the cabin where he'd discovered *Identifying Western Wildflowers* and, before turning to the bookcase, carefully laid the tattered flower book on the kitchen table, opening it to the exact page to which it had been opened when he found it. When he exited the cabin a half-hour later, Michael carried *Tracking and Trapping to Triumph* by Lester Ware and a work/study paper on "Proper Tanning Methods" published by Oregon State University. As an afterthought, Michael also slipped Albert Payson Terhune's *Lad: A Dog* from the bookcase.

He returned three nights later with a flashlight, replacing Terhune's book with *Call of the Wild* by Jack London. As he was leaving, carefully latching the back door and easing the screen door quietly closed, there came two ominous clicks from the darkness. "I reckon that's about far enough," came a voice, "whoever you are."

Michael, still holding his flashlight and *Call of the Wild* raised his hands

A wizened old man hobbled out of the darkness, using a cane in one hand and holding a double-barreled shotgun aimed at Michael's middle with the other. "I don't think one whole hell of a lot of sneak thieves," the old man said.

"Neither do I," Michael said.

"What was you doin' in my house?" the old man asked, his voice ringing clear as wind chimes.

"Borrowing a book, sir."

"What book you borrowin' this time?"

"Call of the Wild. I brought back *Lad: A Dog*.

"Did you like it?"

"Very much. I'd like to have a dog like that myself."

"Who wouldn't?" the old man said. "What else of mine you got?"

"Tracking and Trapping to Triumph and a paper on how to tan hides."

"That book on tracking and trapping ain't no good. I got a better one in the house." Michael, still with raised hands and the shotgun muzzles yawning at his belly button said, "Can I borrow it?"

"Not if you bring anything more of mine back the way the flower book came home. Under God, a book ought to be took better care of than that."

"I'm sorry. If I had any money I'd pay for the book. But all I've got is a dime, and I know a book like that cost more'n that."

The shotgun's hammers were eared down and the muzzles dipped to the ground. "Oh, put your hands down and go back inside. I want to get a better look at you."

The old man followed Michael in, leaned the shotgun in a corner, flipped a light switch and cursed. "Goddamn 'lectricity is out again." He lit a kerosene lamp, then motioned Michael to a chair at the kitchen table.

After they were seated, the old man said, "You sure as hell ain't much to look at."

His visitor replied, "Never was, prob'ly never will be. But I did shave and wash my overalls six days ago, and I took a bath in the creek yesterday."

"How long's it been since you cut your hair?"

"Now that's some harder," Michael said. "But if you got a pair of scissors and a mirror, I'd do it now."

Mikhail Baranovitch left Oscar Perkins' home after daylight, packing a full belly of flapjacks and coffee, as well as London's *Call of the Wild* and a copy of

The Dogged and the Damned

Developing Your Outdoor Skills, from Garden City Books' *Real Book* series.

"Come on back when you want, son," the old man had said. "But do it only when I'm here. Hear?"

Michael heard all right. So when he accidentally dropped and broke his cast iron frying pan on a fireplace rock, he bypassed Oscar Perkins' place.

The bungalow was a faded creamy white, located two hundred feet from the graveled county road and served by a two-track path that appeared to have had little recent use. A sagging and rusted woven-wire fence enclosed an acre and a half surrounding the little dwelling. Quack grass and wild rose bushes sprouted throughout the enclosure. Range cattle had broken through the fence at what must have once been a garden gate, but the broken post had been propped up with triangular supports, and the fence jack-legged along both sides of the breach.

Michael was an expert at reading such places. Once well kept, the bungalow was in benign neglect. Climbing roses crept up the bungalow's sides to the eaves, even snaking onto the moss-covered, shake roof. Two double-sash, twelve-pane cottage windows were, like vacant eyes, cut into the walls on either side of the door. The panes were coated with road dust. Twenty feet from the bungalow's back door was a small woodshed that was boarded on three sides. The woodshed's shake roof was so old that sunlight filtered through gaps in the shingles. Only a few blocks of wood lay scattered on the shed's dirt floor. A rusted single-bit axe stuck from a chopping block. A cross-cut saw hung by a handle from nails driven into a wall stud.

Michael tested the saw's teeth with his thumb and shook his head. Neither did he have a pressing need for an axe. It was a frying pan that he needed, preferably of cast iron.

The back door was padlocked, as was the front. But the first of the vacant-eyed front windows slid up enough for him to slip fingers beneath. The rest was easy. Glancing up and down the road, then across at a dormant sand and gravel operation, he wriggled through the window.

Michael paused to slide the window closed, then toured the cabin. It was neat and clean, its front half given over to a living room-dining area. A kitchen took up one of the final two quarters, and a bedroom the other. A wardrobe stood in a bedroom corner. He opened its door; only a pair of run-over boots (small size), two spare blankets, and a few clothing odds and ends were inside. He took one of the blankets.

In the kitchen, Michael found what he sought—a 12-inch cast iron skillet. Carrying it and the blanket, he started for the window, then stopped abruptly. A bright red Ford convertible was at the gate. The convertible's top was down. A man dragged the wire gate aside while a woman wearing a yellow scarf and a low-cut dress smiled at him from the passenger seat.

Michael reached for the window, thought better of it. Outside, the newcomer dropped the gate, strode back to the convertible, slipped behind the steering wheel, and took the woman in his arms for a passionate embrace. Michael ran to a bedroom window, found it nailed in place. The kitchen window opened, but the opening was too small for a large man to wriggle through. He heard them laughing as they slid from the convertible—the woman's cackle high-pitched, the man's loud and hollow—like the cry of pileated woodpeckers Michael sometimes heard amidst surrounding old growth forests.

He darted for the bedroom as they again embraced. The woman had a hand in one of the man's trousers' pockets. Again came the pileated cry as Michael jerked open the wardrobe door. *No, too small!* He rushed back to the living room to see if he could hide behind the sofa. *No chance!* The woman held up a key ring. The man shook his head and held up a second ring. The woman slipped an arm through the crook of the man's elbow. They started to the house, then the man disengaged and returned to the car long enough to lift a six-pack of beer from the back seat. He staggered on his way back up the walk. She took his face between her hands and standing on tiptoe, smothered it in kisses. A late afternoon sun framed the two. The woman wore no slip beneath her light-colored print dress, but dark garter straps said she wore nylons. While the man fumbled with the front door padlock, Michael tiptoed back into the bedroom and, still carrying the blanket and frying pan, crawled beneath the bed, curling into a ball as far from the bed's edge as possible.

He heard the cabin's door swing open, its doorknob bouncing against the interior wall. "Wha' you think?" the man slurred.

The woman's voice was huskier than Michael would've guessed, judging by her earlier high-pitched cackle. "It looks great, Frankie." A pause. Then, "But so do you."

Both giggled.

Michael could see their feet, the man's were spread; the woman kicked off her high heels, then stood atop the man's black, shiny-toed oxfords. "Take me to zee bedroom," she purred.

Michael saw the hem of her dress rise beyond the drop of the bedspread. There were moans that resembled a Holstein bull he once heard lowing after a cow in heat. "The bed, noodlehead!" she said. "Or are you hard of hearing?"

The hem of the woman's dress fell back into sight. "I want a beer," the man said. "Want one?"

"I guess, if it's the best you can do."

Michael heard a kitchen drawer opened, then bottle caps popped twice, each falling to the living room linoleum.

The sofa squeaked. Michael was glad he'd not tried hiding behind it. An empty bottle fell to the floor with a thump. "To hell with that!" the woman said. "I didn't ride all the way out here for beer."

The man's bottle bounced twice. "Mmmm. That's more like it," the woman said. "We can drink beer later ... if we're still able."

Frankie padded into view—he was visible to Michael only from the knees down. Frankie had one shoe off, one on, and by his erratic steps, he must've been carrying the woman. Her panties fluttered onto the floor.

The man tossed the woman to the bed, kicked off his second shoe, then dropped his trousers. There was more giggling, then a garter fell to the floor, followed by a second.

Frankie's legs were covered by curly black hair. Then the legs were gone and the bed bounced wildly with the addition of his weight. The woman screamed, giggled, laughed, giggled again, then murmured terms of endearment. The bed began rocking, it's springs screeching in protest. Michael stretched out his legs and used the blanket to make a pillow. He closed his eyes.

Then Michael's eyes popped open. Outside, wheels were spinning and gravel spewing. Then there was a gigantic crash! The bed's gyrations stopped. Wheels spun again, and again gravel spewed. Another rending crash!

"What in the hell is going on?" Frankie shouted, leaping from the bed. Again wheels spun, gravel spewed, followed by yet another crash.

"That bitch!" Frankie roared, dashing back to the bedroom for his trousers.

"Your wife?" the woman squeaked. And while Frankie bounced on first one leg, then the other, she screamed, "Tell me! Is it June?" Her question was drowned in another crash.

Frankie pounded barefooted for the door, jerking it open. "You bitch!" he shouted, mostly drowned by the din of another crash.

The woman leaped from the bed and ran to a window. Michael, curious, followed. The front door stood ajar, but he took up a position behind the woman who, when yet another crash came, stuffed both fists to her mouth and whimpered. Michael peered more closely at the naked woman's blonde—almost white—hair and saw the roots were dark.

Outside, dust flew as a tan pickup truck spun it's wheels into reverse, throwing gravel wildly. The red convertible, now a disfigured heap of metal, rocked on its rubber.

Frankie darted between the convertible and the pickup, throwing up an arm to stop the driver. Again, the pickup's wheels spun, dust and dirt and gravel flew and Frankie barely leaped aside as the convertible took another mighty blow. "You bastard!" the driver, her face red and distorted, screamed out her open window. "You goddamned useless no good fart of a man."

Frankie advanced on the pickup, shouting his own obscenities. He tried to jerk open its door, but the lock was down and the woman cranked the window up before he could reach through. It was a good thing he didn't reach inside because the tan pickup spun backwards, with the left front wheel passing over the man's bare toes. He squealed, then burst at a running limp around the cabin.

Again the crash. Again the pickup was jammed into reverse.

A black 1940 Plymouth sedan slowed along the county road and turned into the driveway. But when Frankie burst back around the bungalow brandishing the woodshed axe and began savagely beating out the front windshield of the tan pickup the Plymouth spun backward.

Then the woman in front of Michael, eyes streaming shook her head wildly and while doing so, caught a glimpse of the big man standing behind her. She screamed and fled from the house.

The tan pickup lurched to a stop and the driver's door was kicked open. "My own goddamned sister!" the driver screamed, leaping from the cab. "My own fucking sister!"

Then Frankie had a fistful of June's brown hair and jerked her around. She attacked him with nails and sharp-toed shoes. He dropped the axe and slammed her full in the face with his free fist. "You bitch!" he roared. "You bitch! Bitch! BITCH!"

"Frankie!" the naked girl ran forward, grabbing his arm. "There's a man in the house!"

He shook her off and took aim at June once more. Michael stepped out on the porch, still carrying the blanket and frying pan. Steam rose from the tan pickup. He supposed the radiator was bashed in. Likely it, too, was going nowhere. The black plymouth sped down the county road.

Frankie punched June in the mouth again. Michael ambled down the walk. The naked girl saw him and screamed something unintelligible, then gabbled, "There he is! Frankie, for God's sake, there he is!"

Frankie backhanded her. "Goddamn it, Angelica, will you leave me alone!" June caught him in an eye corner with a fingernail. He swung at her and missed. Michael's hand closed on Frankie's shoulder. Frankie cried, "I told you Angelica—leave me alone! Michael's hand gripped tighter and Frankie released June to spin away. His eyes widened and he stooped, feeling at his feet for the axe. June tackled Angelica, taking her to the crabgrass and rose bushes, where, rolling, they went for each other's eyes.

Frankie came up with the axe, quizzical, uncertain. He swung half-heartedly, but the axe was slapped aside with the frying pan. Frankie said, "What right you got here, you big bastard?"

Michael threw the rolled blanket over his shoulder and advanced, holding out a hand for the axe. Frankie swung. Again the axe was batted aside by a man big enough to wield the cast iron frying pan like a ping-pong paddle.

Screams and grunts and curses came from the women rolling in the grass at the men's feet. June's dress was ripped from bodice to waist. She wore no bra.

It was but a short distance to the smelter road, then only a little way further to the Cow Creek Diner, where the Plymouth driver could reach a telephone. He didn't need the phone, however; a white Chevrolet sedan with a "Douglas County Sheriff's Dept" decal on it's side was parked alongside the diner.

"Warren!" the Plymouth driver shouted, bursting inside. "Warren! Come quick!"

The deputy motioned to the waitress. "Bring Dorsey a cup, Mabel."

The newcomer grasped the deputy's shoulder. "Out at Molly Creason's old place!" he shouted, gulped, then added. "They're killing each other!"

"Sit down, Dorsey. Who's killing each other?"

"I don't know! But this woman was slamming her pickup into a little red convertible!" Again, Dorsey ran out of air. After gulping, he continued, "Then a guy pulled her out of the pickup and started slugging her!"

Warren nodded. "Five'll get you ten, that goddamned Frankie Creason's got woman problems again.

Dorsey pulled on the deputy's arm. "You gotta come, Warren! One guy is swinging an axe at another guy! And this naked woman and the one in the pickup is in a cat fight all over the yard!"

"Naked woman?" the deputy said. "Now you got my attention."

Things were considerably more sedate at the Creason place when Deputy Warren Telford drove into the lane, followed closely by a black Plymouth. But looks were deceiving. Frank Creason was on hands and knees, retching, while two screaming women were held at arms-length from each other by what Warren automatically marked as a big, grubby tramp.

The first thing Warren heard when he stepped outside his cruiser's door was, "You rotten slut! You two-timing sack of...!"

Overlain by, "You wasn't making use of him, you cheap cross-eyed...!" Michael smiled wistfully at the deputy, thrusting the woman with the torn dress his way.

"All right, June," that's enough, the deputy said, taking her by the arm.

The naked woman twisted from Michael's grasp and ran after her sister to plant a kick on the woman's butt. Michael and the deputy pulled the women apart and stood between. The deputy sighed. "Angelica, go get some clothes on."

Michael bent down to pick up the blanket at his feet, shaking it out and draping it over the sobbing, naked woman he now knew was little more than a girl. He also noted red welts on the woman's breasts and all over her face. One ear bled freely, probably from a bite.

"Dorsey," the deputy called to the man standing outside his Plymouth sedan, "see can you set Angelica down for a minute or two 'til I can get some of this sorted out?"

Meanwhile, Michael picked up the frying pan and lifted Frankie to his feet. As he did, June spat fully in her husband's face and made a lunge at him. "You two-timing bastard! You yellow-livered, screw-happy piece of sorry owl shit!"

Whether she was through wasn't plain because the deputy dragged her to his police cruiser and thrust her inside. "You don't look so good, Frank," he said upon his return.

"Did you take a look at what that bitch did to my car? How good would you look after that happened to you. Then this goddamned ape ..." Michael flashed Frankie his best smile. "... stuck that goddamned frying pan in my gut."

The deputy pulled out a notepad and began writing. He didn't bother to look up when he asked, "Using an axe on him, Frank?"

"Hell no! I couldn't reach him. But if I could've, I would've killed the sonofabitch!"

The deputy looked up at Michael, who grinned again. "Name's Telford. Warren Telford. What's yours?"

Michael was struck momentarily mute by the fact that this deputy wanted to be his friend. Then he murmured, "Michael."

"Michael what?" Again the deputy bent to his notepad.

"Michael Bar ..." The rest was cut off as the engine roared to life in the deputy's sedan and its transmission jammed into reverse. The car rocked around on two wheels, then sped for the gate, throwing gravel and dirt over the three men and barely missing the black Plymouth with its driver and the blanket-clad woman

Warren Telford watched June Creason go, then returned to his notepad, writing "Mike Barr—that right?"

"Close enough," Michael murmured.

"Okay, Frank," the deputy said, swinging to Frank Creason, "what happened here?"

Frankie sighed. Angelica jumped from Dorsey's Plymouth and ran to Frank

Creason's side.

Deputy Telford called, "Dorsey, why don't you run down to the diner and call Roseburg. Tell 'em June Creason stole my car and headed off toward Riddle. Tell 'em we'll need another deputy and a tow truck down to Molly Creason's old place on Cow Creek. Then come on back—I might need a ride before this is all over."

"That bitch ..." Frankie began to relate what had happened.

"I don't claim her as a sister," Angelica cut in.

"Why don't you go get into some clothes, Angelica," Deputy Telford said.

When she returned, she asked, "Where'd the creep go?"

Telford looked up from his notepad, then gazed around. "He was here a minute ago. Go see if he's around back."

She shivered. "I don't want to know where he is. I just want to know how he got in the house."

"Why do you think he was in the house?" Frankie asked.

"Are you calling me a liar?" she demanded, stamping a spike-heeled slipper.

"Aww, shit! All I know is all of a sudden he showed up with that goddamned frying pan in his hand and ..." Frankie's eyes widened. "The frying pan!"

"Okay," the deputy said, "where'd he get it?" "And the blanket," Angelica said.

They circled the building, looked in the woodshed, searched the bungalow. Finally, the deputy said, "Check your frying pans. See if one is missing."

Frank Creason spread his hands. "How would I know?" he asked. "I don't cook here. Mom might've known, but I don't."

The more practical Angelica strode into the kitchen. "There's one hanger that's empty," she called. "A frying pan could've hung there."

A bottle cap was popped and fell to the floor. Angelica's face peered around the kitchen doorjamb. "How about you, sheriff, want a beer?"

Warren Telford put his notepad away. "Might as well. Nobody'll get here for an hour anyway."

"Me, too," Frankie called. "I want a beer, too."

Chapter 22

The result of twin contacts with other humans, caught inside Oscar Perkins home and in the middle of the altercation at Frankie Creason's cottage, was that Mikhail Baranovitch—known to Deputy Sheriff Warren Telford as "Mike Barr"—was a recognized presence along Cow Creek. What wasn't available was where he came from, where he'd gone, or where he holed up while out of sight. Naturally the size and strength of the vagrant grew with each telling. Deputy Telford may have been more circumspect when he jotted the incident down in his official report, but in time he enhanced the tale of the surprise newcomer to Cow Creek with each Myrtle Creek to Glendale tavern-telling. Meanwhile, in order to place himself in better light, Frankie Creason's story was of a giant "go-rilla" who might easily climb the Empire State Building to swat airplanes with a frying pan. As for Angelica, of all that day's participants she really *did* see the intruder as nine feet tall, with shoulders as broad as the bumper on a Peterbilt.

June Creason saw "Mike Barr" in a different light, however. After days passed and she'd started divorce proceedings against her husband (naming her sister as corespondent), the woman had time to think more clearly about the affair at Molly Creason's old cottage. As time dulled selected memories and sharpened others, she began to view the stranger's arrival as one of a knight in shining armor riding to her rescue. She forgot the man's week-old beard, grimy knuckles, and wrinkled and soiled clothing. Instead, the woman remembered him as kind-eyed, broad-shouldered, and with the glint of compassion on his furrowed brow. She forgot that the man had been impartial, equally devoted to keeping each member of their sordid triangle from injuring another. Finally she daydreamed about the size of the man's muscles, his tenderness.

Oscar Perkins had, of course, learned all about the Creason affair by dropping by the Cow Creek Diner the morning after. Nor did it take the canny old-timer long to separate the story's chaff from its wheat. He murmured, "Sounds to me like the feller might be a good man to have around."

"I don't know, Mr. Perkins," Deputy Telford said, pausing alongside his own version of the tale to stir cream into a fresh cup of coffee. "He might be the sneak thief we're looking for."

"Oscar," the waitress said, "that sounds like it might be the same guy as the one up at your place."

"Might be," Perkins said, hunching his shoulders and staring into his cup.

"Yeah," Deputy Telford said, not realizing that Perkins had actually *seen* and *talked to* the vagrant. "And probably the same one that's been breaking into places all over the valley."

Fortunately, Mikhail Baranovitch had given his discovery some thought and decided to absent himself for a few weeks. By the time Deputy Telford figured out that Oscar Perkins might shed light on "Mike Barr," the man who was the point of the story was already cresting Dutchman's Butte, west of Cow Creek, and heading down into the coastal drainage of the Coquille River.

"Yeah, Oscar," Warren Telford said, "that description pretty much matches the guy I saw. What'd he take from you?"

The old man shook his head. "Nothing that he didn't bring back."

"Well, did he ask first?"

"Look, Warren, he came here after books. The man wants to learn. I love to see people read." Perkins eyed the deputy. "Do you read?"

"Huh? Yeah, I read. A lot."

"Tell me, what have you read lately?"

The deputy glanced out the cabin doorway, face reddening, then said, "Well, Oscar, he wasn't in the Creason cabin looking for books, that's for sure. There ain't nobody been there who's smart enough to read since Gutenberg cranked out his first bible."

The old man nodded. "But it sounds to me like it's a damn good thing he was there that day or there could've been a bunch higher price of admission to your jail."

Deputy Telford stared thoughtfully at the old man, then asked, "You know where his camp is, Oscar?"

"No."

"Think it's close?"

Perkins shrugged.

The deputy came to his feet. At the door he paused, hand on knob. "Oscar, if you know something more than you're telling and a rash of break-ins starts again in this valley, you'll be partly to blame."

Deputy Sheriff Warren Telford's predicted rash of thievery began in September. The axe disappeared from Frankie Creason's chopping block; bedding was pilfered from Lang's place over toward Canyonville, and a pair of outsized barn boots was taken from the Weaver farm, near Myrtle Creek. The reason? Mikhail Baranovitch had spent most of August building a third shelter in a hollow below Dutchman's Butte and needed to properly equip it—and himself—for the coming winter.

* * *

"Michael," Oscar Perkins asked, "are you stealing things again?" His visitor hung his head, so the old man said, "Why?"

"I built this new place and it needs some stuff."

Perkins nodded. "I can understand that, son. But you do know that it's wrong to steal, don't you?"

Michael looked at him with wide, innocent eyes. "Even if I bring it back when I'm finished with it?"

"How about Frankie Creason's frying pan? Have you brought it back yet?"

"I'm not through with it."

Perkins pulled out a chair and sat down across from Michael. He pushed a pad and pencil toward the younger man saying, "Son, I want you to write down everything you still need and I'll see what I can come up with. Don't stint on the list, but be sure you only put down things you know you need and will use."

Michael worked on the list for several minutes, pausing from time to time to think. Then he pushed the pad back to Oscar Perkins and watched in trepidation as the old man ran a finger down the list. "The rope I can come up with. And the salt and coffee and sugar. I've got an extra coffee pot and as for the shovel, can you use a surplus army trenching tool?"

The guest nodded.

Still the finger scrolled down the list to the end. "I don't see any books on this list. Aren't you reading any more?"

"I ... I thought I could get books from you as long as I brought them back."

Perkins nodded. "You can. But hell, boy, you'd ought to *need* them don't you think? A man always ought to *need* a book."

Michael reached for the pad and pencil and wrote "books" at the bottom.

Perkins pulled the pad back, nodding in satisfaction. "Now," he said, "most of this stuff I can *give* to you; the rest I can *get* for you—like the clothing. But it'll cost you."

Michael turned glum. "I don't have any money."

"Of course you don't. But I've got a woodshed, and I think I'll see if Lanny Riley can dump a load of oak blocks in my yard. You know anybody who could split 'em?"

A broad grin spread across Michael's face. "Me!"

The old man said, "The problem is that somebody else might be looking for you—like Deputy Telford. So the fact that you're working here has to be kept secret." Michael nodded. "This place is far enough away from anybody else that no one'll hear you splitting. But anybody can see you working from the road, so you'll have to keep an ear cocked for cars."

His visitor nodded again.

Perkins continued, "You'll have to keep the pieces you split picked up and stacked in the woodshed, too. That way, prob'ly nobody'll even get it in their head that anybody's splitting wood over here. Okay?"

Michael began splitting Oscar Perkins oak wood on the following Tuesday. It was tough going at first, until he learned to "slab" the oak blocks instead of trying to split them from the heart out as is usually done with fir and pine. Working from daylight to dark, he wrapped up the job as Thursday faded into the sunset. That was also the day Oscar handed him three packages of clothing and a pair of new work boots.

"Clothes all came from the Salvation Army store," the old man growled. "It's where I buy mine. But the boots—nobody carries no size-14 second-hand shoes. So I had to get 'em new."

Michael held up the boots, tears in his eyes.

Oscar said, "If I ever get another load of wood from Lanny, you can come split some more to pay for the boots."

Hunting season rolled around again, and Mikhail Baranovitch squirreled back into his camp, cooking only once per day, always after dark. Then Oscar Perkins received another load of wood from Lanny Riley, and Michael spent the next three days at Oscar's place splitting and stacking.

It was on the first day of his absence that Drew Hamilton and Bill Carlin separated and began climbing, hunting along parallel ridges. Carlin, as it turned out, had drank too much whiskey the night before and had both a towering headache and an unquenchable thirst. He dropped into the narrow canyon between his ridge and the one his partner worked, thus discovering Mikhail Baranovitch's main camp.

Carlin whistled his buddy down and the two men talked about the discovery. Since they were down from Roseburg, neither knew about the rash of petty thievery occurring in southern Douglas County. But both admired the tidiness of the camp, and how well-equipped it appeared.

"You reckon this is a hunting camp?" Carlin asked.

Hamilton shrugged. "How could it be, Bill? A man can't get a vehicle anywhere near it, and it's too close to the road to use otherwise."

"Maybe a hideout camp, you think?"

"Now there's a thought."

After Carlin had tanked up on water from Michael's little spring, the two men parted, still scratching their heads. But that evening, on their way down the Cow Creek road, they came to a sign:

ATTENTION! 500 YARDS!

ALL HUNTERS MUST REPORT

AT GAME CHECK STATION

As chance had it, Deputy Sheriff Warren Telford had also stopped at the check station to talk to the roadblock biologist. The biologist waved the unsuccessful hunters on, but they said they wanted to talk to the deputy. Telford ambled to their vehicle.

The following day Hamilton and Carlin took Telford to the hideout camp. The deputy completed his inventory of the equipment found there by ten o'clock and had compared that inventory against the backlog of petty thefts reported in his end of the county by noon. There were enough similarities for Telford to confer with his sheriff. The outcome of that meeting was for a second deputy to be assigned to assist Douglas County's southern deputy in a stake-out.

Mikhail Baranovitch finished splitting Oscar Perkins' final load of oak wood by the end of the deputies' second stake-out day.

The man was there before Deputy Sheriff Warren Telford heard him, striding through the gloom into his camp with the air of a man at home.

"Hello Mike."

Mikhail Baranovitch paused with one of his new Red Wings still suspended. Behind him, he heard the unmistakable click of a safety pushed to the "off" position on an automatic pistol. Telford stood before Michael's bunk, both hands gripping his 38-caliber automatic at shoulder height, one eye sighting down the barrel. "The rifle, Mike. Drop it."

Michael dropped his carbine and slowly raised his hands.

Chapter 23

"Cynthia," Deputy Sheriff Warren Telford, holding the telephone close, said to the dispatcher, "tell the powers that be that we got the Cow Creek thief. Me and Jocko. We'll be in with him in an hour." Telford listened for a moment, then laughed and said, "Yeah, I'm calling from the Cow Creek Diner. Tell Curly to have a stout cell for this one—he's a big bastard."

Telford sauntered back to the sedan with a Douglas County Sheriff's decal on the door. A crowd of onlookers parted to let him slide into the driver's seat. "Way to go, Warren," one of them murmured. "Looks like he's big enough to heft a gas drum," said another. Telford glanced back through the reinforced security screen at his handcuffed prisoner. Mikhail Baranovitch sat twisted sideways, staring at the floor, seemingly oblivious to the faces of onlookers stooping to peer inside as the second deputy obligingly shined his flashlight on the prisoner.

Telford smiled pleasantly. "You ever get ready to say something, Mike, it'll make our drive to Roseburg easier."

Deputy Jocko Hayes said, "You're sure he can talk?"

Telford nodded. "I know he can. Talked to me at the Creason place, during that brouhaha 'tween June and Frankie; the one I was telling you about."

Jocko nodded. "The one where the sister ..."

"... didn't have no clothes. That's the one."

Irvin Finch was not an imposing figure; what set the undersheriff apart from his contemporaries was an unsmiling, uncompromising manner toward all evil-doers. From toe-headed ten-year-olds shoplifting on a dare to high school teenagers engaged in graduation beer-busts to rapists-murderers who killed for sport, Finch treated them all the same. The man was flint-eyed, tight-faced, slope-shouldered, and mean-spirited. Ordinarily Finch appeared at the Douglas County Jail only to bring in malefactors. But the undersheriff was curious about a sneak thief who'd break and enter a remote cabin's tool shed to steal a battered shovel while leaving a brand-new Disston chainsaw squatting on a nearby shelf. It defied logic.

"He refuses to talk, boss," Warren Telford said as Finch let himself into the interrogation room. Telford perched on the edge of the table alongside the prisoner. Jocko Hayes leaned in the room's far corner. Both deputies held riot sticks.

Finch growled, "Regulations say to stay outside the prisoner's reach. You know that." Telford slid to his feet and eased three feet away.

Roland Cheek

The undersheriff took a wide stance in front of the prisoner who sat hunched in a straight-backed chair, staring at the floor. His hands were still cuffed, this time in front. A heavy silence descended as the undersheriff folded his arms and studied the prisoner. He noted the black ink still on the man's fingers and thumbs and palms and knew the jail staff had taken fingerprints.

"All right," Finch said, "what's your name?"

Mikhail Baranovitch ignored the question; nor had he noted the undersheriff when the man entered the room. Indeed Michael had not raised his eyes from his feet since he was arrested.

"I asked you a question," Finch repeated without raising his voice, "what is your name?" Still no answer, no acknowledgement. "Do I sense antagonism here," Finch murmured. He plucked Telford's riot stick from the deputy's hand, then poked the prisoner with the end. "Are you a tough guy? Do you think you can ignore us?" When the prisoner remained mute, Finch brought the stick down on the back of the man's neck with a thud.

"He blinked," Jocko Hayes said. "That's more than we got."

This time Finch brought the stick down on the prisoner's head. Baranovitch teetered forward, then with immense force of will, pushed back upright.

The undersheriff pitched Telford's riot stick on the table and said, "Lock him up. Put him in solitary. No shower, no food. We'll see what the sheriff wants to do with him in the morning." as Finch was leaving, he added, "Take those boots off him, too, and add them to his effects. They're obviously new, so there's a good chance we'll locate the owner."

After Finch left the interrogation room, Warren Telford sopped at blood oozing from a swelling cut on Mikhail Baranovitch's head. "What was that for?" he asked Hayes.

The other deputy shrugged. "He don't cut nobody no slack. I guess he hates anybody who gets on the wrong side of his law." Telford quit dabbing at Michael's wound and took the big man by an arm. As Hayes also helped the prisoner to his feet, he said, "Finch is bucking for the sheriff's job. And after what happened with that Burdick thing, Bayles might be on his way out."

It took twelve days for the fingerprint analysis of "Mike Barr" to return from the F.B.I. Within the hour, Douglas County Sheriff's Deputies Jocko Hayes and Leland Sanders delivered Mikhail Baranovitch across town to the U.S. Veteran's Hospital. Gladys was first to spot the trio as they entered the lobby, screaming, "Michael!" She leaped from her desk and pounded around the counter to throw her arms around the big man. "Oh Michael! We're so glad you're back!"

The deputies glanced at each other, then eyed the woman. "Ma'am," Hayes said, "we need a formal release signed before we can leave the prisoner."

148

"Oh pshaw," the woman said. "Later. Michael, you look WONDERFUL! What in the WORLD have you been doing?"

The big man smiled and lifted his handcuffs in frustration. "Handcuffs?" the woman said, eyeing each deputy as if they were maggots. "Why is this man in handcuffs?"

Jocko shrugged. "We'll be glad to take 'em off, ma'am, just as soon as I get a release from whoever is in charge here."

Gladys released Michael and stamped to her phone, dialed, and said, "Doctor, we have an emergency that requires your immediate presence at the front desk." A look of disgust crossed her face. "Didn't you hear me, doctor?" she said, voice rising. "We need you NOW!"

A few moments later, a portly, bald, freckled, little man wearing sandals, Bermuda shorts, and a Hawaiian shirt padded around a hallway corner. "Well!" he said, drawing up short. "It's about time you deigned to come back."

"Dr. Henderson!" Michael exclaimed. It was the first words he'd spoken in almost two weeks. He dragged both deputies as if they were puppies on leashes, while striding forward with hands as outstretched as he could get them.

Bryce Henderson glared at the handcuffs, then snarled, "Get those goddamned things off this man."

Jocko Hayes shook his head. "Regulations says we can't do that until you sign a release, Doc."

"I ... said ... get ... those ... handcuffs ... off ... NOW! Get them off or I'll personally kick your asses all the way back to the County Courthouse—DO YOU HEAR ME!"

Jocko Hayes fumbled for the key, unlocked first one cuff, then the other. "You've still got to sign a release, or my boss'll be over here to find out why."

"Then I'll shove a foot up his ass as far as I planned to do yours. Where's this man's shoes? Why is he barefoot?"

"He didn't have any shoes."

"He didn't have any shoes? Are you trying to shit me? Michael, where are your shoes?"

"They took them," the big man murmured. "They were new boots. Red Wings. I worked hard to pay for them."

Henderson stared balefully at each deputy in turn. "So you stole a pair of boots from this man! Weren't they a little big for either of you? Or did your turdhead sheriff want them for a poor relative?" When each of the deputies reddened and shuffled their feet, Henderson thundered, "I asked a question! What happened to Michael Baranovitch's boots?"

Jocko Hayes murmured, "They took 'em the night they booked him in.

Figured they was stolen."

"And that was when?"

"Two weeks, more or less."

"Jesus Christ!" Henderson thundered. "You mean he's been without shoes for *two goddamned weeks!*

"Reckon so," Hayes mumbled. "Wasn't my idea."

Henderson glared at the deputies. "Get the hell out of this hospital before I call our own security. Get the hell out and go bring his boots. In the meantime, I'll be on the phone to your asshole sheriff to grease your getting them." Henderson paused, then added, "And all his other personal effects, too."

Jocko Hayes held out a clipboard. "You've still got to sign this paper, Doc. We can't leave this man without it."

Even the top of Henderson's bald head glowed red. He said to Gladys, "Go page Daniel. Tell him to bring every orderly he can find to the lobby on the double."

When the woman hurried away, the doctor murmured, "The boots. I ... want ... those ... boots."

As Douglas County Deputy Sheriffs Jocko Hayes and Leland Sanders pushed out the hospital's entry doors, loudspeakers sounded behind them: *"DANIEL! ALL ORDERLIES! REPORT IMMEDIATELY TO THE FRONT DESK!"*

Both Dr. Henderson and Mikhail Baranovitch watched the deputies disappear. Then Henderson looked up at his patient and winked. When a wistful smile flashed across Michael's face, the doctor said, "They were *your* boots, weren't they Michael?"

Michael nodded, saying, "I split a whole load of wood for a nice old guy to earn them, sir."

Just then Daniel thundered around a corner and slid to a stop, muttering, "Michael!" Other orderlies soon followed, crowding around, pounding the AWOL patient's back, chattering like magpies.

With the mysterious messaging that seems to permeate hospitals, curious patients began trickling to the lobby, first the most ambulatory, then those using canes and crutches, and lastly individuals able to roll their own wheelchairs.

Gladys stood outside the circle, hands clasped before her, smiling in pure joy at the assembly. Michael pushed between Daniel and John Wilder to take the woman in his arms and hug. "You're special," he murmured. Glady's phone was ringing. She ignored it to hold Michael at arms length for careful appraisal.

Doctor Henderson picked up the phone, listened a moment then plugged a wire into the switchboard. Then he placed a call to the Douglas County Sheriff. When he was put off, the doctor shouted, "I don't think you understand, woman, I want him NOW! This is Major Bryce Henderson from the United States Veteran's Hospital calling and I want action—do you hear? Action!"

Gladys, still holding Michael, said, "Someday I'll want to hear the entire story. But for now, it's just wonderful to have you back."

The big man flashed his most winsome smile. "Lonesome is okay," he murmured, "but it breeds diseases only friends can cure."

Deputy Jocko Hayes brought Mikhail Baranovitch's boots within the hour. Included were Michael's other personal effects: a three-bladed pocket knife, a bottle opener, three marbles, a red handkerchief, a comb with half-dozen missing teeth, and a small folding magnifying glass. Since Dr. Henderson and Deputy Hayes were not on speaking terms, Colonel Y. Herbert Corwin signed the deputy's release form, expressing his personal gratitude that the Douglas County Sheriff's office had rescued Michael on behalf of the federal government.

Michael's old room was occupied by another patient, but Daniel found equal quarters for a patient who'd turned into a hospital folk hero. The cafeteria girls queued at the doorway to their domain to smile and wave and make suggestive remarks as Daniel led the prodigal patient to the stairway. Will Terwilliger caught them in the second-floor hallway to shake the big man's hand. Even Jasper Meacham sourly mumbled that he was glad to see Michael again, "and I hope this time you'll keep your hands out of my pockets!"

Michael's new quarters was a corner room with a southeast exposure. The room sported a splendid view of both Mount Nebo and the entire ridge behind. Michael could even see the band of oaks marking the South Umpqua River. When the patient remembered Daniel and turned from the window, there were tears in both men's eyes. "Glad to have you back, big guy," the orderly murmured. "We were damnably worried about you."

All Michael could do was hang his head, and say "I'm sorry."

But being sorry wasn't sufficient to provide the patient with his old freedom. After first conferring with Dr. Henderson, Daniel returned to bring a suit of hospital blues and explain the revised rules governing Michael's movements. "You'll not be permitted to leave the hospital without being accompanied by an orderly. You can have the run of the main floor—the lobby, the lounge, exercise room, cafeteria. But you'll have to be in your room at ten p.m. and can't leave it before seven a.m. Understood?"

"What about the restroom?"

"Yes, of course. But thats the only reason you can be out of your room at night."

"Can I take a shower?"

"Only between seven in the morning and ten at night."

Michael turned to stare out his window, effectively ending the exchange.

Weyland Jones came down from Sutherlin as soon as he heard. The two men spent half an afternoon with their heads together as Michael unfolded events from his last eighteen months.

It was ten days before Bryce Henderson was able to work Mikhail Baranovitch into his office rotation. The date was Thursday, November 14, 1952. It was two o'clock in the afternoon when Daniel knocked, then led Michael into Dr. Henderson's office. The doctor asked Daniel to close the door on his way out.

It had been raining hard all night, and windblown rain still pounded against the doctor's office window. Mikhail Baranovitch strode directly to stare outside. Henderson chuckled. "I don't believe we'll open it today, son. It's only thirty-six degrees outside right now and that damned radiator is acting up enough that I don't want to freeze."

The patient turned and without being bidden shuffled to the chair across the desk from the psychiatrist. Directly in the middle of Henderson's desktop lay a bulging double-sized expansion file with **MIKHAIL BARANOVITCH** inked across the outside.

The doctor leaned back in his swivel chair, eyes at half-mast, studying the patient. On this day, Dr. Henderson wore a wool shirt and foresters' green corduroy trousers. One by one, the doctor placed his sandaled, white-stockinged feet on his spacious desktop. He said, "What do you want to talk about first, son?"

"How long have you been back, sir?"

Henderson smiled. "I had an eighteen month tour, but I was so indispensable that they kept me for another six months. Then they gave me enough leave to take my wife and son to New Zealand." He paused, thinking. "But we had to have Stan back for school in September, so I decided 'what the hell,' and came back to work. A couple of months, give or take."

"I'm glad you're back, sir."

Henderson nodded, then said, "Remember, I don't like to be called 'sir'."

"Yes sir. I'll try to get it right, but it don't seem natural."

The doctor pointed at Michael's file and the patient's eyes followed. "I've read all the stuff we have on you, Michael. All Dr. Harrow's work, all your military records, what we have from your school."

When the patient said nothing, Henderson said, "So I know all about Aitape, son. The Driniumor, the Yakamul pocket, even your retreat from Nyaparake." He paused for an acknowledgement, received none, then said, "I know how you won your Bronze Star."

Michael said, "Dr. Harrow was a nice man."

"Wasn't he though?" Dr. Henderson dropped his sandaled feet to the floor and said, "I also heard about how you attended the man's funeral. That was a damned decent thing to do, walk all that way out there." The big man's face remained a mask, so Dr. Henderson added, "In the rain."

The patient laid his right arm across his chest, propped the left elbow on it, and leaned a square Slavic chin in the palm--clearly contemplative body language if the doctor had ever been seen it. Even the black eyes took on a certain luster.

"Why'd you leave, Michael?" A veil flowed across the patient's face and eyes; the doctor continued, "Was it because Dr. Harrow died? Or was it because, in his absence, you weren't receiving counseling?"

"I don't know."

"Or was there some other reason?"

To break the silence that ensued, Dr. Henderson pulled his wire-rimmed glasses from a shirt pocket and slid the patient's file nearer to hand. He cleared his throat and said, "Gordon Smith—you remember him, don't you?" When Michael nodded, the doctor said, "Well, he said he's behind on getting the leaves raked before real winter sets in. Says he can use you." When Michael's eyes began to dance, Henderson added, "But can we trust you?"

"Uh-huh. Tell Mr. Smith to give me a rake and I'll have 'em all in piles by next Thursday, when I get to see you again."

Dr. Henderson stood and walked to the window. Rain and wind still pounded upon it. "Next Thursday is Thanksgiving, son." He glanced across his office at a wall calendar and added, "I won't see you again until the twenty-eighth."

"Then I'll sure have 'em all raked up, sir. I'll do a good job. I swear I will."

The doctor placed his back to the window and peered over the tops of his glasses. "But can we trust you not to run away again?"

Michael's black eyes wandered the room before returning to meet the blue ones of the portly psychiatrist. "I'll try, Doctor. But give you my word on it? I don't know."

"Damn it, Michael! Don't you want to walk out of here a free man?" When the patient nodded, Dr. Henderson added, "More than that, don't you want to walk out of here a cured man?"

"Yes."

"Then give me your word you won't run off again."

Michael took a deep breath. "I won't want to leave without your okay, Doctor. But sometimes I just can't seem to live without lonesome."

Chapter 24

A tragedy arising from Mikhail Baranovitch's refusal to pledge not to leave the hospital grounds without permission was Dr. Henderson's consequent refusal to allow the patient outdoors privileges. "The poor dear," Gladys said to Daniel. "All he does is stand in the lobby with his face pressed against the glass like a puppy in a pet shop window."

"The lobby's not the only place he does it," the orderly said. "It's the same thing in the lounge. And when he's awake in his room, he's standing at the window."

"Even the cafeteria girls says he eats his meals standing at the window. Daniel, this has been going on for three months!" When the orderly only stroked his chin, she added, "This simply cannot go on. Surely he can be given *some* kind of outdoor time."

"I think there's a test of wills going on between Michael and Henderson. But I'll be darned if I can tell what it is."

Bryce Henderson knew what it was, however; so did Mikhail Baranovitch. In fact, as week after week dragged by with the morose patient peering out a window and gradually withdrawing into muteness, the entire hospital staff began to talk. Word of the stand-off reached Sutherlin, and one day Weyland Jones sat down in Bryce Henderson's office.

"What's going on?" the farmer asked. "Is Michael's treatment progressing or regressing?"

The psychiatrist spread his hands, palms up. "Weyland, I cannot permit him outside without his pledge that he'll not take the first opportunity to run away."

The farmer's gaze was steady. "And what of your interviews? Has he moved forward in confronting his war experiences?"

Henderson's angered glare met Jones's—rapiers clicking in combat. "He refuses to confront his past."

"And you call that progress?"

"No. You're the one who called anything progress. I choose to call it regression wrought by the fact that he was *Absent With Out Leave* for over a year. I choose to believe Michael must understand there are consequences resulting from such actions."

Jones nodded. "I see. Crime and punishment. The fact that both you and Dr. Harrow disappeared prior to his going A.W.O.L., and he received no counseling

The Dogged and the Damned

at all in the interim has no bearing on the subject as far as you're concerned."

"None at all. I had nothing to do with circumstances beyond my control. If anyone is to blame, it's the federal government."

"You're goddamned right it is," the farmer cried. "In New Guinea. In San Francisco. In this hospital! Surely, Doc, you're not telling me it's *his* fault!"

"And neither is it mine!"

Weyland strode to the doctor's window. "So it's come down to a test of wills? Don't you know you can't win a test of wills with a mental case?" When Dr. Henderson made no comment, Jones added, "Or is it you who's disturbed and not him?" The farmer wheeled back to lean down and peer at the doctor. "So his outdoor privileges is returned and he leaves, what's the big deal? One thing certain is that the man is not violent. He won't hurt anyone."

"But he'll steal from everyone," Henderson replied. "Weyland, that's called kleptomania and it's not acceptable in any society."

"That's right," the farmer agreed. "So what kind of treatment are you providing him for that problem?"

When the doctor hesitated, Jones nodded. "That's what I thought. You're still insisting on *returning* him to society instead of *preparing* him for it. Damn it, Doctor, the way I'm told things are going, you're doing neither. And I'm almighty afraid that you're going to drive one hell of a good man insane through your lack of proper treatment."

"Who, for Christ's sake, is the goddamned psychiatrist here?"

Weyland grinned. "You. So I guess I'd better leave while you dwell on it. But before I go, I'd like to stroll around the grounds with Michael. Will you give me a pass to do that?"

Without a word, Dr. Henderson pulled a pad of passes from a desk drawer, signed his name, then tore off the top sheet to thrust it and a pencil at Weyland. "You fill in the rest of it. Do it in the hall, however, I'm sick to death at sight of you."

Jones grinned again and murmured, "Thanks, Bryce. You always was tough, but you've always been fair."

Weyland found Mikhail Baranovitch staring morosely out the front lobby window. Since Michael had his nose to the window and hadn't seen him, Weyland first went to the front desk and handed the pass to Gladys. The receptionist squealed when she saw it, then clapped a hand over her mouth before blowing a silent kiss to Weyland. The farmer approached his friend. "Let's take a walk, Michael."

The bigger man turned from the window at sound of Weyland's voice, a smile spreading. Then it vanished. "I can't go outside. But we can walk in the halls."

Weyland took him by the arm. "You can walk outside with me; I just turned your pass in to Gladys."

Michael glanced at the receptionist, saw her happy wave, and became animated. Really? I can go outside? And I can do it with you?" Weyland pushed open the door and held it wide as his blue-clad friend bounced through.

Dr. Henderson was busy at his desk when Michael first appeared for his March 13 appointment. The psychiatrist waved him in, telling him he would be a few more moments, then returned to paging through triplicate forms. Directly he finished, pushed that pile of papers aside and pulled the expansion file marked **MIKHAIL BARANOVITCH** near to hand.

Before Dr. Henderson opened his mouth, however, Michael said, "I appreciate very much being allowed outside with Weyland, Dr. Henderson, and I'd like to be able to do it again someday. If I'm allowed out, I'll promise to be good, but if I have to pledge never to leave the grounds, I want you to know I'd like to do that too, but I just can't. Never is a long time."

When the psychiatrist's face remained impassive, the patient said, "Did you know daffodils are starting to bloom? I'll bet early wildflowers are, too. What do you ..." Michael's outburst trickled to an end as Dr. Henderson held up a hand, palm outward.

"Michael," the doctor began, "I'm a beaten man." He held up a hand when his patient started to protest. "I now see that, in good conscience you cannot guarantee that you won't someday walk away from the grounds and not return. Though I don't like that possibility, I must accept it. What I don't have to accept, however, is the probability that the only way you can survive—if you do leave us—is by stealing from others."

Dr. Henderson's pause was pregnant while he waited in vain for the patient to protest innocence. Finally the doctor said, "That's why we're going to work on your understanding that stealing is wrong." Again he paused before continuing, "You do know that taking something from someone else without their knowledge and acquiescence is wrong?"

"Even if they're not using it?"

"Even if they're not using it it still belongs to whoever owns it. And what you don't seem to realize is that they might need it before you decide to bring it back."

"Maybe."

"So, if I return to you the outside privileges you enjoyed before you left, will you at least pledge that, should you leave us again, that you won't steal from others?"

The patient's hesitation was brief. "Yes," he said.

Dr. Henderson nodded. He glanced at the window, the light fixture overhead, the open doorway to his office, then back at Michael. "All right, son, as an indication of your sincerity, I want you to tell me, so I can tell the Douglas County Sheriff's Office, the location of all those things belonging to others that you took while you were A.W.O.L."

Michael's Slavic face remained blank. "I had two other shelters; one was on Middle Creek, almost to Highway 99. The other on a shoulder of Dutchman's Butte. I can pinpoint them if I had the right map."

Undersheriff Irvin Finch was the man designated to pick up the map Mikhail Baranovitch had marked. He wasn't in Dr. Henderson's office for more than a few moments before the psychiatrist sensed the lawman's distaste for people housed within the federal hospital. "No doubt the tools and implements will be rusted," Finch said, "even if we do locate his shelters. And what of the bedding, food, and spare clothing? None of it will be usable after remaining out all winter."

Henderson studied the sharp-faced undersheriff. "And you are suggesting...?" The doctor let his question hang.

"That someone should be responsible for replacing the stolen items."

"And whom should that someone be?"

"Ideally the perpetrator. But lacking that, perhaps the federal government."

Dr. Henderson tapped his fingertips together. "Um, yes. And while you're at it, deputy, how about finding a way to restore what was stolen from Mikhail Baranovitch in New Guinea. Figure out a way for the people of the United States of America to replace the mind that was shattered in a dozen different bloody battles to keep the hopes and homes safe for your victims of Mikhail Baranovitch's rapacious depredations."

Undersheriff Irvin Finch offered a frosted smile. "Unfortunately for you and the patients you serve, doctor, my responsibility is to the people of Douglas County, Oregon. If you have a quarrel with the people of the United States of America, I'm hardly the proper conduit for you."

The top of Henderson's balding head reddened, but he smiled sweetly and said, "That I can see, deputy. And I suspect you are hardly a proper conduit for those in Douglas County who are poor and underprivileged, too."

Mikhail Baranovitch stood beneath the yet-to-leaf-out limbs of a giant oak tree at 7:00 a.m., Monday, March 17th, at the junction of hospital's drive and Harvard Avenue. Clutched in his hand was the single dime he'd carried during the seventeen months of his Cow Creek freedom and the four months of incarceration since. He waited in vain until almost eight o'clock.

He was there on Tuesday, too, in the rain. And Wednesday, Thursday, and Friday. And, assuming that he'd had the misfortune to hit the Roseburg school system's spring break, he stood at Harvard and Hospital Drive the following Monday. This time, a gully-washer rain drummed down. His paperboy friend never, ever pedaled past.

Gladys and Daniel both suggested ordering delivery directly from *The Daily News* offices, but Michael shook his head. He didn't want the newspaper; he wanted delivery by his friend.

So Gladys called the newspaper's circulation department. "No," she was told, "they'd had the same carrier for the Harvard route for the past four years." "No, the carrier for that particular route did not deliver by bicycle, but by automobile. And besides, *she* had not been in school for the past forty years."

"Yes, most of the in-town routes were covered by boys, usually on bicycles, though some chose to deliver on foot."

"Yes, I suppose a boy who lived on the west side, perhaps out Harvard, could pedal a bicycle to school each day, then deliver papers on an in-town route."

"No, I have no idea who might have lived out there two years ago and delivered for us on any in-town route. Perhaps I could run it down if you could tell me the route he covered."

Gladys set the phone back in its cradle and shook her head at Michael. "Sorry Love," she said. "It looks like you're going to have to find another newspaper to read."

Head groundskeeper, Gordon Smith, was pleased to have Michael back. "He might cost me a little more in the hours he insists on putting in," he told Daniel, "but I'll more than make it up by not having to pay three other guys to do the same work he'll do."

Will Terwilliger saw little of Michael after he was again given outdoor liberties. But he told Daniel, "I've never seen a more fit individual as he was when he came back—not for his age. Weighed twenty pounds less than when he left, but he was all muscle—like corded steel. An animal! No end to the cycles he could put the treadmill through. Bench press three hundred pounds like it was Cheerios on the ends of a toothpick. You see his legs? They're like tree trunks. And the muscles on his back ripple when he walks. He's in fantastic condition."

Daniel said nothing, so the therapist added, "If he goes again, I want to go with him."

When he goes again," the orderly muttered.

Chapter 25

From all outward appearances, Mikhail Baranovitch was happy in his restored outdoors freedom. Though he preferred to work alone, he got along well in a crew, whether he was hoeing weeds or carrying irrigation pipe. It wasn't unusual to hear the big man whistling or humming or singing softly to himself, perhaps about Volga boatmen or skies of buttermilk, in sunshine or rain, during wind or mosquitoes. Catch his dark eyes and invariably the face went through a most fascinating transformation, from featureless dough to one of eye-flashing, teeth glistening, dimples-shining radiance.

See the big man outside and see him with sleeves rolled up, trousers tucked into his own proudly worn work boots, ball cap pushed rakishly back and tilted toward his right ear. See him inside and see a man at peace, nodding pleasantly to all, speaking to those who spoke to him.

It was, Daniel could see, as Gladys had told him: all the cafeteria girls loved Michael and wanted to hug him—or at least acted sufficiently so as to make him blush each time he passed through the serving line.

Even Jasper Meacham's sourness failed to dent Michael's easy good humor. "Don't worry about it," he told Daniel. "Jasper is as happy as he's made up his mind ever to be."

It wasn't being outdoors that alone was the source of Mikhail Baranovitch's cheerfulness; the man followed closely the wind-down to the Korean conflict, and when the Armistice was signed, Michael made a point of shaking the hand of every man and hugging every woman he saw, including the startled wives of two patients who were Sunday-picnicking on the grounds with their hospitalized husbands.

Dr. Henderson was pleased with Michael's transformation to ebullience, and after re-reading Dr. Archibald Harrow's 'carrot vs stick' commentary, dated four months before the man's death, he well understood the importance of that observation regarding the patient's treatment. Then, after reflecting on treatment criticism by Weyland Jones, the psychiatrist and his patient initially concentrated on Michael's kleptomania—until one Thursday near the end of August when the doctor brought up studies currently under way on impulse stealing when Michael held up a hand. "I read the definition for kleptomania after I left here last week, sir, and I believe it's inappropriate to pursue this course any further."

"You don't say?"

"Yes sir. Kleptomania, according to this hospital's library dictionary is defined as 'a compulsion to steal having no relation to need or the monetary value of the object.' That's not me, don't you see, sir? I never took a thing that I didn't need; though I will admit I gave no thought to its monetary value."

A slow smile spread across Dr. Henderson's freckled face. "How many times must I tell you not to address me as 'sir'?"

Michael smiled.

"Yes, well, if you feel you've absorbed everything you need to know about the wrongness of taking something belonging to others, then it's time for us to return to New Guinea."

Michael nodded. "If you wish ... Doctor."

"Can you repeat for me your Aitape experiences?"

So Michael spent several hours repeating his story of his Aitape engagements, beginning with the retreat from Nyaparake, moving to the two battles on the Yakamul, and finally their breakthrough crossing of the Driniumor under fire. Then, briefly, he outlined his rescue of Captain Baldwin from behind enemy lines.

At the conclusion, Dr. Henderson nodded and said, "That pretty well squares with the account left by Dr. Harrow. Since you've repeated it to me, it's apparent that the memory of Aitape no longer raises demons for you."

"I don't believe so ... Doctor."

"So where did you go next?"

"Stayed at Aitape for awhile. After it was secured, I guess the powers-that-be decided it was a good place to stage the next campaign from."

"You must have gone to the hospital with your wound?"

Michael nodded. "Yeah. I was there for a week. The hospital was at Tadji Airfield. I got out of there as quick as I could."

"What about your wound?"

"Lower left side. Bullet didn't go all the way through like it did with Captain Baldwin. They got the bullet out with a probe, shot me full of penicillin, coated it with iodine, then left me to try to sleep on my belly. I couldn't with all the planes, though. That's why I wanted out of there so bad."

Dr. Henderson started to ask another question, but Michael had more to add: "Besides, when I did doze, all I could see and hear was Captain Baldwin dangling off my right shoulder while I dashed across the Driniumor, yelling Yankee Doodle at the top of my lungs."

"Do you still have that recurring dream?"

"No."

"What about Lieutenant Gray? Did he ever pay you your dollar?"

The Dogged and the Damned

The question startled Michael, but then he became animated. "He did! When I caught up with him as we staged for Morotai, he dragged a dollar from his pocket. It had 'BAR' written in ink across the face of it. He said, 'I didn't think you had a chance in the world of pulling it off, soldier.' Way he figured it, he said I was lucky and it seemed to rub off on whoever was close. So he wanted me right by his side when we hit whatever the next beach was."

"And that was Morotai?" Dr. Henderson probed.

"Yeah. It didn't work, though."

"Didn't work?"

"I think my time is up. I've been here for a long time."

"Well, Son, as luck has it, I have no further appointments this afternoon."

"I still want to go."

Dr. Henderson nodded, scribbled in his notebook, then said, "All right, Michael. We'll work on Morotai some other time. But before you go, I'd like for you to know that I'm also interested in your life at Butte, your parents, your school activities, your friends, the girls you knew. At the very least, I'd like to know more than such scanty information we have provides." The balding little man leaned across his desk. "There *is* something there that you're blocking out, am I not right?"

Michael took a deep breath and pushed to his feet with the easy grace of a born athlete. "Me'n Barney are going for a walk now. Thank you for seeing me. I'll be back next Thursday."

Bryce Henderson closed his notebook and rolled his chair away from the desk. "Would it be all right with Barney if I walked along with you two? I'm finding these August doldrums to run to boredom, too."

Mikhail Baranovitch disappeared the morning of August 31. Church bells were ringing when last he was seen striding out Harvard Avenue. Mildred Blackman reported a "wild man" at the Canyonville dump a mere two days later. "I'd just closed up our store and decided to swing by the dump that night instead of dropping the bundles of trash off on my way to work in the morning. Then this wild man popped up in front of my headlights and I spun around and got out of there fast!"

Deputy Sheriff Warren Telford investigated, found the shipping container utilized by the "wild man," along with a mattress with gaping holes and missing stuffing, a worn sleeping bag and a ripped wool blanket.

Two nights later, the deputy switched on his heavy-duty flashlight and said, "Hello, Mike. Don't you think this is a tough way to make a living?" Telford held a Smith & Wesson .38 caliber revolver in his other hand.

Mikhail Baranovitch raised his hands.

The Daily News made much of the story, with a one-inch headline on page two:

UMPQUA WILD MAN ARRESTED AT CANYONVILLE DUMP!

The story told of the many "wild man" reports coming into the Douglas County Sheriff's Office from Canyonville residents, and how the investigation progressed until a stake-out brought the "wild man" to heel. There was a photograph with the story, showing a grimy, bedraggled Mikhail Baranovitch as he was being booked into the Douglas County Jail.

The story continued with the background behind this particular prisoner: how he was an escaped patient from the Roseburg Veteran's Hospital, how he'd first came to the Sheriff's Department attention as the Cow Creek Thief, and how he'd been apprehended and returned to the hospital ten months before.

This time, however, Mikhail Baranovitch had succeeded in embarrassing the Federal Hospital Administration. This time, much of Dr. Henderson's discretionary powers relating to the treatment of Mikhail Baranovitch was taken from him.

"It's not easy to live out there without stealing, is it Michael?" Dr. Henderson asked upon his first visit with Mikhail Baranovitch after the patient's second A.W.O.L. adventure.

"It's not easy to live out there by foraging either."

"Maybe it's just tough to live out there, period."

Michael's eyes wandered away. "I'd like to try."

"That's why we must cure you so you can, upon your release, enter society, get a job, make your own way in the world, go where you wish, when you wish."

Michael's dark eyes wandered back to the doctor. "Will that ever happen?"

"Unfortunately your actions are sometimes at odds with your desires."

Michael nodded. "That's true, sir. But I can only do what I must do. I never told you I wouldn't leave; I only told you I wouldn't steal and I didn't."

"So what's your conclusion?"

"That I can't make it with my hands tied."

Dr. Henderson sighed. "Well, son," he said, "it's probable that we won't find out soon what you'll have to do to survive because Colonel Corwin has ordered that you not be given any unescorted outdoors privileges until he expressly permits it." Michael's jaw clinched. Doctor Henderson continued: "I'll try to do what I can for you, Michael, but it's not much. I can of course walk with you on occasion, and Daniel said he'd try to detail an orderly to walk with you at least an hour each week. Weyland also told me, now with his harvest winding down, that he can get away most every week. But there'll be no more garden or lawn work for you, no matter how thick and fast the leaves fall. And there's nothing I can do, nor can I try—unless you'll give me your word that you won't leave. If you'll do that, I'll try to intercede with Colonel Corwin." The psychiatrist waited a few moments, then reached for the patient's file.

Mikhail Baranovitch again tried staring out hospital windows. But this time the man received little sympathy from staff or other patients. Gladys noted his dejection and shook her head; Daniel and the other orderlies ignored him; Weyland Jones visited with him, but attempted no intercession; the cafeteria girls twittered at his approach, but the ease of their banter seemed lost.

Michael tried declining to attend his Thursday afternoon sessions with Dr. Henderson, but soon discovered that he not only lost the occasional walk with the doctor, but he also lost the opportunity to walk accompanied by an orderly.

Again it was Weyland Jones into the breach. "Michael," he said as the two strolled to the river on Easter Sunday. "Aren't you being a little pig-headed?"

Michael's step faltered. "Yes," he said.

"Why?"

"Because it's the only way to protest I know."

"Why do you feel you must protest?"

"Because I want to be outside and they won't let me."

Weyland caught him by an arm, turning the larger man to face him. "How can they? You'll leave. They know it and you know it. What you're doing is forfeiting any hope of walking out of here on your own, with everybody's blessing."

Michael studied the toes of his now-tattered Red Wings.

The Sutherlin farmer shook him harder than Michael had allowed anyone to do since walking away from Coach O'Malley and Stefan Baranovitch. "Don't you understand that Bryce Henderson wants to help you? Don't you understand that Gladys and Daniel and every other person in this hospital is crying out to you—and that includes Colonel Y. Herbert Corwin!" Weyland's eyes snapped and his strong farmer's fingers left red welts on Michael's upper arm.

Michael rubbed his arm and said, "I want to go back now."

"Yeah. Sure," his friend snapped. "Go back and hide and sulk and think the world is after you. You tried it your way and it didn't work. Don't you think it's about time to try it our way? And yes, I said *our* way. It's the right way, man! I was once in your shoes and I know! Henderson can help you—but only if you're willing to help yourself."

Mikhail Baranovitch hurried on his way back to the hospital; though he was mercifully silent, Weyland Jones matched him stride for stride. When the two men arrived at the entrance, Michael flashed a wan smile and muttered, "Maybe you got to treat some men like they was a balky mule. Instead of driving them in, maybe you should leave the gate open and let 'em bust in."

Weyland gripped Michael's hand in both of his own and squeezed until it hurt. A tear trickled down the farmer's face, mirrored by ones coursing down the cheek of his friend.

On his way back past the lobby counter, Michael borrowed a notepad and a pencil from the weekend receptionist and scribbled a note to Dr. Henderson. The man's office door was locked, so Michael shoved the note beneath the door.

The following morning, Bryce Henderson unlocked the door to his office, slipped from his raincoat, and noticed a scrap of paper lying on the floor. He picked it up and unfolded it. It read:

Can I begin treatment again?
Baranovitch

Chapter 26

When Mikhail Baranovitch entered Bryce Henderson's office at three o'clock in the afternoon, April 15, 1954 and took his chair, the doctor silently handed the patient a letter he'd received some months before.

Michael read only a few lines, stiffened, leafed through the letter's several pages, then glanced up at Dr. Henderson. "Do I have to?" he asked.

The doctor shook his head. "You needn't do anything you don't wish to do, Michael. But in my opinion you should read that letter. It lacks all the answers, but it certainly provides clues to the direction we need to go to learn what happened to you in your home town."

To: Major Bryce Henderson
Subject: Mikhail Baranovitch
From: Sylvina Ormansky
Date: October 16, 1953

Please excuse this approach, but your letter was forwarded to me by the present Chief of Police for Butte, Montana in the hopes that I might be better able to respond to your request for information. As fortune has it, I might be the best possible person to do so, since my late husband, Vladimir Ormansky, was, until two years ago, this city's police chief, and had been for over 25 years.

Others of my credentials for responding are: a) 20-year chairperson of Butte's Library Guild; b) former schoolboard chairperson from 1937 until 1945 (during much of the time your patient was enrolled in schools here); c) mother of Anna Karenina Ormansky who was very much in love with Mikhail (we called him Michael) Baranovitch during their high school years; d) served as a second mother to Michael during the many times when the poor boy deemed it difficult to return to his own home.

For your information, Stefan Baranovitch, Michael's father was notorious for his many shortcomings as a parent, a husband, a family provider, and a credit to his community. The man was a hopeless alcoholic; actually the town drunk. In addition, he was, when intoxicated, a noted brawler who several times hospitalized members of the Butte police force sent to arrest him.

However, Michael adored his father, never brooking any criticism of the man, no matter how deserved. (In all honesty, I must advise you that Stefan

Baranovitch had many admirers among the working men of Butte. And when sober, he was known as a loyal, tireless workman who always performed at least as well as any man for his pay, and more than most.)

On the distaff side of the Baranovitch family, Michael's mother, Alexia, was a shy, retiring, absolutely wonderful woman who, it cannot be denied, loved both men of her family with equal passion. Alexia, unfortunately, died—possibly of a broken heart—when Michael went through his unfortunate court-martial affair after being wounded so many times on that dreadful Pacific island. Her death was, I believe, in February, 1945. Please advise her son that Alexia's funeral was held at the Silver Bow County Courthouse and was attended by hundreds.

As often happens in such cases, Stefan Baranovitch was found dead only two weeks after, succumbing during a savage blizzard while staggering his way home from drowning his sorrows.

That completes my understanding of Michael's family background—there were no brothers or sisters.

As for the boy himself, he was a handsome lad, star athlete, studious, extremely well mannered, a courteous gentleman in every way. If my daughter had not fallen so madly in love with the young man, I would've done so myself.

Since my husband, as police chief, was tormented for years by Stefan Baranovitch's drunken tantrums, we first received Michael in our home with a great deal of trepidation. He soon proved our fears groundless and I, for one, expected great things of him, even anticipating grandchildren by him through Anna Karenina.

Unfortunately, something happened—never between those two, but something irreconcilable at school or home (or both)—that drove the boy from everything he loved in the city of his birth. Vladimir once told me he suspected bad blood between Michael's domineering father and his hard-driving, championship-driven football coach, though you must treat that idea with the skepticism it deserves.

You asked for Bulldog Yearbooks for 1941 and 1942 and I've obtained them for your purposes. I've also ordered a "morgue" search of Montana Standard's back sports page files for the years 1939, 1940, and 1941 (enclosed). Through an even cursory examination of the yearbook and newspaper files, you'll readily see that Michael was an outstanding football player who was sought by college coaches across America.

With perhaps understandable pride, I've also enclosed a glossy photo of Butte High School's 1941 Homecoming King and Queen—Michael in his muddy football uniform, and Anna Karenina in her Drum Majorette uniform. Don't you agree they were a splendid couple!

At this point, Mikhail Baranovitch laid Sylvina Ormansky's letter aside and gingerly picked up the glossy photograph. For over an hour, Michael stared through blurring eyes at the photo without really seeing it. Instead his mind went tumbling back....

"Michael, you can't quit the football team—are you out of your mind!" Tears coursed down her face.

He sat on a straight-backed chair in the Ormansky's kitchen, fiddling with a half-empty bottle of Coca Cola. His face was tight and his knuckles white. "It's done, Anna. I'm not going back. What's done is done."

"But why?"

The boy pulled the girl to his side. She straddled him and his chair, sitting back on his knees, facing him. "Why?" she murmured again between sobs.

He shut his eyes. "Because he called my papa a no good bastard."

"Who? I'll kill him myself."

"Coach. O'Malley."

"Oh my God!" She took his face in both her hands and leaned close to brush his lips. "Surely he didn't mean it, Love. After all, he is the coach."

He opened his eyes and smiled a tight, brief smile. "I decked the sonofabitch. And if some of the other players hadn't pulled me off, I would've tried to send him to whatever special hell crazy-mad football coaches are supposed to go."

"But you worked so hard...."

Mikhail Baranovitch / soph / 6'3" / 220 lbs. was listed as the starting right tackle on Butte Bulldog programs for the year 1939. That Baranovitch was two inches shorter and twenty pounds lighter was a given in the psychology of high school football where a 175-pound opposing tackle might read a Bulldog program and think, *Geez, and I gotta face off against a friggin' Holstein bull!*

Michael earned the spot by beating out Joe Demarest, the heir-apparent, who the year previous had been a junior-class understudy to starting tackle Richard Snell. Snell was the arrogant senior who'd beaten Michael senseless with a two-by-four--and paid for it during the following afternoon's practice with a broken jaw and two broken ribs that'd taken the senior out of school for a week and out of Bulldog football for the season's remaining games.

Demarest scrimmaged aggressively against his sophomore competitor. But remembering what had happened to Snell, he scrimmaged fairly. In coach

O'Malley's final analysis, it was Baranovitch's overall speed and quickness that won him the position over the heavier, slower senior's experience. It was to the easy-going Demarest's credit that when Baranovitch was listed as starting tackle for the season's opener, he shrugged and said, "The toughest sonofabitch won."

That first game against the Deer Lodge Wardens was pretty much a pushover against a small school; merely a warmup for the Bulldog's tough schedule. And the sophomore tackle distinguished himself in unanticipated ways....

"Godammit, Baranovitch," O'Malley shouted in the usual post-game dressing down, "three off-sides, a late hit, and a roughing the kicker penalty! What do you have to say to that?"

Though he'd previously heard a few of O'Malley's team-wide post mortems, this was the first time he'd been on the receiving end and he was suitably penitent."I'll try to do better, coach. Honest I will."

Later, according to the eavesdropping third-string halfback Paddy Dougherty, O'Malley told his assistant coach, "Young tackles make mistakes by being too eager. Wait until he gets his timing down, and a little more experience. Baranovitch will tear up somebody else's interior line."

He did, too, roving the Helena Bengals backfield like it was the living room in his own home—until Helena began double-teaming him. The Bengals double-teamed Michael when the Bulldogs were on offense, too, because the sophomore opened up holes a blind Bulldog running back could stroll through.

But O'Malley was too-wise to let an opposing team get away with doubling up on Bulldog linemen, and soon Saunders and Shaugnessey and Modlenski ranged at will through the Bengal line, too. And that game turned into a rout.

But when time came for the post-game dressing down, O'Malley merely growled to his sophomore tackle, "Twenty-five yards in penalties this game, Bar. I thought you were going to do better." Michael nodded and said, "I did. Twenty-five yards is better than forty-five, coach." And O'Malley turned swiftly away to avoid smiling at his budding star.

O'Malley's nickname for Michael—"Bar"—stuck, and his teammates began using it on field and off, until "Bar" became as common as "Mike" when Bulldog players addressed the big sophomore.

Missoula Spartan's tailback jerked Michael off-sides three times with broken cadences on his counts and O'Malley pulled the sophomore, sending in Demarest for the entire second half.

So Michael worked on what O'Malley referred to as the two "P's", peripherals (vision) and patience (mind conditioning). The result? Michael was penalized but ten yards during the remainder of the season, waiting until someone moved in the opponents line before snapping into play.

Left tackle Modlenski sprained an ankle against the Bozeman Hawks and on the Monday following, coach O'Malley called Michael into his office. "I'm starting Demarest at right tackle against Great Falls," he said. "And I want you to take Mod's place at left tackle. Okay?"

Michael shrugged. "Yes, sir. It's okay with me."

"You'll get a chance to scrimmage at left for the rest of the week. Okay? Wanta know why?"

Michael met the coach's eye with a gleam of interest. "Why?"

"Because Wilson is Great Falls' right tackle. He's the odds-on favorite to win Montana's Lineman of the Year. As our left tackle, you'll get a chance to face off against a guy better than you. You'll learn a bunch. Okay?"

Michael stared at O'Malley for two clicks of the coach's wall clock. Then he said, "Coach, there isn't anybody better than me."

O'Malley laughed, lunged to his feet, and clapped his young lineman on the shoulder. "That's the attitude I want to see, Bar. Hang on to it."

Great Falls and Butte were one-two in the polls leading to their match-up on Bison turf. As his team trotted from their locker room for pre-game warmups, O'Malley grabbed Michael's jersey and pulled him aside. "There's three college scouts here to watch Wilson. I want you to make 'em have second thoughts."

The sophomore's face was tight. "I'll do my best, coach."

Whether Michael's best was good enough was, by general consensus, subjective. Without question, however, was the fact that Michael's line-of-scrimmage education took quantum leaps.

Wilson was big—taller and heavier than Michael. He was quick, too, and fast. But not as quick and fast as the younger player. What Elijah Wilson had, though, was the skill to utilize every trick—fair or foul—in an enormous repertoire gleaned from experience. Michael soon thought the man must have four hands instead of two, three feet and six elbows instead of two each. Wilson gouged at Michael's eyes in a pileup, then laughed and tripped him when the angered sophomore came back at the bigger player.

"What's the matter, kid?" Wilson taunted. "Can't take it?"

But the taunts died as a stubborn Slav kept the All-State lineman out of the Bulldog backfield and the Bison tailback quit calling plays through Wilson's position because that damned Slav closed holes as quick as one opened.

Wilson's use of questionable tactics might have been effective against an excitable opponent, but Mikhail Baranovitch was a plodder without imagination; a player who talked to himself between every play, psyching himself up to do his best. And it wore the older player down until late in the game, with Butte leading by two points and the Bison deep in their own territory and the play calling for a pitch-out on an end-sweep going away from his side, Wilson let up for an instant. Enough for Michael to slip around him.

Larimer, the Great Falls scatback was quick, one of the swiftest running backs in the state. His opening was big and he sped through it in an instant, streaking down the sideline. Defensive backs tumbled like tenpins and the Great Falls fans erupted as one, lunging en masse to their feet, screaming as though to awaken the dead. Then Larimer was free! Thirty yards to paydirt!

But what's this? A dark jersey streaked after the white. A big dark jersey! And the player wearing it was overtaking the speedy scatback who thought higher pitched shrieks from the stands were screams of ecstasy. Larimer did a cute double shuffle on the ten-yard line and his reward was that he was hit from behind. The ball popped loose. The hitter recovered Larimer's fumble and the hittee and his Great Falls fans wept.

The scout Hempden, from Washington State College said it best when he told O'Malley in a private post-game conference at the Stockman's Bar, "We can teach kids a lot if they're trainable. But we can't teach 'em speed. Either they got it or they don't. And that kid—what's his name? Barnabitch? He's got it."

Mikhail Baranovitch blinked, and returned to Sylvina Ormansky's letter:

> ... I trust this is all the material—and more—that you requested relative to Mikhail Baranovitch's Butte background. Should you need more for treatment purposes, please do not hesitate to allow me the pleasure of assisting in any way possible. I and my family all loved Michael deeply and have always wished him the best in every endeavor.
>
> We were, of course, deeply saddened to learn of the horror he must have endured on that unspeakable jungle island, and we've wept buckets to learn, through your request, that Michael still carries psychological baggage from the sacrifices he made for his county.
>
> Please convey to Michael that we all love and pray for him.

Michael sat motionless after reading the last page of Sylvina Ormansky's letter. His eyes clouded with tears, then gradually dried. With a jerk, he saw that Dr. Henderson's chair was empty. The patient lunged to his feet and started for the door. On the way, his eyes fell on the wall clock above the threshold and he saw he'd been in Dr. Henderson's office for three hours!

Chapter 27

It was a typical spring day: blustery, showery, sunshiny, sometimes all three at once. Michael noted that Dr. Henderson wore his raincoat as he hurried his approach to the hospital's staff entrance. "Good morning, Michael," he said as he pushed through the door, not pausing to hear the young man's response, striding down the hall to the front desk where he said to Gladys, "Ask Daniel to hold today's patients until later. Michael and I are going for a walk."

And that was it. In moments, Dr. Henderson and Mikhail Baranovitch was strolling hands in pockets along the sidewalks of the hospital grounds. They walked in companionable silence for several minutes before either said a word. Then it was Michael who ventured, "Thank you for sharing Mrs. Ormansky's letter."

"You already knew of your parents?"

"Yes. That word came while I was still in the hospital at Espiritu Santo."

They crossed the river bridge. Finally, Dr. Henderson asked, "I'm curious, Michael, did you know of Mrs. Ormansky's high regard for you?"

"No. She was always decent toward me, but sort of ... aloof. She always seemed so ... kind of haughty. But maybe that was because I was defensive of Papa."

"Aha! It's always difficult, being a teenage boy. Especially in the presence of social inequities."

Michael was still mulling over that when Dr. Henderson said, "Is there any truth in Sylvina Ormansky's belief that there may have been an explosion between your coach and your father?"

He was slow to reply, finally saying, "No. As far as I know, Papa and Coach O'Malley never met, never spoke a word to each other." They reached Harvard Avenue and turned back. I don't think papa ever even saw me play football—ever." He sighed. "The trouble was between Coach and me, and Papa and me."

They strolled to the middle of the bridge amid violent wind gusts. Dr. Henderson, tugged down his fedora, placed both hands on the bridge railing, and said, "Can you tell me about any of it, Son?"

A rain shower slashed in on them from the southwest. Michael turned his face into it. "Coach *insisted* that I go to Notre Dame. Papa hated Catholics. Coach hated anybody who bucked him. That was the heart of it."

"And they put you under a lot of pressure."

"In a way. At first, I could handle it. To tell you the truth, it didn't make any difference to me where I went to college, only that I did. What I figured to do was win a full-ride to someplace where I could go for a business degree. Of course, Papa didn't even want me go to college—he wanted me with him, down in the mines."

"Did you ever entertain any thought to do so?" The sun broke through the clouds, but a light rain still fell through sunbeams.

"Not really. But I didn't tell him so. Not for a while, anyway." Michael wiped his nose with a shirtsleeve. "I had Mama on my side, so I could fend him off. But when he found out O'Malley was pushing for me to go to Notre Dame, he blew up...."

"No-tray what? What's that, a goddamned Catholic college?"

"They have one of the best football programs in the country, Papa. It's someplace in Indiana. Near Chicago, I think. Coach thinks they'll offer a full-ride."

"I don't give a shit if they ride you back there in the fanciest coach that bastard Pullman makes—you ain't goin' to no Catholic school. Nobody in this house even mentions the word Catholic and I'll kick the shit out of 'em."

"Husband," Mama said from the stove where she stirred soup, "so far you're the only one that's said that naughty word. Maybe your mouth we should wash out with soap, eh?"

"You stay out of this, woman; this is a man's business." He returned to Michael, "You wanna go to college, then you can go to the School of Mines, right here in Butte."

"But they don't give scholarships, Papa. I don't have money to pay my own way."

"That way, when you get smart, you get a job as manager, or maybe even foreman. Then you could lord it over you papa."

"I don't want to be a mining engineer, Papa. I want to study business management."

"You want to wear stuffed shirts with ruffles at the collar and gold cufflinks on the sleeves."

"No I don't Papa. But I want to go to college, and get the best education I can."

"Putting two and two together from the 1941-42 Butte High School yearbook," Dr. Henderson said, "it looks as though Butte High School lost their next three games after you left the team."

"Yes, and I'm sorry for that. But there was more problems with the way O'Malley handled the team than just with me."

"What about you? Can you share with me why you left, Michael?"

So the big man wearing only hospital cottons and the little portly man in a raincoat and fedora hat stood amid showers and sunshine while the man in blue poured out the story:

Mikhail Baranovitch sat on a locker room bench, pulling on first one yellow-and green striped high stocking, then the other. All else the young man had on was his unbuckled shoulder pads, a jock strap, and a set of belted hip pads. Others of his teammates were in various stages of dress and undress, suiting up for their big game with Kalispell.

Coach O'Malley slammed the dressing room door on his way in, then paused in front of Michael. "Baranovitch," he growled, "Ryan Shevlan will be in the stands again. That's the third time this year that Frank Leahy sent him to watch your games."

"Michael dipped his head. "Okay, Coach. Thanks."

"I want you to take King's head off. I want you to grind his nose into the dirt. I want you to roam their backfield like you had a deed to the place."

"Okay, Coach. I'll do my best."

"Goddamn it, your best isn't good enough! I want you to get good and damned pissed off. I want you to send their linemen to the sidelines, preferably on stretchers—got that!"

"No, sir. I don't. Yeah, I got it that we've got to beat 'em. And I've got it that I've got to do my part in order for it to happen. I also know that we've got to disrupt their passing attack and I know that in order to do that, I've got to get to their quarterback. But to deliberately hurt somebody?" By the time he was through with the reply, Butte's star lineman had pushed to his feet to go nose-to-nose with his blocky coach.

Michael could see that O'Malley was furious, but by the time a player reaches his twelfth school year, and is a bonifide star who won "first-string all-state" *and* "high school lineman of the year" awards the previous year, and is a hands-down favorite to repeat, there's only so much a coach can do. The older man wheeled and stomped into his office, slamming the door.

King was slippery. The scampering quarterback and Winger, his right end, had an uncanny synchronous ability to improvise, even while raging bulls ranged the Kalispell backfield, and defensive backs swarmed the galloping, weaving end. But the Butte field was cinder-hard, and Butte fans noisy, and they were so partisan it took extra police cordons to hold them back from the playing field. Gradually, King began to wear, especially after being taken down by that goddamned Baranovitch for the fifth time. It began with an interception, then a fumbled snap from center. Later, it was pure fear that manifested itself by the Kalispell star exiting left every time he *thought* that crazy Serb was breaking through on the right.

The final score was Butte 20, Kalispell 13.

O'Malley brought the Notre Dame assistant coach into his team's dressing room, introducing Ryan Shevlan to the Butte players. They paused in front of Mikhail Baranovitch. "Bar, this is Shevlan. He wants a word with you."

Michael was bent forward unlacing his boots as the two coaches paused before him. He stood and held out his hand. Shevlan took it and pumped. "You looked pretty good out there today, kid. How'd you like to play for Notre Dame?"

"I'm sorry, I can't." Michael retrieved his hand during the shocked silence that followed. "My father won't permit me to attend a Catholic school."

O'Malley wheeled a full 360 degrees, spluttering all the way. Shevlan said, "What the hell is this, an aftermath of the Inquisition? How in the hell old are you, boy?"

Michael sank back to his bench and began unlacing his second boot. "I'll be eighteen next month, sir."

"Don't you think you're old enough to make a few decisions for yourself?"

Michael slipped off the second boot, then again pushed to his feet. This time his chin was only inches from the one hanging from the Notre Dame coach's face. "Yes sir, I do. As a matter of fact, that's exactly what I'm doing now." O'Malley could still be heard spluttering in the background. "Sir," Michael continued, "I honor the fine institution you represent, and have the highest respect for their football program, but I've made it my decision not to attend school there."

Both Shevlan and Baranovitch were of a same size. Then O'Malley barged between the two, grasping Michael by his jersey front and pulling him close. "Listen up, you good for nothing shithead. I've never had a player with the talent to get to Notre Dame until you came along. I gave you everything, taught you everything I know, spent extra time with you to be sure your skills matched your talent." O'Malley was panting, but he twisted Michael's jersey tighter to pull his nose down close to his own while the coach gestured with his free hand. "This, just in case it escaped your pea-size brain, is a Notre Dame coach sent all the way from South Bend, Indiana to Butte, Montana to tell you the finest football school in America is offering you a full-ride scholarship!"

Michael reached up to grip the fist O'Malley used to twist his jersey. As he did, the Butte coach snarled, "And you, you snot nose pile of cow turds, you're going to apologize to Ryan Shevlan and take that scholarship offer. Hear?" Gradually, Michael began to squeeze O'Malley fist. Both men's eyes were shooting sparks as the pressure inexorably increased. Then O'Malley lashed out with his left fist, rocking Baranovitch with a blow to the temple. The boy's hand fell away and so did the one O'Malley used to grip his player's jersey.

"You gutless wonder," the maddened coach snarled. "You got no more guts than that bastard Slav old man of yours!"

Where the blow started from was the subject of many debates throughout the next week. But where it ended was never in doubt as O'Malley's head snapped back and he crashed to the floor, sliding half-in, half-out of his office.

Mikhail Baranovitch smiled at the speechless Notre Dame coach. "Nothing personal, sir, but I meant what I said. I'll not be attending your school."

With that, Mikhail Baranovitch opened his locker and pulled his street clothes from their hooks. Then he strode bootless from the Butte locker room, wearing his uniform.

Dr. Henderson was nodding as Michael concluded the tale of confrontation with his high school coach. Throughout the story, his eyes had never left his patient's face. Finally the doctor said, "Let's go on back to the office, son, and get you dry."

Later, as the two men stood by the radiator in Henderson's office, the doctor said, "I'm beginning to get a more complete picture of the circumstances of your early life, son, but there are still pieces to the puzzle."

Michael sighed and turned to face the radiator. "What happened with Papa...."

"And Mama. Seems to me like Stefan should've been pleased at the way things turned out, and with your high school record other schools should've been standing at the door, even though you failed to finish your last season."

"But not when I didn't finish high school."

Dr. Henderson said, "All right, why didn't you finish high school?"

"Well, on December 7, there was Pearl Harbor."

"After football season."

"After football season." The younger man sighed again. "You'd have to know Papa. He was like Coach O'Malley—he had this crazy thing about always having to win. If he pushed and won, he had to push and win again, and again, and again. Like he always wanted me to work in the mines. And I got to seeing if I stayed around there long enough he'd wear me down. That's when we got into this knock-down scrap in the kitchen that went through the living room window and through the neighbor's picket fence. I'll tell you, Doc, I've fought some tough ones since, but never *that* tough!

"When it ended, Papa was unconscious and dripping blood, laying in a bunch of carigana bushes growing in a hedge in the *next* neighbor's yard. I was dazed, not sure which one of us was bleeding more. So I pushed to my feet. Mama stood just behind, holding a rolling pin. She was crying. 'Michael,' she said, 'you better leave. You leave before he wakes up and I'll keep him from going after you.' The next day, I joined the Army."

"I see." The doctor was silent for the longest time. Then he asked, "Do you have the letter?"

Michael reached inside his shirt and slipped the carefully folded pages of Sylvina Ormansky letter from his waistband. "I don't have the picture. It's in my room."

"Keep it, soldier. I'm sure it means more to you than it would to some future graduate student of psychoanalysis, working in a dusty University classroom a thousand miles from here."

Michael's "Thank you, sir," was barely audible.

Dr. Henderson tapped the folded letter for several seconds, then asked, "Was she beautiful?"

Michael's eyes wandered the room. "Which one? The mother or the daughter?"

Dr. Henderson chuckled. "You've answered my question. It was both, right?"

Michael nodded. There was the faintest smile.

"She must have been difficult to walk away from, son."

"The hardest thing I've ever done. Going back after Captain Baldwin was a snap compared to telling Anna that I was leaving and might never come back...."

"Do you mean this?" she demanded. "You've joined the *Army*? Just like that? You're joking, aren't you Michael? What about us? What about our going to college together? What about our children someday? What about ..."

He had no answers. Just that he couldn't stay in Butte. He'd shown up at her home after her parents had both left for the day; the father to the police station, the mother to her library and club activities. He'd caught Anna as she started down the street carrying her school books. He'd caught her long enough for her to see his face and cry out in pain and sympathy; for her to turn back and drag him into the Ormansky home.

"Oh Michael, Michael, what have you done?" He welcomed her blubbering over his injuries during the titanic fight with his father because it left no tears when he told her of the real tragedy—that he was leaving, probably not to return.

She doctored him, dabbing at his cuts and bruises, kissing him. "Darling, what happened? What happened, please?"

"I've joined the Army," he said, making the revelation as cold and impersonal as was possible with the girl he loved.

There was a scene, of course, followed by the thing that he'd never in a thousand years anticipated when she fumbled with the fly on his trousers, saying, "Then before you go, I want you to love me! I want you to know what you're missing when you lay with some inferior wench in a slovenly hut in a far-off country."

He'd pulled her close then, and they'd cried together. But in the end, he'd stood her on her feet and said, "I love you too much for that, Anna."

And he'd left.

Chapter 28

Major Bryce Henderson returned to his desk and threw himself into his swivel chair. "Anna Karenina was one of Tolstoi's major works. Did you know that?"

Mikhail Baranovitch, standing at the radiator, nodded.

"Have you stayed in touch with Anna?" Then the doctor answered his own question: "Of course you haven't. Otherwise the girl's mother would've at least dropped a hint of it." The doctor leaned thoughtfully forward to place elbows to desk. "I'm curious, Michael. Why didn't you at least write to the girl? Obviously she loved you very much."

"Maybe too much," the patient mumbled. "Maybe everybody loved me too much: Mama, Papa, Coach, Anna. Maybe you can get stifled by too much love—is that possible, Doctor? Maybe I just plain got sick of everybody else making plans for what I was supposed to do. Maybe I was being smothered by what other people wanted, instead of what I wanted. All I ever wanted to do was be myself, to make my own decisions, earn my own way. But maybe the people who loved me kept trying to fit the square Slav kid into a round Butte hole. Anna? If you think about it, sir, you'll see, same as I thought I did, that my love—maybe any love—would try to eat me alive. Even Mama, at the end, told me I had to go. I asked her to come with me, told her I'd take her far away, where Papa couldn't find us. But she said, 'No, Michael, I love you, but I love him more. Besides, if I go, too, he'll come for you and you'll either have to kill him or he'll kill you. No, you gotta go.' So I went. And she kept him away, just like she said she would." Tears filled the big man's eyes. "But I'd always have to do it their way if I'd stayed. And doc, I was damned sick and tired of doing it their way!"

Dr. Henderson listened throughout. He nodded once, then said, "But Anna Karenina—I'm not sure how in the hell ..."

Pain etched Michael's face. "Neither am I, doctor. But I thought at the time that I knew it would happen—whatever *it* was." The patient hesitated, then added, "That may not have been my most lucid time ... may have been my biggest mistake."

The doctor started to pull a file across his desk, but his hand slowed, then stopped. It was as if the freckles on the back of his fist fascinated him. His patient drifted to the window. At last, Dr. Henderson said, "Do you wish to know the vast bit of insight that just came to me, son?"

Baranovitch smiled. "I think I'm about to get it, right?"

Henderson, still staring at his knuckles, and without bothering to look up, said, "I believe we will eventually uncover the fearsome tragedy that brought you to this hospital. If so, we will successfully treat it. Of that, I'm sure. But ..." Again, he paused, this time searching for the just-right words.

"Go on, please."

Henderson shook his head and frowned at his patient. "But there's this other thing—an apparent unwillingness to let anyone become a real ..." The psychiatrist broke off suddenly and his eyes lighted. "Is it that you thought we were beginning to stifle you? Is that why you've left us?"

The patient was a long time answering; when he did it was to meditatively drawl "No. I need you, Doctor. I need help you and this hospital can provide. I'd be a fool ..."

"Michael, have you ever before asked anyone for help? Any time? For anything?"

The patient took on a far-away look, then shook his head. "Not that I can remember. Maybe I never felt like I needed it."

"Not even from Anna Karenina?"

The patient stared at his feet before mumbling, "Was I too young then to see it?"

Dr. Henderson pulled his wire-rimmed glasses from his shirt pocket, then opened the second of two expansion files marked MIKHAIL BARANOVITCH. As he did so, he said, "Yet you left us. Twice."

The patient started to say something, then changed his mind, walked to the empty chair across from the doctor, and slid into it.

"You were going to say something, son?"

A fleeting smile swept over the patient's bland face. "It's hard to put a foot in a closed mouth, Doctor."

Again, Henderson nodded. "But we were talking about Anna Karenina, weren't we? What you admitted to me was the age-old conundrum discovered by every man about every woman—that you-me-he-we don't understand them." He chuckled, then added, "Up to a certain age, my boy, men tend not to have thoughts about women, only feelings. Perhaps you aged quickly. Certainly you did if you started thinking about how Anna would manipulate you instead of what you had with her at the time." When the patient remained silent, Henderson added, "Perhaps, a man should not think so much about love—only experience it."

Dr. Henderson unfolded Sylvina Ormansky's letter. "Would you like to respond to this, Michael?"

The blue-clad man shook his head. Henderson said, "Well, I've already written her an acknowledgement and said we'll keep her informed. However that was some months ago. Since then, she wrote a brief note, asking if there'd been any advancement on your treatment. At the time, you weren't attending sessions, so I had to advise Mrs. Ormansky that I was unable to report any further progress. May I now tell her that you've read her letter?"

Michael's head bobbed.

"I can also tell her that progress is being made in your treatment, and that her letter was instrumental in that regard." The patient's eyes seemed like two tiny points of light. "One other thing, son," the doctor continued. "I believe the woman knows very little of your war record. She would appreciate knowing that you served with distinction in several campaigns and I would like to tell her of that."

Michael's Adam's apple jiggled as he swallowed. Otherwise, there was no movement; no apparent feeling—none whatsoever. However, he didn't say no.

Progress Report

Patient: Mikhail Baranovitch

Some advance made in understanding probable early psychological impairment during the patient's youth. Such advance came chiefly because Mikhail Baranovitch willingly returned to analysis. One disclosure surfacing during analysis was the trauma of manipulation by a domineering father on the one hand, and a demanding high school football coach on the other. What seems also to have been uncovered is a possibility that one result of this early trauma was that the patient may have erected a psychological barrier to others coming inside his own personal and very limited emotional boundaries.
Signed,
Dr. Bryce Henderson
V.A. Hospital
Roseburg, Ore.
April 16, 1954

"What will happen at Dien Bien Phu?"

Mikhail Baranovitch's question at the opening of the patient's next therapy session caught Dr. Henderson by surprise. Making a great show of opening Michael's files, the doctor hemmed and hawed and finally said, "Why, those asshole Frogs will lose. That seems obvious now."

"Just like us in the Yakamul pocket, isn't it?"

"Yakamul? Oh yes. Just like when your company was cut off at the

Yakamul."

"Only then, we had less than fifty men inside, whereas the French have fifteen thousand at Dien Bien Phu."

"Same difference, though, soldier. At Yakamul, the Japs had you outnumbered ten or twenty or fifty to one; at Dien Bien Phu the Gooks have the Frogs down by the same odds."

"Wouldn't it be better for them to say, 'This is where we ran,' rather than 'This is where we died'?"

The doctor leaned back in his swivel chair, forehead wrinkling, blue eyes growing oversize through wire-rimmed spectacles. He tapped his teeth with a pencil, wondering if somehow the patient wasn't offering an opening to get back to New Guinea, but he was uncertain how to exploit it. He said, "Perhaps the French lack a commander of your captain's quality."

Michael nodded, seemingly at peace, relaxed in Dr. Henderson's presence like he'd not been since the man returned from Korea.

The doctor cleared his throat and said, "Perhaps we should get on with our analysis of your service record, Michael. Are you ready to proceed to Morotai?"

"Not yet."

"Then Anna Karenina, goddamn it. We were talking about her when we quit last week."

Michael shook his head. "I don't believe there's anything left there, Doctor."

"Then what the hell do you think we should discuss?"

"Why do you swear so much?"

"Why do I ..." Dr. Henderson's mouth fell open, then he smiled. "I see. You want to analyze me."

"Mama always said that swearing was a weak mind struggling to express itself."

"And Mama was right. So that's point one: my mind is weak."

Michael smiled. "What if I penciled out a timetable of our operations against Morotai? You know, when I went in. Where. Then maybe you can supply the why."

"Yes, I think that would be a splendid idea."

"Maybe, too, you can explain to me why the French are in Indo-China."

Dr. Henderson got the connection at last. "I see. But this is something that we'll be prepared to discuss during this session, is it?" When Michael looked thoughtful, the doctor added, "How long will it take you to come up with your timetable?"

"I can have it next week."

"Good. Now what will we discuss this week."

"Do you still have your fishing hat? Maybe you could explain the flies to me; maybe tell me their names and what kinds of materials you used in tying them."

* * *

MOROTAI

Timetable
    Embarked Aitape   *Sept. 10*
    Convoy assembled   *Sept. 11*

    Staged for Morotai landing Sept. 14
    Landed Morotai   *Sept. 15*

Description of Morotai

Roughly 40 miles long and 25 wide. Huge lump of coral. Cliffs rising from sea. Honeycombed with caves. Covered with rain forests and jungle. Drinking water in short supply until one gets to interior.

Strategic importance

Morotai was thought important because it was within air range of Mindanao, which was essential for planned landings in Southern Philippines. That a decision came down to hit the Philippines farther north was apparently not transmitted to the Commanders of the Morotai force, so we rode our LCs into a Morotai hornets nest without knowing that whether or not we succeeded made no difference to either us or the Japanese.

Dr. Henderson accepted Michael's scribbled Morotai timetable, perused it for a moment, then said, "Shit! Sit."

After the patient had done so, the doctor said, "I was given to expect a little better outline of your involvement at Morotai than this ... you got this out of an encyclopedia, didn't you?" He waved the ripped-out tablet page. Embarked for Morotai on ..." the doctor glanced at the page "... September 10. Morotai is forty miles long and twenty-five wide. Holy Christ!"

"Is it so important for you to swear?" Michael murmured.

"You're goddamned right it is! Especially when something pisses me off! It's like a relief valve on my overheated boiler!"

A red-faced Dr. Henderson leaped from his chair and rushed from his office. Five minutes later he returned somewhat mollified and carrying two bottles of

Pepsi Cola. He handed one to Michael, muttering: "Pepsi Cola hits the spot."
Michael chimed, "Twelve full ounces, that's a lot."
The doctor walked to the window, where he morosely swilled from his bottle.
When he finished, he threw the bottle into his wastebasket. "Morotai," he said.
The patient had only sipped from his Pepsi and still had half. "The loading
was kind of tough at Aitape," he said. "Big surf, up over the bung hole of a Zulu
warrior."
"Why do you curse?" Dr. Henderson interrupted.
Michael smiled. "Big swells—the kind that makes an old bosun urp. Half of
my outfit was sick before we even got the fleet assembled. Then it rained like hell
on our transit days. The best place on the landing craft was in the open, and wasn't
none of us dry. But at least it wasn't cold and the soaking felt good." Baranovitch
hesitated, then said, "I sure as hell wished for a little of that rain while pinned to
the beach."
Henderson looked at his patient's timetable tablet paper. "So you landed on
the fifteenth—was that on schedule?"
"Oh yeah, we got there on time, all right. Only we didn't get to the right
beach."
Dr. Henderson had his head down, writing. "Please explain."
Michael shook his head. "Can't. I did hear the coxswain holler to our captain
that he was bucking strong ocean currents." Michael's eyes narrowed and his
mouth corners turned down. Then he shook his head and said, "Besides that,
all the smoke and dust throwed up from the Navy's softening barrage made it
impossible to see anything but an outline of the island."
Henderson looked up. "How far off course were you?"
Again Michael shook his head. "Maybe three, four miles. I do know we
came into a narrow sliver of beach with maybe a couple of hundred yards of
unbombarded jungle behind it. Then some steep cliffs pocked with caves that
glared right down our throat lay behind that. I told Lieutenant Gray that it looked
a touch inhospitable."
Michael smiled dreamily and said, "That was *First* Lieutenant Gray by then.
He'd got the promotion after Yakamul and Driniumor."
"And you, Michael," the doctor said, "why weren't you promoted?"
The younger man shook his head. "I don't know. Maybe somebody heard me
tell Lieutenant Gray to go to hell when he said I couldn't go back after Captain
Baldwin. Probably, though, it was because I was better at taking orders than
giving them."
Dr. Henderson cleared his throat. "Now tell me about your new company
commander."

Michael drifted to someplace distasteful and far away. And his cheeks turned splotchy red. Directly he muttered, "Sarbones was a dirty, rotten, bastard of an excuse for a man."

"Why do you curse?" Dr. Henderson grinned.

There was no lightness in the patient as he growled, "Because there's no suitable nice words to describe the rottenest whelp of a whore-bitch who ever drawed a breath."

Henderson stared at Michael for a moment, then nodded and said, "Where did you two hook up, and how?"

Chapter 29

In the United States Army, basic units begin at the Squad level, consisting of ten or fewer men. Squads are led by a non-commissioned officer, usually a sergeant. Moving up in size is the platoon; it consists of three to five squads and is commanded by a lieutenant. The company is composed of three or more platoons and is commanded by a captain. Battalions, led by lieutenant colonels, is composed of several companies and may number a thousand soldiers. Three or more battalions compose a regiment. Regiments are usually commanded by full colonels. Brigades are composed of two or more regiments and are commanded by brigadier generals. There are normally three brigades in a division. Divisions, usually totalling ten to fifteen thousand men, are commanded by major generals.

The force chosen for the Morotai Campaign was a combination of the 31st Infantry Division and the 128th Regimental Combat Team from the 32nd Division. The combined force was designated the Eleventh Corps and code-named *Tradewind Task Force*.

Mikhail Baranovitch's Morotai tale was a long one, beginning in mid-morning and continuing without break until shadows began stealing around the buildings, lawns, and gardens of the Roseburg Veteran's Administration Hospital complex. Neither analyst or patient felt hunger. There was no drowsiness nor incontinence. Very little eye contact was lost between Michael and Doctor Henderson. There was almost no body shifting, nothing but the evident fascination of both men....

When Mikhail Baranovitch was released from the hospital at Tadji Airdrome and returned to active duty, he was ordered to report to the *Tradewind* staging area near Aitape Harbor. The date was August 27, 1944, two days after Japanese action in the long, four month battle for Aitape was declared terminated. Corporal Baranovitch was routed to Company H of the First Battalion, 128th RCT. Company H was a largely green company replacing Company G, the devastated "Baldwin Bunch," who'd been all but destroyed during the retreat from Nyaparake and in the Yakamul "pocket".

The first soldier Michael recognized upon entering the Company H compound was Lieutenant Stanford Gray. "We had word that you were released and assigned to us, Bar," the Lieutenant said, holding out a hand. "Welcome back."

Michael dropped his duffel bag, saluted, then gripped the other's hand.

"Hmm," he said, eyeing the single silver bar on his friend's shoulder epaulets, "you made first 'looey'."

Gray's grin was lopsided as he reached down for Michael's duffel bag. "Bottom of the barrel. Last of the breed. Ugly duckling made good despite all efforts to the contrary."

Gray motioned for Baranovitch to tag along. "I want you in my platoon, big guy. I want the best B.A.R. man in the whole U.S. and A. Army on my side when we hit the next beach."

Michael smiled. "You'll have to find me another tool then, sir. I lost mine on the other side of the Driniumor."

Lieutenant Gray paused. "That was a fine piece of work, Bar. Captain Baldwin I mean. I didn't think you had a chance in hell ..." He trailed off, reached into a shirtpocket and handed the corporal a dollar bill. "I owe you this." The officer grinned. "And I want to tell you that I've never enjoyed paying a gambling debt so much in my life."

The two men ambled between rows and rows of tents. Michael asked, "How about 'the Bunch'? How many made it?"

The transformation was startling as the lieutenant seemed to age in seconds. Michael peered closely at the graying hair over his friend's temples.

The lieutenant took a deep breath. "Drew took a stateside hit. He's okay, but he'll spend the rest of the war smelling magnolia blossoms. You probably saw Kotynski in the hospital. We got him back early last week. Rogers and Hammerstein both made it—you probably knew that. But our new commander took them into Headquarter's Company. I guess he likes classical music."

Michael laughed. "Can either of 'em play a radio?"

The officer shifted Michael's duffel bag from one hand to the other. "We may get 'em back when he finds out their real names." The two friends strolled along the rows of tents once more. "Doorman made it, and is here. So's Wallace." He shook his head. "That's about it, I guess. I heard Bjorkun and Trilby went right to the field hospital. But I was told neither of 'em pulled through." He paused. "That true?"

Michael nodded. "Kotynski told me that when I came in."

A shadow flitted across the lieutenant's twisted face. "I'll tell you this much, Bar—I'll never again see a platoon I command so butchered."

They approached a larger tent; one with the Stars and Stripes fluttering from an extension of the tent's center pole. A sentry stood outside the entry flap. "In here, Bar," Lieutenant Gray said, motioning the big man toward the headquarters tent. "Better introduce you to our new captain. You're something of a celebrity, you know."

The Dogged and the Damned

The lieutenant dropped Michael's duffel bag, saying, "Permission to enter" to the private on duty.

The sentry saluted, wheeled smartly and disappeared inside. "Lieutenant Gray, sir," Michael heard him say through the canvas.

"What does he want?" another voice replied.

The private reappeared. "Your purpose, sir?"

"To introduce a new arrival," Gray said, eyeing Michael.

The private disappeared. "Lieutenant Gray says it's to introduce a new arrival, sir."

"Convey my regrets, but I have more important things to do."

Michael heard the private's heels pop together at the same time the man's "Yes, sir!" drifted through the canvas.

The sentry reappeared. "The captain regrets that he's otherwise engaged."

Gray glanced at Michael with an amused expression. "Very well. If there's an opportunity, you might tell Captain Sarbones that Corporal Baranovitch has reported for duty."

"Private!" the tent voice snapped, "Escort Lieutenant Gray and the corporal in."

The sentry took a deep breath, then motioned to Gray and Baranovitch to follow. Inside the tent, the private saluted and said, "Lieutenant Gray and Corporal Baranovitch, sir." On his way out, the sentry eyes swept over the corporal with interest.

Lieutenant Gray and Corporal Baranovitch both came to attention and saluted as the captain waved a palm in the direction of his brow and pushed indolently to his feet. "At ease," he growled. As his visitors spread their feet and melted into easy positions, their superior raised an eyebrow.

Lieutenant Gray took the cue. "Captain Sarbones, I'd like you to meet Corporal Baranovitch, the soldier I told you about who's a ring-tailed ..."

"I get the message, Lieutenant," Captain Sarbones drawled in what Michael categorized as a cultured schoolmaster's voice. "This is the man who returned across enemy lines to rescue his former captain."

"Yes, sir. And that's hardly all, sir. He won a Silver Star at Buna. Got a couple of coconut bunkers ..."

"I said I get the message, lieutenant. Please! There's no need to reiterate the litany."

Captain Sarbones was neither tall, nor short; he was neither fat, nor thin. He was dark-faced, with prominent cheek bones and facial muscles, as if he spent most waking hours with his jaws clenched. Michael thought of his high school classmate, Tommy D'Orsay. D'Orsay was Butte's top distance runner and a state-

187

class miler. Tommy came from a big family who lived up a canyon off the road to Pipestone. All the kids traveled three miles out their mine's access road to the schoolbus route. It was said none of 'em—boys *and* girls—ever walked those miles; they ran. For all the years Michael could remember, there was a D'Orsay boy running the Butte Bulldog's distance races. And every D'Orsay owned facial bones that stood out like mountain ledges.

"So this is Mikhail Baranovitch, the Slavic 'lone wolf'," Captain Sarbones said, striding around his desk to hold out a limp hand to the corporal. Sarbones' palm was moist. The officer retrieved his hand quickly, saying as he did, "Welcome to *my* company, corporal." Then he wheeled and strode to *his* side of the desk. After he'd seated himself, Captain Sarbones said, "Lieutenant Gray, you're dismissed. I'll keep the corporal here a few moments longer."

The lieutenant snapped a salute, did an about face without looking at Michael, and left.

Sarbones leaned back in his canvas chair and stared up at the corporal. Uneasy, Michael slowly came to attention. "Corporal," the captain said, "I believe I told you earlier that you may rest at ease." Michael relaxed.

Still, the captain stared up at him. Finally the officer said, "You do speak, do you not?"

"Yes, sir."

The officer interlaced his fingers across his flat stomach and leaned farther back. "I'd like to clarify something, soldier. I will not tolerate lone wolves in my command. Not even for rescue missions. Is that clear?"

Michael's face turned as impassive as an empty dinner plate. "I guess so, sir."

"Headquarters feels your old company might've been inclined to take matters into their own hands rather than follow orders."

Michael's eyes lifted to a spot on the tent wall a foot over the captain's head. Unable to help himself, he again drew to attention.

"There are, what? a half-dozen holdovers? That kind of attitude can infect an entire company, corporal. And I shan't permit it. Is that understood?"

"It is, sir." Then he asked, "Is that all, sir?"

Sarbones voice dropped a level, turning silky. "And finally, Corporal, I don't know what kind of deal you had with Captain Baldwin, but I want the same kind of deal for myself."

"Deal?" Michael murmured.

Sarbones' eyelids drooped and stayed there. He finally grunted, "I thought you were brave, soldier. Now I find you are merely stupid."

Michael said nothing, rocking almost imperceptibly from his heels to the balls of his feet and back again, his Slavic face as blank as a whitewashed fence. "Get the hell out of here," Captain Sarbones finally said.

Michael's salute was crisp and his about face impeccably smooth. On his way past the sentry, he winked and the private winked back.

Specifications for Landing Craft Infantry was thus: Displacement 387 tons. The craft was almost 160 feet in length and 24 feet wide at the middle. Its "skin" was steel plating, ¼-inch thick. LCIs were built for a top speed of 16 knots and drew five feet when fully loaded. Armament was light—four 20mm guns. The craft was powered by two sets of diesel engines with twin variable-pitch screws, producing up to 1,600 horsepower. Fully fueled, without cargo, the LCI carried 110 tons of fuel oil, 240 tons of lube oil, and 37 tons of fresh water. It had an endurance range of 8,000 miles. There was a crew of three officers and twenty enlisted sailors. Loaded for war, the Landing Craft Infantry carried six Army officers and 182 enlisted troops.

Along with the rest of his companions in Company H, First Battalion, 128th Regimental Combat Team, Michael embarked on LCI 316 at Aitape Harbor early in the morning of September 10, 1944. Seas were heavy, with giant swells. At least half the company was seasick before LCI 316 even cleared the harbor's breakwater. The rest was sick by noon of their first day—except for two: Captain Sarbones and Corporal Baranovitch. However, neither corporal nor captain sought to fraternize.

As each LCI was loaded, the craft pulled out into the ocean staging area, circling to await others of their convoy. With the troops and crew of LCI 316 sick en masse, it was not a happy voyage throughout much of the next three days, though the seas did moderate as they approached their target.

"Word is out that it's Morotai, Boys," a still-debilitated Lieutenant Gray said. That's only halfway to the Philippines, so we'll have to avenge Bataan after putting this one to bed."

A heavy rain fell; all three men crouched against a bulkhead were wearing ponchos. "What's Morotai like, Lieutenant?" Sergeant Rufus Black asked.

"Piece of cake. We're after a couple of all-weather airfields I guess. They're inland, of course, with some swamps and coral ridges between our beachhead and where the air jockeys want to park their toys. But the word is that Morotai is lightly defended, with mostly slant-eye headquarter's troops."

Mikhail Baranovitch laughed.

Lieutenant Gray threw his corporal a quick smile. "Report is the Navy will begin bombardment at nightfall. We're supposed to be going in come morning."

The drumming rain moderated. Michael stood to peer over the bulkhead at the heaving sea. A destroyer sliced through the water off their starboard beam, racing past the lumbering transports, circling their charges like a shepherd dog guarding a band of sheep. Another destroyer bird-dogged the transports abaft, and Michael could see two more slicing through the waves, one on the port side, another at the lead. As the flatbottomed LCI rolled sickeningly, Baranovitch wished he was on one of the destroyers. He knew each carried as many troops as could be stuffed into its hull and would debark them when the LCVPs returned to the fleet after their first sorties to the beach.

Several hours later, Lieutenant Gray paused beside Baranovitch as the corporal cleaned and oiled his weapon. At the time, the B.A.R. lay on a shelter half in twelve pieces. Gray glanced up at a sky filled with stars that were unfamiliar to men raised in the Northern Hemisphere. "But the stars came out and danced about 'ere again I ventured near," quoted the officer.

Michael muttered, "Cremation of Sam McGee."

Gray crouched down and chuckled. "I didn't know you're a Robert Service aficionado."

Michael flashed a brief grin. "I'm not sure what that means, but I like 'Sam McGee'."

"You hear 'em, Bar?"

The larger man nodded while fitting the Browning's barrel to its action housing, tightening screws with his fingers. "Been hearing 'em for awhile. Sounds like distant thunder, don't it?"

Gray stood, then leaped to perch upon a crate. "This war won't last a lot longer, soldier. Can't. What you gonna do then?"

The corporal shook his head. "First thing I'm going to do is drop in on Mama and Papa. Mama says Papa is going downhill. I want to get another good look at 'em before I head off somewhere else."

"And where is else?"

"I dunno. I ..."

"Lieutenant!" It was Captain Sarbones. He'd approached unseen and unheard. Michael looked to see if the man had removed his shoes. He hadn't.

Lieutenant Gray jumped down from his packing crate, saying, "Yes sir."

"Follow me." The order was peremptory. Unfortunately, the two officers were still within earshot when the captain angrily said, "Fraternizing with enlisted men isn't the kind of action I expect from my officers, lieutenant."

Gray's reply was muted, but Michael knew it was a "Yes sir."

"You would do well to follow my example and retire to your quarters. We must appear calm in the lull before approaching action. Men who see nervous officers are almost certain to become nervous themselves."

"Yes sir."

"Now get the hell out of my sight."

Michael heard the lieutenant's heels pop; knew Gray had snapped off a brisk salute. Meanwhile, Michael slipped the B.A.R.'s stock into place and picked up the magazine to wipe off any oil residue. He heard, rather than saw, the captain pause before him. "I hope to hell, soldier, that you know how to put that back together."

Michael's private smile was his answer.

"And I hope to hell you'll know how to use it when we hit the beach."

The corporal fed the magazine into the machine and locked it into place. Then he uncurled his legs and pushed to his feet. After first glancing around, Michael leaned forward until his nose was only inches from Sarbones forehead. "You got any problems with the way I use this weapon tomorrow, sir, why you just come to me then and we'll see if your concern is worth discussing."

Anger flashed in the captain's eyes.

Michael crouched to pick up the shelter half and his oily rag. When he stood again, he said, "Right now, though, I gotta get my beauty sleep. It might make it easier for you going in, Cap, if you did the same."

Chapter 30

Despite what Mikhail Baranovitch told Captain Sarbones, he did not get his beauty sleep the evening before the Morotai invasion. Instead, the corporal stood near the fantail of LCI 316 as it plied the Pacific night. For much of what seemed the brief hours of darkness he stared down at the churn of their wake as it unfurled in a roiling florescent murmur. As his eyes sharpened with the darkness, Michael tried to identify silhouettes of ships around them. He knew, of course, that LCI 316 wasn't the only company-size, beach-dumping transport in the fleet surrounding them; he'd counted at least twenty others before dark. He calculated that number to translate into around four-thousand troops in the first wave—not counting cargo-carrying LCIs. Or that some might be loaded with ammo.

He spotted a couple of big transports, some of which he knew carried over a thousand men and their equipment. From past landings, Michael knew their beaches would also swarm with smaller LCPs, LCVPs, and LVTs. And, though he made out none in the uncertain light, he prayed that somewhere among the outspread armada were a few of the brawny but lovely, lumbering LSTs and LCTs to drop their bow ramps into the sand and disgorge tanks to simplify pillbox reduction. Even at this advanced period in the war, with foot-sloggers carrying flame throwers and bazookas, it was still the tanks that could carry a given day without men having to die for the doing.

Just as the eastern darkness began to fade into amber, Michael spotted an aircraft carrier on the far-off horizon; saw its outline shorten, and knew it was turning into the wind to launch planes. Dive bombers! Wave after wave turned ninety degrees over LCI 316 like angry hornets heading for the rolling thunder of big guns ahead. Japanese fleet, Michael wondered? As the sky turned lighter in the east, Michael saw a seaman standing almost at his shoulder, could make out facial features. Michael gazed seaward again; saw smaller patrol craft taking up sentry duty around the landing fleet, freeing the destroyers to run on up to the landing grounds to engage their guns.

"God, it's gettin' plumb noisy!" the seaman said, and Michael realized the thunder was indeed much nearer.

There was more daylight now than needed eastward, so some spilled west. LCI 316 chugged past several small vessels who made only enough way to keep them on course. A few steamed away from Morotai.

"That's the Tanager," the seaman said. "She's a fast minesweeper. She was at Wakde and Hollandia, too." Michael stared after the retreating vessels. The seaman slapped his hands together and said, "If they're clearing out, it means their work's done. Leastways we won't have to worry about Nip mines on our way in."

"Where'll they go from here?" the corporal asked.

"Probably do outside picket duty until Morotai is secured. Mostly sub patrol, or watch for the Jap fleet's picket ships. Provide early warning, that sort of stuff." Michael pointed. "What's that one? A transport?"

"Yeah. Soon as we get through, they'll pull in closer and start loading the little bugs." (It was in a 'little bug', a Landing Craft Vehicle Personnel—or LCVP— that Michael hit the beach at Aitape.)

The first-wave fleet of LCIs worked around and through other transports rolling hove-to amid the swells. Michael shook his head at the probable seasick agony of the transports' hundreds of homesick G.I.s. The fleet salvos became thunderous as the LCIs motored in. The corporal turned to peer forward, but could make out no capital ships, though there were wisps of smoke rising on the northern horizon.

The seaman followed his gaze. Leaning elbows to the fantail rail, he said, "There's the *West Virginia*. She's a resurreck from Pearl. Bet the Nips never expected her to be out here in this war, throwin' her sixteen-inchers around."

Michael cupped his hands to shade his eyes and was about to ask "Where?" when he spotted puffs of smoke, then heard the accelerated roar of the big guns over the rolling thunder, and finally could make out the battleship's outline.

"Yippee!" yelled the seaman as their ship motored past an oil tanker and an ammunition ship, each with torpedo boats and destroyers circling attendance.

Battleships, cruisers, escort carriers. Michael had never seen so many ships in his life, more than he thought could possibly exist in the entire world! Salvo after salvo after salvo spewed from the capital ships as LCI 316 steamed between the big guys and headed for the island. He'd never before realized that one could actually *see* the huge sixteen-inch shells as they traced their trajectories—at least until they entered the blue-black haze from what the seaman said was their target island.

"What's your name?" Michael shouted, leaning into the seaman's ear.

"Smitty!" the other shouted back. "What's yours?"

"Bar!"

The seaman's eyes flickered to the weapon the dog soldier carried slung over his shoulder. He flashed a mouthful of white, saying, "Well, we're inside the fifteen arc. Battlewagons can lay off fifteen, sixteen miles—outside the range of anything the Nips have for coast guns, and hammer 'em."

"What about carriers?"

Fleet carriers will stay back. The *Franklin* back there was closer than I expected, but I guess they're not catching much from Nipponese air. Besides, they'll be protected by their own air cover, and by the Jeeps."

"Jeeps?"

"Escort carriers. There's one over there. If the Nips do come up, the escorts and the battlewagons will probably siphon off any Zeros before they get out to her."

Michael saw Captain Sarbones come on deck, saw the officer spot him, saw the officer turn toward the bow.

"There's a cruiser up ahead. It's a 'heavy'. That means were comin' on up to ten miles, but it looks like we're not going to see Morotai, no matter how close we get."

The sun was beating down out of a clear sky, but Michael could see the sailor knew what he was talking about: despite a steady breeze, the island was shrouded in an immense plume of smoke and dust. The sea had settled considerably during the night, but their landing craft was still buffeted by waves and chop kicked up by the steady roll of capital ships as they fired broadsides at the distant beaches, and by the constant wash of ships patrolling back and forth before Morotai's landing grounds.

"Five miles!" Smitty shouted as LCI 316 moved past a destroyer that was firing its four- and five-inch guns as fast as they could reload.

LCI 316 heeled to port and Smitty said, "Well, soldier, I gotta get on my own gun mount." He held out his hand. "Wish you luck. Send me a Nip flag if you get an extra." Then he was gone.

It looked to Michael as though all the LCIs were staging to the left, outside of what could be a harbor. He glanced again at the island. If anything, it was more shrouded in smoke and dust and clouds and stink. A flight of divebombers swept overhead and Michael followed them until they disappeared into the huge plume towering up from Morotai.

"Get any sleep?" It was Lieutenant Gray.

"All I needed."

Amusement glittered in the officer's eyes. "We're supposed to gather at the ramps in fifteen minutes. We've got the starboard side ramp. That's the right side, to you landlubbers."

Michael nodded.

"Here's the deal," the lieutenant continued. "I want you with Draeger's squad. He hasn't been in combat before, but I've talked to him about it and he's tickled pink to have you and your B.A.R. I'm sure he'll listen up when you've got something to say. If there's any problems, let me know and I'll fix it."

"There'll be no problems, Lieutenant."

"We're after an airfield—we're *always* after an airfield. Our sector is Beach Red. It's on the left side of the beachhead and it's got a hundred yards of sand, a low seawall, and a jungle swamp behind it. Our job is to secure the beach and keep the Nips from working us over from the jungle. Our beach is supposed to be the staging area for supply buildup. That's why we've got a couple more machine gun crews and four more B.A.R. men in the first wave—to secure fast and hard."

The lieutenant laid a hand on Michael's stripes. "I want you to lead the first wave, Bar. I want you to be off and sprinting for the seawall before the ramp even hits the sand. Then I ..."

"Or water." Michael grinned.

"Or water. But I want your covering fire while the rest of us are getting up to you. Okay?"

Michael nodded.

"There'll be two more B.A.R. teams right behind you. I've made Smith—the dark one—your mule."

Michael shook his head. I'll pack my own bandolier, lieutenant. You can send Smith with some backup bandoliers if you want. But I don't need to be worrying about somebody else on my way across that beach."

Lieutenant Gray gripped Michael on his muscle stripes again and said, "The captain has made it plain that he wants it by the book, big guy. That means you have to have a mule to carry your magazines."

Michael shrugged.

Just then, came a soft flutter and a thump. Both men wheeled—and were flung belly-first against the fantail rail as a huge fountain of water rose from a heaving ocean. Another thump came from farther out to the starboard side, and another waterspout. Somebody yelled, "My God! Look at 283!" and Michael gripped the rail with all his strength as another flutter came just behind his fantail perch, heaving up the 316's stern until Michael heard the prop whir as it came out of the water. Then he felt their ship heel over, peeling to port. Their 283 sister LCI looked dead in the water; men were plunging overboard. He saw another LCI hit—a huge red flame as it seemed to pause in the water, then explode.

Michael whirled. The lieutenant was gone. He whirled again as another waterspout rose fifty yards behind the fantail.

Then he whirled back, trying to pinpoint where the withering artillery fire was coming from. But they were entering the smoke and dust plume and he could see little more. He realized, however, that the Navy's capital ships were no longer firing, and knew they must've stopped when the LCIs headed in.

Shit, this might not be any fun!" Then he was startled to realize it was his own voice he'd heard.

LCI 316 heeled farther left in the smoke, probably north by west, right into the worst of the smoke and haze. As the 316 did so, they pulled away from the main assault wave. Michael checked the massed assault fleet for a last time, saw another LCI hit, then the plume enveloped them.

He shuffled forward, heading for the starboard bow. As he passed the wheelhouse, he heard the coxswain shout, "If we keep on this bearing, captain, I'm not sure of the target beach in all this smoke!" Then Michael spotted Lieutenant Gray and shoved through the milling throng of hesitant soldiers.

"Here he is, lieutenant," Sergeant Draeger called across the helmets of his squad. The sergeant clapped Michael on his back and said, "Come on big guy. We're up front."

Michael slipped his helmet on as the 316 picked up speed. The haze began lifting. "Where's Smith?" he murmured.

As if by magic, Private Smith materialized at his side. Smith was strung with a bandolier of B.A.R. clips. Michael grasped the bandolier and lifted it over Smith's head. "I'll take this one. You go round up a couple more for yourself."

"Two!" Smith cried. Hell, Bar, they weigh twenty pounds each. You want me to carry forty pounds AND my combat pack?"

Michael grinned. Smith was almost as big as he was. He slipped the B.A.R. from his shoulder and handed it to the other. "Try that on for size, private. It weighs twenty pounds, too. Forty pounds for you, forty for me, and we'll make a war out of this yet."

Smith whirled away in search of two more bandoliers of 30-caliber B.A.R. box magazines.

"J-e-e-e-sus!"

Michael looked where the lieutenant pointed. There was a thin strip of beach, with a wider band of jungle directly ahead. Towering over both was honeycombed cliffs that appeared several hundred feet high. Then, two waterspouts erupted on their right, and the 316 slewed left. He heard a whump and a clang from the stern and when he looked, a giant waterspout towered behind the 316.

"They're on us now!" Lieutenant Gray shouted.

Michael stared up at the oncoming cliffs. And when he squinted just right, he saw a couple of tiny figures run across the front of a cave mouth.

Their LCI heeled right, but Michael never knew if they'd taken a near miss off port bow or whether the roll came from evasive action. A waterspout dead ahead! He eyed the cliff again. Lieutenant Gray stood at his side. "Looks like a piece of cake," the corporal murmured.

Gray nodded. Another waterspout off to their right. "The new captain is lucky to have such an easy baptism," Michael added.

"The new captain isn't going ashore with us," Lieutenant Gray said as yet another waterspout geysered up farther out. Gray's smile was thin. "He'll stay aboard to oversee the beach fighting while hurrying our supply buildup from the convoy."

"But we dasn't show any initiative on our own," Michael said.

"Exactly."

The cliffs loomed nearer, as if those caves rushed at them, instead of the other way around. Michael could no longer see the beach or the jungle beyond, hidden now behind the starboard bow ramp. "Maybe we'd ought to stay on board, too, in order to make sure we follow directions without screwing up," the corporal murmured.

Lieutenant Gray clapped him on the shoulder and pushed away, Sergeant Draeger took his place and the rest of Draeger's squad crowded forward. LCI 316 slewed left and a waterspout towered up, drenching them. Smith-the-Dark wormed his way to stand alongside Michael. He wore a faint smile, along with two bandoliers of .30 caliber B.A.R. clips, as well as a combat pack and a slung M-1 Garand.

Then Michael saw no more as he tucked his nose to the buttons on his khaki blouse. He heard, though—the muffled explosion dead ahead, and the clinking and clanging of shrapnel and perhaps small arms fire rattling against the bow ramp. Then, too, there was the drenching cascades of incessant, near-miss waterspouts.

He also felt the grind of LCI 316's flat bow hull as it rode up on the ocean floor, and heard the whisper of the bow ramp as it slipped at freefall into the surf.

And with a full-throated cry, Mikhail Baranovitch charged down the ramp as it thudded to a stop in four feet of Pacific Ocean surf. The big man plunged on, splashing through the surf exactly as he twice splashed across the Driniumor, shouting "YANKEE DOODLE WENT TO TOWN RIDING ON A DONKEY!"

And all the way through the surf and across that beach he tasted bile, heard the din of exploding shells, saw terror in the steady rattle of Nambu fire from the distant line of green, smelled the acrid smoke of battle, and felt death hovering around him....

Chapter 31

Straining with everything he had, Mikhail Baranovitch surged from the surf onto wet sand. The crackle of small arms fire came from the jungle ahead and, while still running all out, Michael sprayed the line of dark green. He was on dry sand now, still singing *Yankee Doodle* at the top of his lungs and sprinting madly for the seawall and the shelter it afforded.

He heard a cry from behind, heard the chatter of a Nambu ahead. Then his B.A.R. went dry and he put his feet on full automatic and turned his mind to shoving a fresh magazine into place. He hit the seawall, fell behind it, squirmed a few feet left, then popped up to spray the jungle on his right front. Smith-the-Dark flopped beside Michael as the corporal dropped to prop his back against the bank. He took the box mag Smith offered, then crawled a few feet further left to pop up and spray the left jungle. Blood dripped from Smith's fingers as the private handed him yet another clip saying, "Sarge went down."

Michael glanced at the beach and saw the sergeant wasn't the only one down. "What about you?"

"A scratch. Look!" Blood dripped from the man's fingers as he held them up and wriggled them.

Again Michael popped up and sprayed the forward jungle. The Jap machine gun was on him almost before he dropped behind his shelter. He grinned at Smith and pointed with his chin. "Long as they're after us," he said, "they won't be after them."

Other soldiers, some wounded, all scared, were flopping behind the seawall. Other waves were coming on from LCI 316. Michael crawled six feet right to pop up and spray the general location of the Nambu.

Michael pointed at Smith's bloody hand when the private handed him another clip. "That your pitching arm?"

"Huh?"

"How are you with grenades with your left hand?"

Smith looked stupidly down at his bloody fingers. "Maybe I can throw okay," he muttered, "I don't know."

"Maybe you can shit little green apples, too. But maybe you can't. You feed me your grenades."

Michael unhooked two of his grenades while staring up and down the ragged line of soldiers huddled against the seawall. "YOU BASTARDS GONNA KEEP

THEM GRENADES TO TAKE HOME FOR YOUR KIDS TO PLAY WITH? he shouted. "NOW'S THE TIME TO USE THE DAMNED THINGS!" With that, he pulled the pin on both his grenades, leaped up and sprinted along the headwall, throwing his best pitches.

The Nambu opened up, then went silent as Michael's first grenade exploded. He had two more out, pins pulled, and flung into the foreboding jungle when other men began following his lead. A ragged line of explosions cut like slashes into the jungle.

When Michael threw himself prone, there was Smith-the-Dark handing him first one grenade, then another. "Goddamn it," Michael said, "I planned to work my way back to you."

"Then you better give better instructions, Corporal"

Suddenly there was a roar at the beach and all seawall heads turned. Half the bow of LCI 316 was gone! The explosion occurred as the landing craft had backed only a few feet from shore. Sailors were leaping over the side. Almost absently, Michael pulled the pins on two new grenades, then leaped up to fling them. Smith handed him his last two and both men sprinted along the headwall to where the corporal had left his B.A.R.

Lieutenant Gray wormed his way to Michael's position. "Looks like you're squad leader, big guy. Draeger took one in the head." When Michael nodded, the lieutenant added, "They had him on the boat headed out when it took the hit." Just then another explosion struck the 316 and the men watched it heel over and half-submerge, stuck on the bottom.

"You reckon our captain will be running this company from out to sea?" the corporal murmured.

"They'll be turning those big guns on us next," Lieutenant Gray said. "We've got to get into the jungle."

Michael nodded. "What's your plan, sir?"

"I'll gather groups of effectives at each end—say a couple of hundred yards down, both ways. Corcoran will handle the right. I'll take the left. I'll want you here, Bar, in the middle, stirring up enough hell they won't guess we're coming at 'em from the ends."

"Speak of the devil," Michael murmured, waving along the seawall. Captain Sarbones crawled toward them.

"What, may I ask, are we doing hiding behind this embankment?" Sarbones said without preamble.

"Right, sir," Gray said. "We're about to do a flanking action from each end. Corporal Baranovitch will serve as our decoy."

Roland Cheek

"I'm countermanding that," Captain Sarbones said. "We'll hit them with everything we have right here in the middle."

"That's where they'll expect it, sir."

"We'll be going into a machine gun," Michael murmured.

"Are you afraid, as well as stupid, corporal?" Sarbones said.Smith-the-Dark rolled over to stare, eyes wide, up at the captain.

Michael leaped up to fire a long burst back and forth into the jungle. A Nambu opened up milliseconds after Michael dropped back to his knees. "No, sir. Alive. That's what I am."

"Our plan, sir, is to mount a two-pronged ..."

My plan, lieutenant, is to mount a combined assault from this point. I suggest you organize it and get it underway, or I'll replace you with another platoon commander."

Michael said, "There's no other officers left, captain.

Sarbones' eyes never left Michael's face, but he said, "Lieutenant, I gave you an order!"

"Yes sir!"

As the lieutenant crawled away, Captain Sarbones murmured, "Would I be wrong in suggesting that we're on a collision course, corporal?"

Michael thought about the captain's question for several seconds, then wagged his head. "Not from my point of view, we're not."

The captain glared from beneath beetled black brows, his facial muscles ticcing. Considering that the officer had recently escaped a sinking landing craft, then fled across an open beach under hostile fire, Michael thought he seemed remarkably untouched. The man's suntans even held a semblance of a crease and appeared little soiled. The corporal's eyes found their way to the captain's glare. His bland Slavic face turned to one of amusement. He said, "But whether we collide or not, you plan to put me in my place, right?"

Captain Sarbones began crawling left, along the seawall. He paused and called back, "Tell Lieutenant Gray that I'm sending everyone from the left to join his assault."

Michael took a deep breath. "And you'll monitor the assault from the left point. Is that right, sir?"

Sarbones crawled away.

The assault was scheduled to jump over the seawall at 1200 hours. But at 1150 hours, Japanese artillery hidden in honeycombed cliffs took note of the pitiful buildup going on beneath them and began ranging on the invaders' huddled ranks. First, it was the soft sigh, then the flutter, like dove wings at a water hole. Then the earth and sand and guts of the beach's dead and dying churned and rained down

200

upon the pitiful remnants of seawall huddlers—perhaps platoon-size from the two hundred original men of Company H; fifty men, total. "And one of them had to be that chickenshit captain," Michael muttered.

Again the sigh and flutter—closer this time! Michael didn't even bother to duck as he and Smith-the-Dark hurried along the seawall, to the right, in the direction Lieutenant Gray sent them—away from Captain Sarbones command post on the left.

"I want a covering fire across our front, Bar," Gray had said. "Pour it on when I wave, and don't stop until we hit the jungle.

It was awful: the wave; the leap up and over the seawall. The headlong dash for the jungle. The Nambu. The crackle of Jap small arms. Grenade eruptions. Rebel yells and Manhattan yells and even one Chiricahua yell. Above it all, the steady hammer of his B.A.R. Then his squad and his platoon and what was left of his company was into the jungle. And Mikhail Baranovitch and Smith-the-Dark sprinted forward, too.

All left of Company H was little more than an extended squad. Lieutenant Gray was in forward command, with Corporal Baranovitch as ranking noncom. Ted Kotynski had survived the dash into the fringe of jungle below the cliffs, as did the Hargesheimer portion of Rogers and Hammerstein. The Rogett part of the team was lying wounded in Captain Sarbones command post—behind the beach seawall. Enemy artillery still ranged from the cliffs above their heads, but the guns either could not depress sufficiently to fire down upon them in their jungle sanctuary, or the Japanese staff dismissed the remnants of Company H as too insignificant to waste artillery rounds on. Instead, they kept up a steady barrage on invasion barges farther out in the bay.

"Hell, they dropped us in the wrong place," the lieutenant said upon his return from company command.

"Sarbones took us off course," the corporal said. "I heard him giving orders to the 316's pilot."

Lieutenant Gray shook his head. "An army captain can't give orders to a naval officer in command of his own vessel."

Michael chuckled. "He's a hard man to refuse."

"He's an asshole."

"That from you, sir, is bitter criticism."

"When I was back there, Regimental Command was screaming on the radio that we're in the middle of the Nips strongest defenses."

"Maybe we ought to pull another Driniumor," the corporal murmured.

"The problem is, our beach—Beach Red—is only now being occupied with our backup team. And the way I get it, it's far from secured. That means if we manage to break through on our right, we still might not be able to hook up with any of our own guys."

Both men had their helmets together, conversing in whispers. "The way I get it is that Division Command may want to reinforce us for a cliff assault—the Jap guns up there are killing re-supply."

"Hell, lieutenant, they'd have to send in a battalion. And how can a battalion get here when the enemy commands the bay?"

Gray shook his head. "The Navy needs to give that cliff another working over, but for some reason—maybe they're low on the big stuff—it ain't gonna happen."

"That's bullshit about taking that cliff. You know that, sir."

"Oh hell! I know that. You know that. The only one who doesn't know that is our own goddamned captain. For some inexplicable reason he ..."

Both men cocked their ears. "Oh shit!" Lieutenant Gray groaned at the rising clamor of screaming and shouting in the jungle before them.

"What is it?" Smith-the-Dark asked.

"Visitors," Bar said. "We're about to get visitors." When Smith-the-Dark still looked confused, Mikhail Baranovitch shouted up and down the line, "Banzai! Every mother's son of you guys better unlimber and get ready."

"We can't hold here, Bar," the lieutenant muttered. We need a better field of fire."

"And to get dug in," Baranovitch muttered.

"Sarbones wouldn't stand for it if he knew we were going to fall back. So we won't tell him."

"Fall back?" the corporal said.

"The seawall. It's our only defendable position.""That won't give us much time to get ready, even if we fall back now."

"But at least all of us will be there. Maybe I can get our remaining machine gun set up back there first. And we've got two B.A.R.s now—your's and Boudoin's."

"Put us on the perimeters, the MG in the middle."

Lieutenant Gray nodded. "You take the right. I'll get the left."

Michael caught the lieutenant as he started to move away. "You get the right. I'll get the left. It's the left that Sarbones will jerk around, and I'll make sure it won't happen to my side."

Gray clapped him on the shoulder and ran to the right.

They came within the hour, hundreds of them, first slipping through the jungle; then when they received fire, crashing forward in an all-out assault. At Michael's first B.A.R. burst, the men of his wing fired clips, then fled for the seawall. Michael stayed to fire one more burst, then waving Smith-the-Dark ahead of him, pell-melled to their defense line.

Captain Sarbones met him there. "What in the hell are you men doing here?"

Michael saluted with military precision. "Fighting Japs, sir. That's what they're paying me to do, sir. What about you, sir?"

"Here they come!" Private Williams shouted from down the seawall. The center-mounted machine gun opened up from behind its sandbags and Michael heard Boudoin's B.A.R. over the din of general fire.

"Beggin' your pardon, sir," Michael said as he whirled to lay down a magazine of 30-calibers on the screaming line of mustard-clad Nips who were waving their rifles or machetes or, in one case, a Samurai broadsword."

Smith-the-Dark had his M-1 over the top of the bank, pouring steady, fast-as-his-finger-could-pull-fire into the oncoming horde. Without looking up, firing his Garand one-handed, he handed a magazine up to Michael. When the corporal ejected the old mag and took the new one from his bandolier jockey, he glanced at Sarbones. The captain crouched with his back to the seawall, eyes closed and both hands over his ears.

The banzai charge faltered only a dozen feet from Company H's line, then melted back into the jungle. Lieutenant Gray materialized seconds later. "What do you think, Bar?"

Captain Sarbones picked himself up. "I'm in charge here, Lieutenant."

"I dunno," Michael said, ignoring the captain. "You think they'll be back?"

"Maybe they got what they want by throwing us out of the jungle. Maybe we'll pose no threat to the cliff. What do you think?"

"Maybe."

"Lieutenant, will I have to put you on report?" When Michael smiled at the lieutenant and the lieutenant smiled back, Captain Sarbones snarled, "*I'm* the one asking questions, and the first one I'll ask is who authorized this retreat?"

"Retreat, captain?" Lieutenant Gray said. "There was no retreat. We merely maneuvered for better defensive positions."

"Lieutenant, for your information, Division Command is vitally interested in that strip of jungle you and your men just vacated. I told them we would hold it until they could get reinforcements in here—probably by 800 hours tomorrow. Since you unilaterally made a command decision not to even *try* to hold that ground, you can have the pleasure of leading an assault to retake what has now been designated 'Sector Pleasant'. Is that clear?"

"Perfectly, sir," Lieutenant Gray said. "Have you told them the enemy just attacked in battalion strength?"

"Are you refusing an order, lieutenant?"

"Not at all, Sir. But do they know Company H is now down to twenty-three effectives?"

The captain waved a casual hand. "One American fighting man is worth dozens of those from inferior races."

Lieutenant Gray turned to stare up at the foreboding cliffs. "You do know, Sir that, if you follow through with this order, you're sending the remainder of your company to their death."

"Cannon to the right of them," Michael murmured. "Cannon to the left of them. Into the jaws of Death rode the six hundred."

Captain Sarbones glared at the corporal. "Lieutenant, this man has no business at a command conference. Send him to his duty station immediately."

Lieutenant Gray spread his hands. "This *is* his duty station, captain. I ordered him to take over defense of this sector just as the banzai began."

Captain Sarbones drew himself up. "Very well," he said, "you leave me no choice. Corporal, consider yourself under detention. You will surrender your weapon to Private Smith, and accompany me to my Command Post. Lieutenant Gray, you will expedite your orders."

Mikhail Baranovitch was placed under the arrest of two sailors from the destroyed LCI 316—one of whom was Smitty, the swabby Michael had visited with just before the invasion began. The two sailors had found their way across the beach and were commandeered by Captain Sarbones to augment his headquarters staff.

Smitty wanted to talk, but Michael brushed him off to stare down the seawall, where his lieutenant prepared for a foredoomed assault.

Lieutenant Stanford Gray led the attack over the seawall at 1700 hours on September 15, 1944. He was one of only two casualties, killed within ten feet of his futile one-man charge. Smith-the-Dark made a brave attempt to rescue Lieutenant Gray's shattered body. But he, too, was felled by a barrage of Nambu bullets from two directions. No other men of Company H even so much as raised their heads above the sand embankment.

The first LCVP nosed into an approach to Sector Pleasant at 0800 hours on September 16, as planned. The Japanese artillery was ready, turning the runup of small landing craft into one of brutal carnage. If a craft succeeded in making it to the beach to drop its bow ramp, the narrow stretch of sand turned into a killing ground for each three dozen soldiers suddenly disgorged into the mouth of Hell.

The radio constantly crackled in Captain Sarbones Command Post, demanding to know where Company H was; why the company produced no covering fire.

Mikhail Baranovitch, confined to the post, heard the radio exchanges, until he could stand it no longer. Then he shrugged off his naval captors and sprinted out along the seawall to the B.A.R. Smith-the-Dark had dropped.

"ALL RIGHT, YOU SONSABITCHES!" he shouted to the beaten men crouched at the seawall. "WE'RE GONNA RETURN THEIR FIRE! AT THE COUNT OF THREE! ONE! TWO!" His "THREE!" was lost as the battered bastards of Company H rose to a man to pour fire into the jungle.

Michael ejected a clip, fumbled for another, then saw Smitty at his side, firing an M-1. He grabbed the swabby's blouse and pulled him down, shouting, "Goddammit man, don't they teach you nothing at Annapolis? You're not supposed to stay up all the time!"

Smitty grinned as Michael roared again down the line. "ONCE AGAIN! GO!" After that, the fire of the men of Company H became more sporadic as each man loaded and leaped up to fire when ready.

Captain Sarbones wormed his way up to Michael. He smiled at the corporal, but Michael could see the smile failed to reach the man's eyes, and barely even reached his nose. "That was good work, corporal. Now, if you can get these men moving forward ..."

Michael popped up to finish off a magazine. When he dropped below the seawall, he said, "Can't. I'm on detention." He pointed to Smitty, as the swabby fired an M-1 clip. "See, here's my jailor."

"Corporal, you're off detention. As of now. You're the senior noncom in Company H and I'm ordering you to get these men moving over this seawall. Do it now!"

Michael leaned his B.A.R. against the embankment, then murmured in a deceptively soft voice. "Tell you what, Captain Sarbones, why don't you lead us? If you'll be out front like a real officer would, I'll follow you through to the devil's workplace myself."

"It's you I'm ordering to lead this attack while I coordinate the incoming reinforcements!"

"But if you won't lead it, then I'm washing my hands of you."

"Are you refusing to follow orders? Are you demonstrating cowardice in the face of the enemy? Are you ..."

"Careful now, captain."

"I'll see you court martialed. I'll see you—you're a ... a yellow coward!"

Mikhail Baranovitch slowly came to his feet. Grasped in one hand was the front of Captain Sarbones shirt. His fist began from somewhere deep in New Guinea; in the Butte Bulldogs' locker room; in the home where he was born. The fist exploded through the feeble waving arms of Captain Sarbones and found a home against nose and teeth and cheekbone—and it was a *big* fist!

It might have been lucky for Michael that Smitty and Ted Kotynski and the wounded Chris Mellman tackled him to the sand when he went for the unconscious Sarbones again—just as a Nambu swept its angry wasp sting over his head. But the big corporal did succeed in ripping the twin captain's bars from the epaulets of the bloody Sarbones' starched shirt. And when he stood to heave the silver bars far out into the sand, the Nambu had passed on.

Mikhail Baranovitch stared up and down the seawall line, then roared, "WHAT THE HELL DO YOU SONSABITCHES THINK YOU'RE DOING? RETURN THEIR GODDAMNED FIRE!"

Then he turned and walked out onto the sand, and into the Pacific Ocean....

Chapter 32

After nine straight hours, Mikhail Baranovitch's story of Morotai and the circumstances leading up to his being charged with refusal to obey a direct order, cowardice in the face of the enemy, and striking a superior officer was complete. From ten-thirty in the morning until seven-thirty in the evening the patient had stared at and through the freckled, balding psychiatrist while speaking softly and steadily about his most terrifying war experience.

For his part, Dr. Bryce Henderson silently listened, occasionally scribbling on a notepad. But even while scribbling, the doctor usually stared in fascination at the younger man, occasionally shaking his head in frank sympathy.

After finishing at last, Michael continued to sit as he had throughout, elbows on his chair's armrests, hands clenched in his lap, shoulders slumped, head seemingly held up with some indefinable force of will. A giant tear welled and slid through the stubble of his right cheek.

"Where's Barney?" the doctor murmured.

"I don't know."

"Is it that you don't know because you no longer need him?"

"I don't know."

Dr. Henderson picked up his pencil, tapped the eraser on the notepad in front of him, dropped the pencil, and said, "Are you hungry?"

"No."

"Are you nauseous?"

"Maybe a little."

"Michael, this is important—could you repeat this story again?"

The younger man dabbed at his eyes with a knuckle, then straightened, lifting his head higher. "I think so."

Dr. Henderson pushed his chair back. "I have to piss; how about you?"

"I'm okay."

When Dr. Henderson returned, Mikhail Baranovitch was still sitting as he'd left him. "Come along, son. Let's go get something to eat."

Michael twisted to stare up at the doctor's office clock. "The cafeteria is closed."

The pudgy man's eyes twinkled. "Well, I don't know about you, but I want a root beer float and a cheeseburger with fries. Want to come along?"

"Where?"

"There's a drive-in out on North Stephens, a couple of miles from here."

"I can't. I can't leave the hospital without Colonel Corwin's okay."

Dr. Henderson chuckled. "I believe you can if you're accompanied by me. I *know* you can if he never finds out about it."

They passed by the night desk, where Dr. Henderson told Carla that he and Michael would stroll about the grounds. Once outside, it was simple; they walked around to the rear parking lot, climbed into Dr. Henderson's new Jeep and headed north, to the Garden Valley Road.

"They call it a 'CJ'," the doctor said. "A Willy's-Overland Civilian Jeep."

Michael said, "I was in a Ford Jeep once. At Saidor. Did you know Ford made Jeeps."

"Absolutely. I've driven several of them; some in India, one in Burma, a couple stateside." Henderson turned his vehicle east on Garden Valley, motored up and over the bridge crossing the new Interstate Highway. Then waited for a green light before turning left on North Stephens.

"Two root beer floats," Dr. Henderson said to the carhop, "and," looking appraisingly at his passenger, "three cheeseburger deluxes with fries."

After the carhop left, the doctor said, "You were lucky to be picked up, with Japanese artillery commanding the bay."

Michael nodded. "I didn't think ..." His eyes turned vacant as he stared through the windshield. Then he tried again. "There was a bunch of LCVPs buzzing around—so many of 'em the Japs couldn't get 'em all. Rescue boats, too, I guess. One of 'em picked me up on the way back out, I guess. I don't know."

"What happened at Morotai? How long before they secured the island?"

Michael shook his head.

"What about Captain Sarbones?"

"I don't know." Then the big man added, "Don't care, neither."

The men sat in silence until the carhop brought their order and affixed the aluminum tray to the driver's side window. Dr. Henderson paid and, after they began eating, said, "What about the court-martial, Michael?"

Mikhail Baranovitch sighed. "It didn't happen right away. I was out of it for a long time because of the Morotai wounds. Then after it was clear that I would pull through, there was Okinawa and Iwo Jima, and I guess they just never had time to work it in. By then, Captain Baldwin must've been pulling strings because this major—a guy named Thomason—came to see me at Espiritu Santo and said he'd been assigned my defense."

Michael paused to drink. "This float is *good!*

"And was the court-martial held at Espiritu Santo?"

"No. It was supposed to come off in San Francisco. By then, Major Thomason had researched my war record, and what happened to Company H at Morotai.

He'd lined up Kotynski and that seaman, Smithson—the ones who stopped me from killing the sonofabitch—to testify. I guess Captain Baldwin's senator father-in-law took an interest in the case, too. And when next I seen Major Thomason, he said the Military Tribunal took one look at my record, then did a voice vote before presentation, and shoved the whole thing under the table."

"And what's your opinion of that, son?"

Michael murmured. "I don't have an opinion on that, sir. By then, I was past caring what happened—ever."

Dr. Henderson was a long time in responding. When he did, it was thus: "Michael, is this a state of mind that you've just reached—understanding that you were past caring? Or is it a state of mind in which you're still engaged?"

The younger man was silent throughout the remainder of their meal. The carhop had taken their serving tray and Dr. Henderson drove onto North Stephens before he replied: "I guess I'll have to think on that one for a while, Dr. Henderson. Do I still not care? Is that what you asked? If so, I imagine you want an honest answer. Well, whether I care or not might hinge on whether I'll ever be free again. Is that fair?"

The doctor pulled into the parking lot and shut off the Jeep's engine before *he* replied. "Yes, Michael. I would say that's fair. But I'll also say you made a giant stride today toward freedom. Now if you can just hold on to it, you'll have me in your corner."

Mikhail Baranovitch nodded into the darkened Jeep's interior. He asked, "Who else do I need?"

Dr. Henderson opened his door and stepped onto the parking lot pavement. "Colonel Y. Herbert Corwin is one. If I sign a release order, he must also countersign it."

Over the next few weeks, Major Henderson grilled Mikhail Baranovitch about his war experiences: Buna, Endaiadere, Giropa Point, Salamaua, Saidor, Aitape, Nyaparake, Yakamul, Driniumor. Henderson spared nothing. Neither did the man he grilled hold anything back. Finally they talked again of Morotai, with the doctor taking copious notes. At last, during the fourth week after Michael's Morotai breakthrough, Dr. Henderson threw down his pencil and said, "Michael, I believe your progress is superb. From all reports you are getting along splendidly. Terwilliger tells me you're in top physical form. Daniel says you're reading voraciously. Everyone tells me you are courteous and engaging with others, sometimes even bantering small talk with them."

The patient seemed to swell with pleasure.

The psychiatrist appeared to ponder. "If you were to win your release, what would you do?"

Michael moved up to perch on the edge of his chair. "Go to Montana. Find a job. Spend as much time as possible outdoors."

"What kind of job would you seek?"

Michael's eyes wandered to the window. "I don't know. I never finished high school, so I don't have much of an education. But I do know how to work. Maybe they need somebody loading lumber in boxcars, or unloading heavy freight trucks. Maybe I could get on with some Forest Service trail crew, so I could be outdoors all the time." The younger man's eyes clenched, then popped open to engulf Bryce Henderson. "I don't know, Doctor, but I'll find something. I'll make good, I swear. Just give me the chance."

Dr. Henderson smiled. "I'll see what I can do." Then he stood and shook the big man's hand as he dismissed him.

That's why it came as a blow to both Dr. Bryce Henderson and Mikhail Baranovitch when Colonel Y. Herbert Corwin chose not to countersign Michael's release form. Instead, the commandant recommended that the patients privileges be extended to permit him to work around the grounds.

"You understand, Major," Colonel Corwin said, "this is merely a procedural check—allowing Baranovitch to prove himself beyond all doubt before we release him."

"Do you understand, Colonel," Henderson spluttered, "that it'll be easier for Mikhail Baranovitch to find employment in the summer, than if you release him during the winter."

Colonel Corwin waved dismissively, "Then perhaps we'll hold him until *next* summer, Major. Maybe you have confidence in Mikhail's recovery, but all I want is to be equally as sure."

"There's nothing I can do, Michael," Dr. Henderson told the crestfallen patient. "Colonel Corwin is the ultimate authority at this institution. And he insists on further proof of your recovery. That proof, in his mind, can only come if you have the freedom of the grounds without abusing that privilege."

Mikhail Baranovitch grew more rigid as Dr. Henderson explained Colonel Corwin's reservations. Finally the patient said, "Does he suggest I join Gordon Smith's grounds crew?"

Henderson nodded. "That's exactly what he suggests, Michael. Do you wish me to talk to Gordon?"

"So he wants me for slave labor?"

Dr. Henderson's eyes widened. "Michael! You must not think that way! Colonel Corwin is sincere in believing we should do a final check before your release."

The patient's face was hard—stretched tight over cheekbones and jaw line. He spat, "Do you agree with him? I don't!"

"This is not a question of agreement or disagreement; it's a question of following orders."

Michael's laugh was harsh. "But you said I'm no longer in the army. So I'm no longer required to follow orders."

Dr. Henderson jumped to his feet and rushed over to slam his office door. When he returned, it was to stand at his desk and eye his patient. "Michael, you're heading down the wrong path." He took a deep breath. "While it's true you're no longer in the army and need follow no spit and polish, or attend close-order drills, it's equally true that you were *committed* to this institution by military order until the institution releases you as restored. While it's true that you no longer need salute and say 'yes sir' and 'no sir', there are still rules you must obey and regulations you must follow. What we're looking at with Colonel Corwin's demand is merely a formality, perhaps a month or two or three, at most. Comparing what you have to lose by being obstinate with what you have to gain through being a little more patient is so ludicrous as to be absurd."

The patient pushed wearily to his feet. "That makes me out to be stupid if I refuse to work as slave labor—right?"

Dr. Henderson sighed. "Can't you look at it as the opportunity to get outside; the single thing you've been after for months."

"You can tell Corwin to shove it up his ass." The big man strode to the door.

As he turned the knob, Henderson said, "All right, Michael. I'll tell Corwin you refused the groundskeeping duty. But you still have freedom to walk the grounds at your discretion."

Mikhail Baranovitch slammed the door on his way out.

Chapter 33

But Mikhail Baranovitch did *not* have the freedom to walk the Roseburg Veteran's Hospital grounds alone.

"Wait a minute, Dr. Henderson," Colonel Y. Herbert Corwin said, holding up a hand. "Let's back up—Mikhail Baranovitch *refused* our offer to let him join Gordon Smith's grounds crew? And he actually *told* you we were doing it because we wanted him for *slave* labor?"

"Goddammit, Colonel, you're taking this out of context," Bryce Henderson said. "The only reason I'm filling you in is because Michael himself told a half-dozen other patients, and I was afraid word would get back to you through the rumor mill."

"Well, I for one don't see how I'm taking it out of context if Baranovitch is spreading the rumor himself!"

Henderson threw up his hands. "He's distraught because he anticipated release. I tried to tell him ..."

"Why, pray tell, did the man anticipate release? We want to see him cured before releasing him. And when I hear tales such as these being bandied around, it seems clear to me that he's hardly a rational patient ready to fit into society."

Bryce Henderson's face reddened. "I considered him cured, and I believe I can demonstrate improvement through even a cursory glance at his file."

"Improvement, yes, Doctor," Colonel Corwin said, standing at his desk. "But cured?"

"I'll stake my reputation on it!" Henderson flared back.

Colonel Corwin shook his head and smiled. "Major, you are free to stake your reputation on anything you wish. But please! Leave my reputation and the reputation of this hospital unsullied. Consider this an order—Mikhail Baranovitch is not to be released until *I'm* satisfied he can readily meld into society."

The portly, balding, freckled subordinate clicked his sandal heels together, saluted smartly, did an abrupt about face with his brightly colored Hawaiian shirt flaring behind, and marched to the colonel's office door. Before he reached it, the colonel added, "And Bryce, I'm also revoking Mr. Baranovitch's freedom to walk the grounds unescorted."

Henderson thrust out a rigid arm. "Jahwol, mein Fuhrer!"

Within minutes of receiving Colonel Corwin's rescission order, Dr. Henderson tried to reach Weyland Jones. "This is an emergency, Kitty. Please. I know it's at the busiest time of year for you folks, but I do need to talk to Weyland as soon as it's convenient. Yes, yes. I know it might be late in the evening, that's why I want to give you my home number. Yes. I know, Kitty. But it's about Baranovitch. Weyland will know I wouldn't call him if I didn't believe he could help with a serious problem. Please. I'll be ever so grateful. Thank you."

"I would rather take a beating than tell you this, Michael, but Colonel Corwin became upset with your response to his not signing your release and has rescinded his approval for your outside privileges."

The big blue-clad man nodded. "Don't worry about it, Doctor. I've had worse things happen to me." He thrust out his jaw and pointed at it. "Tell the colonel that he'll have to take a better shot if he wants my attention."

Both men stood just inside the door of Dr. Henderson's office. "Michael, you mustn't let this momentary setback reverse the splendid progress you've been making."

The big man patted the smaller one's shoulder and smiled. "Like I said, don't worry about it. I wasn't planning on going outside anyway, no matter what the overstuffed, would-be bird colonel says."

Dr. Henderson squeezed the big man's bicep. "We'll continue our therapy sessions, Michael, no matter what. Same time, same station."

Weyland Jones arrived the following day. The farmer was told by the colonel's gatekeeper that Colonel Corwin was 'unavailable'. "No, I'm sorry, Mr. Jones, I'm not sure *when* you could see him."

The next morning, notice was served by the Roseburg legal firm of Gadis, Luther, Scriver, and Adams that they were acting in behalf of Sutherlin farmer Weyland Jones who sought an immediate meeting with the Roseburg Veteran's Home Commandant. The meeting was scheduled for ten the following morning in Colonel Y. Herbert Corwin's office. Weyland Jones was accompanied by Stephen Scriver, one of the legal firm's principals. Following that meeting with Colonel Corwin, Weyland Jones and Dr. Henderson met For lunch. "I don't know, Bryce, Corwin has a snit going over something. He refuses to let us look at Michael's records. Says it's all privileged information, in order to protect patients under treatment."

"But you've already seen the records," Dr. Henderson protested.

"Calm down, Doc. I know that. You know that. But I could hardly let Corwin know that without compromising you."

"Hell, I'll make a copy for you. That bastard can't pull rank on me in one of my own cases."

"What about you? I don't want to see you hurt."

Henderson laughed. "I've already got enough time in to retire. He can't do a thing to me and he knows it. What we've got to do is shake him loose on this for Michael's sake."

"Another beer, boys?"

Weyland nodded at the hovering waitress. "Make it two more Raniers on tap. When you come back we'll order." After the two men placed their order, Weyland lit a cigarette and said, "Scriver says there's nothing we can do about Corwin refusing to sign the release, but he says a damned strong case might be made about not relaxing Michael's restrictions—If we can prove he's improving through treatment."

"He is, dammit!" Henderson said, pounding the table hard enough to make their mugs jump.

Weyland nodded. "Scriver thinks Corwin is paranoid over the bad press he got for Baranovitch's last escape. He says just the fear of bad publicity by our threatening litigation over the hospital's failure to follow accepted procedure might drive Corwin to relent. What do you think? The bastard doesn't like bad press, does he?"

The doctor nodded. "He's got the backbone of jellyfish." Then he said, "Have you time to talk to Michael while you're down?"

The farmer shook his head. "And I won't have time for a while, dammit. You'll have to keep him informed."

A week later, the hospital's head psychiatrist received an imperious summons to the Commandant's office. When Dr. Henderson was ushered in, Colonel Corwin stood at an open window. The Colonel barked, "I don't suppose you have any idea how Weyland Jones obtained a copy of Mikhail Baranovitch's hospital records?"

"What records, colonel?"

"His treatment records!"

"Do you mean a Sutherlin farmer has one of our patient's records? No! Whose?"

"Don't toy with me, Major. You know whose."

Dr. Henderson said, "Well, sir, I can't imagine how they could be Mikhail Baranovitch's records. Why I was just examining those myself a few minutes ago."

"Copies! They're camera copies!"

"Camera copies? Are you saying Weyland Jones broke into my office and photographed Baranovitch's records? Those are confidential!"

Colonel Corwin strode from the window to stop inches from his head psychiatrist. "You are on thin ice, Henderson," he murmured.

Major Bryce Henderson clicked his sandal heels together and saluted. "Colonel, am I to assume this is some sort of interrogation?"

The colonel returned to the window. "If I could prove what I know happened, Henderson, you'd be out of here in a minute."

"Colonel, if you'll be kind enough to share with me why I'm here in your office at this moment, I'll take it upon myself to leave in less than your prescribed minute."

"It would appear, Major, that you have become too close to this patient."

Major Henderson frowned. "I hope not, Colonel," he said at last. "But I certainly honor the man as a bonafide American hero, and I'm very proud of the progress this institution made in curing him. In addition, I deeply regret that you inhibited that process."

"Please leave." As Dr. Henderson turned for the door, the colonel added, "And please convey to Mr. Baranovitch my personal pleasure in re-instituting his outdoors privileges."

"I don't know how you did it, Dr. Henderson," Mikhail Baranovitch said during their next session, "but I know you did."

"That's absurd, Michael," the doctor said, leaning back in the swivel chair to better view his patient. "It was Weyland who came to your rescue once again. Did you know he brought an attorney in on your case, even threatened Colonel Corwin with litigation in order to force him to be more lenient with you."

The big man chuckled. "You're not the only one I get information from, Doc. I got a letter from Weyland."

The doctor jerked forward in his chair! "A letter? God no. If the colonel got hold of that, he'd crucify me!"

"The letter said you stuck your neck out for me. Don't worry, I tore it into small pieces and flushed them down a toilet. But not before I read it all. The rest of it said I should listen to you in order to plot a strategy for my release."

"The latter part of that letter is good advice."

The very next day, Mikhail Baranovitch applied to Gordon Smith, asking to join his groundskeeping crew.

Michael found his way outdoors for the first time in several months; it was the evening of July 4, 1955. He stood in the field to the east of the main hospital building and watched the annual fireworks display atop Mount Nebo. Afterward, he returned to his room thinking of Morotai and the fleet fireworks he'd watched from LCI 316 as the landing craft threaded its way between capital ships that were raining fire onto the island. And how that bombardment wasn't sufficient to save his friends during the invasion. As a consequence of those memories, the blue-clad man wondered how well—or even *if*—he would sleep that evening. He was surprised and gratified, come morning, to find he'd slept soundly the whole night through.

As anticipated, Gordon Smith was eager to have Michael back on his crew. The big man took up where he'd left off, frenzied to work, always on time, always tackling any job with cheerful willingness. Gordon started him with a reel-type mower, assigning him the task of keeping the lawns mowed around the Hospital's Main Building and Building 16, next door.

The real reason Michael was assigned that particular close-in task was because Gordon was ordered to keep the patient where he could be surreptitiously monitored. But Michael, being Michael, tackled his task with such zeal that he soon ran out of work and crossed the street with his machine to mow around the buildings to the east, though that grass had been barbered only two days before.

Smith found Michael poaching grass by the carpenter's shop in mid-afternoon. So he took the patient's mower and handed him a hand trowel and an edger tool. Then he pointed him back across the street to manicure the hospital lawn at the sidewalks' edge. Within a week, Gordon Smith was pleading with Colonel Corwin for more latitude in how and where he could use the new man.

"Dammit, colonel, there's only so much can be done around these main buildings and Baranovitch hits what there is to do with so much sweat and blood that I can't find anything else for him. Besides that, we need help moving sprinkler pipe and he'd be perfect for that job."

The colonel rubbed his nose while peering down it. "Very well, Gordon, use Baranovitch where he's most needed. But I want him under surveillance every minute."

"I can try, colonel."

"This is not a Robert Bruce saga, Gordon. If at first you don't succeed, you don't get to try again."

So Michael began moving sprinkler pipe. Afterward, the chief groundskeeper gave him a splitting maul, and when senior members of the grounds crew cut down a diseased maple tree, and sawed it into blocks, Mikhail Baranovitch split those blocks into suitable pieces for fireplace use in the brick bungalows that provided administrative housing.

Autumn came, and growth of the lawngrass slowed as leaves began falling. So Gordon took away Michael's mower and splitting maul and gave him a rake that he was allowed to keep in his room. Michael raked from daylight to dark, seven days per week.

"I'll be a sonofabitch if I know how he does it," Gordon told Bryce Henderson. "I swear, if a leaf falls on these grounds anytime during the night, the guy hears it and takes after it when daylight strikes." The groundskeeper shook his head in wonder. "He's a damned one-man gang, blessed if he ain't."

One day, Gladys called to Michael, "Hon, do you know you now have over three hundred dollars in your envelope. What are you going to do with all that money?"

"Well, if I had my freedom I'd invite you out on the town."

The peel of her laughter awakened two dozing loungers, including one who'd drooled down the front of his hospital pajamas. "Wouldn't that be something?" she cried. "It's a good thing you don't have your freedom, or I might take you up on it."

Michael blushed. "I was just teasing."

She patted him on the arm. "So was I, Hon. I'd have to ask Fred first." To explain, she told him, "Fred is my husband. But since all he ever does is lay on the couch and watch TV, he'd probably tell me to go ahead." Then they both laughed together, though Michael's was more choke than chuckle.

There came a rare early snow in December, and Gordon Smith issued snow shovels to his crew, assigning Michael to keep the sidewalks of the Main Hospital building snow-free.

"Hell, he's out there before daylight," Gordon said. "He told me he didn't want any ice buildup on *his* sidewalks. Said there was Gladys and the cafeteria girls to think about. Then he told me he worried about the old guys here who're crippled or maybe just too frail to walk on icy sidewalks."

When Dr. Henderson shook his head, Gordon added, "I know this, Bryce— when Michael Baranovitch is here, it sure makes my job a bunch easier."

"Why don't you tell that to Colonel Corwin?"

"Oh I have, Bryce, I have. He told me not to worry—that Baranovitch would be with us for a while."

On the fifth of January, 1956, Bryce Henderson again applied for release for Mikhail Baranovitch. Again, the application was turned down by Colonel Y. Herbert Corwin, with the proviso that Michael's status could be elevated to that of "Trustee"—the rating just under release.

"That means, Michael, that you can ride the bus downtown, go to a movie," Dr. Henderson told him. "It means you can climb Mount Nebo any day you wish, visit Weyland on his farm. The only proviso is that you have to let them know at the desk where you're going. And you must return to the hospital each night—

unless you're given an overnight pass."

Michael shifted in his chair. "Who issues overnight passes?"

"Well, Colonel Corwin has that exclusive privilege."

"I won't ask him, you know that."

"Yes, dammit!" Henderson growled. "I do indeed know that. But I also know you're growing better by the day. And I know the mere fact that he's elevated your status to that of the most privileged means he can't keep you here much longer."

Michael stood, reached over the desk to shake Dr. Henderson's hand. "I want to thank you, doctor. You've helped me a lot, and I want you to know I'll go to my grave remembering it." After the big man had gone, Dr. Henderson stared at the hand Michael had shaken, then down the empty hallway where the blue-clad man disappeared.

The following Monday, Michael withdrew fifty dollars from the savings Gladys hoarded for him, then boarded the City Transit bus for downtown. After leaving the bus, he strolled into a sporting goods store, gravitating to their military surplus section. There, he picked out a plywood packframe designed originally to carry a 30-caliber machine gun, then bought a packsack to hang on the frame. He also picked up two shelter halves that, when snapped together, made a pup tent. He added a hundred feet of ¼-inch nylon rope, a surplus down-filled mummy bag designed for use by ski troops in Alaska, a Swiss Army knife and a surplus water canteen.

After that, he went to the J.C. Penny's store, where he purchased two pairs of Levi jeans, four pairs of wool socks, a wool shirt and a flannel shirt, then found himself without sufficient funds to buy a pair of work boots.

Mikhail Baranovitch did, however, have enough money to buy a ticket at the Star Theater where he watched *The Robe*, a touching movie about the crucifixion of Christ; a movie that brought tears cascading down Michael's cheeks. Then, carrying his packages, he rode the bus back to the hospital.

The next day Michael withdrew an additional twenty-five dollars from the envelope Gladys kept for him and again boarded the bus for downtown. When he returned the following evening, he wore new Red Wing work boots with foam rubber soles. He also carried a surplus Army poncho.

"Michael, Gladys tells me you've withdrawn seventy-five dollars from the groundskeeping wages she holds for you." Dr. Henderson tapped his fingertips together as Mikhail Baranovitch met his eyes.

"Yes sir, I have."

"Can you tell me what you plan on using it for?"

"I went to a movie!" The excitement in the blue-clad patient's voice was clear. "It was about Jesus and the Crucifixion, and how Roman soldiers gambled for Jesus's wool robe while he hung on the cross."

"Are those new boots you're wearing?"

"Yes."

"I see." The doctor seemed fascinated by his own tapping fingertips. "You do know, Michael, that, if you'll stay until spring, there's no way Colonel Corwin can keep you any longer."

"No sir, I don't know that."

"Um, yes. Well, son, Gladys tells me you still have two hundred and thirty-eight dollars and seventy-five cents left."

The patient's eyelids dropped until he was barely squinting across the desk at his counselor.

"You may wish to withdraw the rest of it," Dr. Henderson said, "should an emergency arise."

Michael's eyelids clicked up. "If I take it all, might that not cause suspicion?"

"Probably no more so than the packages Daniel tells me you've accumulated in your room."

Though he'd arrived at Dr. Henderson's office only minutes before, Michael stood and walked around the psychiatrist's desk, held out his hand for what the doctor feared was the last time. "Again, thank you, doctor, for all you've done. And for all you've tried to do."

That very evening, Michael packed all other purchases except the boots in his backpack, then tied one end of the ¼-inch rope to the packframe, opened a window and lowered the bundle to the ground. Then he gathered up the wrapping paper, discarding it in the restroom wastebasket. Within minutes, he walked out the front door, studied the grounds carefully to make sure there were no loiterers about on this cold and rainy January evening, then shouldered his backpack and headed off at a brisk walk for the Umpqua River.

He crossed the bridge, selected one of the most dense cedar trees growing along the sidewalk, climbed up inside the spreading branches, and hung his backpack ten feet from the ground. Michael was back in his room a short time later, sound asleep.

The following morning, Michael timed his approach to Gladys to coincide with the City Transit schedule, withdrawing all his money from Glady's desk. "Oh Michael, please don't do anything foolish," she said as she handed him the envelope. He came around her counter to hug the woman, murmuring, "Thanks for being you." Then he was gone.

Dr. Henderson knew about Michael's monetary withdrawal within minutes.

"Did he say where he was going?"

Gladys shook her head. "All he said was 'Into town'."

Dr. Henderson advised Gladys not to mention Mikhail Baranovitch's withdrawal to anyone else until asked about it.

Daniel did ask about it the following morning. Soon after, Colonel Y. Herbert Corwin knew of Michael's absence. He also knew of the patient's new boots, his surplus backpack, and the packages that had disappeared from the patient's room two nights before. Shortly thereafter, one of the janitors brought in several pieces of wrapping paper from the "B" Ward restroom. Two sales slips were found wadded up within the paper, one from Penny's and one from Sportsman's Surplus. By then, Mikhail Baranovitch had been gone for twenty-six hours.

"Henderson, do you know anything about this?"

Colonel Corwin hadn't waited for a summons to fetch the psychiatrist, but had loomed suddenly in Dr. Henderson's office. The doctor looked up mildly at the distraught commandant. "About Baranovitch? Other than that he's gone, not a thing, colonel."

"Doesn't he realize he was nearing release?"

"Obviously not. I imagine all he could see was a life sentence staring him in the face."

"Couldn't you make him understand that I planned to sign his release in the spring, for God's sake?"

"Oh, were you? Since you neglected to mention it to me, how could I advise him of it?"

Colonel Corwin kicked Henderson's waste basket skittering across the office. "Confound it! Now he's shit in his own nest. How can I ever sign his release?"

Dr. Henderson leaned back in his chair, but he was examining his fingernails when he murmured, "The patient may have signed his own release, colonel."

By late afternoon, a VA Hospital investigator had identified most of the purchases Mikhail Baranovitch had made at Penny's and Sportsman's Surplus. He'd also discovered Baranovitch had taken a bus downtown; but the driver couldn't remember exactly where Michael had exited the bus.

"Do we notify the sheriff's office?" the investigator asked.

"Oh God, no!" Colonel Y. Herbert Corwin exclaimed. "We want to keep the lid on this one or the press will get it."

But the press already had it! That afternoon's Roseburg newspaper headlined:

UMPQUA WILD MAN ON LOOSE AGAIN!

Chapter 34

Chuck Little was an enterprising newspaperman whose diligence and patience at last paid off. The man his colleagues called "Little Chuck" had, since Mikhail Baranovitch's previous hospital escape, expected that someday the "Umpqua Wild Man" would again bolt. Cognizant of ink splashed previously on Baranovitch's escapades, Chuck Little set about cultivating sufficient hospital attendants to ensure that when the next Baranovitch's disappearance occurred, a "Chuck Little scoop" followed. After eight months, however, the reporter had nearly given up hope. Then he received a tip from his fishing buddy, hospital orderly John Wilder.

The story following the headline was scanty—only a few column inches because the V.A. Administration's first response was to stonewall Little's request for information. But that first headline crumbled the stonewall's barricade. And the day following the January 18 story's break found the V.A. Hospital's administrator both accessible and cooperative:

NO WORD YET ON THE "WILD MAN'S" WHEREABOUTS
Chuck Little
Daily News Staff Writer

"No word yet on Mikhail Baranovitch," said Colonel Y. Herbert Corwin, Commandant of Roseburg's Federal Veteran's Administration Hospital.

"We, of course, hope and pray that the young man will return of his own accord. After all, he was merely days from being judged fully restored and suitable for release from our facility."

Baranovitch apparently walked away from the Hospital grounds sometime Monday morning and has not been seen since.

The recluse, sometimes known as the "Umpqua Wild Man", especially since his arrest eight months ago while scavenging in a refuse dump near Canyonville, has multiple escapes from hospital detention. The "Wild Man" achieved much notoriety during rashes of petty thefts during previous attempts at freedom.

That second day's story told of a period when residents of southern Douglas County felt they weren "under siege" because of the "Umpqua Wild Man's" thefts from homes in the Cow Creek Valley. And the story told of Deputy Sheriff Warren Telford having been in on both previous arrests of Mikhail Baranovitch.

"Fucking rubbish!" Bryce Henderson cried, wadding up the newspaper's front page and throwing it in a corner.

Gordon Smith rubbed his eyes with a thumb and forefinger. "Yeah, and I'll have to find three other men to replace him."

The phone rang on Dr. Henderson's desk. "What?" he barked into the mouthspiece. It was Gladys. "Colonel Corwin would like to see you, doctor."

"When?"

"I think he'd like to see you now."

Corwin turned from the window as Dr. Henderson entered. "Thank you for coming, Doctor. Please be seated."

Both men took chairs on opposite sides of the colonel's desk. Dr. Henderson folded his arms and said, "What is it you wish from me, Colonel?"

"Baranovitch. I'd like to talk about Mikhail Baranovitch."

"And you think I can help you?" the doctor asked.

"Bryce, I'm hoping we both can help the hospital."

"My primary concern right now," the doctor said, "lies with our patient, not the hospital. Nor with its administration."

Colonel Y. Herbert Corwin laid both of his hands face down on his immaculate desk and said, "You haven't been exactly cooperative on this entire case, have you, doctor?"

"If you mean, have I put more concern into Mikhail Baranovitch than in Y. Herbert Corwin, the answer is an unqualified yes."

Corwin's hands slipped back across the desk's surface until he could grip the edge. "Dr. Henderson, I've never questioned that. Nor have I questioned its obvious rightness. What I wish to talk about is not the past, but the future."

Dr. Henderson nodded, his lips compressing. "You want me to keep the lid on Michael's analysis."

"I would rather you didn't talk to the press."

The psychiatrist laughed. "I have no intention of talking to the bloody goddamned press for fear I'll call them the asshole sonsabitches they are."

Colonel Corwin seemed satisfied. "I have reason to believe this reporter, Chuck Little, may try to contact you for information on your treatment. You, of course, have the obligation to refuse requests from all reporters on confidentiality grounds."

The stubby psychiatrist stood. "I shall refuse them, colonel, because they are the earth's offal—and because I still have a foremost obligation to my patient. Beyond that, I'll give your request some consideration."

The Dogged and the Damned

Colonel Corwin nodded. "Let us hope," he said, "that we never hear from the Slav again."

Dr. Henderson sighed. "That, too, is my most fervent wish." He turned for the door. There, he paused and said over his shoulder, "But alas, ours, I fear, are fools' wishes. We've sent him out of here a hunted man when we should've sent him on his way with our blessings. And by God, the newspapers will make such a mockery of him that it would drive even one of us insane!"

Money, Mikhail Baranovitch found, wasn't all it was cracked up to be. He bought a safety razor, blades, and a bar of soap at the Dixonville store. Then when pausing for a drink from an outside faucet, he overheard the proprietor telephoning the dispatcher at the Douglas County Sheriff's Office.

The fugitive fled across Deer Creek, into the foothills to the south. It was from those foothills that he saw the patrol car pull up to the store and the proprietor point to Deer Creek.

There was no way, of course, that half-hearted, foot-slogging pursuit could catch a fleeing man in Mikhail Baranovitch's condition, especially in forested hill country, and especially amid a steady rain such as that beginning to fall.

He kept angling east, toward the peaks and valleys of the Cascade Mountains. Within a day, the traveler bumped into a large stream that seemed to be rising with the drumming rain. He took shelter beneath a bridge across what the roadsign said was "Buckhorn Creek," and ate the last of the V.A. Hospital's cafeteria biscuits he'd confiscated on his final morning there.

There were many homes along the larger stream, and a good graveled road with considerable motor traffic, mostly logging related: log trucks, tool trucks, logging "crummys" that hauled crews to the jobsite. But there were other vehicles, too: farm trucks, family sedans, a school bus, a pickup truck carrying three barking dogs in its box.

After nightfall, Michael headed downriver. He'd not been hiking long when he approached an even larger river. There was also a highway junction. He lit a match, then another, while reading the sign proclaiming this as the only place in the world where two rivers collide head-on. Michael wished he could see the rivers better.

He crossed the Little River Bridge and within five minutes strode the main street of a hamlet called "Glide." He stood beneath the porch roof of the little store and wished for daylight as his belly growled overtime.

The sky lightened around seven-thirty. But a fog, not uncommon during winters in the Umpqua country, settled in and Michael remained more or less obscure on the store porch. Interior lights switched on at eight a.m. and the door

223

was unlocked. The proprietor stepped outside to look around, saw Michael, spotted his pack, and said, "What do you want?"

"I'd like to buy a few groceries, sir."

The man was slender, stooped, probably well into his sixties, with a wrinkled face that appeared to be practiced in the art of frowning. He peered over his octagonal glasses and said, "You're that nutcase that escaped from the Roseburg mental hospital, aintcha?" When Michael said nothing, the storekeeper said, "I don't think I want to sell you anything, even if you do have money. Go on, get out of here."

Michael sighed, shouldered his pack and headed off east, circling the school where yellow buses disgorged shouting, running children. In only a short distance, fog swallowed him and he circled back to the Little River Bridge. He peered from behind roadside brush near the bridge when a sedan with a Douglas County Sheriff's Office decal drove up to the Glide Grocery and two deputies clambered out. A few minutes later, they drove on east, up the North Umpqua Highway.

That night, Michael broke into the Glide Grocery and took two loaves of bread, three cans of tuna fish, several cans of soup, a large jar of peanuts and two pounds of bacon. He left a ten dollar bill lying on the counter.

Back beneath the Buckhorn Creek Bridge, Michael took stock: Obviously he was being hunted; obviously his money had no real advantage to a man on the run and could actually lead to added danger if he tried to obtain supplies through legitimate means.

Michael really wanted to flee into the mountains further east, but during the brief time he'd been free, he could see the snow line halfway down the higher ranges he coveted. It was clearly still winter up there and inaccessible to him for some months. That meant he must hide somewhere in the lower elevations. Still, he was loathe to abandon thought of reaching those distant mountains. With a course charted, the big man went to sleep as diesel trucks loaded with logs rumbled across the bridge.

That evening found Michael in search of refuge, striding up the Little River Road. He turned up the little-used Cavitt Creek Road without knowing why, and bivouacked near Cavitt Falls. With only occasional traffic along the remote road, he felt isolated enough and safe enough to set up his little pup tent, enjoying several uninterrupted hours of solid sleep for the first time since leaving the hospital. Through the man's resting hours, he was unaware of the headlines carried on the front page of Roseburg's afternoon paper:

WILD MAN STRIKES GLIDE GROCERY

The Dogged and the Damned

The story, bylined by Chuck Little told how proprietor Cason Jakeway had, the morning before, turned the "Umpqua Wild Man" away. "I told him I didn't want him in my store," said Jakeway. "Then the S.O.B. comes back in the middle of the night and steals a hundred dollars worth of groceries and leaves a ten dollar tip!"

Little's story also told how the "Wild man" had made purchases at the Dixonville Store. And the reporter quoted Undersheriff Irvin Finch as advising people dwelling east of Roseburg to be on the lookout for an escaped mental patient who could be "bewildered" by his unexpected freedom.

Dr. Bryce Henderson tore that page from *The Daily News*, wadded it up, and deep-sixed it, muttering, "Corksoakers."

Henderson wasn't the only one disappointed in the story: Mikhail Baranovitch picked up a two week-old copy from the garbage can at the Glide Ranger Station when next he ventured to civilization....

Michael awoke refreshed and ready to explore farther up Cavitt Creek. It was near snow line when he found what he was looking for—a small copse of trees tucked far back in a spreading maze of blackberry bushes. The copse was on a piece of flat ground across Cavitt Creek, near a couple of other creek junctures. The spot wasn't easy to get to, especially during high water brought about by torrential rains. But a few hundred yards upstream the man found a fallen tree that spanned the creek, providing access to his soon-to-be hideout. He was quickly at work developing a shelter similar to the one he'd used a few years earlier in the south of the County.

Hunger drove him forth again. He knew, of course, that he'd soon need to become self-sufficient, but in the interim he would either have to buy his supplies, or obtain them by other means. Three nights later he was at the Glide Ranger Station. But the old newspaper story about the Umpqua Wild Man made him switch targets. He again broke into the Glide Grocery, making two trips from there with his backpack filled. This time he left no money.

GLIDE GROCERY HIT AGAIN BY WILD MAN!

This time Chuck Little's story was relegated to the inside pages while the newspaper covered issues of larger import:

Douglas County Sheriff Conrad Bayles had successfully weathered a storm of criticism over his department's handling, some years previously, of the "Burdick Affair." At that time, two thousand rounds of ammunition was fired by his police force into the barricaded home of a mentally deranged man while the man's tear-streaked wife pleaded with the sheriff to allow her to go inside and talk her husband into surrendering.

But when sufficient evidence surfaced to indicate massive financial fraud within his department, Bayles was forced into early retirement. The County's Commissioners quickly appointed Undersheriff Irvin Finch to fill the last years of the deposed sheriff's term. At his swearing-in ceremony, the professed law-and-order Finch pledged to show malefactors no mercy, no matter their social status, economic position, or political favor.

It was at this point in the ambitious new sheriff's career that complaints began trickling in from the country east of Roseburg: an axe taken from a U.S. Forest Service pickup at the Wolf Creek Campground, a shovel from a fisherman's pickup parked at Rock Creek. There was a pound of coffee purported stolen from a small cabin on the Buckhorn Road, and utensils apparently taken from the kitchen at the Glide Ranger Station. More ominous, a 30-30 rifle and a box of ammunition disappeared from the window rack of a pickup truck parked at the Lone Rock Bar, and a Remington single-shot .22 caliber rifle disappeared from the closet of a summer cabin on Little River.

Paranoia, apparently riding the crest of media frenzy, exploded. Letters to the editor poured into *the Daily News* office decrying the lack of police protection in outlying rural areas.

Glide Isn't The Same headlined one letter-to-the-editor.

Officers Slow Action Draw Wrath of Reader headlined another.

KRNS's popular "Voice of the Valley" call-in radio show attracted dozens of respondents when host Dick McCrae featured a discussion of the "Umpqua Wild Man."

Meanwhile, ensconced in his quiet camp on Cavitt Creek, Mikhail Baranovitch remained oblivious to the media furor occurring thirty miles (as the crow flies) west. Through the remainder of January, throughout February, and into March the reclusive escapee avoided detection.

Michael set rabbit snares. More important, he found winter chinook salmon occasionally migrating up Cavitt Creek and by judicious use of his 30-30, was able to obtain an occasional one from the pool below Cavitt Falls. He shot a deer. He butchered a rancher's domestic sheep. He even took a bucket of milk from a compliant milk cow standing in a far pasture corner from her barn. God, did it taste good!

By late-March, Michael was ready to move. He stashed much of his camp in a hole dug beneath a big fallen tree, carefully wrapping each piece of equipment in black plastic liberated from tattered remains of a tarp used to cover a "fed out" haystack.

The Dogged and the Damned

When he set out for new horizons, Mikhail Baranovitch left after nightfall, striding strongly down the Cavitt Creek Road, his camp, except for its bark-roofed shelter, was completely gone. The blackberry bushes were taking on new life, obliterating the trail into the abandoned camp, and even vine maple, willow, chinquapin, and poison oak were beginning to sprout new leaves.

Michael hoped to be past Glide and past the fishing mecca at the Rock Creek Narrows before daylight, but as much as he hurried, growing light still caught him at the Lone Rock Bridge. Michael could see heavy lowering clouds drifting down below surrounding mountaintops and knew rain was in the offing, so he tucked in beneath the bridge to wait.

He was at Susan Creek the next morning, hiking all night in the rain. And he cleared Steamboat Creek, with its fishing lodge and tourist cabins, the following morning. On the fourth morning after leaving Cavitt Creek, Mikhail Baranovitch peered through a screen of small cedar trees at the Dry Creek Store, wondering if he dared? Finally, around five in the afternoon, after the fugitive had shaven and changed clothes, two forest service pickups and a logging crummy filled with a cutting crew stopped at the store for gas, cigarettes, beer, and salami slices. Michael left his backpack and strolled into the store as part of the mix, trusting that each person there would think he was part of the other bunch.

He hurried to buy a one-pound can of coffee, a loaf of bread, some Slim Jims, three-day-old rolls, a quart of milk, two cans of Pepsi, and a handful of Hershey candy bars. Then he paused at an Umpqua Forest map hanging on the wall and became so intrigued that he almost failed to exit with the logging crew as they laughed and joked their way from the building.

Caps Illahee, Michael thought. That's got a nice ring to it. He shouldered his backpack and trudged up the river to the graveled road winding up to an open flat where, back in days of yore, Umpqua Indians once gathered for horse races.

Conveniently, there was an unoccupied forest service gazebo-style shelter on Caps Illahee, too. Michael examined the quaint round building made from peeled, weathered logs, the fireplace on one side, and the small stack of firewood the last user had left out of courtesy for the next.

Michael slipped from his backpack, took a quick walk around the area in the fading light, then returned, built a fire, dug out a piece of jerky, a Slim Jim, a dinner roll, and his quart of milk.

When the first rays of sun fell on the shelter the following morning, the occupant, still sleeping the sleep of the dead, was rudely awakened: "Well pilgrim," came a deep booming voice, "looks to me like you got a pretty nice wickiup."

Chapter 35

The fugitive, still in his mummy bag, sat up, momentarily dazed. A man, apparently astride a saddlehorse, bent over his saddlehorn to peer under the shelter roof. The man chuckled, then said, "Howdy." When Michael leaped from the bag and gripped the half-wall of the quaint shelter, he saw another horse shuffling behind. A gray-haired little lady sat its saddle.

As the fugitive ducked down to grab his trousers, the first rider said, "Sorry to wake you up, pilgrim. We didn't know anybody was here—we're just riding out to check on our cows is what we're doing." When Michael still said nothing, he added, "Our ranch house is just up the road a little ways."

Michael said, "Is this your building?"

The man on the horse laughed—booming it out as if he wanted God and the world to hear. "No, no. B'longs to the forest service. Anybody's welcome to stay in it for a day or two. That's what they built it for—lost pilgrims."

Michael slipped on a shirt, opened the half-wall's gate, and stepped from the shelter barefooted. The man on the horse appeared as large as Michael, though much older. The man leaned down and offered a gnarled hand. "Name's Purley White." Waving toward the woman, he said, "That there is Jenny. She runs the outfit."

The horseman's eyes had never stopped roaming since Michael popped upright in the sleeping bag. He shrewdly said, "No horse. No car. You must be packing a load on your back."

Michael murmured, "I'd invite you in for coffee, but I don't have any made and ..."

Purley White's voice boomed. "Already had so much my eyes shaded to black. Ate breakfast, too. Planning to stay long?"

"I ... I don't know. I just like to look at things the way God made 'em." Michael moved closer to the horse, holding out a hand to touch its shoulder. "This is as close to a horse as I've ever been."

Again, the big man's laugh boomed through the forest glade. "Well, boy, me'n Jenny makes up for your lack of horse sense. We been breaking and runnin' ponies on this flat for fifty years."

"Purley," the woman said, "if we check on them cow brutes on Big Oak Flats, we've got to get a move on." She cantered her gray horse back down the shelter's little spur road, then onto the graveled main road.

The big man chuckled again. "Duty calls and that woman's second name is

228

duty." Purley White reined the big sorrel around and, with a wave, clattered after his wife. Michael watched them through the trees and across the big meadow until they disappeared. Then he thought about his problem.

He felt he couldn't take a chance the Whites hadn't recognized him for a fugitive and so, must move. The way he reasoned, he'd have to be away from this shelter by the time the two horseback riders returned. He wondered if there'd been a telephone at the store—wished he could remember. What if the riders phoned his description to the county sheriff? Even if they phoned in his whereabouts, it would still take the sheriff's office two or three hours to put an officer up here. He had a little time.

Mikhail Baranovitch bent to kindle a fire in the fireplace. As he did, he filed the name 'Big Oak Flats' in his memory bank. He vaguely remembered seeing it on the U.S. Forest Service map hanging in the Dry Creek Store. He also recollected a place called Pine Bench and thought it was on the same side of the North Umpqua River as Caps Illahee. But wasn't there a creek—Boulder Creek—between?

As their horses jogged down the Illahee Road, Jenny White said to her husband. "Do you think that he might be the one was in the papers a while back; the 'Umpqua Wild Man'?"

"That's what I thought when I first saw him, Jens." The horses jogged a few feet further before Purley added, "He didn't look too wild to me."

"Can he be trusted, though?"

Her husband growled, "Jenny, there was a lever-action rifle leaning 'longside that fireplace. He woke up sudden and the first thing he *didn't* do was reach for that gun. I think that alone makes a good start toward trust."

"Do you think we should report him?"

"Why? He ain't a-botherin' us. As long as he don't bother us we can leave him be." They jogged on. He added, "And if he does bother us, we'll prob'ly handle it ourselves—just like we always have."

Mikhail Baranovitch found the big ponderosa trees on Pine Bench delightful. There, he discovered another forest service shelter, this one constructed in a chicken coop style, with three shingled sides and an open front. The shelter sported a rock-lined fire pit just outside the opening.

The man dropped his pack and wandered away looking for water. He found it shortly, a clear spring gushing from just below the top of a cliff that dropped away on the bench's west side. After drinking his fill, Michael returned to the shelter to unpack his meager belongings. With the road more than three miles away, and a thousand-foot drop into Boulder Creek to the west, He felt Pine Bench offered more security than he'd had since leaving Cavitt Creek.

A soft rain began falling during the night. The next morning the man took his 30-30 along on an exploratory hike. At three in the afternoon, he shot a blacktail doe on a mineral lick near a rock overhang that looked as though it'd been used often as a campsite. For how long was indicated by Indian artwork evident on the rock's rear wall. He shouldered the deer and carried it back to his Pine Bench camp. Early the following day Michael skinned the deer and cut the meat into strips for drying.

He built his smoke house about three hundred yards from his camp, utilizing a hollowed out tree where a long-ago fire had burned at its base. The fugitive employed chunks of fir bark and remnant black plastic brought up from Cavitt Creek to enclose the tiny smokehouse. Then he lashed together drying racks made from rhododendron branches. After building the drying racks, he laid strips of deer meat on them. Finally the man kindled a small fire inside, to which he fed only wood chips in order to keep the fire low.

Afterward, he fleshed the deer hide with his Swiss Army Knife, then submerged it in the creek to let the water soften the hide and soak off the hair. Two days later, while the deerskin was still moist, Michael rubbed ashes and deer brains into the hide to cure it. Late that afternoon, as he tended his smoker meat, a woman said, "You'd do a lot better with green hardwood chips." He was so startled that he knocked over one of the drying racks. The little gray-haired lady, Jenny White, helped him pull meat strips from the fire. Noting his quick glances, she said, "Go on about you; there's nothing to be frightened of." When he remained mute, she said, "We've guessed who you are, so it's worth nothing for you to worry about that."

"Why are you here?" Michael muttered without looking at her.

"Why am I here? I'm riding the trail back from Medicine Creek. We'll be bringing our cow brutes through here on the way to Mountain Meadows along toward the end of the month. I just wanted to make sure the trail is open."

"Where's your horse?"

"She's tied back at your shelter. Why?"

"Why do you say green hardwood chips are better?"

She chuckled. "Fir chips have resin or pitch in them. They'll implant that taste into the meat."

"Even when the fir chips are dry?"

This time the little lady laughed aloud. "Mister, you want a lot of smoke and very little heat. The way you're doing it, you're not smoking the meat; you're cooking it. If you cook it, it'll last maybe a week in this weather. And I suppose you hoped to keep it longer."

He dropped his eyes and shut his mouth.

She clapped her hands. "Well, that's done. Now come along; I want to talk to you about that deer hide."

Michael trailed her like a puppy. When they reached where the doeskin lay on the ground, she said, "I see you've been rubbing it with brains and ashes."

"Yes."

"But don't you know, as it dries, that you must work it back and forth across a rod or pole to keep it stretched and soft?" She pointed to the hitchrack where her gray mare was tethered, "that pole will do, but you ought to be working it now, or at least wetting it some more with a towel or rag—you can't soak it again without spoiling it."

All he could say was, "Yes, ma'am." She smiled for the first time. That she was tough, Michael conceded. But he saw, too, that she wasn't much more than a slip of a woman—and had certainly been beautiful when she was younger. He studied her through lowered lashes and decided that she's softening into everybody's grandmother, especially when she smiles.

"All right, now, I'll tell you a better way to tan a hide." His eyebrows shot up. "After you soak the hide enough to slip the hair, then while it's still moist you cut holes all around the outside, then lace it together with a cord and pull it up like a drawstring sack. Then you throw tanning plants in and fill it with water. The best plant of all to use might be alumroot, but it's hard to come by this time of year. Alder bark is good and so is oak bark. Oregon grape works, too, and mistletoe."

Michael held up a hand. "What do you do, ma'am, pack the bag with the bark or plants, then fill it with water?"

"Half full of your tannin plants will do. Then fill it with water and let it hang for a week. Then when you take it down to empty out the tannin, you need to work the hide as it dries."

When it was obvious she'd told him everything she felt compelled to tell, Michael murmured, "Thank you ma'am. I bet I could learn a lot from you and your husband."

She laughed as she untied her saddlehorse and pulled herself into the saddle with some effort. "I'll bet you could, too."

She reined her mare away, then wheeled back. "You don't seem so 'wild' to me," she said.

Mikhail Baranovitch would've pulled stakes immediately after Jenny White left his camp, had not he been helplessly involved with smoking meat and curing the deerskin hide. But he berated himself for letting the Whites sneak up on him—twice.

That's why, while returning from his smoker on the very next day, he threw up his hands in dismay to find Purley White working the deerskin hide back and forth across the shelter's hitchrail.

"There's the pilgrim!" the old man boomed, giving the deerskin one last flourish. "Jenny sent me over with a couple of quarts of huckleberries." The old man waved a casual hand to the shelter, at the two Mason jars of homecanned huckleberries standing beside Michael's bunk. "She canned 'em herself. Picked 'em up at Grassy Ranch last summer. We allus make a sashay up there for hucks and to check on the cow critters when the berries are ripe."

Movement caught Michael's eye; it was a bluetick hound lying sprawled in the shade of a tree. The dog lazily scratched an ear. "That's Old Blue," Purley said of the hound. "Dan's comin' up behind you."

Michael twisted to see what might have been the ugliest dog on the face of the earth. Dan sniffed his boots and walked away in apparent disdain. "What kind of dog is that?"

"Black and tan and airdale cross. His nose ain't the best, but he don't take no for an answer—as you can see with the beatings he took."

It was true; one eye was gone and, if his muzzle was any indicator, it must've been strained through a mesh window screen. Michael murmured, "At least he took his wounds all from the front."

"Jenny figured you didn't have no fruit nor vegetables. She said you looked a little peaked, like maybe you was close to scurvy. That's something a body has to watch for in the wintertime in these mountains."

"I'm very obliged to you people."

The old man leaned against the deerskin and the hitchrack and the horse. "She says for you just to leave the jars in the shelter. If somebody else don't take 'em first, we'll pick 'em up when we drive through here."

Michael nodded.

Then the old man said, "A forest service trail crew will be coming through any time now. They cut out and waterbar the lower trails about this time of year, then move higher, come summer."

"I see."

"There's another shelter over on Big Oak Flats, but it's right off the road, and likely there'll be people in and out of there any time."

Michael's face was a mask.

"There's some of these shelters scattered around the high country, but the snow's too deep up there now."

The old man turned to check his saddle cinch. "Nope, was I you I'd look for a good spot a ways off the main trails, where there's water and wood, and where rain can't get to you. Maybe cook only after dark so no daytime trail crew can smell your smoke."

Michael moved up to the hitchrail in interest. Purley White said, "Maybe I'd look up Medicine Creek, from where the trail crosses it. I'd look for a shelving overhang that stands out over the creek and has a sandy floor back in it for about ten feet. I'd make sure I wasn't under that overhang if a gully washing flood came along, but it's too late now for any snow-melt high water comin' down a south-facin' slope."

"And how far up Medicine Creek do you think a man ought to look?"

"Oh, maybe a quarter mile. Maybe a little more. If there was a hideout cave there, it should show up by then."

Meanwhile, far to the west and northwest and southwest, Mikhail Baranovitch was on a rampage. Every break-in from Drain to Glendale was attributed to the "Umpqua Wild Man." Every armed holdup—even if committed by masked teenagers who stood no larger than five-foot, six—was blamed on the escaped mental patient. Even graffiti scribbled with spray paint on schoolhouse walls was blamed on the deranged hospital escapee. Sheriff Finch, purportedly beside himself at the one-man crime wave, vowed vengeance, assigning more and more deputies to investigate the malodorous deeds of Mikhail Baranovitch. The news media had a heyday and Sheriff Irvin Finch received the ink he coveted. By solving most of the cases, however, and uncovering other malefactors, it seemed obvious that Mikhail Baranovitch had gone mysteriously blank. So to keep wires hot, the press engaged in a rehash of the "Umpqua Wild Man's" history. Concurrent with the fresh media wave came a flood of sheriff's office press releases outlining the strategic planning for fall and winter, when the Umpqua Wild Man would be driven to strike lowland regions, where domiciles were filled with innocent women and harmless children.

The hidden cave on Medicine Creek proved to be exactly the kind of place Mikhail Baranovitch wanted. Plentiful water was but a few steps away, and a perfect bathing pool just downstream, around the bend. Wood was abundant in the surrounding forests, too: dried limbs, pitch-filled stumps. No rain could beat beneath the wide overhanging ledge; no mattress could be softer than the sand upon which he unrolled his sleeping bag.

The only pebble to irritate the perfection lay in the fact that someone else knew where he'd taken refuge. And with that thought, Michael decided he would scour the surrounding country for another suitable hideaway.

But the fear of someone else knowing his location didn't prevent the fugitive from visiting the trail when he heard the lowing of cattle on their way to Mountain Meadows. They came singly, sometimes two abreast crowding each other. They were led by an old brindled cow who'd been over the trail twice a year throughout her lifetime. Michael counted over a hundred cows and calves. Then Purley White spotted him.

The big-hatted old man reined his sorrel horse to a halt, crying, "There's that pilgrim!" Then he dug in his saddlebags and handed Michael a roll of newspapers. "Thought you might want to read about what you been up to while you were gone."

Dan and Old Blue trotted up to smell Michael, then Jessie was there, handing down a sack of whole potatoes. "They're starting to grow sprouts, so you'll have to down 'em pretty quick."

"I don't know how to thank ..."

"Do you have any salt?" she interrupted.

"A little," he said. "I took some water from the Soda Springs and boiled it down to get what I have."

"Look," Purley said, "this ain't a-working, what with our piece-mealing dribbles to you. We'll be home in a week. That'd be a good time for you to pay us a visit."

"I can pay," he blurted. "If I could find a place to spend my money, I could pay. Or I can split wood!"

Chapter 36

Mikhail Baranovitch was so starved for vegetables he chunked two of the potatoes and ate them raw, skins, sprouts and all. Then he kindled a tiny fire, poked small sticks into the ends of three more spuds and thrust the other ends in the sand near the fire. As they roasted, the big man thought of his new friends, Purley and Jenny White, whom he now trusted.

He gazed around at his hideout and decided it was sufficiently secure to allow him to turn it into a home. So, for the first time since leaving the V.A. Hospital, he took the glossy photo of the Drum Majorette and her football-playing boyfriend and propped it on a ledge where he could see it from anywhere under the overhang. Now that he had a home, he could begin shaping its furnishings. Tomorrow he would start with a chair, perhaps a bunk, maybe a table. Right now, though, he would read the roll of newspapers Purley White had given him.

That's when he discovered he'd broken into a home in the North Douglas community of Elkton and stolen a bundle of stock certificates worth several hundred dollars. Then he'd stolen wheels from a car parked at a trailhead to Fish Lake on the South Umpqua, and broken a window and stolen cigarettes and beer from a grocery store out the same Garden Valley Road he'd once walked on the way to Dr. Harrow's funeral.

On and on went the litany, with copious ink devoted to the rising anger of Sheriff Irvin Finch and his promises to apprehend the "Umpqua Wild Man" if it was the last thing he did.

The United States Veteran's Hospital came under fire for their permissive treatment of patients. So hot and heavy did that tide run that influential Roseburg citizens began worrying about public support for a facility that employed upwards of a hundred local citizens and returned thousands of dollars to dozens of local businesses each month. After all, so it was said, the city of Roseburg had lobbied extensively during the depths of the Great Depression, besting several other Pacific Northwest communities in competition to obtain the hospital. They'd even raised a local bond issue to buy the land on which the facility was located, donating it to the federal government as the sweetener to obtain the medical center.

Chalmers R. Station, *The Daily News* Editor, penned a thoughtful editorial about the value of the Veteran's Hospital to Roseburg and Douglas County, detailing its history. Michael found that slice of information fascinating. Then the widely respected editor went on to explain how the hospital provided much needed services to the men debilitated by the shock of war.

"Much is owed these gallant men who defended our shores against the march of evil," the editor wrote. *"And small we who benefitted the most would be if we turned our faces from their plight."*

The editor focused on the topic at hand: *"Mikhail Baranovitch was one such soldier, ravaged by the tide of war. Obviously the man has not yet been rehabilitated, and it's entirely possible mistakes were made in his treatment. But we citizens of Douglas County cannot second-guess the intent; whatever treatment was accorded to Mikhail Baranovitch was made in his behalf by trained specialists in whom we must place our trust."*

And finally, in a newspaper near the bottom of the pile, a short letter-to-the-editor that had been circled in pencil came to Michael's attention:

Reader Questions Sheriff's Focus

Am I alone? Am I the only one wondering why, after accusing the so-called "Umpqua Wild Man" of crime after crime that was later proved the man had nothing to do with, is our sheriff diverting so much of his department's funds to the case of a confused mental patient who by all reports has already disappeared? If Sheriff Finch is driven by genuine concern and compassion, that is one thing. But I fear his real interest is in how much ink he can milk for a case that has the inordinate attention of a paranoid public.
Weyland Jones
Star Route
Sutherlin, Ore.

Michael laid the papers aside and turned his potatoes. He thought of Sheriff Finch, and how the man had used a nightstick on him for no reason during the night of his first arrest; how the man had ordered his new boots taken from him. Would his life always be filled with Irvin Finches? Or Captain Sarbones? Or Coach O'Malleys? Or even Papa? He sighed. Where would it all end?

Michael followed the trail to Mountain Meadows. He wondered about the abandoned forest service lookout there—the only lookout station he'd ever visited where one must travel for miles *downhill* to reach! The view from the lookout was spectacular, however. It was like being in the bottom of a huge bowl, with clear vision to the bowl's rim that was miles on all sides.

Though the abandoned building was locked, it was easy enough to throw up a shutter on its ring of windows and peer inside. He laughed. A glass pane was missing from one window, allowing him to reach inside and unlock it.

As most lookouts had, there was an alidade on a stand in the middle of the room. The circular alidade—a surveying instrument used for pinpointing the location of wildfires—rotated over a map that was as round and flat as the cardboard holding uncooked pizzas. Michael studied the map for a long time before leaving the building as he'd entered it.

He took the trail down to the North Umpqua River, and found the hot springs used by Indians for centuries, and white settlers for decades. Had the day not been blistering hot, he would've paused to soak at the springs; instead he chose to swim in the river.

That the river was shallow was a surprise. Then he remembered the deep diversion ditch filled with swift-flowing water he'd crossed on a plank bridge during his journey down to Mountain Meadows. He decided there must be a dam somewhere upstream. Right now, though, the alidade map showed a big flat on the other side of the river with the intriguing name of "Thorn Prairie." And beyond that, Lemolo Falls.

He licked his lips at thought of salmon schooled below the falls on Cavitt Creek. And he hoped they would also school below another falls. The man piled his clothes atop his backpack, then shouldered the load and waded across the shallow North Umpqua River.

He soon climbed onto Thorn Prairie, striking an old wagon road that snaked down the sloping flat from the east. Along the way, Michael passed through grazing cattle, noting the same brindled cow that led Purley and Jenny White's herd on their way upriver. Finally he located the trail down to Lemolo Falls.

The octagonal-columnar igneous rock that formed a buttress for Lemolo Falls was spectacular; so was the pool beneath. But It was obvious the present trickle of water spilling into the pool at its bottom was a mere shadow of what once roared over the lip. Nor were there salmon in the pool.

Michael took a seat on a driftwood log and pondered. The trail down from Thorn Prairie appeared to be seldom used. Driftwood for a fire was plentiful. The pool looked inviting, the sky clear, and there were few mosquitos. In short, it looked like a great place to make camp for the night. And he still had two potatoes.

The following day, Michael trudged back through Thorn Prairie, through Purley's and Jenny's cows. Something in the wagon road caught his eye; a piece of chipped obsidian protruding from the soft pumice soil at his feet. He dug around it with his fingers. It turned into a perfect spear point, perhaps five or six inches in length and an inch and a quarter in width. He fondled it with reverence, tested its edge—*ouch!*

Back at the Mountain Meadows Lookout, Michael studied the alidade map more closely and saw there was another falls downstream from where he now stood; Tokatee Falls. But this map was clearly more ancient than the power development that seemed to dominate this portion of the North Umpqua country. For instance, he knew there was a power generator near Soda Springs—he'd heard it while boiling out salt. And the big ditch he'd crossed on the way down to Mountain Meadows came from somewhere and went to somewhere. What else was going on along this river? Again he studied the map.

The following night, Michael discovered Tokatee Lake, Tokatee Dam, the nearby Diamond Lake Ranger District headquarters, and the California-Oregon Power Company encampment. Using considerable stealth, he entered the Copco commissary and helped himself to sufficient stores to get him back to his hideaway. Mid-day found him admiring the dwindled Tokatee Falls from the bottom up.

Still no fish.

The following night—one filled with lowering clouds and rain—Michael groped his way down the graveled roadway to the Soda Springs Dam, and the last generator for the power project. Poking around at daylight, he discovered the trail he sought—the one up to the mineral lick where he'd boiled out salt. Deciding to do so again, Michael made a hideway camp away from the forest service trail, then began the laborious process that would take him days to get a teaspoon of salt. While waiting for his mineral water to boil down to a few flakes of salt the fugitive found what he should've first discovered long ago—migrating fish were blocked at Soda Springs Dam.

The man's heart beat faster when he spotted the first giant fish leaping. They were in a school, finning only enough to maintain station alongside others of their kind. Salmon. Giant fish! Michael lay quietly on a rock studying the fish and pool, as well as the possibility of a project workman showing at any moment.

That night, he decided the little dam, and the powerhouse below had no maintenance worker or attendant or security personnel stationed there full time. The next morning, shortly after daylight, Michael trudged up the trail to Medicine Creek carrying a twenty-pound salmon and enough salt to flavor it.

He'd also discovered something else at Soda Springs that might prove beneficial: cattails grew there! But Michael couldn't remember what he'd once read about cattails. Couldn't one eat the seedpods, the stems, and particularly the roots? But how does one prepare the seedpods and stems? And how does one even obtain the roots?

"Indians used to dig 'em out with a sharp stick," boomed Purley White. "But it looks to me like a number ten shovel would work better. Or even an axe."

"You know, watercress is abundant now," Jenny said. "It makes wonderful salad dripped with a little bacon grease and sprinkled with crumbled toast."

"I don't know what watercress looks like," Michael said.

She laughed. "Then come with me out to the spring and I'll show you."

Purley walked with them. "I'll bet there's a lot of watercress growing along Medicine Creek, if you look in the shady spots," he said.

Michael had knocked timidly at the weathered board-and-batten ranch house in mid-afternoon of an overcast early June day. He was visiting, so he said, to learn how to prepare cattails but, in reality, the man was after as much information as he could glean from what he sensed was the most knowledgeable outdoor folks he would ever meet.

"There was somebody down at the shelter," he said. "I planned to stay there, but there's a red Jeep station wagon there and I was afraid to get any closer."

"Did anyone see you?" Purley asked, pulling him inside.

"No. Not that I know of. I left my pack down at the barn, under some hay."

"I'll bet you'll stay for supper, won't you?" Jenny asked. "You're probably starved for a home cooked meal."

"Well, I ..."

"Now that's settled," Purley boomed, "come on in and sit awhile. Tell us what you've been doing. Where you've been."

The ranch house's living room furniture was covered with pelts of cougars and bears and smaller furbearing creatures: bobcats, raccoons, mink, marten, even a skunk. A fanned-out eagle wing was pinned to a wall.

Later, Michael told them how he was trying to tan another hide using the method Jenny had told him about: tying it in a giant drawstring sack filled with alder bark and chinquapin nuts mixed with the sack full of water. "It's been hanging now for three days, and already the hide is taking on a darker color."

Purley stared at a pouch Michael had made to go on his belt. "What's that?" he asked.

"It's an Indian spear point, I guess," Michael said, slipping the obsidian piece from its sheath. "I found it on Thorn Prairie, in amongst your cows."

"Oh, isn't it beautiful!" Jenny exclaimed. "But that's not a spear point, is it Purley?"

"Nope. It's the finest obsidian knife I ever saw, though."

Michael handed it to him. The old man tested the edge with his thumb. "Sharp, too," he said without looking up. "You know that well-knapped obsidian holds an edge good as steel?"

"No sir, but I know it's sharp. I used it to flesh my last deer hide and it works better than my pocket knife."

Both Whites laughed.

Michael ate ham and mashed potatoes and red-eye gravy and fresh strawberries and peach cobbler until he could not eat one bite more. Then he rolled his sleeping bag out in the hay of White's barn. And the next day, when he left for his Medicine Creek camp, he carried a packsack overflowing with fresh garden onions and radishes, ten pounds of flour, a slab of bacon, a pound of butter sealed in a Mason jar, another jar of precious huckleberries, two pounds of coffee, a pound of salt, and an unopened can of Log Cabin syrup.

When he tried to pay, the Whites became indignant. "Just neighborliness is all it is," Jenny said. "Anybody likes my cooking as well as you gives a woman goosebumps."

The last thing Purley gave him was another roll of newspapers. "We can read, pilgrim. And we know there's a pack of lies in them papers about how 'wild' this here 'Umpqua Wild Man' is."

The last thing Jenny told Michael was that the Indians used to dig camas bulbs and dry them for later use. She said the blue camas ought to be in bloom at Big Camas Meadows now.

Chapter 37

Mikhail Baranovitch ate his first camas root amid moonlight, while eyeing the sleeping Big Camas Ranger Station. He used a requisitioned number 10 shovel to fill his packsack with the tasty roots and at daylight was swinging along the pumice flat known as Fish Creek Desert. Shortly thereafter, Michael entered a stand of stately Douglas fir trees that caused him to lean on his liberated government shovel and stare above in awe. Each tree was four or five feet through at eyeball level, each a hundred feet to the first limb! In his travels through this North Umpqua country, he'd been more or less enveloped in forests with trees of extraordinary size. But nothing like the symmetry of these! In fact, the fugitive was sufficiently enthralled that he almost missed the sound of a power company pickup grinding up from the Tokatee complex, barely taking concealment behind one of the huge trees. He needn't have bothered; the driver looked neither right nor left, ignoring the forest much as a Kansas native might drive by a cornfield without admiring the Divine nature of individual cornstalks.

Back at his enclave on Medicine Creek, Michael ate a few more raw camas bulbs, boiled and pulped some into mush, roasted a few, then gathered the rest into a bundle that he hung from an oak branch to dry.

After considering the camas roots, their ease of digging and storing, along with the nutritional value of the bulbs, Michael returned to Big Camas and dug two additional packsack loads. He bundled one and hung it from a chinquapin tree growing in the middle of dense brush; the other he packed back to Medicine Creek.

Still in a harvesting and storing mode, Michael dug cattail roots from the mineral waters at Soda Springs. From Soda Springs, it was but a couple of hours to Caps Illahee. The White's hay meadow was still nodding in the afternoon breeze, so he knocked at the ranch house to ask when the couple planned to begin cutting.

"Gonna start in a couple of days," boomed Purley.

Then Jenny timed in with, "But you'd better not try to help."

"What! I want to!" the young man protested. "I can work. I know how to work!"

She laid a hand on his arm. "Mike, there are others coming to help—our son Dan and some of his friends."

"Way we figure, boy," Purley said, "there ain't no way you can go unnoticed if you join up with our work gang."

"But I want to do something for you people!"

"Just continue to be our friend," Purley said, chuckling at the younger man's earnestness. "You'll get even, if 'even' is what's needed."

Jenny added, "Besides, we like you."

That evening, Mikhail Baranovitch tucked his feet under Jenny White's table. And during the night, he slept in what little hay was left in the White's haymow. Between, Michael peppered his friends with questions about edible plants, their preparation, proper storage, and when they should be harvested. He mentioned that he was working at fashioning a pair of calf-length moccasins from one of the hides he'd tanned, and was thinking about trying a jacket and trousers.

"We got an extra awl, don't we Jen?" Purley asked.

She nodded, adding, "And some waxed thread, too."

While Jenny rummaged for their extra sewing awl, Purley disappeared to the barn. When he returned, he brought a square of thick bullhide he said would make better moccasin soles than any of the deerhides he'd seen at Michael's camp. When Michael left the White's ranch, he also carried a copy of Jerome C. Wallace's *Edible Plants of the Northwest*, in third edition. And tucked inside his shirt was the latest U.S. Forest Service map of the Umpqua National Forest.

Intrigued by names on the Umpqua Forest map, Mikhail Baranovitch set out for "Rough Creek" in "Devil's Canyon." As far as the fugitive was concerned, the canyon was not as forbidding as he'd expected. On his way out of Rough Creek Michael chanced through a place called Lonesome Meadows where he discovered several dead Hereford cattle lying in bloated random among a forest of huge western red cedar trees. "What could've killed them, Mr. White?" he asked Purley a day later.

"Was there any larkspur around, boy."

Michael shook his head. "No. I looked, too. But there was a bunch of live cows feeding there and I didn't know what to do. Tell me they weren't yours."

"No, no," the old man boomed. "Charley Howell, over on the Rogue, has grazing rights there." Purley said, "How long again was it you seen 'em?"

"Yesterday," the young man said. "I came right here soon as I could."

"That's one hell of a walk, boy. From Lonesome Meadows to here in one day. You sleep any last night?"

"No. I was on the road by then, so I could see well enough to keep moving."

Purley nodded. "I'll try to get word to Howell about the dead cows. Meanwhile, you come on up to the house and let Jenny fix you a bait of vittles. After that, you can curl up in the fresh hay we fetched up."

Though Michael was infatuated with the huge Lonesome Meadows' cedars, he had a superstitious dread of the place and never returned. But as he'd fled from there, he'd passed through the lower end of another place of awesome beauty. Upon his return, Fish Creek Valley fulfilled its promise, and Mikhail Baranovitch spent several days subsisting on camas roots and the schools of small trout so abundant in the little headwaters creek that flowed there.

Upon leaving Fish Creek Valley, Michael climbed Rattlesnake Mountain, then drifted through Whitehorse Meadows and the Rolling Grounds. He climbed Black Rock Mountain until he could gaze down into the South Umpqua watershed, then drifted west to Hemlock Meadows and the headwaters of Little River.

The end of July found him back at his Medicine Creek overhang, contentedly sewing a second pair of moccasins and fashioning a jacket of tanned deer hides. During the last few months he'd learned that the olfactory leather-like leaves of evergreen ceanothus made a suitable substitute for soap; that he could scour pots and pans with jointgrass; that early Utah Mormons ate mariposa lily bulbs—and that he could, too.

Michael thought it must have been their camp. Huckleberries were ripe and he'd grazed his way from Balm Mountain to Bradley Lake without spotting his friends. He thought the Whites were up here somewhere, though; Purley said they always packed horses into the high country above Caps Illahee for a week or two of picking and canning huckleberries during late summer.

Jenny had scoffed at that. "*I* pick huckleberries. *I* can huckleberries. *He* takes his hounds out cougar hunting."

Purley grinned. "We've always made most of our living from bounty hunting for varmints—she didn't tell you that, did she? Oh we made some from cows, and some from guiding pilgrims. But most of it was from varmint hunting."

Michael had been fascinated to learn that Purley had actually guided Zane Gray for fishing on the North Umpqua. "I thought Zane Gray wrote about the Rogue," Michael said.

"That's right, Purley boomed. "He *wrote* about the Rogue, but he *fished* the Umpqua." Michael was still thinking about that when Purley added, "I asked him about that one time, and he told me he wasn't about to ruin the Umpqua by writing about it, too."

Mikhail Baranovitch had found signs of a recent camp at Bradley Lake and was heading for Grassy Ranch when he crossed fresh horse tracks leading toward Reynolds Ridge. He turned that direction. He was still lost in thoughts of Zane

Gray and *The Riders of the Purple Sage* when Jenny White poked her head out of a huckleberry patch and said, "Well, you certainly aren't a bear, though as much noise as you were making, I wondered."

She had an extra bucket, so he helped her pick throughout the remainder of the afternoon. When Jenny and Michael straggled up to the White camp at Reynolds Ridge Shelter, Purley had a pot of pinto beans bubbling over the firepit. Cornbread was also mixed and ready to pour into the Dutch oven.

Jenny said, "The cook's been busy." Then she waved a hand at their visitor and said, "Looky here at what the cat drug in."

"You know," Purley said, straightening from the fire and waving a big serving spoon at the younger man, "you keep showing up all over this country, someday you'll know it as well as us."

Michael slipped out of his heavy backpack, and while opening it said, "I brought you folks a little something special." With that, he pulled out two cans of Lucky Lager beer and a quart bottle of Cabin Still whiskey.

"That's the same kind of beer we got in our ice box at home, ain't it Jenny?" Purley boomed.

"Yes, and didn't you bring a bottle of that same kind of whiskey home just before we packed up for here?"

"Where did you get that?" Purley asked, his smile fading for the first time since Michael had met him.

"It came out of your house," Michael said. "That's all the beer that's left after two guys let themselves in and started swilling it. But they hadn't even started on the whiskey when I pointed out what they were doin' wasn't proper."

Purley dropped to a block of wood, while Jenny crowded close.

"They took it out of the house while I was on my way up from the timber behind the barn. They got in their car and took off before I could catch 'em and I thought I'd lost 'em. Then they pulled into that round forest service shelter and when I got there, they'd already downed a beer apiece and punched the top on another. One of 'em said, 'Who in hell are you?' But that's the last either of 'em got to say before I took their beers away, gave 'em a spanking, and put 'em to bed."

"Are you shittin' me?" Purley demanded.

"No sir. They had a .22 rifle in their car, and a knife bigger than most of the machetes I saw in New Guinea. By the time they woke up, I had one of 'em in the trunk and a rope around the other one's neck. I made that guy drive down from Caps Illahee while I held on to the rope from the back seat." Michael blushed. "You see, sir, I never learned to drive a car, so he had to drive." The young man saw his friends wouldn't make fun of him, so added, "I never had a car of my own and neither did Papa. Nor did I ever run into no Army General that needed a man my size to herd his Jeep. Then I was in the hospital ever since Morotai and...." He trailed off.

"Mike, what did you do with them?" Jenny said.

His smile was faint. "Made 'em drive up Copeland Creek and out the powerline road on Big Oak Flats. Then I shot out the tires on their car and put the almighty fear of God in 'em." He wound up grinning at both of his friends. "I'm pretty sure they'll never go back to Caps Illahee."

Purley picked up a beer, dug in his trousers for a pocket knife, opened a blade, and poked a hole in the top of the can. Silently he handed the beer to Michael, then picked up the other can for himself. Jenny wiped out a tin cup with a dishtowel and held it out. "Is that whiskey fit to drink?" she asked.

Chapter 38

"We finally have a fix on Baranovitch," Sheriff Irvin Finch told his assembled deputies in the enforcement division conference room at the Douglas County Courthouse. "His prints were on a car belonging to a man named Harrison Shilling that was left on Big Oak Flats, up the North Umpqua River, near Illahee Rock. Shilling said he and a companion, Wolfgang Draeger, was overpowered at gunpoint while camped at a forest service shelter on Big Oak Flats. Then Shilling said they were made to drive out a powerline road, beaten, their tires shot out, then left to find their way back to civilization. They claimed their attacker was a crazy wild man. As a result, I had their car dusted for fingerprints and Baranovitch's was lifted in two places."

Sheriff Finch turned to a U.S. Forest Service map of the Umpqua National Forest, pinned earlier to the wall. He pointed out Big Oak Flats, then drew a circle that included Caps Illahee, Pine Bench, Big Camas Ranger Station, and the Tokatee encampment. "Our quarry is somewhere in this area. I'm dispatching Talbott, Carmichael, and Hayes up there to make inquiries and investigate for petty burglaries. The rest of you can relax your scrutiny around Glide and the Little River drainage—obviously the fugitive isn't there. Any questions?"

Jocko Hayes raised his hand. "What level of force are we to employ in apprehension, Sheriff? Are we to try and take him one on one? Do we shoot if we have to?"

Irvin Finch stared down his straight and slender nose. The man's eyes were as flat as half-squeezed grapes. "Baranovitch is armed and known to be dangerous. The answer to that question seems readily apparent. On the other hand, he is an escaped mental patient and, as such, might engender sympathy from do-gooder elements. You should, of course, always try to call in reinforcements for a take-down. But if circumstances fail to warrant that option, then I'll expect you to expedite the arrest using such proper means as is appropriate." The sheriff added, "That kook has been an embarrassment to this office for seven months. *I want him bad!*"

Jocko Hayes was forty miles up the North Umpqua Highway before he realized Finch had not answered his question.

Purley White was splitting wood when the deputy sheriff drove up to the ranch house. The old man paused, fished a red handkerchief from an overalls pocket and wiped his brow. "Howdy," he called. "Come on up here and sit awhile. That's what I aim to do."

Jocko Hayes took a block of wood alongside the one Purley perched on and, gazing out across the distant vista, said, "Lord, this is some view."

"I thought so," Purley said, "when I took the homestead back in ought-eight."

The screen door behind the two men slammed and there was Jenny, holding out two cups of coffee. "There's cookies in the oven; they'll be out in a couple of minutes. Purley and his wife exchanged guarded glances as Jocko beamed.

"Indians ran their horses up here," Purley said, waving at the huge hay meadow. "And the forest service wintered their strings up here for a few years—until the big snow of '17 caught 'em without any feed." Jocko sipped from his mug as Purley continued, "After that big die-off, the ranger in charge asked me if I'd put up hay for 'em and I said 'shore,' because up until that time they'd been refusing to deed me my homestead. The reason why was they didn't want any homesteads messing up their forest, see? They claimed my homestead wasn't suitable for agriculture." The old man snorted at the memory, then burst out laughing. "So when I got my first check from 'em for the hay they bought, I went up to Portland and got me a meeting with the Regional Forester. Had me a lawyer, too."

Jocko blew across the top of his cup of coffee, then took a sip.

"Well, I got my homestead deed right after that."

Jenny returned with a plate of cookies and the coffee pot. "He'll talk your leg off, Sheriff. What can we do for you?"

Jocko took a cookie. "I'm going around warning folks about the 'Umpqua Wild Man'." He saw no flicker of recognition on either of the Whites. "We have reason to believe he's in this area, and ..."

"What makes you think that?" Jenny asked.

"Well, actually there was a disturbance over on Big Oak Flats. We know the Wild Man stole some stuff from a camp at Snuff Shelter and vandalized a car—we lifted his fingerprints off the car."

"I see."

"Either of you folks seen anything strange? He's a big guy, Mr. White—as big as you. He's an escaped mental patient from the V.A. Hospital in Roseburg and he's armed and dangerous."

Purley threw off the remainder of his coffee and said, "Me and Jenny, we been followin' that case through the newspapers, and it seems to us that this here Umpqua Wild Man has been accused of a whole bunch o' stuff he didn't do."

Jocko's face reddened. "Yeah, I guess that happened. But," he winked, "you know the media."

Jenny said, "Most of the accusations look to us like they started with the sheriff's office."

"We may have been quick to conclusions," the deputy said.

"Tell me about the two guys on Big Oak Flats," Purley boomed.

"I didn't say there were two guys," Jocko Hayes said, eyes narrowing. "How did you know there were two guys?"

Jenny said, "We had a report that two men driving that same car was seen breaking into our home while we were up picking huckleberries. Purley assumed there were two men, as did I."

Jocko pulled a notebook and pencil from his shirt pocket. "Did you report the breaking and entering?"

"Was going to," Purley said. "But we ain't got to town."

"What was taken?"

"Near as we could tell, just beer and whiskey."

"Who reported seeing them do it?"

Jenny said, "There was a note on the door. We don't know who wrote it."

"Can I see the note?"

"I burned it."

"How do you know the car on Big Oak Flats is the one?"

"They took the license number. It was on the note."

Deputy Hayes gazed closely at the couple. "And you just happened to amble over to Big Oak Flats and see the car?"

"Sheriff," Jenny said. "Big Oak Flats is only six miles from here. We graze cows there in the spring and fall. It's common for one or the other of us to walk or ride through Big Oak Flats to check on the grass."

"Uh-huh," Jocko said, pocketing his notebook. "Now let me recap what's been said here: You folks had a report of a couple of guys breaking into your house and stealing beer and booze. You even had a report on the license number of their car. Then, by chance, you find that car over on Big Oak Flats with all its tires shot out. Is that right?" Both Jenny and Purley nodded. "But you just haven't got around to reporting this affair, though you intended to do so."

"Don't have to now, Sheriff," Purley boomed. "Now that you're here, you can take the report back to Roseburg with you."

"You could've phoned," Jocko said. "There's a telephone down at the Dry Creek Store."

Jenny held out the plate of cookies. "Won't you have another one, Deputy? In fact, take a handful."

It was George Talbott who discovered that someone had taken camas bulbs

from the meadow near the Big Camas Ranger Station.
"We just figured it was some left-over Indians," the station guard said, "maybe Klamaths or Modocs. Anyway they did it at night, over a couple of weeks. We wouldn't have known, except the blue of the blossoms kept fading from the meadow. Then I went out and checked and found somebody'd been digging."
"Anything missing from the station?" the deputy asked. "Any tools or food or personal gear?"
The station guard laughed. "God almighty, who could tell? With us moving lock, stock, and barrel down to Tokatee, everything up here is in such a turmoil that they could take stuff away in a semi and nobody'd be the wiser."

Milo Carmichael struck paydirt at the Tokatee Falls Copco encampment. "Yeah, maybe three or four months ago—I can't remember 'xactly when," the camp tender said. "Anyway, somebody broke into the storehouse and took some stuff. Wasn't much, so we didn't bother to report it. But I paid closer attention. Whoever did it never came back, so we just figured it was a transient."
"And you can't remember when?" the deputy asked, scribbling a note.
"No. But Joe Tibbets said he thought somebody poached a fish or two below Soda Springs."
"Where can I find this Tibbets?"
"Maybe headquarters could tell you. He quit a month ago. Said he was going back to Oklahoma."
"Shit. What can you tell me about somebody poaching? Did he see him?"
"Not that I know of," the camp tender replied. "But there's been reports off and on about poaching there for years. Maybe this time Tibbets dreamed it, for all I know."

On his way back downriver, Deputy Sheriff Jocko Hayes stopped by the White Ranch. As chance had it, Purley was gone, but Jenny was feeding chickens.
"Good afternoon, ma'am," Jocko said, doffing his hat.
She dusted her hands. "Let me gather the rest of the eggs, deputy, then we'll go up to the house and I'll make some tea."
Later, balancing a saucer on one knee and cup on the other, Jocko said, "We know he dug camas roots at Big Camas, and we know he dug cattails at Soda Springs. We even think he might've taken a fish or two below the dam. We have his prints from the alidade at the old lookout at Mountain Meadows. We know he was at Big Oak Flats and I've got a darned good hunch he was here at Caps Illahee when two yahoos broke into your house and stole beer and whiskey. What I'm asking, ma'am, is can you tell me anything?"

Jenny White looked down her nose at the deputy for several seconds, her face as inscrutable as a that of a Chinese Mandarin. Finally she said, "Sheriff, I'm so disgusted with the press releases coming from your office, and the way they're used in the media, that even if I knew something of the whereabouts of the so-called Umpqua Wild Man—who I suspect is not half as wild as you would have us believe—I would not tell you."

Jocko shrugged and smiled. "Well, that's telling it like it is, ma'am. It confirms what I suspected, though. You do know that it's a crime if you harbor a criminal, do you not?"

She drew herself up, voice rising, all four feet, eleven inches. "Are you accusing me of ..."

"And it's equally a crime if you aid and abet a fugitive."

"You mean like the 'underground railroad' that spirited slaves to freedom from Georgia. Or are you talking about the French Resistance that tried to help downed allied airmen flee a Nazi concentration camp?"

Jocko held up a hand. "Hold on, ma'am. I'm accusing you of nothing."

"You are, too," she spat back. "It's lucky for you that Purley isn't here."

Jocko turned to look at the barn. "Where is he, by the way? Out to warn the Wild Man?"

As a matter of fact, Purley White was at that very moment straddling a block of wood in Mikhail Baranovitch's Medicine Creek lair, scribbling a note. He'd arrived minutes before to find Michael gone. Expecting as much, the old man had taken out a pencil and paper and begun to write when the subject of his scribbling said, "I saw your horse." He hopped across the creek to join the older man.

"You're getting good enough at pussy-footin' that you're surprisin' me, ain't you, boy?"

Michael grinned. He dug into a rock crevice and brought forth a sack of roasted pine nuts. "I might should've dried 'em a little longer," he said.

Purley took a handful. "They know you're up here, boy."

The revelation came as a blow. Michael moved a second block of wood nearer his friend, then dropped on to it with a thump. "Here?" he mumbled. "They know I'm right here?"

Purley shook his head. "Naw. But they took your prints off the car on Big Oak Flats and so they know you're in these parts. They just don't know where. They might even think Jenny and me know more'n we're tellin'."

Michael leaped to his feet. "I don't want you two to get in trouble!"

Purley's laugh echoed around the cavern. "Ain't likely, boy. What we ain't telling would fill up a couple of books. What we do tell don't make it worthwhile to wet a pencil nub."

It was with a great deal of gravity that Michael shook his elderly friend's hand as Purley made to mount his horse. "Tell Jenny goodby. Tell her I appreciate everything you two have done for me."

Purley swung a leg over the saddle cantle, then said. "There ain't no reason to run off half-cocked, boy. Just lay low for awhile, maybe take a little sashay over to the headwaters of the Willamette or the Rogue. Then when you come back it'll all be dyin' down." Michael smiled and waved. And when the last hoofbeats of the sorrel horse faded, he began dismantling his Medicine Creek camp.

It took Mikhail Baranovitch the better part of two months to move the contents of the Medicine Creek camp to the one on Cavitt Creek. Moving only at night, following the pavement when he could so that no tell-tale size-14 shoe prints would be left to attract wonder and attention, the big man shuttled load after load the fifty-five miles from Medicine Creek to Cavitt Creek. He hid from every approaching headlight, took fright at voices emanating from nearby campgrounds or cabins.

As expected, the fall rains began by the end of September, interrupting his plodding journeys. But of far more consequence was the advent of deer season, commencing in early October. With deer hunting in full swing, all *predictable* encounters went by the wayside. Hunters could be *anywhere*.

Remembering that it'd been deer hunters who'd years before discovered his earliest camp on Cow Creek, Michael squirreled back into his Cavitt Creek camp and stayed put.

Sheriff Irvin Finch withdrew the observers he had watching the White Ranch at the end of October. "Might as well," Deputy Renfro Rogers said. "Hell, they knew we was there. That little old lady even once brought us out a plate of sourdough biscuits to munch on." And with end of hunting season, Sheriff Finch also recalled the undercover officers he had posing as deer hunters and canvassing the area centered on Soda Springs. Mikhail Baranovitch's Medicine Creek camp went undiscovered.

"If he was ever up in that country," George Talbott said, "he ain't now."

With his decision to call in his deputies, Sheriff Irvin Finch also put out a press release that the "Umpqua Wild Man" had been driven from Douglas County, and that citizens could now feel at ease.

Chapter 39

No one was more pleased than Colonel Y. Herbert Corwin, Commandant of the local United States Veteran's Hospital when the Douglas County Sheriff stepped down the search for escaped mental patient, Mikhail Baranovitch. "Look at this," Corwin said, handing his chief psychiatrist the latest *The Daily News.* "Finch says they've traced Baranovitch to the remote Tokatee Falls area and believe that he slipped over the Cascades."

Dr. Bryce Henderson read the news release, muttering "That socktucker."

"I'm sorry," Colonel Corwin said. "What did you say?"

"I said the sheriff is an asshole."

"Please, Bryce! Even if I agreed with you, it's hardly a diplomatic position for us to take when our star is rising in the East. May our patient succeed in avoiding his cross forever."

Henderson grunted, pushed back his chair and said, "if you've no further need for me, Colonel, I have another patient to see.

"Do you think he truly did get away?" Gladys asked as the psychiatrist trudged by the reception desk.

"Hell, no!" he replied, abrupt and angry.

Mikhail Baranovitch dreamed of returning to Montana. Secure in his Cavitt Creek camp, he thought he had enough food for a couple of months. If he could avoid detection through the remaining winter, he could then dash across the Cascade Mountains into Eastern Oregon, and thence home. Without pursuit, and with his outdoor skills, the fugitive thought he could make it across Oregon and Idaho even if he had to walk every step of the way. On the other hand, he still had money. Maybe if he got to Bend, or up on the Columbia River, he could buy a bus ticket.

But there was this other problem: he was lonesome. Until he met Purley and Jenny White, he had a full-time job obtaining food. With the White's help—and friendship, and most of all their knowledge—he'd learned much about nutritious wild plants and their preparation. Then with the abundance of late summer and fall, and the effort he'd put into the harvest, he'd found he could focus less on survival and more on the pleasure of his infrequent visits to the White's Caps Illahee Ranch. There, Mikhail Baranovitch found stimulating conversation and a cornucopia of books. Not only did the Whites have a wealth of outdoors knowledge they readily shared, both husband and wife had a bunch of stories to tell: exciting tales, wonderful tales, tales of the Old West, of Zane Gray and the old Umpqua mountain man, Bill Bradley.

Michael heaped coals on the lid of a broken Dutch oven while his memory worked overtime. He'd discovered the cast-iron pot at a dump behind the Big Camas Ranger Station. There'd been only an inch-long triangular piece broken out of its wall and he'd been able to wad up aluminum foil and fix it in place with clips made from abandoned forest service telephone wire. He sighed. He missed his friends. There was Dr. Henderson and his other friends at the hospital: Weyland Jones—what a fine buddy *he* was—and Gladys and Daniel and Will Terwilliger! How he'd love to chat with them again. A tear slid down the big man's face. The absence of human contact, he decided, was like vultures pecking at the eyes of his spirit.

December morphed into January. Mikhail Baranovitch ate the last of his camas roots in early February and the last of his jerky three days later. It was on Valentine's Day, 1957 when Michael decided he'd like mutton for a change of diet. It was during a soft rain that he downed the yearling ewe on a ranch along the Buckhorn Road.

He thought he'd chosen well. The band of sheep was in a back pasture, well screened from road or dwellings by treeless hills. What he'd not reckoned with was that Jeremy Marsters skipped school that day and was holed up in a cave he and Ralph Coogan had dug the previous summer. The cave, well hidden by a patch of willow brush was a bare fifty yards from where Michael killed the ewe.

The sound of the .22 Remington never awakened him, but the drumming, bawling flight of the remaining sheep alerted the slumbering boy. Ten minutes later, a breathless Jeremy Marsters burst through the front doorway of his parent's farmhouse. "The Wild Man!" he screamed. "The Wild Man is back!" Seconds later, Jeremy's mother was on the phone to the Douglas County Deputy Sheriff in Glide. And twenty minutes after that, Deputy Renfro Rogers drove into the Marster's yard. Andrew Marsters and a neighbor, Lucien McDonald waited. The men carried deer rifles.

Following Jeremy's directions, the posse converged on the hidden pocket where Mikhail Baranovitch was finishing his work by burying the sheep's remains. Only a little trampled grass would've been all the posse might've found had not they topped the low ridge just as Michael slipped on his backpack and picked up his rifle and shovel.

"HALT!" the Deputy cried. The two farmers threw up their rifles.

Instead of halting, Michael raced away at a zig-zagging run, heading for some distant timber. Lucien McDonald got off a quick shot at two hundred yards; Andy Marsters raised the muzzle of his .30 caliber Stevens, then lowered it. "God, look at him run! And with a full pack!"

UMPQUA WILD MAN RETURNS!
By Chuck Little
Daily News Staff Writer

Andrew Marsters's farm along the Buckhorn Road was the latest to feel the outlaw brunt of the Umpqua Wild Man when the fugitive mental patient from the Roseburg Veteran's Hospital was spotted shooting and butchering a yearling ewe.

"When we surprised him, he took off running," Marsters said. "He was like a deer, heading for the ridgeline between our place and Fall Creek."

Sheriff Irvin Finch pledged quick action to halt the Wild Man's depredations. "Obviously he has just returned to the County and this time we'll bring him in or I'll want to know why."

Sheriff Finch said he was mobilizing his deputies to blanket the Glide-Little River area. "If he's there, we want to make it so hot for him that he'll break from cover."

The front page *Daily News* story went on to recap Mikhail Baranovitch's multiple escapes from hospital detention; it also speculated on how ineffective his treatment had been. The story recapped how the aggressive Sheriff's Department had, the summer before, driven the "Wild Man" from the County.

"Cokesackers," Dr. Bryce Henderson muttered as he wadded up the latest news story and directed it at his wastebasket.

Colonel Y. Herbert Corwin waxed indignant that a shot was actually fired at the mental patient. *"Mikhail Baranovitch is an unfortunate human being,"* the Hospital Commandant told Chuck Little in an interview. *"The man is in jeopardy purely because of his battle fatigue, and those mental disturbances caused by it."*

However, Colonel Corwin declined to make other members of the hospital staff available for interviews relating to Mikhail Baranovitch's treatment, or the man's behavior while incarcerated. Even a phone call from the newspaper's editor failed to provide his reporter with more access.

Meanwhile, the roads around Glide and Little River crawled with Douglas County Sheriff's vehicles. Regular patrols were implemented as far up as snowline, including periodic night patrols on side roads, until Mikhail Baranovitch was barely able to cook meals without detection.

The Dogged and the Damned

"I dunno, Sheriff," Deputy Renfro Rogers reported, "but when I stopped to piss up there above Cavitt Falls, I thought I smelled smoke. Mind you, I couldn't place it, but it stands to reason he could be camped up there somewhere."

"What about a stake-out?" the sheriff asked. "If he's cooking at night—and he must be—he'll douse everything when he sees or hears a vehicle coming."

"What I think would be better, Sheriff, is to put a nighttime foot patrol on Cavitt Creek, and maybe to walk the Jim Creek Road. What do you think?"

"He might be farther up Little River," the sheriff replied. "Damn him!"

"I'd like to try a foot patrol, though. But I'll need somebody on standby in a patrol car. Give me Jocko and we'll get this guy."

"All right," Sheriff Irvin Finch snapped. "But no letting it out to the media. They're already all over us because I mentioned that I might bring in bloodhounds."

It was three nights later when Deputy Rogers again smelled smoke in nearly the same place. This time, however, the Deputy had trudged up the Cavitt Creek Road instead of riding in the comfort of a heated County Law Enforcement sedan. By creeping closer, Deputy Rogers even spotted the fugitive's campfire and plotted its position in a dense patch of young trees across Cavitt Creek from the road. Then Rogers hightailed it back down the road to join Jocko Hayes.

At four o'clock in the morning, Sheriff Irvin Finch was alerted. He arrived at his office fifteen minutes later. After hearing Roger's story, Finch studied the map, asked about patrol routine, and ordered that the same procedures be maintained so as not to alert the fugitive that a take-down was in the offing. While swilling nerve-jangling black coffee, and with more map study, the sheriff decided more surveillance would provide more information. The following night, he ordered his most trusted deputy, Undersheriff Milo Carmichael, to accompany Rogers on a second nighttime trek up the Cavitt Creek Road.

Unfortunately for the officers, Mikhail Baranovitch did not need to cook for three more nights. Then he lit a small fire in order to boil a pot of coffee.

"We got him, Irv!" Carmichael crowed. "He was right where Rogers said he was. "Let's take him down in the morning."

Finch smiled at the phone. "Not in the morning, Milo. I want to bring the newspaper in on this one. Let's make it at one o'clock ... no, say two. We'll assemble our team at Cavitt Falls. I'll bring more deputies up with me to go with you and Rogers. Hot damn! This time we've got the bastard!"

It was a quarter past two by the time Douglas County Sheriff Irvin Finch arrived at Cavitt Falls with the *The Daily News* reporter, Chuck Little. The sheriff was trailed by two other patrol cars filled with deputies. And it was nearly three o'clock by the time Finch had unfolded a map on the hood of his sedan and finished explaining his plan.

Undersheriff Milo Carmichael was to take three deputies in his vehicle past the suspect's camp until they reached a footlog across Cavitt Creek that Rogers had earlier spotted. They were then to silently take positions above Baranovitch's hiding place. Carmichael and his men were allotted thirty minutes to accomplish their objective. Meanwhile, Deputy Renfro Rogers, along with Deputy Tuck O'Neal, was to remain out of sight at a lower road bend to ensure that, should the fugitive break free, he would remain securely bottled. "There's no chance he can cross the creek—not while its up like it is now," the sheriff said, staring at the rampaging falls.

At precisely 3:30 PM, Sheriff Irvin Finch, accompanied by Deputy George Talbott and newspaper reporter Chuck Little would park the sheriff's Chevrolet on the road directly across Cavitt Creek from the fugitive's hideout. At that time—3:30 PM—Sheriff Irvin Finch would use a bullhorn to demand the surrender of the "Umpqua Wild Man." Due to the anticipated close confines of Mikhail Baranovitch's hiding place, each deputy was issued autoload riot guns in twelve-gauge caliber.

Chuck Little wriggled with delight as Carmichael and his carload of deputies left the Cavitt Falls Campground. To be in on a ground-level scoop of this magnitude would be a once-in-a-lifetime opportunity for a cub reporter on a small-town daily! Once again, the reporter his friends called "Little Chuck" thanked the sheriff for his trust and thoughtfulness.

Mikhail Baranovitch was startled to hear the whine of an approaching vehicle; he wrinkled his brow, trying to recollect if there had been a patrol earlier in the day. He peeped from his hiding place as the sedan motored by—only the driver, so there's nothing to worry about. Only a couple of miles to the snowline, he'll be back in a few minutes.

Fifteen minutes later, Michael was growing restless. The Sheriff's Department sedan hasn't returned. Why? What was that? Rustling? Like at the Yakamul, when the Japs closed in. Damn the creek—it's too noisy to hear anything. The fugitive picked up his .30-30 Marlin and moved outside his shelter, nearer where he'd heard the noise. *Up the hill and to the left!* He darted back inside his shelter, picked up a box of .22 rimfire ammunition, and snatched his Remington single-shot .22. Just then, he heard another approaching vehicle. He grabbed a few slices of remnant meat, slipped the butcher knife into its scabbard and slung its belt around his neck.

Another Sheriff's car! He knew then that he was being surrounded! He threw the sling of the .30-30 over his head as the second car pulled to a halt on the road across from his camp. Douglas County Sheriff Irvin Finch's mega-voice boomed through the bullhorn:

"MIKHAIL BARANOVITCH! YOU ARE SURROUNDED! COME OUT WITH YOUR HANDS OVER YOUR HEAD! REPEAT! YOU ARE SURROUNDED. YOU HAVE NO CHANCE FOR ESCAPE! YOUR ONLY HOPE IS TO SURRENDER PEACEFULLY! REPEAT! GIVE YOURSELF UP!"

Sheriff Irvin Finch grinned across the seat at Chuck Little, more than a little proud of how authoritative he sounded. Deputy George Talbott slid from the rear seat to take a position at the sedan's rear. Finch, noting the fearlessness of his deputy, opened the driver's door and stepped out, again lifting the bullhorn.

"MIKHAIL BARANOVITCH! THIS IS YOUR LAST CHANCE! YOUR ONLY HOPE IS A PEACEFUL SURRENDER! YOU ARE ..."

Michael took a deep breath, then burst from his shelter, taking huge leaps through the head-high, clawing, clinging blackberry bushes, heading pell-mell for the creek.

"There he goes!" yelled someone behind him.

Then Mikhail Baranovitch heard no more because he was singing at the top of his lungs:

"YANKEE DOODLE CAME TO TOWN ... RIDING ON A DONKEY!"

Chapter 40

Mikhail Baranovitch's audacious move stunned the sheriff and his deputies! Bounding up and through the tearing, clinging blackberry vines, leaping into the flood, surging across with his great strength, all the while his **"YANKEE DOODLE DANDY!"** mixing with the bullhorn's **"GODDAMN! HE'S COMING THIS WAY! HOLY SHIT! SOMEBODY DO SOMETHING!"**

Who fired the first shot was a subject of debate long after, but the first shotgun blast from behind Michael's camp took out a patch of grass just over the surging fugitive's head! The second flattened a rear tire on the sheriff's patrol car as Michael lunged up the bank. The third cut limbs from a tree over the prone and scrambling Finch's head. The fourth came from George Talbott's gun as he reflexively returned fire on those firing upon him.

"CEASE FIRING! CEASE FIRING! YOU'RE KILLING ..."

"MIND THE MUSIC AND THE STEP!" Baranovitch roared as he scrambled to the bank top, brandishing his puny single-shot .22 like a Browning Automatic Rifle. **"AND WITH THE GIRLS BE HANDY!"**

Another shotgun blast came from the fugitive's rear, this time blowing out the driver's side window on the Chevrolet!

"STOP FIRING! STOP FIRING!" Finch shouted again through the bullhorn. **"CARMICHAEL, STOP YOUR MEN FROM FIRING! DO YOU HEAR ME!"**

An eerie silence fell over the battlefield. Finch rolled over to peer beneath the length of his patrol car, at its sagging rear tire, at Talbott's boots. The sheriff, not realizing he was still holding the bullhorn, blasted into the silence, **"DID WE GET HIM?"** Finch glared at the horn, then threw it aside. He noted the reporter lying, hands clasped over his head, amid mud and water in the ditch across the road.

"Talbott!" the sheriff cried. "Did we get him?"

Talbott's boots shifted by the right rear wheel, but there was no response. Then Talbott fell heavily to the graveled roadway. His eyes looked as wide as saucers and stared directly into the slitted ones of Sheriff Irvin Finch. "I've been shot!" the deputy said, as if in wonder.

Mikhail Baranovitch charged into the forest beyond the Cavitt Creek Road and paused. He was bleeding over much of his body from the knife-like blackberry thorns, his clothes clawed and ripped. Behind him came shouting and he knew

258

pursuit was close and inevitable. He pulled his pocketwatch from his buckskin trousers, knowing the timepiece would be water-soaked and useless. However, he expected the watch would've stopped while he was in the creek—and he was right: 3:38 PM. That meant, on a cloudy day like the present, darkness was only a couple of hours away.

He decided there was no way they could catch him before nightfall. But he wondered what then? They had his entire camp, everything he owned except a knife and two rifles. Setting out to climb the forested ridge between Copperhead Creek and the adjoining drainage, Michael soon settled into a ground-eating pace. Tears streaked down his cheeks at thought of Anna Karenina's picture tucked into dry corner of his tiny shelter.

"Carmichael!" shouted Sheriff Irvin Finch through cupped hands. "Get over here. NOW! Leave one of your guys to guard the camp in case he tries to double back. But I want you here. We've got one of our own down!"

The radio was one thing on the sheriff's car still operable. "Rogers," the sheriff called, "be alert. He could try circling around you and down to the lower road." Rogers acknowledged, then the sheriff asked the Glide deputy if he had any competent friends he could call in for assistance in monitoring the Little River Bridges?

The sheriff's next transmission was an effort to get out to his headquarters, but radio reception from the Cavitt Creek Canyon was too weak for that. Finch called Rogers again to ask if he was able to reach outside contact from the Falls?

"Negative, sheriff," the deputy replied. "I think I could tap into the relay on Mount Scott if I could call from the Little River Road."

"Never mind. I'll be down there myself in five minutes. We've got an officer down and I'll want to get an ambulance up to meet us."

"An officer down?" came the query. "Who?"

"Talbott!" was the reply. "If you see that sonofabitch who did it, shoot first and ask questions later!"

Chuck Little tucked his rolled-up jacket beneath George Talbott's head, then unzipped the stricken officer's jacket and unbuttoned the wool shirt. When Finch joined him to look in on Talbott's wound, the reporter asked, "Are you sure Baranovitch shot him, sheriff?"

"One hole," the sheriff said. "Our guys all had buckshot."

"Could there have been ..."

"I said Baranovitch did this, Chuck."

Little pushed to his feet and walked around the car. "And did Baranovitch do this?" he asked.

Finch followed him. "Look, Chuck, you have to help me on this. I'm looking out for you; you've got to look out for me."

The reporter mumbled, "I'll do what I can." Carmichael's car sped around an upper bend and slid to a stop.

Finch assigned Deputies Hayes and Brown to stay with the sheriff's damaged patrol car, then he and Carmichael and the reporter helped the wounded Talbott into the back seat of Carmichael's vehicle. Finch, Carmichael, and Little climbed into the front seat of the undersheriff's car for the ride down to Rogers's location. After commandeering Rogers and his car, Finch delegated O'Neal to remain at Cavitt Falls, while Carmichael was sent back to pick up the other two deputies and take over the task of trying to block the Little River bridges to Mikhail Baranovitch.

"Tell whoever you got over at the camp—who is it, Schreckingust?" the sheriff said. "Anyway tell him that we'll need some uncontaminated clothing to provide scent for the bloodhounds."

"Bloodhounds?"

"You're damn right," Sheriff Irvin Finch replied. "If I can get them, they'll be up here in the morning."

The Daily News for February 21, 1956 had already been put to bed; was in fact being read across Douglas County by the time Chuck Little returned from the bungled capture of the "Umpqua Wild Man." Little's chief worry was how to keep the lid on the Cavitt Creek affair until the following day's paper hit the streets. On the ride down Little River to the North Umpqua Highway and the ambulance rendezvous, Little talked turkey with Sheriff Finch. Their agreement was that Finch would release nothing to other media until Little was able to break the story. Little's quid pro quo was favorable treatment in *The Daily News* for Sheriff Irvin Finch.

By the time *The Daily News* went to press with Little's story, Mikhail Baranovitch, traveling through the night, had crossed the mountain divide near Buck's Peak and dropped into the North Myrtle drainage. Striking a graveled road, the fugitive hoofed steadily down it until he came to a farm gate. Michael studied the muddy, well-used track filled with prints of truck tires. A patch of briars grew by the gate. Michael cleared a place for himself amid the briars and settled in to wait.

As luck had it, he had only to wait a couple of hours before a flatbed farm truck loaded with sawlogs destined for a valley mill ground down a hill to the gate. Michael watched as the driver opened the gate, drove through, then closed the gate. It was while the man clambered back into his truck cab that Michael hitched a ride atop the logs. He dropped from the truck at the first stop sign in the town of Myrtle Creek. Within minutes, the fugitive was climbing the hills to the north....

Chuck Little's scoop on the great Cavitt Creek shoot-out broke on the afternoon of Friday, February 22:

UMPQUA WILD MAN BREAKS THROUGH CORDON

DEPUTY WOUNDED IN SHOOT-OUT
by Chuck Little
Daily News Staff Writer

In a blazing gun battle reminiscent of the OK Corral or the Sands of Iwo Jima, escaped mental patient Mikhail Baranovitch, known widely as the "Umpqua Wild Man" once more escaped capture by Douglas County Sheriff's Deputies.

During the latest escape, however, the one-time soldier, a Yugoslavian immigrant, wounded Sheriff's Deputy George Talbott and may have signed his own death warrant.

"I've issued a 'Shoot-To-Kill' order on the poor man, Sheriff Irvin Finch regretfully told The Daily News. But we have no choice. Baranovitch is armed and dangerous, and probably mentally unbalanced to where he no longer understands the difference between right and wrong. He's not only a threat to my deputies, but a serious danger to every honest citizen of Douglas County."

It was just before dark on Thursday when Douglas County Sheriff's Deputies surrounded the camp of the reclusive Baranovitch and gave the fugitive every chance to surrender. Instead, in a hail of gunfire, the nine-lived Baranovitch chose to shoot his way to freedom.

The front-page story was supported by vivid photos of the sheriff's command car with shot-out window and flattened tire, demonstrating beyond a shadow of doubt that a gigantic firefight had indeed taken place. Included was a photograph of the wounded deputy sitting up in his hospital bed.

Deputy George Talbott is reported resting comfortably in Roseburg's Mercy Hospital. Wounded in the lower left abdomen, the deputy is expected to fully recover from his harrowing ordeal.

Talbott, this reporter surmised, was in Baranovitch's direct flight path. *"I got off one shot before he got me,"* Talbott said.

Then the story moved beyond the battle to Sheriff Finch's plans for apprehending the "Umpqua Wild Man." *"We'll get him—it's just a matter of time,"* the sheriff said. *"We've got him boxed in the Little River area, and that's where we plan to contain him."*

The sheriff went on to explain that even as *The Daily News* reporters interviewed him, two bloodhounds have picked up the fugitive's scent and are tracking him into the hills between Cavitt Creek and Deer Creek.

"He can't get away," the sheriff said. "I've even requested search helicopters from the Army Command at Camp Adair. We'll get him—have no doubt of that. When he shot my deputy, he signed his death warrant."

Chuck Little's story hit the big time when the Associated Press decided the "Umpqua Wild Man" was sufficiently newsworthy to pass along their wires. Soon, newspapers in Chicago and Houston and Salt Lake City ran sordid accounts of the "Wild Man." Even the *Washington Post* and *New York Times* carried the scoop.

But a problem surfaced when Chuck Little was called into the office of the much admired editor for *The Daily News*, Chalmers R. Station.

Station was a big man, with a heavy mane of snow white hair. He habitually wore narrow wire-rimmed glasses that he peered over when upset or angry. The editor was peering over his glasses when he told Little, "Close the door young man, and take a seat." Little did so gingerly. He'd entered the office anticipating congratulations for his scoop, but he turned wary with the unsmiling way the old gentleman studied him.

"Mr. Little, I understand you were along with the posse when they surrounded Mikhail Baranovitch's camp."

"Yes sir, that's correct. Sheriff Finch invited me along because I've demonstrated such profound interest in the Baranovitch case."

The white thatched editor said, "And you reported the affair accurately?"

The reporter sensed that a trap lay buried ahead. Still, there could be but one answer to the question. "Yes sir. Certainly."

"Did you know doctors serving in Mercy Hospital's Emergency Room removed a .22 caliber bullet from Deputy George Talbott's abdomen?"

"Yes sir, I do." The reporter thought he could see where the trap lay. He began to sweat.

"Can you explain to me why you've not reported that fact in your copy, young man?"

"I must have overlooked it, sir. I'll include it in my next dispatch."

The Dogged and the Damned

The editor picked up a file and opened it to spread several glossy photographs before Chuck Little. The reporter turned physically ill. "These are your photographs, are they not?" Chalmers Station asked.

"Yes sir."

The editor was grim. "So you certainly were there."

"I was." The reporter's reply was a squeak.

"Then, young man, if Mikhail Baranovitch was armed with a .22 rimfire rifle, who fired the shots that blasted the Sheriff's sedan?"

Little murmured, "It was confusing when the battle was going on, sir."

Chalmers Station snapped up the photos and slid them back into the file folder. "I imagine it was," he said. The editor glared at his reporter until the younger man at last looked at him. "What were the deputies armed with?"

"Riot guns, sir."

"All of them?"

"Yes sir. As far as I could see."

"What gauge?"

"Twelve gauge, I think."

"All of them?"

"Yes sir, as far as I could see."

"Yet you inferred that Mikhail Baranovitch, armed with a .22 rimfire rifle caused all the damage to Sheriff Finch's car?"

Little swallowed. "I'll write a clarification, sir."

Chalmers Station said, "You'll do no such thing. *I'll* write the clarification. But I won't call it a clarification, I'll call it what it will be—an effort to right a grievous editorial assassination. Don't you see what you've done, Mr. Little? You've portrayed a lie. First, you've made a confused mental patient out to be a violent criminal. Secondly ..."

Little broke into his editor's angry dressing-down, "But he did shoot Talbott, sir!"

"Secondly, you've painted the Sheriff's Department out to be white knights when they're obviously bumbling idiots!"

Little said, "May I go, sir? I'm working against a deadline right now."

Chalmers Station snarled, "As far as Baranovitch shooting George Talbott— how many shotgun blasts were fired at the man before Talbott was wounded?"

Chuck Little spread his hands. "I haven't any idea, sir."

"Mmm-hmm," the editor mused. He picked up a newspaper that carried the breaking news. "It says here that Talbott said he got off one shot before Baranovitch shot him."

"Yes, that's what he said."

Chalmers Station's brow wrinkled. "Then tell me, who fired first?"

"The first shots came from across the creek. One of them got the tire. That's the one that sent me rolling from the car. And it's a good thing I did, sir, because the next one came through the driver's window."

"And both of those came before George Talbott fired his weapon?"

Little nodded. "Yes, I think that's right."

The editor spun his chair so that he stared at a Charles M. Russell print of a hunter scratching his head while looking down at a bighorn ram lying dead on the edge of a perilous cliff. Station spun back. "Use your head, young man. Baranovitch leaped from his hiding place and charged at the fewest men confronting him. Several shots were fired from behind; wildly enough to cause you and, I imagine, Sheriff Finch to take cover. Baranovitch charged across the creek and up the bank, topping out only a few feet from where Deputy Talbott crouched behind the patrol car."

Little's eyes had the same calculating gleam as his editor's.

"Now, Mr. Little, at some point during this fracas, Deputy Talbott fired his weapon. With his refuge taking repeated hits from across the creek and Baranovitch apparently wading the stream, is it possible that Talbott could have even *seen* the quarry?"

"No-o. No, he couldn't until Baranovitch popped out on top."

Chalmers Station nodded. "You are at last following my line of reasoning— the one you should've followed—the one any good reporter would've followed from the outset!" Little's eyes again fell, but the editor allowed no respite. "Now tell me, Mr. Little, how far was George Talbott from the edge of the road when Mikhail Baranovitch appeared to him?"

Little murmured, "I don't know sir, I was in the ditch with my head covered."

"Then," Chalmers Station's voice turned silken, "guess!"

"Maybe eight feet."

"And you think he could've missed ... with a shotgun?"

"It doesn't seem reasonable, sir."

"It certainly doesn't! Talbott never fired at Baranovitch! Of *that* we can be sure!"

Both men were silent as they took each other's measure. Finally the white-thatched editor said, "Now put yourself in Mikhail Baranovitch's shoes. You're being repeatedly shot at by men using twelve-gauge shotguns. You pop atop the road and what do you see? A man standing there with a twelve-gauge shotgun leveled your direction. What in God's name do you think any trained soldier would do? Wait to get cut in half?"

Chuck Little stared at his editor in frank admiration. The old boy had developed the probable scenario for the entire Cavitt Creek shootout, and he'd done so with only the clues afforded by the photographs. There's one thing he doesn't know, though, the reporter thought.

"Tell me, Mr. Little," Chalmers Station said ominously, "did you strike any sort of arrangement with Sheriff Finch to suppress an accurate account of what really went on up there?"

Chapter 41

Mikhail Baranovitch was starving. He'd long ago consumed the few scraps of mutton he'd snatched from his camp as he dashed for freedom. Though rested and well-fed prior to the dash, he'd burned enormous energy during his flight over Buck Peak and down to the North Fork of Myrtle Creek. In addition, it had been raining steadily since yesterday and only a ripped deerskin shirt and tattered trousers lay between him and nakedness. To make matters worse, one worn-through moccasin sole had broken loose at the toe and flopped when he walked.

Michael's matches were rendered useless during the surge across Cavitt Creek. He desperately needed a place to hole up out of the rain, where he could strike a fire with flint and steel—if he could first find the flint.

The fugitive dropped back down to the South Umpqua River after fleeing the town of Myrtle Creek. He gathered a few remnant rose hips, chewing them methodically, knowing them to be rich in vitamin C despite their seedy tastelessness. While doing so, he watched traffic across the river on the new Interstate highway for unusual police activity. There seemed to be nothing out of the ordinary. So, during the night, he crossed the South Umpqua River on the highway bridge, heading for a patch of cattails he'd spotted before nightfall. The distance proved to be deceiving, for the cattails turned out to be teasel weed and he struck out again.

Michael did, however, find a switch engine idling at the huge Roseburg Lumber Company complex at Dillard, and a pipe and a couple of stick matches in the vacant engineer's seat. It was the matches that he wanted. He watched the night shift leave the mill at 1:00 a.m.—according to the clock on the lunch room wall. And he was pleased after the men had gone to find a couple of full lunch boxes belonging, he supposed, to night cleanup men. Cannily, he took only a sandwich from one and a package of cookies from the other before fading into the night.

He re-crossed the highway bridge before daylight, then discovered a tumbled-down old sheep shed up a narrow canyon to the east. One corner of the shed was still standing, with its roof sufficiently intact to afford meager shelter. Though soaked from the incessant rain, Michael gathered fallen oak leaves and dead grass by the handfuls, stuffing his tattered clothing with them for warmth. Then he fell into an exhausted sleep.

The fugitive shivered under the crumbling sheep shed all the following day. When the rain tapered to mere sprinkles, he struck a fire with one of his two matches, and dried his ragged shirt and trousers. Hunger drove him from the shelter before daybreak. Shortly thereafter, Michael found an abandoned cabin. The cabin hadn't been used for some time, with broken windows and door ajar. But there was a small, rusted sheet metal frying pan and a couple of cans of food from which mice had eaten the labels. One proved to be beets, the other lima beans. All else the cabin contained was a filthy wool blanket lying wadded-up on rusted bedsprings.

Still wistfully thinking of Montana, Michael turned east, up Roberts Creek, then down Tucker Creek to Dixonville. The man studied the store where he'd made purchases that began his long flight from the V.A. Hospital and police authority. It was while lying sprawled atop the ridge, debating whether to chance a nighttime break-in, that he spotted the cattail marsh near the white farmhouse where rose vines climbed a sidewalk arbor.

He'd had better tools to dig cattails with than his butcher knife, but he still obtained an armload of roots and shoots during the following night. He also discovered the farmhouse had a nearby root cellar stocked with Mason jars filled with canned fruits and vegetables. For the first time in six days, Mikhail Baranovitch filled his belly.

While the fugitive stuffed himself with raw cattail shoots and roasted cattail roots, topped off with canned peaches and corn and peas, *The Daily News* editor Chalmers Station inserted an apology to the newspaper's readers:

THE NEWSPAPERMAN'S DUTY
by Chalmers R. Station

A newspaper—any newspaper, even muckraking ones of dubious credibility has an obligation, a responsibility, a duty to report the truth as they see it. However, the truth is not always obvious and mistakes are sometimes made.

In the case of The Daily News a grievous error was portrayed in this newspaper's reporting of the infamous Cavitt Creek shootout between seven members of a Douglas County Sheriff's posse and escaped Roseburg Veterans Hospital patient Mikhail Baranovitch.

During that gun battle, Baranovitch apparently carried a .22 rimfire rifle while the entire Sheriff's posse was armed with 12-gauge automatic shotguns.

Unfortunately photo captions accompanying the original story of the patrol car damaged during the shootout, as well as the story itself, implied that the fugitive Mikhail Baranovitch was responsible. In fact, armed as he was, it would've been physically impossible for Baranovitch to have accomplished that feat.

The damage to the patrol car, as it turns out, was entirely caused by errant gunfire from sheriff's deputies carried away by the explosive nature of the fugitive's escape.

Let it be said, however, that Mikhail Baranovitch did in fact shoot Deputy George Talbott during the melee. That is the truth. Also true is that the bullet taken from Talbott was fired from a rimfire .22 rifle.

As far as is known, the bullet that struck Talbott is the only one fired from Mikhail Baranovitch's weapon.

There currently is a "Shoot-To-Kill" order out on Mikhail Baranovitch, brought about largely, one suspects, by the mayhem wrought during that gun battle, much of which should actually be attributed to errant fire from the deputies' guns.

This newspaper deeply regrets any other portrayal of the events.

Chuck Little was removed from the assignment to cover the Baranovitch case, and another staff writer, Maxine Marble, named as his replacement. However, America had been titillated by reports of the "Umpqua Wild Man" and his escapades. An Associated Press Staff Writer was assigned to report on the chase. As a result, regular AP wire service reports with Roseburg datelines began running in newspapers across the land.

Initially, fiery letters-to-the-editor zoomed into Chalmers R. Station's in-box; many of those letters cast figurative stones at what their writers perceived as sloppy police work by the Douglas County Sheriff's Office.

Officers Draw Wrath in Baranovitch Case, said one. **Reader Says Glide Isn't The Same**, penned another.

But with *The Daily News* editor's apology over his newspaper's coverage of the shootout, the tenor of both letters-to-the-editor and hometown talk radio began to change. One letter struck a humorous note:

... Douglas County should be proud of the fact that they possess the only citizen in the United States who beat the high cost of living, the bankers, car salesman, their mother-inlaw troubles, and the Bureau of Internal Revenue.

Dick McRae's popular "Voice of the Valley" radio show received calls from listeners who asked to present their views on the so-called "Umpqua Wild Man" instead of addressing whatever subject was chosen as the day's topic.

Mikhail Baranovitch moved even farther east, up Deer Creek across the divide leading down to Buckhorn Creek. He was in deep trouble. He needed clothing, blankets, shoes. All the money he had left in the world was tucked beneath a rock at his Cavitt Creek camp. Neither was living off the land an option: he was moving too fast and too far to permit taking a deer and spending the time necessary to tan and work up the hide.

The fugitive was hungry by day, even starving. And cold. And wet. God, how cold and wet and ragged and wretched! But sometimes at night he was rich! Sometimes, during the brief periods before shivering and moaning, twisting and rolling, he would dream. Those dreams contained images of the big and small things he desired trotting across his eyelids: gloves, new Red Wing boots (size-14), the mountains of Montana, a spool of waxed sewing thread, a strawberry milkshake, a wool stocking cap and a sou'wester rain hat. In his dreams, a mare and foal stood in a meadow, ears alert, while a gigantic snowcapped mountain towered in the background. He saw a Ford army jeep and a knee-length blanket coat and a down pillow for his head. There was a sandy beach running for miles along the lapping waters of an azure bay. There were fishing poles and a pretty girl's dimpled knee. A plate of bacon and eggs. Coffee, aromatic and delicious...

One night he made a foray down Buckhorn Creek to Little River. He found the bridges still patrolled by special deputies sworn-in by the Douglas County Sheriff Irvin Finch for the great adventure of capturing or killing the "Wild Man of the Umpqua."

Bloodhounds, two days behind Baranovitch, trailed him up into the snow on Buck Peak, then followed him down into the North Myrtle drainage before losing his scent amid brambles alongside a farm gate. Sheriff Irvin Finch called off their handler, Springfield dog trainer Buford Wallace. Wallace, who provided bloodhounds for police work throughout the Pacific Northwest, concurred. "Not much use bustin' our butts during this rain."

With Baranovitch's flight direction determined, Finch ordered a special alert for the south end of Douglas County, going on radio and television news programs to appeal for help from listeners and viewers.

INCLEMENT WEATHER HAMPERS SEARCH FOR WILD MAN
by Maxine Marble
Daily News Staff Writer

Douglas County Sheriff Irvin Finch said today that bloodhounds had definitely determined that escaped mental patient Mikhail Baranovitch is headed for the same South County haunts where he initially achieved notoriety as the "Umpqua Wild Man."

"Residents of the Cow Creek area should be especially vigilant," Finch said, "and report any incident of missing property or unlawful entry onto private property."

A full week has gone by since Baranovitch shot and wounded Deputy George Talbott in the heavily timbered area along Cavitt Creek, southwest of Glide. Though the fugitive has not been sighted again, Sheriff Finch is confident that his department is "running him to ground, and that he'll soon make a mistake."

Finch said he thought Baranovitch's escape through his police cordon, and his subsequent flight over a mountain range and into the South Umpqua Valley exhibited the man's enormous vitality and courage. "I'm beginning to think we may have a big task ahead of us in eventually overtaking him."

Colonel Y. Herbert Corwin wanted information. "Bryce, suppose the sheriff's department succeeds in capturing Baranovitch, they'll want to bring him here, won't they?"

The pudgy, balding, frecklefaced man said, "That's a logical assumption, I'd suppose."

"Then he'll be a model patient for awhile. But eventually we'll lose him again, won't we?"

"Not if we turn him loose like we should've done a year ago."

Colonel Corwin sighed. "There is one other alternative, Bryce. We could put him up on Ward 'D'."

Henderson's face flamed as he lunged to his feet, overturning his chair in the process. "No!" he shouted. *We* could not put him on Ward 'D'. Maybe *You* can. But so help me God, if you do I'll do everything I can to expose the way you've fucked up his treatment for the past three years!"

The commandant remained calm throughout the psychiatrist's outburst. "Please be seated, Bryce. I've been in touch with Washington on this thing and they're in agreement that if, in fact, Baranovitch is taken alive, he should not be interred here."

The red-faced man righted his chair. "Foist off the problem elsewhere, eh? Why do you find it so difficult to believe the poor bastard is ready to re-enter society?"

"Come now, Bryce, after the way this affair is being dragged through the media? How can we release him?" Corwin slid a copy of the March 1 edition of the *New York Times* across his desk. It was turned to page three. "The Baranovitch affair is making *national* news. Our entire Veteran's treatment program is undergoing scrutiny because of it."

"What has that got to do with whether the man is cured or not?" Dr. Henderson shot back, ignoring the *New York Times*.

"Every media attack dog in America will be watching to see how this will be handled, Bryce. If we were to release him, those same dogs will be in his face every minute of every day. That, in and of itself would drive any sane person mad. Admit that."

Henderson pounded Corwin's desk. "You can't keep the man under lock and key forever, Herbert! You just can't!"

Colonel Corwin shrugged. "It would appear that the affair is out of our hands."

Henderson's eyes narrowed as he debated simply retiring now, even with his son into his second year of college. The commandant interrupted his thoughts when he pushed an envelope across the desk. "You may find this amusing, Bryce. A pity that we can't simply adopt its proposal and wash the Administration's hands of the entire problem."

Henderson stared at the envelope for some time as he brought thoughts of retiring from his life's work back from resignation's brink. Then he reached for the envelope.

To whom it may concern:

I've been following the regrettable Mikhail Baranovitch affair with considerable interest through the Salt Lake Tribune and would like to offer a simple solution: I own an 18,000 acre ranch in Southeastern Utah; if you people could find a way to do so—and would find it in your heart to do so—you might parole the unfortunate Baranovitch to my custody and the man could have the run of my ranch for the rest of his life.

The signature at the end leaped out at Dr. Henderson:

Bradley L. Baldwin
RR3
Monticello, Utah

"Why not?" Dr. Henderson said, his face a mask as he slid the envelope back to the commandant.

Colonel Corwin laughed. "Wouldn't *that* solve our problems, to release a berserk wild man on a bunch of Mormon farmers and Navaho sheepherders?"

Henderson leaned back in his chair, at once thoughtful. "What if it could be a legitimate cure for Michael?"

"Michael?" the commandant murmured. "Oh, you mean Mikhail." The colonel wagged a finger back and forth. "Not hardly. We're not in the business of releasing our patients to the custody of private citizens who have no relationship to the patient."

"What if this man—Baldwin was his name?—what if he did actually have some relationship with Baranovitch?"

Again Corwin wagged his finger. "Even if he did, Bryce, we'd still have to get approval from Washington. And I can assure you such approval would *not* be forthcoming after everything that's gone on out here." The commandant shuffled through a stack of newspapers, all with reports relative to the Baranovitch case, then said, "It's academic anyway; Baranovitch has no listed relatives."

The moon hung tethered to the hills, a full, golden moon; the kind of moon that turns men insane and causes dogs to howl without reason. Michael paused while butchering the sheep to gaze up, wondering if the same moon shone with the same intensity on the mountains of Montana.

Nearby, a tiny fire crackled. He'd kindled it by striking the chunk of chert against his knife blade. He'd found the stone while clambering up to Jack Mountain. The ensuing sparks into the incendiary cattail "fuzz" gathered earlier held, then burst into flame. To the sheltered tiny blaze, Michael added small dry twigs gathered from the low branches of Douglas fir trees. Larger branches were propped in tiny teepee fashion until he had a cheery blaze going; it was the kind of blaze that was perfect for roasting slices of sheep liver.

Later, a dense fog rolled into the hill country bounded by the North Umpqua River on the north, Little River to the east, Buckhorn Creek to the south, and the busy North Umpqua Highway to the west. Because of the fog, Michael felt safe in taking shelter in a copse of small firs on the north slope of Jack Mountain. He remained there for three days while he roasted all his mutton.

For the first time since escaping the Cavitt Creek trap, the fugitive felt warm, lying on the charcoaled earth where his fire had been, with the raw sheepskin thrown over top.

Meanwhile, Sheriff Irvin Finch was furious. "What do you mean Baranovitch was at Dixonville!" he shouted at Jocko Hayes. "You know as well as I do that he's somewhere down below Myrtle Creek."

Hayes shrugged. "I'm only repeating what I saw, boss. I know this old lady reported that somebody stole some canned fruit from her root cellar. She lives across the road and up a ways from the Dixonville store. So when I went there to check on her report, I saw she had a marsh close to the house and I checked that out, too. Somebody had been in it for cattails—like we know Baranovitch did up at Soda Springs."

"What about fingerprints?" Finch asked, settling down. "Why didn't you see if there were fingerprints on the jars he left?"

"Two of 'em are in the car, boss. They looked to me like somebody moved 'em aside to get at the jars behind."

BLOODHOUNDS AGAIN TO BE ON THE WILD MAN'S TRAIL
by Maxine Marble
Daily News Staff Writer

Douglas County Sheriff Irvin Finch informed The Daily News that as soon as the poor visibility brought about by the present air inversion lifts, the hunt for Mikhail Baranovitch, the "Umpqua Wild Man," will resume.

Sheriff Finch said his office has learned Baranovitch is back in the Dixonville vicinity and *"may be trying to cross the Little River bridges to get into the wild and forested country to the east.*

"As soon as we get a fresh fix on the fugitive we'll bring in bloodhounds once again. But this time," the Sheriff added, *"I'm wary about making predictions because the man's mental condition makes second-guessing the fugitive's intentions about where he's going near impossible. In short, we've got to run him to ground, and the man is in such superb physical condition that's proven to be a difficult task."*

The Sheriff said he's once more applied to the Army Command at Camp Adair for helicopter support. *"If we can flush him, then we can drop deputies in his line of flight. With bloodhounds in pursuit and helicopters blocking his path, perhaps this time we'll get him."*

But with every passing day of Mikhail Baranovitch's freedom, more public support swung in the fugitive's favor. Letters-to-the-editor questioning the handling of the Baranovitch pursuit turned to torrent. KRNR's talk show addressed the "Wild Man of the Umpqua" question at least two days per week. Most of the criticism focused on Sheriff Finch's "Shoot To Kill" order. Finally, on March 8, the sheriff stepped down his "Shoot to Kill" to the lesser one of "Fire Only When Fired Upon."

In mid-March, Douglas County Special Deputy Brian Paulson, coon hunting with his Walker hounds on Jack Mountain, discovered Mikhail Baranovitch's camp. The ground was still warm where a fire had been. Though the week-long fog had yet to lift, Sheriff Finch ordered in the Bloodhounds. He also requested that a helicopter be placed on "standby."

Again, Mikhail Baranovitch eluded pursuit by simply outrunning dogs and men. It was during this latest flight that the fugitive had the inspiration he hoped would save his life....

Chapter 42

Mikhail Baranovitch lay atop the hill, studying the valley below. His lever-action .30-30 rifle lay by one side, the single-shot Remington .22 by the other. Above him, the Stars and Stripes snapped and crackled in the breeze. The man lifted his head to gaze west to the sunset. Another half-hour until dark, he decided; about right to make it down off this ridge and close to the first houses. He was glad the fog had finally lifted, but suspected the better visibility would put him in more peril. He wrapped his two rifles in the sheepskin, tied them with twine taken from a bale of hay in an isolated barn. Then he took another look at the sprawling Veteran's Home Hospital, and began trudging down from Mount Nebo.

It was after midnight when Mikhail Baranovitch, moving through the sleeping hospital with the ease of a man familiar with his own living room, cut his hair with a pair of scissors taken from the unoccupied information desk, shaved with a razor left lying on a restroom sink, outfitted himself with two blankets and a pair of oversized shoes (he had to cut open the toes) from a storeroom. He showered and shit and soaped and spit, and when he shuffled from the shower room carrying his ragged clothing wrapped in one blanket and wearing another with a corner flipped over his head, Larsen Volkamen, the sleepy night orderly, hardly glanced his way.

Michael took a length of rope and a raincoat two sizes too small from one of Gordon Smith's storage sheds. And just before daylight, when the food delivery vans arrived at the cafeteria's rear door, Michael was waiting in the shadows until the delivery men disappeared inside.

By full daylight, Michael was hunkered down in a patch of blackberry bushes along the South Umpqua River, eating fresh bread and drinking quarts of fresh milk. And when a soft rain began falling that afternoon, he donned his too-tight raincoat and smiled up at the dark and heavy-bellied clouds.

OREGON SHERIFF AGAIN DRIVEN INSANE BY WILD MAN
By Dempsey Portiso
AP Special Correspondent

Roseburg, Oregon

Douglas County Sheriff, Irvin Finch, is slowly being driven insane by an escaped mental patient from a nearby V.A. Hospital. "The guy's a magician," Finch complained. "He's a sorcerer. He can be here today, then miles away in another part of the county tomorrow."

Mikhail Baranovitch, a U.S. Army veteran with mental problems has undergone treatment at the Roseburg Hospital for most of a decade, but periodically, according to Sheriff Finch, sees himself as a guerilla resisting Nazi occupation of his native Yugoslavian homeland.

During his first escapades, Baranovitch, nicknamed the "Umpqua Wild Man" in initial press reports, was a harmless recluse with a penchant for pinching tools needed for survival from unoccupied summer homes. But in this, his last dash for freedom, the "Wild Man" wounded a sheriff's deputy in a shootout reminiscent of the Earps and the Clantons at the O.K. Corral.

Since that time, well over a month ago, the Douglas County Sheriff's Department has left no stone unturned—bloodhounds, search helicopters, special deputies—in an effort to apprehend the illusive "Wild Man", all to no avail.

"We're especially handicapped," Sheriff Finch recently said, "because we've responded to the pleas of County residents and will attempt in every way to take Baranovitch without violence."

When asked if that means he's ruling out deputies firing if fired upon, Finch said, "I'm not goin that far. Naturally, if another gun is fired at you, your automatic response is to shoot back. I have no trouble with that."

Mikhail Baranovitch was dwelling in comparative comfort on the federal hospital grounds. He found a crawl hole that led beneath the commandant's residence; there he stockpiled stolen supplies taken in before-daylight raids on delivery trucks and storage lockers. In one corner of the crawl space, he had his choice of soda pop. In another, he stored candy bars and sweet rolls and sandwich meat wrapped in butcher paper and secured in galvanized buckets requisitioned from the groundskeeper's sheds. He had bread and blankets and butter and milk. For a fugitive nocturnal being, Mikhail Baranovitch was doing quite well, sleeping by day, roaming the grounds and hallways of the Veteran's Hospital by night—a cat-and-mouse game in avoiding the night orderlies.

But search as he might, Michael never felt secure enough to enter the housekeeping wing where he might find suitable clothing, or even locate the needle and thread that would enable him to make clothing from his blankets.

Unknown to the fugitive, his very success at disappearing into the mists engendered outsized images until the name Mikhail Baranovitch began to take on mythic proportions, enough so the fairminded editor of *The Daily News*, in a spirit of honesty, felt he must counsel caution:

The Dogged and the Damned

UMPQUA ROBIN HOOD
By Chalmers R. Station

One of the strangest public responses to the tragic Mikhail Baranovitch affair is the way people are beginning to view a case attracting so much attention all over the nation. This widespread interest is resulting in much discussion and expression of opinion, and it is from these things that one finds the very human characteristics causing us at least to be strange in our psychological reactions.

Baranovitch is a mental patient who escaped from the Veterans Hospital where he was being treated. He is an exceedingly able and crafty woodsman. He has been eluding law enforcement officers sent to capture him for more than a year. Baranovitch has committed multiple petty thefts from private property holders throughout much of Douglas County. But because he is mentally ill, complaints were dropped, his rights restored, permitting him to be eligible for a pension. His condition made him a ward of the Veterans Administration.

Many "Tales" Heard

The Veterans Administration has come in for much criticism because 'Big Mike' has been allowed to escape. A measure of criticism perhaps is justified, yet there are some exonerating circumstances.

As a patient in a mental hospital shows improvement in his condition, his liberties are increased. Because of more and more freedom, the patient often is either fully restored or is brought back to the point of release from the hospital.

So, 'Big Mike' was, I imagine, given an increasing amount of freedom from restraint.

But often patients have relapses. What happens in Baranovitch's case, apparently, is that his relapses cause him to resume his imaginary role as a guerilla leader and he takes off for the hills where, by the very nature of his illness, he seeks to elude pursuit.

In such activity he captures the public imagination and sympathy.

Most of us, too, would like to get away from the tensions of living, income taxes, committee meetings, banquets and the like, and live the 'simple life' of the hills.

Because Baranovitch is doing the things so many of us wish we could do, we have admiration for him. We create strange tales, which are repeated until a lot of people get to believing them.

For example, we were told in all seriousness that Baranovitch has found a gold mine, that his pockets are filled with gold nuggets, that when he steals guns, food, ammunition, clothing, etc, he always leaves gold in payment.

Unfortunately readers, though the story is a good one, we have yet to hear of anyone who was paid for anything that was stolen.

That's the truth. Mikhail Baranovitch is not a modern day Robin Hood. Instead, the poor man is merely a misguided, mentally ill escapee from the Veterans Hospital in Roseburg.

We all need to have sympathy for the poor man, and wish him the best. What we need not do is believe the man is larger than life; that he's some mythic, God-like persona from the pages and pageantry of Mount Olympus.

As lucid and accountable as was Chalmers Station's editorial, it spurred a spate of letters suggesting otherwise.

For instance, a lady named June Creason wrote from Riddle that Mikhail Baranovitch had once saved her life in an altercation with her former husband:

"This total stranger appeared as if by magic, and pulled my attacker away, then kept my attacker at arm's length until the sheriff's deputy arrived. I know positively that the man vilified as the 'Umpqua Wild Man' is far different from the one portrayed. I know he's gentle and kind, not beastly and mean."

June Creason's neighbor, Oscar Perkins, also felt Baranovitch to be unique:

"Here you got this paradox—a genuine mountain man with an insatiable desire to read and learn. Yeah, I know the man is no saint. But neither is anyone else I ever met. Mikhail Baranovitch is one of the kindest people I ever knew, and I believe the man would give anyone the shirt off his back, even without them asking first."

Both Jenny and Purley White weighed in from the North Umpqua country:

"If it hadn't been for the intervention of Mikhail Baranovitch, our home would've been vandalized in our absence by ruffian out-of-state vagrants who more than likely would've stolen us blind. Unfortunately for our friend, who at the time was being bitterly slandered throughout the news media, the beating he gave the thieves brought the attention of our so-called law and order sheriff down on his head and he had to again flee for his life.

"Whatever else might cause complaint to be lodged against this good man, accusing those of us who know Mikhail Baranovitch for what he is of being misguided citizens is the lowest form of editorial baloney."

Then from Sutherlin came another letter from Weyland Jones:

"No matter how 'fair' an editorial writer may pretend to be in addressing the sordid affair of the 'Umpqua Wild Man', the truth is that being treated unfairly has been a way of life for Mikhail Baranovitch.

"How many know Michael (as he is known by his closest friends) received four Purple Hearts in battle during World War II? (Three, for God's sake, sent every other warrior in American uniform home for the duration.) How many know the man is a certified military hero, winning both the Silver Star and the Bronze Star for heroic actions in the face of death on the island of New Guinea?

"How many recognize that nothing less than a Gestapo-like vendetta is being waged by our own County Sheriff against a man that is in every possible way superior to the individual appointed (yes I said 'appointed'—not 'elected') as our County's chief law enforcement officer?"

One would think it inevitable the Veteran's Hospital hiding place of the "Wild Man of the Umpqua" would be discovered. It was mid-April and Julian Hoerner pushed a reel mower around the commandant's quarters when he noticed a strip of worn grass leading to a crawl space beneath the brick building. The workman paused to examine the crawl space cover and it fell off in his hands. Behind the cover was Mikhail Baranovitch, forefinger to lips, shushing him.

A terrified Julian leaped to his feet and backed away as Baranovitch scrambled from beneath the building, dragging only his single-shot rifle with him. Julian didn't shush!

It took almost twenty minutes for the excited, stammering Julian Hoerner to get across to Gordon Smith that he'd discovered Mikhail Baranovitch beneath the commandant's quarters. Another fifteen minutes passed before Smith made an investigation and found probable cause to believe Mikhail Baranovitch had, indeed, been hiding on the hospital grounds.

Five minutes later, Smith barged into a hospital staff meeting with Colonel Y. Herbert Corwin's secretary holding his arm, trying to stop him. When the outraged colonel began berating him, Smith shut him up by crying, **"BARANOVITCH!"**

Ten minutes later, a stunned Colonel Corwin was faced with a dilemma, whether the staff should try to apprehend Baranovitch, or whether they should alert the Douglas County Sheriff's Office. "He's been gone an hour by now. Hoerner never saw which way he went. Hell, he could be up on Nebo Ridge now, heading for Lookingglass."

The colonel placed both elbows on the desk and sank face to hands. At last he said, "No sheriff; not now anyway Gordon."

"This ain't gonna stay quiet for long, colonel. I told Hoerner to wait for me in the tool shed. But he may have told somebody else by now. Or somebody different may have spotted Baranovitch running. Any way you look at it, you'll not keep the lid on for more than a couple more hours."

"Will that be enough to conduct a thorough search of the grounds? I just couldn't face him being arrested here at the hospital."

News of the "Wild Man's" whereabouts spilled from the Veteran's Hospital grounds early enough so quick copy could be splashed on the afternoon paper. An angry Sheriff Irvin Finch was ushered into Colonel Y. Herbert Corwin's office shortly thereafter. Gordon Smith was there to provide up-to-date information on the hospital staff's own investigation. The hospital's head psychiatrist was also on hand.

"It offends me no end, Colonel Corwin," grated Sheriff Finch through clinched teeth, "to have to get my information about Mikhail Baranovitch's whereabouts through the daily newspaper." The commandant held up his hand, but Finch ground on. "How dare you! How dare you let an entire day elapse after the fugitive's location is discovered before allowing the Sheriff's Department to be advised? What makes you think ..."

The pudgy, balding, freckled man at the window turned and said, "Perhaps this administration's lack of alacrity in providing information to you, sheriff, also indicates this same administration's lack of confidence in the way you've conducted the entire 'le affaire' Baranovitch. Why should you," Dr. Henderson added, "be surprised that someone else might employ the newspaper to disseminate information? Or do you deem generating media hue and cry to be the sole province a county sheriff?"

Finch turned slitted eyes at the psychiatrist, taking in the bright Hawaiian shirt and the scotch plaid knee-length walking shorts that brushed the tops of the man's argyle stockings. The sheriff sneered, "And you! If I ever saw one who belonged in a nuthouse, it's you. All of you!"

Colonel Y. Herbert Corwin had remained seated throughout Finch's entry and tirade. Again he held up a hand. "Please be seated, Sheriff. You too, Bryce. Then we'll discuss this matter rationally, between men of good intent."

Sheriff Finch perched angrily on his chair's edge, but Dr. Henderson merely turned to gaze out the window. "I'm here on an investigation, colonel," the sheriff snapped. "I want to know how long Baranovitch has been in hiding at this Hospital and why you people sheltered a known criminal."

"For one thing, sheriff," Colonel Corwin said, "we didn't know Mr. Baranovitch was hiding here. For another, we have every intention—should a patient be delivered to this facility—of providing shelter and treatment for any soldier in need. This includes Mikhail Baranovitch."

"Do you think because this is a federal institution that you are immune to the laws of the land? What you did by not immediately notifying my office of the fugitive's whereabouts verges on criminal negligence."

"Nothing would please us more, sheriff, than to have Mikhail Baranovitch under treatment at this hospital, at this time. We sincerely hoped we could officially bring the man back into treatment without further ado to your overstressed department. What we attempted was to ensure that the man was no longer on the grounds before reporting him. Unfortunately, the newspapers obtained the story before we completed our investigation and notified your office."

"Even if you'd found him and officially logged him into the hospital," Sheriff Finch said, "I would've been obligated to take him from you until the Talbott case is adjudicated."

Some of the colonel's composure slipped. "*If* that scenario had indeed occurred, sheriff, and you attempted to take a legally committed patient from this facility without our approval, then you might find it a case for *Federal* Courts and *Federal* Marshals."

The commandant and the sheriff glared at each other. Then Finch said, "Colonel Corwin, I'm here on a criminal investigation. Am I to assume you'll not cooperate?"

"On the contrary, Mr. Finch," the colonel said, "Gordon Smith is available to lead you to the fugitive's recent hiding place, and will remain there while you do an inventory of items recovered therein. Also standing by is the individual who discovered Mikhail Baranovitch. Julian Hoerner will, of course, be available for your interview."

After Finch's and Smith's departure, Dr. Henderson said, "Well done, Herbert. He's an arrogant bastard who deserves to be kicked in the balls by a balky mule."

The commandant visibly preened. But he turned steely when Dr. Henderson asked if the colonel *really* meant it when he told Sheriff Finch that Mikhail Baranovitch would be welcomed back to the hospital?

"Don't be ridiculous, Bryce," Corwin said. "What I told the sheriff was merely dissembling to assuage the man's temper. No, Mikhail Baranovitch will not be welcomed in this hospital again, and that's final."

A faint grin flashed across the doctor's face as he wagged his head and headed for the door.

Colonel Corwin cleared his throat. "I assume you'll be returning to your office. Before you go, however, I want another word with you."

Dr. Henderson faced the commandant, his face glum.

"I know the news media will be all over this thing of Baranovitch hiding here on the grounds. They're insidious, those reporters, and insistent. That's why I'm ordering all records of Mikhail Baranovitch's treatment sealed. In order to do so, they'll have to leave your possession. Daniel and Miss Spencer are in your office as we speak, removing the files from your cabinets. I trust there'll be no overt display of petulance on your part."

"On the contrary," Dr. Bryce Henderson said as he strode from Corwin's office. "Now I don't have to feel dirtied because I failed to act."

As anticipated, the Associated Press had a field day with the disclosure that escaped mental patient Mikhail Baranovitch had actually hidden from authorities for several weeks on the very grounds of the hospital from whence he'd fled.

As the furor from Mikhail Baranovitch's latest escapade faded, Chuck Little asked for an audience with his editor and had the request granted.

"Sir," the reporter began, holding up a copy of a Chalmers Station editorial, "it says here in your editorial that Mikhail Baranovitch is eligible for a pension. Is that true?"

The stern, white-thatched editor said, "Of course it's true. Otherwise I would not have included it."

"But sir, I've been unable to find any evidence that he's receiving one. It's possible he didn't even *apply* for one. It's even more possible that, in his condition, that he didn't know he *could* apply for one. And sir, its entirely probable that no one bothered to tell him!"

Chalmers Station's countenance turned even more grim. "What are you doing investigating anything about the Mikhail Baranovitch case, Mr. Little. You've been removed from that assignment."

The cocky 'Little Chuck' came out in the reporter's reply. "I've been investigating on my own time, Mr. Station. I want to re-establish my credentials as a newsman." He paused. "You see, sir, I feel so badly about the way I treated Mikhail Baranovitch that I want to make up for it."

The editor was gruff. "You don't *make up* for bad reporting by reporting badly from the other side."

"But how about reporting 'goodly' from the other side, sir?" He waved a page with Weyland Jones letter-to-the-editor circled in red. "If there's truth here about Baranovitch's war record, that's certainly something that should be told in depth. And sir, excuse my French, but there's one hell of a lot of truth there about the man's war record."

Chalmers Station studied the young reporter. "All right, Mr. Little, tell me what you have."

Chapter 43

Though stooped, the stranger was broad-shouldered and lean-hipped, tanned, taller than a casual observer would think. His were clear eyes, a sharp nose, and firm jaw. An eagle, Gladys thought. She watched from beneath lowered lashes as he limped from the entry doors to her reception desk. The way he carried himself, despite the limp and the cane, was of a man in command. His suit was of a natty green whipcord. She thought it Pendleton Wool. His boots were of expensive western cut, with sharp toes and a fresh shine.

"Hello. May I help you?"

His smile was as infectious as hers. "I'd like a minute with Colonel Corwin. My name is Bradley Baldwin and I've been in correspondence with the colonel about Mikhail Baranovitch."

Gladys jotted the man's name down and disappeared. When she returned, her smile was gone. But when she told him Colonel Corwin's secretary advised her the commandant could not be disturbed, the visitor's smile remained unchanged.

"Perhaps someone else familiar with the Baranovitch case?" he murmured.

She was obviously embarrassed. "I'm very sorry, sir, but Colonel Corwin has specifically ordered that no one on staff is to talk to you."

The bemused smile remained, but the gaze turned piercing. "Ma'am, I'd like to help Mr. Baranovitch, not harm him. And if I were a wagering man, I'd wager that a sharp lady like you might let that pencil you have stuck in your hair slip and jot down a name of someone who's also knowledgeable and sympathetic to Michael."

Mr. Baldwin's use of "Michael" galvanized her. The note she pushed across the counter had "Weyland Jones" scribbled on it. He stared down then up, eyebrows raised. She reached for the note and added "Sutherlin" to it.

Gladys glanced around, then handed a telephone book to the countertop. "Certainly, sir," she said loudly. "You may look at our phone book."

He found the number and jotted it down, all the while with the same bemused smile. Again, she looked around, saw no one, and said, "I ... I could maybe let you use our phone."

The eagle-look softened. "Thank you ma'am. But I believe I'll pass on that one. I've always made it a practice not to waste an asset."

"Good luck," she whispered as he turned away.

* * *

Mikhail Baranovitch again was bone weary, hungry, demoralized. He'd fled from the hospital grounds, dashing first for the river and the bridge that would allow access to the country he knew so well. But by the time he reached the bridge, the man was having second thoughts. He decided they would expect him to head for Nebo Ridge, then work east toward Glide. Or maybe drift south to Cow Creek. So Michael fled west, following the South Umpqua River to the vicinity of Point of Rocks. Then he climbed from the river bottom to hike up the San Souci Road.

By midnight, at the end of that first day, Michael peered down at the San Souci Ranch. With the advent of daylight, he skirted the scattering of ranch buildings to strike further west, away from roads, drifting into a forest heavy to scrub oak, with only a few madrones and firs. He passed occasional bands of sheep and looked longingly at them. But he'd abandoned everything in his precipitous flight from the cave beneath the commandant's bungalow, even his butcher knife. Other than the ragged clothes he wore and a half-dozen .22 shells rattling in a pocket, Mikhail Baranovitch's only possession was the Remington single-shot rifle he carried in first one hand, then the other. What use to kill a sheep without the means to butcher it? He had to find a knife. And matches.

By midday, Michael struck the Melrose-to-Lookingglass Road along Champagne Creek. He turned north, sticking to the ridges, drifting in and out of scrub oak. To the west he could see a line of mountains. But between his present location and those mountains were valleys filled with roads and homes and vehicles and people. He *had* to find the means to sustain himself! Before dark, Michael gazed down on a busy road fork, with several white frame houses clustered there, and a store with gas pumps. He turned west. Lowering dark clouds were dropping below those western mountains.

Rain had begun falling by the time Mikhail Baranovitch located the old Swedish Lutheran Church in Elgarose and found the crawl space beneath. It'd been two days since he'd eaten and he was nearing exhaustion. Though homes were nearby, and roads on three sides of his refuge, he lay beneath the church all the next day, drawing the half-inch manilla rope he used for a belt tighter and tighter.

Shortly before dark, as Michael readied to exit his hiding place, a car drove into the weed-filled parking lot, followed by another. Then another, and another, and another. He decided it must be Wednesday night; prayer meeting night. So he lay there for another half-hour, until singing began. Then he scrambled into brush behind the church.

If they're in church, Michael reasoned, then it's likely nobody's home. So he turned into the first lane he came to, one with a bungalow squatting back from the graveled county road. Though it was still twilight, he could see no lighted yard light or porch light. Neither were there children's toys scattered outside. No dog barked at his approach.

Inside the unlocked home, he quickly pocketed a handful of matches, and a butcher knife. He found no bacon, but discovered ham slices in the refrigerator. He grabbed a jar of jelly and a half-loaf of wheat bread. Then car lights flashed on windows panes and Mikhail Baranovitch fled.

Further up the road, he discovered a cattail swamp. There was a shovel in the corner of a nearby barn, and he was able to spend the waning hours of the night digging cattail roots. Daylight found him hidden amidst a copse of young firs, stuffing his growling belly with cattail roots and stalks, topped off with ham and jelly sandwiches. That evening, Mikhail Baranovitch plodded toward the Coast Range Mountains to the west.

Sheriff Irvin Finch neared the end of his patience. "What the hell do I have to do to get you guys off your ass and find this nutcase that's making fools of us?"

Jocko Hayes said, "Maybe he isn't as crazy as we thought." Then he asked, "When do the dogs get here?"

Finch threw a folding chair against the wall. "They were supposed to be here yesterday. I've got a good mind to fire that bastard and bring in bloodhounds with a handler who's more responsive."

Sheriff Finch put out another press release asking citizens near Roseburg to be alert.

"... Especially be alert to any cattails growing near your home. Mikhail Baranovitch is known to have harvested cattails for survival food."

The press release brought a spate of letters-to-the-editor with a different reaction than the one the sheriff sought.

"He can have my cattails if he wants," one woman wrote. *"In fact, if he knocks on my door I'll serve him the biggest platter of roast beef and mashed potatoes he ever saw in his life."*

Another writer penned:

"Let me get this straight, we don't want this 'mentally impaired' guy running around stealing a couple of eggs out of our chicken coops, or an apple off our trees. But now the poor S.O.B. can't even harvest survival food grown by God? What in the hell kind of police state are we running?"

The morning after the sheriff's department press release ran in *The Daily News*, Arvid Bloomquist told his wife, "Aye t'ink somebody, they dig cattails beyond that barn, Hella. What you t'ink, the sheriff, we should call?"

"No! You tell that sheriff if he wants cattails, to find someplace else to dig them. Tell him ours are already taken."

"Mr. Jones?"

"Yeah."

"My name is Bradley Baldwin and I'm calling from the hotel here in Sutherlin. May I come talk to you about Mikhail Baranovitch?"

"Hell no, you can't!" Weyland shouted into the telephone. "Three of you bastards wanted to talk to me just yesterday. Good day!"

Bradley Baldwin took the receiver from his ear at the 'click'. He tried again. There was no answer. Baldwin swung open the phone booth door and limped to the lobby desk. "Do you know a man named Weyland Jones?" he asked the receptionist.

"Sure do, hon'. Ever'body knows Weyland."

Thirty minutes later, Baldwin steered the rented Ford up the winding Jones driveway. Lights were on at the farmhouse. Lights also gleamed from the barn. An outside light was switched on. Weyland Jones emerged from the barn carrying a pitchfork."

The stranger saw a tall man with a long neck as stringy as a celery stalk and protruding eyes with lids that stretched to cover them. His cheeks were brown as cuspidor swill, and shiny and pitted. The hair, thrusting from beneath a baseball cap, appeared prematurely white. "Mr. Jones?" Baldwin said, as he swung from the car.

"What's it to you, mister? Are you the guy who called a few minutes ago?"

"I am," the stranger said. "I was also Michael Baranovitch's commanding officer at Buna and Aitape. He saved my life; now I'd like to help save his."

"Baldwin?" Jones said. "*Captain Baldwin?*"

"I am."

The pitchfork clattered to the barnyard and the lanky farmer strode forward, his hand outstretched. "I was Mendendorp. I was at Buna, too. A hell of a place."

Bradley Baldwin's smile was faint. "Worse for you Mr. Jones. You didn't have Michael Baranovitch around to ease most of the terror."

It was after midnight when the three men gathered around Bryce Henderson's kitchen table while the not-quite awake psychiatrist's coffee pot percolated. Henderson wore only polka-dot undershorts and seemed unconcerned. "That's one thing about being in a man's own home," the doctor growled, "he can wear what he wants." Both Baldwin and Jones appeared amused.

"Dr. Henderson," Baldwin said, "Weyland tells me you considered Michael psychologically restored and signed a release form for him."

"I did. That shithead colonel wouldn't countersign it."

"Did he give you a reason?"

"He said he needed further clarification that Michael was ready to re-enter society."

"Is that normal practice for an administrator to need more proof than the patient's analyst?"

The doctor got up to turn the stove burner down. When he returned he looked thoughtful. "No, it's not. But anything's possible with that bastard."

The doctor placed three cups on the counter and returned for the coffee pot. "If you're asking if there's some crookedness going on, I'll have to come down on Corwin's side—he's too innocent an idiot to be involved in anything underhanded." As the doctor poured, he added, "On the other hand, if you're asking if there's some lunacy going on here, I'll tell you that asshole commandant has a corner on the market."

Baldwin said, "Could I have just a glass of water, please. Coffee and me never got along."

Dr. Henderson nodded. "Michael said you were a polygamist."

"Come on Doc!" Weyland protested. "Michael said no such thing."

"Okay," the doctor said, filling a glass with tap water. "But he did say his captain was a Mormon. Same thing."

Baldwin chuckled along with the others. He asked, "What will it take to budge Colonel Corwin?"

Henderson waved at Jones. "You tell him, Weyland. You tried and got nowhere."

"We talked about it while driving over here, Doc. I told him Corwin had a broomstick up his ass about this and wouldn't budge."

"To make matters worse," Henderson mused, "he's been embarrassed now, and with all the national news coverage he's washed his hands of the whole affair."

"Like Pilate," Baldwin said.

"How's he washing his hands?" Jones asked.

"He says Washington is going to take over the case. Says Baranovitch is embarrassing the entire Veteran's Administration treatment program and that Washington told him there's no way that if the poor sonofabitch is taken alive they'll let him return to the Roseburg hospital."

Baldwin took a sip of water. "But you feel he's cured?"

"I'm sure he *was* cured," the doctor said. "But I don't see how he still could be, after what he's gone through with that ding-a-ling sheriff after him."

Baldwin tapped his fingers on the formica tabletop. "I'm not hearing any ideas for helping Michael."

"Captain Baldwin," Bryce Henderson said, drawing himself up as if he was in full-dress uniform, "don't think I haven't worried over that." He took a big mouthful of coffee and shook his head. Coffee dribbled from a mouth corner. "If there's a way, I don't see it. Hell, everybody's for him now—except that bloody fool of a sheriff and that double bloody fool of a hospital commandant. What it comes down to is we're up against the twin problems of officaldom's pride and a system that says you've got to go by the book."

Baldwin nodded. "So Mikhail Baranovitch can't win out through commonsense and logic?"

The doctor's lips pursed and he shook his head as Baldwin murmured, "And Michael can't win by trying to circle around them?" Both Weyland Jones and Bryce Henderson waited to see what would come next. "So maybe the only thing left to do is go at 'em."

"Like the Yakamul Pocket?" Henderson said.

"Like the Yakamul Pocket."

Henderson topped off Weyland's and his coffee, then rummaged for a bottle of whiskey to top off the top. He waved it at Baldwin and grinned when the Mormon rancher shook his head.

"A little sugar?" Henderson asked Jones.

"A little."

After Henderson took his seat, he said, "Okay, it's agreed that we go at them. How?"

Baldwin sipped again at his water. After he ran a sleeve over his lips, he said, "I wrote a letter to Corwin, asking if there was a way to get Michael released to my custody. I told him in the letter that I owned a rather large ranch and that the young man could have the run of that ranch for the rest of his life."

"I read the letter," Henderson growled. "You've got to know the only reason the bastard showed it to me is so he could have somebody to laugh with. There's no way he would've ever considered such a thing. Now there's no way he *could.*"

Baldwin nodded. He pushed his chair back, crossed his legs and began swinging the top one. "I'd like to see Michael's files."

Henderson said, "Now we're getting somewhere. However, those files are privileged, captain. You must know that."

"I do. I'd still like to see them."

Henderson laughed. "Hell, I'd let you see 'em if I could. The problem is that Corwin had them removed from my office and sealed. There's no way *anyone* will ever see those files again—if they even exist now."

"How about an independent psychological examination?"

Henderson spread his hands. "You can do it, of course. It would probably take a court order. But without Michael's treatment records as a baseline for psychological movement, it probably wouldn't legally be admissible."

"Aren't we missing something here?" Weyland said.

Baldwin and Henderson looked at the farmer. "What?"

"Bryce, *I* have a copy of Michael's files. Hell, you made photostats when we were having that first snit with Corwin—at a big risk to yourself, I might add."

"That's right!" Henderson cried. "I'd forgotten."

"Let me ask you, Weyland," Bradley Baldwin said, "was there a copy of Dr. Henderson's release form in the mix?"

Weyland shook his head. "I don't know, Captain. I don't remember." He glanced at the doctor. "Would there have been, Doc?"

Dr. Henderson glared at the tabletop. He finally said, "I doubt it. Wasn't that before I'd fully completed my analysis? Even if it was after that, I would've made it out in duplicate. That's the way they go to the commandant's office. After he countersigns, he usually keeps one, while the other enters the process."

Then the doctor lifted his head and grinned. "But I could make out another...."

Chapter 44

Chuck Little's rehabilitation as a valued staff writer for *The Daily News* came through a three-part series on the "Umpqua Wild Man" that ran on consecutive days, beginning May 14, 1957.

Little began the series with a bombshell:

"Though eligible for a Veteran's Disability Pension, Mikhail Baranovitch never received one penny from the federal government for the impairments he'd received in service to America. The reason, as it was explained by a Veteran's Administration spokesperson, was that no record exists that Mikhail Baranovitch ever applied for his rightful pension."

"Little asked the obvious question: How could a psychologically impaired individual be expected to apply for his own pension?" The reply:
Someone—perhaps a relative—must apply for it in his stead."

The reporter then took the next logical step by pointing out that, in Mikhail Baranovitch's case, there are no relatives.

"Then," the spokesperson said, "some caring person within the Veteran's Administration must apply in Mr. Baranovitch's name."

Little wrote:
So that's it in a nutshell. Apparently there was no 'caring' person in any of the four Veteran's Administration Hospitals to whose care Mikhail Baranovitch was assigned during the past 12 years."

Little continued on with an analysis of how much money Mikhail Baranovitch should have accumulated during those 12 years:
The man was a corporal while on active duty, receiving $69 dollars per month. Because he was also engaged in combat in a war zone, Mikhail Baranovitch received an additional five dollars per month. Add three more dollars for his three years of service and the young soldier was receiving the munificent sum of $77 dollars per month.
Disability pensions, I'm advised, are prorated at 60% of active duty pay. That works out to $45.20 per month, or a total of $542.40 per year for 12 years—or an overall total of $6,508.80.

The tragedy of the "Wild Man of the Umpqua" affair is that the man should actually have had the means to purchase anything he needed to survive alone in the wilds—but didn't because the system failed him.

With no other alternative left to him, can we be surprised that the man resorted to the only other means available to him—stealing what he needed.

One wonders who wouldn't, were they to be placed in the same circumstances? The problem for most of us in Baranovitch's shoes is that we would probably have to steal more, and still wouldn't, couldn't, and shouldn't survive.

Chuck Little's second full-page story in *The Daily News* featured Mikhail Baranovitch's heroic war record.

Serendipitously, those records became available through a cautious approach to *The Daily News* Editor Chalmers Station, through Weyland Jones' legal firm. Both Jones and a nameless man who used a cane monitored the reporter while Chuck Little studied a photocopy of Mikhail Baranovitch's hospital files. When the man with the cane filled in blanks spots in Baranovitch's war record, the reporter introduced himself. But the nameless man merely shook Little's hand and said, "My pleasure, young man."

Jones closed the files after the Aitape Campaign, but Chuck Little had sufficient information to send him scurrying to the War Department Records Division for verification.

Coming on the heels of the revelations about Mikhail Baranovitch's missing pension, the detailed report on the man's war heroism and his subsequent breakdown on the Morotai beach evoked great public sympathy. That, coupled with the fact that he had been recommended for release by his treating psychiatrist, brought a storm of criticism to both the Veteran's Hospital Administration and the Douglas County Sheriff's Department.

Another result of Little's revelations took its genesis from a letter-to-the-editor by one Wanetta Williams, who confided that she was tacking a note on her door, inviting Mikhail Baranovitch to come inside for pie and milk.

Shortly thereafter, similar notes became common kitchen door decorations on half the homes in Douglas County. And Sheriff Irvin Finch sensed his popularity sinking into a political morass wrought by a Slavic madman who, the sheriff told his chief deputy, "probably couldn't wipe his own ass without help."

Colonel Y. Herbert Corwin let himself into Dr. Henderson's office, waiting imatiently until the doctor arrived for the day.

The Dogged and the Damned

Henderson was anticipating the confrontation, so he evidenced no surprise when Colonel Corwin closed the office door and said, "I've told Daniel there are to be no interruptions."

Henderson slipped from his windbreaker, hung it on the coatrack, and did the same with his beret. Then he dropped into his swivel chair and waved a hand to the seat across his desk. "All right, what can I do for you, Herbert."

Corwin remained standing, his face mirroring anger and disappointment. "I counted on you to behave honorably." When the doctor merely stared, Corwin said, "The files, Bryce. How did the newspaper obtain access to the files?"

"I can't imagine. Why don't you ask them?"

"I depended on you, Bryce. You know that."

"And Mikhail Baranovitch depended on us. If I somehow let you down, then consider that we're the ones who let him down."

Corwin paced back and forth for several seconds. At last he said, "I wish to talk about those files—only those files."

Henderson eyed the commandant with contempt. "And I wish to talk about Baranovitch's pension. What happened to it?"

Corwin's shock was unfeigned. "Surely you can't think what you appear to be thinking! If guilt is there, it belongs equally to both of us—neither of us applied for his pension, did we?"

"But I'm not the one who blocked his release, therefore I'm hardly culpable." Henderson chuckled. "Did I touch a nerve, Herbert? Are others asking what you did with his pension money?"

"You know I would never be guilty of such a thing as you're inferring!"

"Yes, I know that. And you know that I know that. But I imagine there are a bunch of people out there who don't know that. They're also the ones who will be so shocked with what I believe they'll learn about the treatment of Mikhail Baranovitch that you'll be fortunate to survive the accusations." Corwin buried face in hands. "At least tell me how you got access to the locked files."

"After you locked them? I didn't."

"Then you talked to the reporter against my expressed wishes."

"I did not."

"Then how ..."

"What about Michael's pension? How did you use it?"

Thirty miles west, the subject of the two hospital men's discussion toiled through a land that might've provided the backdrop for *Tobacco Road* or *The Grapes of Wrath*. Mikhail Baranovitch, after first trudging through the scattering of small farms and rural homes known as Elgarose, had climbed the steep mountain front of the Coast Range. It was a surreal land, savaged by catastrophic wildfire only a few years prior. It'd taken the starving, hallucinating fugitive two days, following logging roads, to clamber through the old burn. Finally he reached ancient old-growth forests and the still-standing abandoned homesteads that dotted a poverty-stricken landscape of red-dirt roads and little else.

True, the not yet crumbled homesteads provided shelter for a fugitive staggering from lack of hope, companionship, future. But his real concern was food. Real food. Survival food. *Any* food. The hunted Mikhail Baranovitch was starving amid a sterile land of nothing but ancient forests; a place that had already defeated an entire generation of American failures fleeing the Great Depression.

Mikhail did find a rhubarb patch behind one homestead, and ate so much of the tart stalks that he had the shits for a week and was listless for another.

He ate mushrooms, though he wasn't sure whether some were deadly. He killed an occasional grouse with his little .22, but the gun was too small to kill deer or elk. And with the homesteaders gone, there were no sheep or goats or chickens or pigs.

Michael threw a fir cone at a single fence post—the only one still standing on the old homestead where he loitered. Earlier, he'd almost tumbled into the crumbling homestead's old water well—fifty feet straight down to water and no way to crawl back up. The well had been covered with half-rotten planks that were hidden by weeds.

Michael was lonesome. God how he was lonesome. Hallucinating, he thought he might make it past the armed guards on the Little River bridges and reach his friends at Caps Illahee. But when reality set in, he knew there was no hope of reaching Illahee; he was too near the end of his tether.

He'd stolen nothing since a half-pound of butter before climbing from settled country to this mountain fastness. And the rich butter had made him sick. Now he was almost out of matches and had only three .22 shells remaining.

Michael's buckskins were little more than scraps; his shoes had fallen apart so badly that no amount of rope could hold them together. Hope was gone. No flint, no cattails, no will to go on. He pushed slowly to his feet. If I can get to the Whites, I might still make it, he thought. But that thought was merely a dream; the reality a nightmare.

He again staggered through Elgarose, without even sufficient will to steal what he needed, passing at least a dozen homes that had welcome notices for him tacked on their kitchen doors. When daybreak came, he squatted beneath a bridge that spanned a tiny fast-running little creek. Cars and school buses and logging trucks rumbled over that bridge. And if he stood, he could make out the roof of a chickenhouse-style home only a hundred yards away—one with small children playing in the yard—and an invitation to Mikhail Barnovitch on the door. All day, the fugitive broke small chunks from twigs and tossed them into the bubbling water. Occasionally he tried chewing on one before tossing it. Then he drew up the rope spanning his middle. These days, the rope ends slapped against his knees as he staggered on.

The third and final installment in Chuck Little's "Wild Man of the Umpqua" series ran on Thursday, May 16, essentially a recap of the history of Mikhail Baranovitch's escapes from detention at the Roseburg Veteran's Hospital, and his efforts to remain free.

Much ado was made of the Cavitt Creek gun battle, and the futile efforts of Sheriff Irvin Finch to apprehend the wily outdoorsman. Equal ado was made in recapping Baranovitch's missing pension and the thousands of dollars of which the deserving soldier was "cheated."

The problem was, where was Baranovitch?

On Tuesday, May 21, Colonel Y. Herbert Corwin received a wire from the Veteran's Administration Headquarters in Washington, D.C. requesting Mikhail Baranovitch's hospital records. The records, the wire went on to explain, was requested by the Senate subcommittee with responsibility for Veteran's Administration oversight.

Corwin pounded into the hospital's head psychiatrist's office. "Bryce, you've got to help me on this!"

Dr. Henderson took one look at the telegram and said, "So? Send the files."

"I destroyed them!"

Henderson was still laughing that afternoon when he slipped the windbreaker over his Hawaiian shirt and headed home.

Two days later, when Washington admitted the Baranovitch files had been misplaced, Senator Malcolm Young (R. Utah) suggested that the Undersecretary for Veteran's Affairs contact Dr. Bryce Henderson of the Roseburg V.A. Hospital for a report on what happened to the missing files. Gerald Rapp, an assistant to the undersecretary was on the phone within minutes. As a result, Colonel Y. Herbert Corwin was placed on extended leave. Meanwhile, during the subsequent investigation, Major Bryce Henderson was elevated to "Acting" Commandant.

She was there, straddling his knees, her lips brushing his. He moaned and shifted on the sand. There was a dusky island girl doing the hula—not that he'd ever seen one, but he'd heard plenty from the other guys; even seen a movie clip once about how the Hawaiian people had gone all out to help rebuild the spirit of the U.S. Navy after Pearl Harbor. Again, there was a mare and foal in a green paddock with a snowy mountain peak rising behind. And there were dozens of strawberry milkshakes, this time joined by platters of steaming French fries.

He awoke with a start! After several minutes, he pushed laboriously to a sitting position, ran a hand over his face, dragging fingers that were caked with grime through a ragged, filthy beard. His near-empty bowels had tried to move the day before while he was too far gone to drop his tattered trousers. "Mama," he moaned, then wondered why he did so.

He thought of that Great Falls tackle—what was his name? Wilson? Yeah, Wilson. He was tough, but he wasn't half as tough as Captain Baldwin. Or Papa. Or Coach O'Malley. In fact he wasn't as tough as me. Then his thoughts turned to the way things happened—when his coach and his Papa asked more of him than he could give. Michael dozed again, this time while sitting upright. When his eyes flickered open, he sighed and struggled to his feet. He could only stagger a few yards before pausing to rest. He actually waved at a passing car, but the driver speeded up instead of slowing down. And he collapsed in the barrow ditch as blessed unconsciousness took him.

Later, somehow, he wound up at the forks of two rivers and spent the night there. When daylight came he managed to wade into the South Umpqua, tattered clothing and all, and lie down.

He was sitting up sputtering, with just his neck out of the water when the blue Dodge pickup pulled to the riverside and began backing a trailer into the water. Michael could see two heavy salmon rods sticking out of a plywood boat. There was an outboard motor hooked to the transom. The driver climbed from his pickup and stood by the water's edge. "You know, old man," he said, "drowning is a sure cure for bad habits."

Michael looked across the river at where the North Umpqua spilled into the South Umpqua to make the main river.

"Come on," the man called. "You may need a bath all right, but my buddy and me, we need to go fishing worse." A second man opened the Dodge's passenger side door and pulled on a pair of knee-high rubber boots.

"I dunno what's going on, but he don't want to move," the first man said. "Maybe he can't."

The head thrusting from the water had the appearance of an emaciated biblical prophet, with prominent cheekbones stretched over a face that had both beard and hair hanging below the water line. The eyes were so sunken into hollows that one could not discern their color. The head of the prophet truly did look "wild."

"Mikhail?" Jocko Hayes muttered. "Mikhail Baranovitch, is that you?"

Michael's eyes were glazed. "Where's Barney?" he asked.

Chapter 45

BARANOVITCH CAPTURED!
Chuck Little
Daily News Staff Writer

Mikhail Baranovitch has been captured alive and unhurt!

Baranovitch, who hardly needs any identification to readers in Douglas County, was apprehended at 8 a.m. this morning, May 21.

He offered no resistance, and was taken into custody by off-duty Deputy Sheriff Jocko Hayes who, along with friend Raymond Potter, were on their way to a morning of salmon fishing at the Forks of the Umpqua.

"Baranovitch was just sitting there in the water," Hayes said, "right at the boat launch. All that was sticking out was his head. Me'n Ray had to wade in and help him to his feet—he was so weak he couldn't do it on his own. His only possession was a rusty single-shot .22 rifle, without ammunition."

Baranovitch's buckskin clothing was in tatters. He wore no shoes. He appeared emaciated and a physician has been called to the Douglas County detention center to provide a medical examination for "Big Mike."

Sheriff Irvin Finch at last was able to call off an extensive search for the "Umpqua Wild Man," and not a moment too soon for his beleaguered department.

"The public interest in this case far exceeds anything I've ever experienced, or ever even heard about. I'm not sure what kind of 'hero' Mikhail Baranovitch is, a folk hero or a military hero, but I can assure you if the man confounded the Japanese half as much as he was able to disconcert this Department, the war would have dragged on twice as long without him."

Sheriff Finch said he was extremely pleased that Baranovitch was taken alive and unhurt; pleased that he and his deputies "exercised the correct combination of reserve and restraint to bring the patient in for the kind of help and treatment he deserves."

The question now, according to Finch, is where Baranovitch will go next. "The Veteran's Administration has requested that we hold Mr. Baranovitch while he's undergoing medical treatment for his present debilitated condition."

A spokesperson for the Roseburg Hospital said arrangements are currently under way for the ultimate disposition of the patient—probably another V.A. Hospital in another state.

Baranovitch, now 33 years of age, was grievously wounded at least four times in New Guinea battles during World War II, and was awarded both the Silver Star and the Bronze Star for extraordinary valor in the face of the enemy.

U.S. Army Major Bryce Henderson, Acting Commandant at the Roseburg Veteran's Hospital said, "That the man once said to be a Yugoslavian immigrant, but who, in fact, was born and raised in Montana and was an all-state high school football star, was brought in without serious injury is but his due for all his heroic services to this country."

The two men stopped at the cell bars. Deputy Sheriff Jocko Hayes said, "The only thing he said since we first saw him sitting in the river was 'Where's Barney?' If I didn't know better, I'd think he couldn't talk. But I was there when he broke through our cordon, singing Yankee Doodle at the top of his voice. Then, too, I heard him one time we took him back to the V.A. Hospital. He talked up a blue streak with his doctor and the receptionist, and all the staff and half the patients. Only reason I'm telling you this is I don't want you to feel bad if he don't say nothin'."

Mikhail Baranovitch sat on a wooden cell bench, eyes on his bare toes. "They gave him some jail clothes," Hayes said. "They look too small to me, but he's a big guy, even if he is a skeleton. Maybe what they give him was all they had. Don't look like shoes was part of the mix, though."

The second man ignored the deputy. "Hello Bar," he said.

Baranovitch never raised his eyes from his feet, but he said, "Pasqueflowers only grow in undisturbed soil."

Bradley Baldwin smiled, tears in his eyes. "And Aldo Leopold said 'The right to find a pasqueflower is as inalienable as free speech'."

Mikhail Baranovitch continued to study his toes.

Baldwin said, "Michael, we're going to get you out of here. Me and Weyland Jones and Dr. Henderson. It may take a few days, but you can count on it, Son. Meanwhile, you've got to eat as much as you can as quickly as you can. Will you do that?"

"Yes." The undernourished prisoner struggled to his feet and shuffled to the bars. "I'm sorry you have to walk with a cane, Captain. I just couldn't do any better than I did."

Bradley Baldwin reached in and squeezed Michael's shoulder, then remembered where he was. Deputy Hayes acted as though he saw nothing.

* * *

A new pair of Red Wing boots in size-14 triple E was delivered to Mikhail Baranovitch later that day. Accompanying the boots were Levi jeans and a Pendleton wool shirt in suitable sizes, two pairs of undershorts, a vee-neck polo shirt, two pairs of cotton stockings, and a St. Louis Cardinals baseball cap. Also included with the packages was a belt and a Swiss Army knife that was to be held at the jail desk until the patient's release.

Mikhail Baranovitch was taken from his cell block on Tuesday, May 28. The release occurred with bewildering speed. Two U.S. Marshals simply appeared at the desk at 8:00 AM with properly executed forms transferring the prisoner to federal custody.

Alerted at the last moment, Douglas County Sheriff Irvin Finch rushed to the jail to offer his best wishes to the man who had so confounded him. As a final goodwill gesture, the sheriff held out the glossy photograph of Anna Karenina and her football playing boy friend, saying, "This came from your Cavitt Creek camp, son. I thought you'd like to take it with you."

Then the two marshals whisked the patient into a waiting automobile and drove away.

Inquiries to the Veteran's Hospital elicited no information. "We're as bewildered by his disappearance as you are," Acting Commandant Bryce Henderson told reporters. That afternoon's *Daily News* headline read:

BARANOVITCH TAKEN FROM JAIL

DESTINATION NOT REVEALED

Chuck Little
Daily News Staff Writer

Mikhail Baranovitch, the so-called "Wild Man of the Umpqua," who has been in and out of the news for several years because of his desperate escapades in living off the land has been transferred out of the county.
Destination Unknown
Baranovitch was moved from the Douglas County Jail Tuesday by U.S. marshals assigned to the transfer. The place of transfer was not reported to Sheriff Irvin Finch, whose deputies captured Baranovitch last week after the mental recluse had been at large for 15 months. Finch said the patient had taken capture philosophically, but expressed a wish not to be returned to the Roseburg Veteran's Hospital.

Relief In High Circles

Sheriff Finch expressed relief that the controversial Hospital escapee was finally out of sight and mind. "The man certainly captured the public's imagination during his long flight from enforcement personnel. His unique combination of daring and fortitude, coupled with a measure of strategic genius and the pure unpredictability of the mentally unbalanced made him the foremost apprehension challenge of my enforcement career."

Baranovitch also proved an embarrassment to the Veteran's Administration with his repeated escapes from detention. And it is said that a request went from the Roseburg Hospital to Washington, asking that Baranovitch be assigned to another hospital in an undisclosed state.

The "undisclosed state" was revealed a few days later in yet another *Daily News* scoop:

MIKHAIL BARANOVITCH TAKEN TO UTAH
Chuck Little
Daily News Staff Writer

Mikhail Baranovitch, who has made much news over the last six years because of his three escapes from the Roseburg Veterans Hospital and his solitary life in the Douglas County forests, has been taken to a Veterans Administration Hospital in Utah.

This information came from a VA official, who asked not to be identified. Baranovitch was taken from the Douglas County Jail to Eugene where a Military Air Transport Service plane was to take him to the Utah hospital. One such hospital is located in Salt Lake City.

Officials at the Roseburg Hospital said they could not provide any information relative to the patient's future location because it is against regulations.

Baranovitch was taken from the Douglas County Jail Tuesday by United States marshals, almost before the sheriff himself was notified of the transfer. "We're just happy to see a final dispensation of this case," Sheriff Irvin Finch told reporters. "Our only hope is that the best interests of this poor mentally disturbed American soldier will be served."

The pudgy, freckled, balding little man in the clashing Hawaiian shirt and

The Dogged and the Damned

Scotch-plaid shorts slid his sandaled feet from his desktop, slipped glasses from his nose, laid the latest issue of *The Daily News* on the commandant's desk, smiled sardonically, and muttered, "That cookstinker!"

Chapter 46

"This thing has more twists than a sidewinder, sir."

The white-thatched editor gazed at the reporter for several seconds before murmuring, "I imagine it does."

Chuck Little laid the sheaf of papers he clutched on the conference room table. "I've been following all Baranovitch leads, sir. And they're becoming clearer by the minute. Perhaps you'd allow me to explain." The editor nodded.

"Well, Baranovitch never went back to the hospital here, but he was logged in to the hospital in Salt Lake. He's no longer there, though. At least there's no record that he was ever assigned a room at that hospital. Trying to unravel the process, sir, it seems the treating psychiatrist at the Roseburg facility, Dr. Henderson—who's now the acting commandant—signed a release form for Mikhail Baranovitch over a year ago. Essentially, it said he was cured. But the form was never countersigned by the commandant at the time, Colonel Corwin."

"Perhaps Henderson countersigned when he became commandant?"

"No sir, I've checked and regulations preclude that. Both the treating psychiatrist and the commandant must sign—and they must be different people."

"Go on."

"Well, suppose the Salt Lake commandant signed off on Baranovitch's release the moment he arrived there? After all, it was originated here by the case psychiatrist, needing only the commandant's signature. There's nothing I could find in the regulations requiring the case psychiatrist and the administrative signatory to be from the same hospital. Only that they must be from the patient's hospital at the time of signature."

"Unusual for them to be different, though." Chalmers Station spun his chair to study his busy workfloor through the conference room windows. When he spun back, he stroked his chin—a sure sign the editor was deep in thought. "What else do you have?"

"Well, sir, I contacted Weyland Jones, the Sutherlin farmer. You'll remember he was the one who let me look at copies of Mikhail Baranovitch's treatment records?" The editor nodded. "Well, Jones told me he no longer has the records—that they went with Baranovitch to Salt Lake to replace the ones that disappeared."

"Disappeared?"

"Yes sir. I think Colonel Corwin destroyed those records when things began to grow hot for him as the Baranovitch case drug on. You see, sir, it was Corwin who blocked Baranovitch's release a year ago, despite the fact that the treating doctor was convinced of the man's restoration."

Again, Station stroked his chin. "Wasn't there some question of impropriety in the patient's pension?"

"Yes, but since no record exists that Baranovitch ever applied for his pension, I can't verify anything but government stupidity."

The white-thatched editor wagged his head. "What a pity. That could've solved everything."

"Anyway, sir," Chuck Little said, "Corwin is thought to have destroyed the records to cover his ass—sorry sir—himself. But then an order came from Washington that a senator wanted to see Mikhail Baranovitch's treatment records and Corwin no longer had them. That's when he got sacked."

Chalmers Station's eyebrows shot up. "Did you say a senator? Who?"

Chuck Little smiled at the clean way he'd set the hook. "He's Malcolm Young, senior senator from Utah, sir. Vice-Chairman of a Veteran's Administration subcommittee. Apparently the guy has taken an interest in the case. He's big cheese, sir."

"All right. Now why do you think a United States Senator from Utah is interested?"

The reporter shook his head. "Can't be all coincidence." He ticked his fingers. "Young is from Utah. "Baranovitch went to Utah. And the commandant for the Salt Lake City Veteran's Hospital is a member of the same Morman 'Stake' as Senator Young."

"Really?" the editor said. "My, young man, you've been thorough."

Little swelled with pride. "Right now I'm working on the angle that the guy with Weyland Jones—remember him? The one with the cane?—has something to do with this."

Chalmers Station nodded. "That seems probable. Have you any idea what?"

"I have a lead. Deputy Sheriff Jocko Hayes told me the guy visited Baranovitch in his cell block, and that Baranovitch referred to him as 'Captain'."

"And you feel there's a military connection between this man and Mikhail Baranovitch?"

"Yes sir, I do. If you'll look at my second series installment, there was reference to Baranovitch being awarded a Bronze Star for saving his captain's life. According to Major Henderson's psychiatric files that Jones let me see, the captain's name was Baldwin. According to military records, Captain Bradley Baldwin was—and is—a Utah native. And get this, sir, the man is married to Senator Malcolm Young's daughter!"

"I see." Again Chalmers Station spun to take in *The Daily News* workroom. When he spun back, the editor said, "Tell me, Mr. Little, what do you propose to do with all this?"

"Sir, I believe we're on the cusp of something very big. I'd like leave to go to Salt Lake City to try to nail down whether there's been collusion between their hospital commandant, Colonel Wallace, and Senator Young."

"If so," Chalmers Station mused, "Then Major Henderson would have been in on it."

That gave Chuck Little pause. Then he muttered, "I guess he'd have to be, wouldn't he?"

"And what of the U.S. Marshals? Would they have been complicit?"

Little nodded. "Perhaps. But not necessarily so. They may have merely followed orders."

The editor spun his chair all the way around without pausing to look at the workroom. When the chair came to rest, Chalmers Station asked, "And what would the purpose of all this complicity be, Mr. Little?"

"That's what I'd like to find out, sir. What if it's illegal?"

Station's eyes shifted, then returned to the reporter. "No, Chuck, there may be nothing illegal about it. But return to my question, will you: Why are all these people going to all this trouble? Where's the financial gain? Who will it benefit?"

"Well, aside from Baranovitch ..."

"What's that? What did you say? Who did you just mention?"

"Baranovitch. He's the one I can ..."

"Is there anyone else coming clear in your picture, Mr. Little?"

A troubled look spread over the reporter's face. Then it was replaced with one of pure bewilderment. "No, sir."

Chalmers Station nodded. "They're doing it for Mikhail Baranovitch alone. They're doing so in an attempt to right two decades of wrongs that's been done to the unfortunate man. What they're doing is noble and fine and deserves to succeed."

"But sir, what about the truth?"

A faint smile creased the editor's face, then was gone. "Mr. Little, you have the makings of a fine reporter. You write copy fluently, and you religiously adhere to deadlines. You're a good researcher and you obviously can develop a network of contacts. You're young enough to still believe in yourself. You have a conscience that might be construed as moral fiber. You are curious, passionate in what you believe, and outraged by dishonesty. All those attributes are to your credit. But you have one weakness that you must learn not to overlook: you are impetuous.

You still have yet to learn what is truth and what is not. And most of all, you need to understand when parallel truths are in conflict."

"I'm not sure I understand."

"Of course you don't—you haven't lived long enough. Because of that fact, and because I believe you'll make a fine newspaperman, I feel an obligation to explain.

Chuck Little sank back into his chair, his face a mask.

"You will agree," the editor asked, "that Mikhail Baranovitch took some blows that were undeserved, will you not?"

Little nodded.

"Because of his perseverance and determination and integrity of spirit, the man survived despite being damned at every turn.

Little nodded. "Dogged, but damned; that's him."

Chalmers Station stroked his chin. "Yes, that's right. But there are some people out there trying to right that wrong. That's the truth. Do you understand?"

"I think so ..."

"Chuck, I just told you that's *the* truth. The *only* truth. Now do you understand?"

The reporter's eyes widened. "You want me to suppress my investigation!"

"Now you've just taken quantum steps toward being the fine newspaperman I expect you'll someday be. During the course of your career, you'll discover many such cases where overall truth can better be served by omitting small details that might deflect from, or confuse, overall truth."

"But sir ..."

"Now let's look at another aspect that you might be overlooking—our readers." The editor paused to allow his reporter to collect himself, then continued: "Our readers have followed your stories about Mikhail Baranovitch for years; in part—*with one glaring exception*—because you've always been truthful with them. They've formed images in their minds about Mikhail Baranovitch. They were able to do so because you helped them understand the man, his character, his doggedness, the damnable way he was treated.

"But Mikhail Baranovitch has somehow escaped; he rode off into the sunset to disappear, like a mythic being, the way he deserves to disappear while he's still a man of their dreams instead of something much less."

Chuck Little's eyes were wide. Give the lad his due, the editor thought, he's listening. "Don't you see, Chuck, by pursuing the avenue you're presently following, you risk destroying a myth—that is also a truth—both Mikhail Baranovitch *and* the way he's thought of by *Daily News* readers. You may be doing so in the name of truth, but if you continue you'll be destroying a much greater truth and risk destroying a most deserving individual."

Now it was Little who stared out at the workroom. When his eyes found their way back, he said, "Sir, I see what you mean. And if I'm an honest journalist, I'd have to agree. But you need to know learning that difference might be the hardest thing I've ever had to do.

the end

About Roland Cheek

There are, perhaps, febrile savants who reject any notion that a person can acquire the writing art outside the hallowed halls of academia.

There's dissent, of course, with the less-learned pointing out that storytellers held audiences spellbound for millenniums before Oxford or Harvard was more than a forest enclave where wild turnips sprout. Those same dissenters may also believe academic life to be poor training ground for obtaining the kinds of riveting experiences readers find entrancing.

Roland's particular PhD came from God's own University of Wild Places and Wilder Things. His *Culture* might best be described as the *Campfire* kind, backed up against the inky black of star-filled nights, regaling saucer-eyed guests with tales of wilderness adventure, while horses stamped on picket lines and coyotes howled at a rising moon.

But can he write?

You judge. His doctoral thesis came during three decades of narratives about those wild places and wilder things; wonders saw, heard, smelled, tasted, and felt; crafted for Outdoor Life, Field & Stream, and Sports Afield. His column was syndicated over two decades to 17 newspapers, and he hosted a coast-to-coast radio show with 210,000 listeners, airing on 75 stations across America. Then he turned his attention to books: six novels and six wildlife and adventure nonfiction titles, all self-published to great success, all adventure-flavored with real-life experiences.

What's the point?

That one can live adventurously, write adventurously, and publish adventurously despite academic disdain for anyone succeeding outside the comfort of their cloistered clique.

Other Books by Roland Cheek

nonfiction

Montana's Bob Marshall Wilderness

Learning To Talk Bear
- so bears can listen

The Phantom Ghost of Harriet Lou
- and other elk stories

Dance On the Wild Side

My Best Work Is Done at the Office

Chocolate Legs
- sweet mother, savage killer?

fiction

Echoes of Vengeance

Bloody Merchants War

Lincoln County Crucible

Gunnar's Mine

Crisis On the Stinkingwater

The Silver Yoke